CLEAN CUT

CLEAN CUT

THERESA MONSOUR

G. P. Putnam's Sons

New York

G. P. Putnam's Sons
Publishers Since 1838
a member of
Penguin Putnam Inc.
375 Hudson Street
New York, NY 10014

Library of Congress Cataloging-in-Publication Data

Monsour, Theresa.
    Clean cut / Theresa Monsour.
        p.   cm.
    ISBN 0-399-14968-6
        1. Police—Minnesota—Saint Paul—Fiction. 2. Women—
Crimes against—Fiction. 3. Saint Paul (Minn.)—Fiction.
4. Serial murders—Fiction. 5. Policewomen—Fiction.
I. Title.
PS3613.O6485 C57   2003   2002069755
813'.6—dc21

Printed in the United States of America
10 9 8 7 6 5 4 3 2 1

BOOK DESIGN BY MEIGHAN CAVANAUGH

This book is dedicated to my husband, David, with all my love.

ACKNOWLEDGMENTS

Thanks to my:

husband, David, and our sons, Patrick and Ryan, for supporting me in this great adventure;

mentor, John Camp, who encouraged and helped all along the way;

doctor friend Marilee Votel-Kvaal and nurse sister-in-law Rita Monsour for their medical advice;

brother, Joseph Monsour, and sister, Bernadette Monsour, who have faith in me;

father, Gabriel Monsour, and late mother, Esther, for raising me right;

police pals Sergeant Mark Kempe and Officer Randy Barnett, who answered my questions;

agent, Esther Newberg, and editor, Leona Nevler, for being wonderful to work with;

past and present editors, reporters and other colleagues at the *St. Paul Pioneer Press,* for creating a newsroom that nurtures writers.

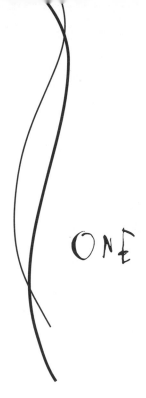

ONE

Despite the rain, Finch stayed.

All day ninety-degree heat had cooked the garbage cans behind the restaurants that lined the street. The stink of discarded food mingled with the smell of the prostitutes' sweat and perfumes. Musk and pickles. The men who usually drove up and down the street hunting for hamburgers and hookers had stayed away. At dusk came the rain, making a sizzling sound like meat hitting a hot pan. One by one the women left their corners, a parade of bored sentries abandoning their posts.

But Finch stayed.

She was the only daughter of western Wisconsin dairy farmers. At fifteen, she had been crowned princess in a county pageant and waved from a paper-flower float. Even then she knew she wasn't the prettiest, that she got by on her hair and her breasts. On her seventeenth birthday she decided that even though she was only a little pretty, she shouldn't have to put up with all the farm crap. All the family crap. She scribbled a three-word note to her mother and thumbed her way to St. Paul.

Now twenty-three, she waved to johns from the city's sidewalks. She wasn't even a little pretty anymore.

"Hey, Finch. Call it a day?" asked Charlene Rue. She and Finch shared a corner and were always the last to leave the street; their pimp wouldn't have it any other way. He told them the ugly ones had to stay out later because he couldn't stand looking at their faces in the daylight.

Together, the pair ducked under the awning of a secondhand store. A sign in the window said ANTIQUE PARLOR, but it was a junk shop, specializing in chipped dinner plates and broken table lamps. Rue took one last drag down to the filter and flicked her cigarette into the gutter, where a stream of water carried it and a string of French fries into the sewer. She was fat, and older than Finch. She'd dressed up her short brown hair with a garage-sale braid clipped to the back of her head, but the rain made the hairpiece stink like a wet dog. Rue yanked the braid off and stuffed it in the back pocket of her shorts. "Come on," Rue said. She set her umbrella down on the sidewalk, pulled another cigarette out of the pack tucked in her bra and lit up. "Let's pull the plug. I'm drownin' and so are you."

"I can't go yet," said Finch, using the bottom half of her pink tank top to wipe the water from her green eyes. The rain made her pale skin appear shiny and translucent, like the inside of a seashell.

She took a pull from Rue's cigarette and handed it back to her. "Gotta turn one more trick."

"Whatever you say, darlin'," Rue said. She slipped in and out of an accent that was vaguely southern. She handed Finch her yellow umbrella. It had a busted spoke and sagged at one end. "Don't lose it and don't get sick, or Sully'll beat your bony behind."

"What about you?" asked Finch. The ugly ones looked out for each other.

Rue spotted a rolled-up newspaper resting on the junk-shop stoop. She picked it up, unfurled it and held it over her head. "I'll make a run for the house," she said. Finch watched her go and smiled; the braid in Rue's back pocket looked like a tail.

As soon as Rue was out of sight, Finch folded up the umbrella. The thing was useless. The rain had already soaked her through to her skin, and her long, red hair hung in heavy strands. She felt like she was wearing a wet mop on her head. On nights like this, she thought about slicing it off, getting a dyke cut like some of the other girls. Sully liked her hair and wouldn't allow it, said she'd be even homelier if she cut it. "Who'd want you then?"

He used to call her pretty. She sometimes wondered when she'd crossed the line. Had there been a particular day when she'd woken up suddenly ugly? Or had it been a gradual thing, like aging? Had there been a middle stage when she could have rescued her looks? Would her face have lasted longer on the farm, or faded even faster? It didn't matter. Now all she had was her hair and her breasts.

Sully had long red hair, too. He kept it pulled back in a ponytail to show off the diamond earrings that studded his lobes. When they were out together—buying condoms at the pharmacy or beer at the liquor store—people mistook them for siblings. She hated that but Sully got a kick out of it. Called her "Sis" and pinched her ass in public, and watched their faces.

If they'd seen what he did to her in private . . .

When they didn't bring home enough money or when they mouthed off to him or when he was drunk enough or high enough or feeling mean enough, Sully LePlante beat his whores with plastic clothes hangers. The white one was for the white women, the black one for the black women. He saved a special red hanger for Finch.

"To match your hair, baby," he said when he used it on her, and he used it on her a lot. Some of the other pros called her "Flinch" behind her back.

She hadn't yet met her quota for the evening and she wasn't anxious to feel the sting of that hanger against her buttocks and thighs, so she stayed on her corner after Rue and the other hookers had left.

Finch stepped off the curb and tried to make eye contact with the driver of a maroon station wagon. It sped by, kicking up a jet of water that barely missed her feet. Several minutes passed. A semi rumbled up the street. She waved; he slowed and honked but didn't stop. Window-shopper. Two men in a pickup truck followed.

"Get off the street, you stupid cunt!" one of them hollered out the window. They steered into a puddle, splashed her legs and laughed.

A white van crossed the street. The front passenger-side window was missing. A plastic Target bag was taped over the opening. She recognized the car. Didn't waste her breath. They were from the neighborhood, and people from the neighborhood would like to run her over. Run all the pros over. She fiddled with the umbrella and popped it open again, for something to do.

She figured it was raining on the farm. Since it was June, the lilacs would be done. Her mother's pink peonies would be in full display, the dark green stems bending from the weight of the heavy flowers. She fingered the crucifix hanging around her neck, a Confirmation gift from her parents. Instead of throwing it away with the rest of her past, she clung to it like a drowning woman clutching a life ring. She never took it off, even when Sully complained that it spooked the johns. Like a thousand other nights, she thought back to the note she had left in her mother's sock drawer. Finch wondered if she should have left clean. No note. No nothing. Those three words. What good were they? They only kept her from ever going home again. Three words. Ten letters: "Dad raped me."

She saw another car coming down the nearly deserted road. One last john, she thought. One last trick.

He peered through the windshield of his black Chevy Suburban. The wipers struggled to keep up with the downpour. The car radio was tuned to a hard-rock station: Friday night, and a weekend of the Rolling Stones had started, kicking off with their *Exile on Main Street* album. He bobbed his head to "Tumbling Dice" and brushed a shock of hair from his eyes. *GQ* handsome, but with an angry edge. Whenever he entered a room, he looked as if he'd just come from an argument. He wasn't a wheat-colored blond with blue eyes. He was a winter blond: gray eyes and almost white hair. He favored dark or neutral clothes. Color photos of him looked identical to black-and-white ones.

He came to a red light and stopped. What was that noise? He turned down the radio and held his breath so he could hear it again. Buzzing. The fly was back. Damn. Deal with it, he told himself. Handle it. He inhaled deeply and gripped the steering wheel. The wedding band on his left hand bit into his flesh. He imagined he was wrapping his fingers around the submissive throat of a tiny woman. He exhaled. Slowly.

The light changed, but he didn't notice. The driver of the car behind him honked once and then pulled around to pass him. He snapped to attention and stepped on the gas. The St. Christopher medal and coach's whistle, both dangling from chains draped over his rearview mirror, swung wildly and smacked against the windshield. In the rear storage area of the big vehicle, a half dozen soccer balls bounced around.

Driving west toward the Minneapolis city line, he scanned the corners but found nothing on the drenched, darkening streets. He braked at a traffic light and looked to his right through the windows of a Burger King restaurant. Maybe they were inside, drying off and waiting for the downpour to let up. All he saw through the window was an old man in a T-shirt hunched over his coffee cup like a human question mark. The light changed. He drove on, searching.

"Jesus Christ," he muttered to himself, not in prayer but in frustration. He stopped himself. He looked at the religious medal hanging from his mirror. He knew the engraved words by heart: "St. Christopher, protect us." He wondered if he swore too much, then set aside his moment of Catholic guilt. His life was neatly compartmentalized and piety belonged in another box, to be opened later.

The buzzing again. He turned up the radio, let the guitar riffs drown it out.

He thought back to the accident of several weeks ago, in the spring. That's what it was, an accident. He had gotten too rough. If she hadn't liked it rough, Miss Accident, what was she doing hanging out in that kind of bar? She had been a slut, anyway. Deserved it. Like that nurse in the incident during his fellowship. Miss Incident. Neither had been his fault, really. As long as it hadn't been deliberate, then there was nothing to confess. Nothing to reconcile. He was clean. Blameless.

Certainly he was usually more in control than he had been with those two, able to take things to a certain point and then pull back. Sometimes he miscalculated the boundaries of the women he laid, especially the bar pickups and the prostitutes. With strangers, you don't know how far you can take it. He always tried to ease them into it. He would start with a little rough handling. A couple of slaps. Some shoving. He'd grab their hair. Couldn't keep his hands off the hair. Before he was really satisfied the way he wanted to be satisfied, they were pulling on their clothes and sobbing or screaming at him.

"You sick bastard! What's your problem?!"

He laughed and repeated the question out loud: "What's your problem?"

Miss Accident and Miss Incident had gone beyond miscalculations. They'd died on nights when his life's problems had sent him spinning out of control. Miss Incident had been the night his father succumbed to cancer. Miss Accident happened after his wife miscarried his son. That same anxiety he'd felt those other two nights was working his gut now, but he didn't know why. There'd been no new train wrecks in his life, no new catastrophes. Yet for some reason, in the back of his throat, the coppery taste of adrenaline mixed with the smoky flavor of Scotch.

For some reason, the buzzing in his head was worse than ever.

The rain refused to let up. He was ready to quit the hunt and go home to his bottle of eighteen-year-old Macallan and forty-year-old wife. On any given day he far preferred the former to the latter. A bottle of single malt didn't whine or complain or ask where he was when he should have been coaching the kids' soccer game. It didn't demand to know why he hadn't come home all night or ask for explanations when there were buttons missing from his shirt and mud on his shoes. Scotch didn't ask for much, save the occasional splash of water.

He was pulled from his whiskey reverie when something caught his eye. A flash of yellow, a beacon in the rain. She was soaking wet and the only thing more pathetic than her skimpy pink outfit was her broken umbrella. She was petite. He liked that. He could see her nipples under her saturated shirt. He liked that, too. She had hair that reached all the way down to the small of her back. He liked that best of all.

He navigated the Suburban to the curb and rolled down the front passenger-side window. Standing on her toes, she poked her head in, dripping water onto the leather interior. The last of her mascara was running down her cheeks in brown rivulets; they looked like muddy tears.

"Hey, baby, lookin' for a date?" she asked.

He hated hooker-speak. Why not call it what it is? How about the direct approach: "Hey, mister, want to pay me to wrap my mouth around your organ?" Or "Hey, big guy, I charge reasonable rates for sexual intercourse."

"Get in," he said flatly.

She folded the umbrella and shook it a bit. She jerked open the door, climbed in with a little hop and slammed it hard. He winced but said nothing as she leaned forward and squeezed water from the hem of her shirt onto the carpet. Like most whores, she looked prettier from the curb. Up close, he could see the freckles fighting the acne for space on her face. The pimples were winning. There were tired circles under her eyes and fine lines creeping across her forehead. By the time she hits forty, her face will need a lot of work, he thought. Still, she had fabulous, long hair.

Then he noticed the small crucifix around her neck. Catholic. It made him uneasy. She saw him staring at it and quickly tucked it under her tank top. She turned around in her seat and tossed the umbrella on the car floor behind her. She spotted the lab coat he had thrown on the backseat.

His jaw tightened as he watched her eying his name tag. Damn, he thought. He should have stuffed the coat under the seat before leaving work for his excursion.

"You a dentist or somethin'?" she asked.

"Or somethin'," he said.

He sounded snotty and sarcastic, and sarcastic customers made her feel stupid. She wanted a sharp comeback: "What's the *A* on your name tag stand for? Asshole?" She laughed.

He didn't like it at all. He was supposed to be in charge, piss her off, make her mad. The bitch was the one laughing. In a smooth move that was almost reflexive, he slapped her across the face with the back of his right hand.

She yelped. "What the fuck was that for?" she cried, holding her left cheek with her hand. He could see it was red, see the stripes from his fingers. Her skin marked easily, and that aroused him. He could also see she had her right hand on the door handle, ready to open it. He didn't want her to leave. Things were getting interesting.

"I'm sorry," he said, slipping into his best altar-boy face. "God, I don't know what got into me. I had a really bad day. Stay. Please stay."

He sounded genuine; the sarcastic snot was gone. She slid her right hand off the door handle and looked at him. She noticed how handsome he was, how well built. He had to be at least six feet tall. She guessed he was in his mid-forties. He smelled good. Clean. Most of her customers were paunchy old men who, on their best days, smelled like Old Spice and onion rings. Still, he had hit her. Only Sully could hit her. She straightened her back, sitting as tall as she could with her slight frame. "You had a bad day. Big deal. Join the fuckin' club. That's no reason to haul off and . . ."

"Look, let me make it up to you," he said, quickly interrupting her. "Whatever you usually charge, double it."

The rain was slowing. He pulled away from the curb, veered into the left lane and made a squealing U-turn around the concrete median and headed east, back toward downtown St. Paul.

"Hey, where're we goin'?" she asked, an edge of panic in her voice. "I've got a parkin' lot one street over."

"I want something more than a blow job," he told her. "Don't worry. I'll pay for it."

"Where are you takin' me?" she asked. She was frightened. She couldn't read this guy. Couldn't get past the pretty hair and eyes.

"What can I call you, anyway?" he asked, trying to lighten things up. "What's your nickname? Please don't tell me it's 'Red.'"

She laughed nervously. "Finch. That's what the other girls call me. Finch."

"Finch? Well, that suits you," he said, his voice smooth and soothing. "You are a delicate little bird."

"Okay," she said. She had to get down to business. "Where's the cash?" she asked. "I haven't seen any paper yet."

When he stopped for the next red light, he reached into the right pocket of his windbreaker and pulled out a money clip stuffed with folded fifties. He peeled off three of them and threw them on her wet thighs. "You'll get the other half when we're through," he said. "Okay, Finch?" She picked up the bills and paused with them in her hands. It looked like she was doing some adding in her head. Math probably wasn't her best subject in school, he thought sardonically.

She was mentally tallying what her total day's earnings would be with his contribution and dividing it by her hours on the street. The little game she played with herself made her feel better. She thought of herself as a contracted professional paid by the hour, as opposed to a common prostitute paid by the sexual act. "That's cool," she said, stuffing the bills into the pocket of her shorts. She leaned forward and turned up the radio volume.

They cut through downtown St. Paul and drove south across the Wabasha Bridge, crossing the Mississippi. They took a right after the bridge and passed a recreation area along the riverfront, following the Mississippi until they were in the thick of Lilydale Regional Park. "I don't like it here," she said. "It's too creepy." She told herself she'd messed up; it was too late to bail out. On one side of Lilydale Road were thick woods that ran along the river. On the other side were tree-covered bluffs dotted with caves, where teenagers partied all summer and homeless men hung out.

He pulled off the road, turning into a sandy clearing on the river. The rain had stopped. Some daylight was lingering. Without saying a word, he turned off the ignition, slipped the keys into his pants pocket and got out of the driver's seat. He slammed the door hard behind him. Finch sat for a minute, reassured herself he was tame—he wore a lab coat with a name tag, for God's sake—and followed him outside.

A lone picnic table in the middle of the clearing was covered with carved initials and messages. "Black Magic Woman 7-24-95." On one side of the clearing was a railroad bridge that crossed the river and snaked through the park. On the other side were four massive concrete pillars anchoring the tower of a high-voltage power line. Spray-painted in script on the pillars: "Wellcum to my garden! Black Magic Woman." Down a small hill that led to the river's edge, a decrepit fishing boat moored close to shore. The boat appeared dark and unoccupied. Across the Mississippi was an old power plant.

He was in back of the vehicle with the gate open, rifling around for something. Several soccer balls rolled out. He quickly picked them up and threw them back in. He pulled out a picnic blanket with wool on one side and waterproof canvas on the other. He shook off some cookie crumbs and laid it wool-side-up on the wet, sandy ground.

"Strip," he said.

"What?"

"Take off your clothes."

"It's your money," she said with a shrug. She kicked off her sandals, stepped into the middle of the blanket and started peeling off her damp tank top.

It had stopped raining and the heat had returned. He wiped sweat from his forehead with the back of his jacket sleeve. He took off the jacket and tossed it on top of the picnic table, and then sat down at the table to watch her as she wrestled with the wet shirt. The straps were tangled in her hair.

"How 'bout giving me a hand here?" she asked.

He didn't answer or move. He watched. She pulled the shirt hard over her head. Her necklace flew off and landed on the ground at his feet. She didn't notice. He thought about picking it up for her, but didn't want to make the effort. He decided at that moment she was stupid and clumsy, and he didn't like stupid, clumsy people. She dropped her shirt in a wet knot on the blanket. He stared at her breasts. Small, he thought, but nicely shaped. He got up from the table and started toward her.

She was looking down to unzip her shorts when he slapped her so hard she thought his hand was a brick. She fell backward, stunned. She scrambled to her knees to get up and run, and he slapped her again and again. She couldn't catch her breath enough to scream. When she finally sprawled flat on her back, he leaned over her smiling, grabbed her by her hair and pulled her to her feet. He held her an arm's length away from him, by the hair on top of her head. For an instant she couldn't feel the ground; her toes swung in the air. She regained her footing and whipped her arms around like a cockeyed windmill, finally finding a voice to scream. "You son-of-a-bitch!" she shrieked.

He laughed. She couldn't believe he was laughing. She had been slapped around by johns before, but not like this, not with such perverted relish. "You goddamn sick bastard! Nut case! What in the fuck is your problem?"

"I knew you had a good fight in you," he said. "Redheads always do."

"Fuck you!" she said, and spat in his face. The spit was mixed with the blood oozing out of her nose and split lips. He didn't like being spat upon. Didn't like it at all. He pushed her backward onto the blanket and fell on top of her.

She screamed.

"Go ahead," he said. "Who'll hear you?"

She pulled her right arm out from under him, reached up and gouged his face with her nails. Deep, bleeding scratches. He didn't even grimace. He looked right through her, as if she didn't matter. She retreated to the one place she had left. She shut her eyes and started praying under her breath. "Our Father, who art in heaven, hallowed be thy name . . ."

This wasn't what he wanted to hear. This wasn't the time or the place for prayers. He wanted screams. Screams muffled the buzzing.

"Thy kingdom come, Thy will be done . . ."

The walls separating the different sections of his compartmentalized life were losing their structural integrity, threatening to collapse. He had to shore them up. Shut her up.

"Stop it!" he growled. "God doesn't give a damn about whores." He wrapped his right hand tightly around her throat and with his left, pulled down her shorts. He put his mouth to her ear:

"The fly shall marry the bumblebee," he whispered.

At the water's edge, in the waning daylight, another man watched through the fishing boat's porthole.

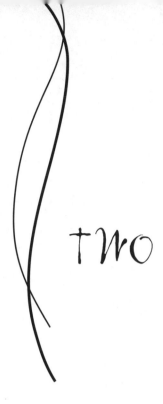

two

Paris Murphy rolled over with a groan and reached for the ringing cell phone, inadvertently knocking it off the nightstand. "Aww, man," she mumbled.

Under the bed and still ringing.

"Answer the phone," the naked man said into his pillow. He was sprawled out facedown, taking up three-quarters of the bed. At six-three, he couldn't help it.

It kept ringing. She stretched her arm down and felt around the floor with her fingertips.

"*Please* answer your fucking phone," he said.

The phone stopped ringing. She rolled back over to look at him. He's pretty damn gorgeous, she thought. Curly brown hair, broad shoulders, smooth back. Men don't realize how much women appreciate a nice back, she reflected.

The naked man flipped onto his back and opened his soulful brown eyes. "What if it's your mother? Do you want her to come knocking because she didn't get an answer? All we need is for her to find me here, screwing her daughter."

"Number one, my mother doesn't come knocking. She thinks my house could sink and she doesn't know how to swim," Murphy said, running her fingers through her hair.

"And B, she would be thrilled if you and I . . ."

"You mean number two," he said, smiling and scratching his crotch.

"What?" she said, resting on her elbow.

"The last time I checked, babe, number two followed number one. B doesn't follow number one."

"I'm trying to make a point," Murphy said, laughing.

"That point would be?"

"That point would be that my mother would be thrilled to find out we're sleeping together," she said. "You *are* my husband."

"But we're supposed to be separated," he said, pushing her down and rolling over on top of her.

"This doesn't feel too separated to me," Murphy said. She gently raked his back with her nails.

"Give me a minute and I'll show you some real separation," he murmured, forcing her thighs apart with his knees. He kissed her. His tongue darted into her mouth.

The ringing resumed.

"That could be work. I'd better get it," she said, rolling him off her and getting out of bed to search for the insistent cell phone. She found it and sat naked on the edge of the bed to answer it. "Hello . . . Ah, man. Not Finch. Shit. Did anyone pick up LePlante on this? . . . No kidding? What time Friday?"

Her husband reached over from behind and cupped her left breast with his left hand.

"Damn it, stop it," she told him, putting her hand over the mouthpiece.

"Look, I'll be right down there," she said into the phone.

She set the cell phone on her nightstand and stood up.

"Have I told you lately how much I hate your job?" asked her husband as he lay back in bed.

"Not for at least five minutes," she said. She yawned, stretched her arms over her head and walked over to her dresser.

Murphy was tall for a woman, at five feet ten inches, but small boned, giving the illusion she was petite. She had a small waist and narrow hips, but larger than average breasts. She worried they made her look fat. They didn't. She carried herself like a hockey player. Quick. Graceful. Ready to slash. She never smiled at strangers. Most men kept their distance. Even though by her age—thirty-six, six years her husband's junior—most women need makeup, she didn't need a thing. Her eyes were almond-shaped and colored violet and framed by lashes so long and thick they looked fake. Her olive skin was a gift from her Lebanese mother, as was her long, black hair. She usually wrestled it into ponytail behind her head for work, but sometimes, in her off-hours, let it go free.

There weren't too many off-hours for her—or her husband, an emergency-room doctor at a downtown hospital. They knew it was one of the many problems in their on again–off again marriage of eight years.

More ringing—

"That's *your* phone, Jack," she told her husband. She pulled a pair of panties out of her dresser drawer and stepped into them.

He groaned and reached over to the nightstand on his side of the bed, and picked up a cell phone. "Jack Ramier here."

Murphy always liked the way that sounded. "Ramier here." She smiled to herself. God, she missed having him around regularly, especially at night.

"Yes . . . yes," he said into his cell phone. "No. No. Don't worry about it. It's not a problem," he said, smiling at his wife. He put down his cell phone.

"I thought you weren't on call this weekend," she said. She scanned the floor for her jeans. They were under the bed. She pulled them out, shook off the dust balls and wiggled into them.

"I'm not, but they need some extra help in the E.R. They're stacked up in the hallway like firewood," he said. His clothes were folded in a neat pile on the nightstand. He sat naked on the edge of his side of the bed and pulled on his socks.

Mr. Methodical, she mused, starting from the bottom and working his way up. That's how he did everything. It drove her nuts. She wished he'd put his baseball cap on first. Just once. For variety.

"It must have been one hell of a Friday night around town last night," he continued, slipping into his boxers. "What's your Saturday-morning mayhem, my desert flower?"

She loved it when he called her that, even though his tongue was firmly planted in his cheek.

"I've got a dead hooker," she said distractedly as she rifled around in her dresser drawer for a bra. Her own insensitivity gave her pause. She didn't like it when the job did that to her. She didn't want to be another prickly homicide cop. Too many of those already.

"Knew her?"

"Yeah. Wisconsin girl," Murphy said. "Sexually abused as a kid. Ran away. Ended up on the street."

"Ended up dead," said Jack.

"Yeah," said Murphy. "Ended up dead."

How about dinner back here, tonight?" Murphy asked, as they walked down to their cars.

They stopped in the parking lot. She looked down and dug in her purse for her car keys; she didn't want him to see her face when he answered. A "Yes" wouldn't necessarily mean much of anything, other than that he missed her cooking. A "No" would speak volumes.

"Absolutely," he said. He opened his car door and slid into his silver BMW. "I'll bring some champagne."

She looked up and smiled. An "absolutely" accompanied by champagne was very promising.

"Meet you back here at six," he said. He smiled back at her and pulled on his baseball cap.

"Here" was her floating home, a houseboat moored on the Mississippi below the Wabasha Bridge, across the river from downtown St. Paul. She'd bought it after she and Ramier had split the first time. He kept the Dutch Colonial they had purchased together in St. Paul's Macalester-Groveland neighborhood. She'd hated cutting the grass and doing routine home maintenance, but what he didn't know was that she would mow a football field now to have him back. The riverfront had its charms, but it couldn't match the heat of his arms and legs wrapped around her at night.

The riverfront also had its dangers, as poor Finch had discovered Friday night, Murphy thought as she rolled down Lilydale Road in her Jeep Grand Cherokee. She snapped on the radio. Her favorite rock station was playing some old Rolling Stones tune. "Let's Spend the Night Together." She flicked it off impatiently. She hated the Rolling Stones.

Snaky Swanson curled up in the bowels of the fishing boat and wept. When he went off his Risperdal, he imagined snakes were following him. These were not ordinary snakes. Schizophrenics rarely suffer from dull delusions. They sang, read poetry—William Blake—and when the St. Paul Saints were at home, delivered play-by-plays of the baseball game. This wasn't always a bad thing. Sometimes Swanson found his slithering pals good company. They could be entertaining and even made him laugh out loud on occasion with their dry, reptilian wit. He found their observations on the human condition to be insightful. Mostly he found the snakes annoying, however, and so stayed on his antipsychotic medicine as well as he could while living on the streets. The Risperdal made him tired, a problem when you're moving from one home under a bridge to another. Sometimes he started doing so well he forgot why he was taking the medication, and stopped.

He had been taking it lately, however, and that was why he was weeping. He was perfectly sane and healthy, and clearly remembered that the night before, he had watched a man murder a woman along the shore. He had been too terrified to do anything, even yell, as he peeked through a grimy porthole. He felt weak and vulnerable himself and was certain if he tried to stop the killer, he would be the next victim. All he could do was watch while the woman tried to fend off her attacker, her skinny white arms thrashing. When she screamed, he covered his ears. He hardly slept that night, feeling guilty for his inability to help.

Come dawn, he heard a train screeching to an emergency stop. Not much later, sirens. He looked through the porthole. A lone train engineer standing over the white, waxy figure on the ground. It wouldn't be long before the cops would arrive, swarming around the body and the riverfront like blue vultures. They'd find him on the boat and blame him. At the very least, he had done nothing to save her, and he was trespassing to boot. He could be arrested and thrown in a jail cell, and he didn't like sharing such close quarters with his slithering friends.

"What am I gonna do? What am I gonna do? Oh, God, help me!" he whispered to himself. He wrapped his arms around his backpack as he continued to watch through the window and listen to the sirens. Louder, closer. Finally the engineer turned to take the steps back up to the train. That was his chance. Swanson threw his backpack over his shoulder. He slipped into the brown water, waded the short distance to shore and ran into the woods.

He had one person in the world he could trust with his secret, and he wasn't sure it was her weekend to work at the soup kitchen.

Four squad cars and a hearse from the medical examiner's office blocked the dirt turnoff leading to the murder site. Beyond them were vans with call letters belonging to three television news stations and behind them was the beat-up Ford F150 pickup truck belonging to the *Pioneer Press* police reporter. No company name or logo decorated the sides of the cop reporter's truck—it was his own—but a bumper sticker clearly reflected the owner's attitude: SOME PEOPLE ARE ALIVE ONLY BECAUSE IT'S AGAINST THE LAW TO KILL THEM. Murphy pulled up behind the truck and dodged the television cameras and reporters. Two uniformed patrolmen were keeping them on the paved road, away from the dirt turnoff. A television news helicopter hovered overhead.

"Hey, Murphy?" hollered the newspaper reporter, a tall man in his late twenties with a shoulder-length brown mop and John Lennon eyeglasses. "Who creamed the dairy queen?"

"Lose the attitude, Cody," Murphy said as she brushed past him. He was dressed in his usual Hawaiian shirt and jeans.

The murder scene was deceptively festive in its yellow color scheme. Yellow police tape was staked around the body, a crime-scene photographer in a yellow polo shirt snapped pictures, all pulled together by a yellow Union Pacific train stopped on the railroad bridge at the side of the clearing. A glum train engineer sat in the middle of the steps spanning the twenty feet from the railroad bridge to the ground below. Erik Mason, an investigator for the medical examiner's office, was talking to a couple of uniformed patrolmen. Evans Bergen, the night guy in homicide, was standing around with his hands in his pockets. Murphy thought he was a worthless turd. He was the master of undertime—got to work late and left early. He was young, short and had blond hair that was already thinning on top.

Then there was the body itself. Finch was on her back on a plaid wool blanket. Her face was battered and bruises dotted her throat. On the blanket next to her was her tank top, and on the ground next to the blanket were her sandals. Her shorts and panties were tangled around one leg. A wad of bills was sticking out of her pocket.

"Finch," said Murphy, carefully stepping over the police tape. She crouched down to get a better look at the hooker's body. Mason started toward her. "Semen?" Murphy asked, without looking up.

"Yup," said Mason.

"Hair?"

"Got some."

"Skin?"

"Loads of it. She clawed a good chunk out of him."

"Good," she said.

"We'll give her a full workup," Mason said. He was a tall, athletic-looking man in his late thirties with short, walnut brown hair and hazel eyes. Like Murphy, he was a runner. She hadn't worked with him for a while and she was glad. He attracted her and she didn't need that. He drove a sapphire XK8 Jaguar convertible, a $75,000 car. Rumor was that he bet the horses.

"It won't take a forensic genius to figure this out," said Murphy, standing up.

Bergen walked over. "Why does the media give a crap about this case?" he asked, nodding toward the road where the crowd was gathered. "Since when do they give a damn about a dead whore?"

Murphy cringed. To be reduced at life's end to two hard words, *dead whore*, was cruel. "Finch tried to leave the life," said Murphy. "The newspaper did a profile of her. She grew up on a dairy farm. She even won a beauty pageant."

"Bergen says her pimp has an airtight alibi," Mason said, peeling off his latex gloves as a couple of other staff from the M.E.'s office started loading Finch into a body bag.

"Yeah," said Murphy. "Airtight." LePlante had been in a bar on West Seventh Street most of Friday afternoon, shooting pool and boozing it up. He cracked a cue over another drunk's head and spent the night in detox. He was still sleeping it off Saturday morning. "He doesn't even know Finch is dead, not that the sleazebag would give a rat's ass one way or the other," Murphy said. She looked over at the M.E.'s staff guys as they pulled a bag over Finch.

"Hey—wait!" she yelled. "What the hell?"

She knelt on the ground next to the bag and carefully lifted Finch's head.

"What's wrong?" asked Mason. He crouched down next to Murphy.

"Finch never cut her hair. That asshole, Sully, wouldn't let her. Ever," said Murphy. "I saw her on the street a couple of days ago. She was bitching about how this hot spell was miserable with long hair."

"So?"

"So someone gave her a pretty shitty haircut." She turned Finch's head so Mason could see that a wide section of the young woman's long red hair had been sloppily chopped from the back of her head.

"Now *that* is weird," said Bergen, looking down with his hands still in his pockets. "Hair fetish?"

"I'd say so," Murphy said.

Mason stood up. "I'll give you a call when I have something. You'll be out on the street all day?"

"Yeah. I have to talk to some of the other ladies," said Murphy, setting Finch's head back down. "I'll give you my cell-phone number."

She stood up and looked around the immediate area. She'd have some people sweep it, but it wasn't very promising. This ratty part of Lilydale was especially isolated. When she was a uniform, she'd occasionally come across a teenage couple pulled into the clearing. Busted up a kegger along the shore here once. She looked down the small hill to the river. The power plant and the fishing boat were possibilities. Street people set up camp anywhere they could.

Bergen shuffled next to her. "Need anything from me?" he asked. "I want to file my end of the paperwork and hit the road."

"Go," Murphy said, waving him away. "I'm on it."

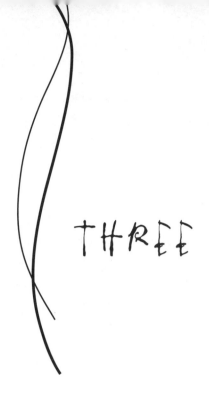

THREE

Dr. A. Romann Michaels used his hands to wipe the steam from the mirror. He was damp and pink after a few Saturday-morning laps in the pool and a long, hot shower. He still had a slight headache. Nothing too serious. He'd had much worse, and he had something to take care of it. He took a drink of Scotch and shuddered. Hair of the dog. He set the glass down on the bathroom counter and leaned closer to the mirror. "Bitch," he said. He ran his fingers lightly over the scratches on his left cheek and glumly studied the three red stripes. They were deep and wouldn't fade quickly.

He needed a story for his family.

His two girls were attending a soccer camp in Denmark, and his wife had decided to stay longer at their Lake Superior cabin. The two of them had just spent a week there, joined by the queen mother. The entire vacation was an unpleasant haze. He couldn't stand being alone with the two of them for such a long stretch, even with Scotch as a buffer, so he'd driven back early. Work was a good excuse. Plus he did have a soccer tournament coming up. As the coach, he had to show up whether his daughters were around to play or not.

As far as the clinic was concerned, he'd come up with something by Monday to satisfy his gossipy staff. He could tell them he'd taken a spill into some bushes while biking. Something like that.

More bothersome than the scratches was the burning knot in the pit of his belly. Things had gotten out of hand last night. He was sure no one had seen the girl and the park would be empty by dusk. Despite being drunk, he still had managed to collect his souvenir. He had to wash her hair, of course. God knows what kinds of things could be crawling around in it.

"What's your problem?" he asked himself in the mirror. "Hell, what problem? I don't have any problem." Then, more honestly, "Maybe a couple."

He slipped the red hair out of the plastic bag.

Michaels's problems, like nearly everyone's problems, could be conveniently blamed on crappy parents.

His parents were rich.

He'd played on the lawn of a Summit Avenue mansion that had been in his mother's family for two generations and eventually passed on to him. The place was a rambling 1880s Queen Anne with a high-pitched roof and gables, turrets and towers. A greenhouse squatted on the east side, a sleeping porch on the west and a swimming pool in the basement. The house was in a neighborhood bordered by two Catholic colleges and sprinkled with churches. He and his parents walked to mass together on Sundays, strolling past other historic Victorian homes.

He was an only child and his mother and father lavished *things* on him. A massive train set complete with a miniature Bavarian town, a hand-carved rocking horse imported from Italy, radio-controlled cars and boats and chemistry sets. Private French instruction, private fencing lessons, private tennis classes, private everything. He attended Catholic elementary and prep schools in Minneapolis and plush summer camps in northern Minnesota.

He wanted for nothing, except sane parents. Behind the wrought-iron fence, behind the leaded-glass windows, behind the Irish lace curtains, the banker and his pious wife fought like demented dogs.

As a boy, he would sit watching as his father and mother hurled insults and objects at each other. He learned to study the level of Scotch in their glasses to anticipate the severity and duration of the evening's fight. They drank out of tumblers with painted pheasants on the side—funny how those fragile items were always spared in his parents' mad scramble for ammunition—and when the booze covered the hen resting on the ground, it would be a brief battle. When the whiskey reached as high as the cock in flight, the boy knew it was time to take cover behind the couch. They would slap and punch each other, scratch and claw, kick and flee to opposite corners like spiteful children. The banker usually won. He once dragged his wife all the way up the stairs to their second-floor bedroom by her long, golden, beautiful hair. The son loved his mother's hair.

Their battles always ended in the bedroom, finishing the fight with a good fuck. They never shut the bedroom door.

Michaels coped. When he was very young, he saw a television report about a girl who fell down an old well. Her playmates ran for help, leaving her alone. The girl said she wasn't afraid until she looked up and saw daylight beyond her reach, so she stopped looking up. She imagined she was sitting in a cardboard box in her bedroom. He'd admired the girl's survival technique and, as it turned out, spent his life using it himself. As long as he didn't look up and see the daylight, as long as he properly boxed his life and compartmentalized his world, he could keep everything under control.

When he was a child he looked up from the hole at times, and it made him envious and angry. Once he was sitting in the backseat of the car after a dinner party. His father was driving, half in the bag and yelling at his mother. His mother was drunk and crying. They were at a stoplight in downtown St. Paul. It was winter and snowing. A family was standing outside the bus depot—mom, dad, three kids. Each carried a suitcase held shut with twine. They were laughing; he wanted to be them.

The older he got, the more Michaels isolated himself. He didn't go to other kids' houses because their families were normal. He didn't bring friends home. He stayed on the fringes of social circles at school. His only playmates were his cousins—most of them had equally screwed-up families. He participated in sports that emphasized individual events; he was not a team player.

He decided to braid the red hair before he washed it so that loose strands wouldn't be lost down the drain. That would be wasteful. He fished a rubber band out of one of the bathroom drawers and wrapped the band around one end of the twist of hair. Then he carefully separated three sections and started braiding. The work relaxed him. Calmed his nerves. He used to help his mother brush and braid her hair. In her sober moments—she used up most of them when he was young—she held him on her lap and let him play with her long braid while she read nursery rhymes:

"Fiddle-de-dee, fiddle-de-dee,

The fly shall marry the bumblebee.

They went to church and married was she.

The fly has married the bumblebee."

He and his mother laughed over that one. She nicknamed him Buzzy and he called her Bee. He imagined he was a fly walking down the aisle in a tuxedo, with a bee bride on his skinny fly arm. Sometimes the bee had his mother's face and hair. Sometimes it looked like his favorite cousin. The one from Iowa. A little younger than he. Long blond hair and gray eyes like his. She'd let him play with her hair, wash it, braid it, tie ribbons in it. She was the only other person who called him Buzzy. She liked the rhyme. His daughters used to like it too, but they pushed him away as they got older. Said they were too old for nursery rhymes. Too old to let him do their hair.

Despite the drinking and the fighting he could have turned out normal, or a little screwed up the way most people are a little screwed up. But then she killed herself, Bee did. Michaels blamed himself. He thought he should have said yes. The fly should have married the bumblebee.

He was a junior in high school. He had gotten home late from swim practice, the smell of chlorine still hanging in his hair. Michaels found her in his bedroom, sitting on his bed with one of his childhood books. The nursery rhymes. "Buzzy, come sit on Bee's lap," his mother said. His father had slapped her around and then left to find a hooker, something he'd been doing more and more. The boy had heard his father tell his mother she wasn't pretty anymore. Her face was puffy. Her figure was gone. Her hair had thinned. Her beautiful hair.

"Buzzy," she said, patting the mattress. "Come." He stood in the doorway and stared. One sleeve of her dress was torn and hanging by a thread on her shoulder. Blood oozed out of the corner of her mouth. Her lipstick was smeared around her upper lip like a pink moustache. His father had really done a number on her this time. The boy walked into the room. She smelled like Scotch. She was lit. Of course.

He stepped closer. "Mom . . ."

"No. Bee," she said.

"Bee, maybe you should go to your own . . ." Before he could finish, she pulled him down next to her and kissed him on the mouth. Lipstick and blood and whiskey. He felt like vomiting. She pushed him down onto the bed and crawled on top of him. His mother's soft form pressed him against the mattress. Repulsion and panic locked his limbs. He shut his eyes, opened them again and rolled her off him. "Jesus Christ!" he yelled, bolting up from the bed.

"Don't swear," she said drunkenly. "It's a sin."

"A sin? You're coming on to me and you're worried about my swearing. You're fucking nuts."

"No, Buzzy." She sat up and grabbed his wrist with both hands, trying to pull him back onto the bed. He wrestled his arm away from her, drew it back and slapped her. She fell back on the mattress, crying.

He ran out of the house, his face hot and red with rage and shame. He drove to the side of town where he expected to find his father cruising the streets, and instead found his first hooker. He didn't kill her, but he beat the hell out of her and got away with it. That made him feel better. More in control.

When he got home early the next morning, four police cars and an ambulance were in front of the house. The neighbors stood watching on the sidewalk and in the street. Michaels's father sat on the front steps, his arms wrapped around his bowed head as her body was carried out on a stretcher. The garbage man had found her floating facedown in the backyard pool. She'd emptied a medicine cabinet into her stomach.

Michaels never told anyone what had happened the night before.

His father filled in the backyard swimming pool.

When he got to the bottom of the red braid, he took another rubber band and wrapped it tightly around that end. He filled the bathroom sink with warm water and opened the cupboard below to look for shampoo. A tangle of curling wands and electric hair rollers fell out, a reminder that his oldest daughter had staked a claim to the hallway bathroom in an annoying burst of adolescent independence. They had long blond hair, his daughters did, and had strict standing orders from him never to cut it short. He didn't give a damn about what they wanted. His wife got a short haircut once and it made her look like a lesbian, he thought. It had sent him into a rage. Jennifer's long blond tresses were the best part of her, the only part he could tolerate. She grew it back, promised never to cut it again.

He squirted a dab of shampoo into the sink, swished it with his fingers and gently turned the red braid around in the sudsy water. He rinsed it under the tap and patted it dry with a towel. He picked it up and sniffed. It smelled nice and clean. He rubbed the braid against his cheek. So silky. He shut his eyes, cradled the braid in one hand and stroked it with the other. Michaels thought about the redheaded whore. She had gotten to him. Her crucifix startled him, and her desperate recitation of the Lord's Prayer almost stopped him. Almost. Something about her was gnawing at him in an unfamiliar way. What was he feeling? Was it genuine remorse or simply fear of getting caught? Isn't guilt some awkward combination of the two? Is it immoral when there is too much of the latter and not enough of the former? Is one emotion worth a trip to the confessional and the other not?

He'd have to think about it. He set the braid down and took another drink of Scotch. He noticed a strand of red hair caught under his wedding band. He pulled off the hair and tossed it in the toilet. The ring had never felt comfortable on him in all his years of marriage. It seemed too tight, binding. Such a nuisance and so meaningless, he thought. He soaped his hands with a squirt of the shampoo. He twisted and pulled until the band came off. He held his wedding ring in the palm of his right hand for a moment, reflecting on its weight and shape and color. A simple gold circle. It felt light in his hand. Insubstantial. Like his marriage.

He set his ring down on the counter and caught his image in the mirror, the wild-eyed naked man staring back at him. "What's your problem?" he said.

He waited for an answer.

"No, seriously, I really want to know!" he shouted. "What is your problem?"

He threw the last bit of Scotch into the face of the angry man. The amber liquid ran down the mirror like dirty tears. A whore's tears. He found the image disturbing. He filled the empty glass from the tap and hurled some water at the dripping Scotch. It fell short of the mirror and splashed all over the counter. "Pathetic," he mumbled. He filled it again and threw the water harder. The glass flew out of his hand and struck the mirror, shattering it.

Now I have to think up a story for this as well, he thought.

He tucked the braid into a fresh Ziploc bag. He sealed it shut partway, squeezed the air out by pressing it against his chest and zipped it the rest of the way. Still naked, he tiptoed around the broken bits of mirror on the bathroom floor, walked down the hallway to the attic stairway, and up.

Treading barefoot on the wood floor, Michaels navigated his way around a rocking chair and an end table. Though it was morning, it was already warm in the attic. His feet left damp prints that quickly evaporated and disappeared in the heat. He bumped into a child's red bicycle, knocking it over. His old bike. He bent over and picked it up. There were still playing cards in the spokes. He squeezed the bike horn. Nothing. He was disappointed. He glanced at the collection of ancestral portraits stacked against a large trunk and steered clear of an unsteady-looking tower of coffee-table books. "We need to get rid of some of this shit," he muttered under his breath.

He stared wistfully for a moment at an infant's highchair. The back of the seat was decorated with the crooked decal of a clown holding a bunch of balloons. He remembered when his older daughter, as a toddler, had sloppily plastered the sticker on the chair to surprise her younger sister. Now the edges were peeling. He tried to press them flat but they curled back up.

Small windows at each end of the attic let in the morning light and illuminated the dust hanging in the musty air, making it look like a swarm of fireflies.

From a corner laced with cobwebs, he pulled out a Victorian hatbox decorated with roses and violets. Cherubs danced among the blooms.

He lifted the cover and placed the bag of hair inside, next to the other bags of hair.

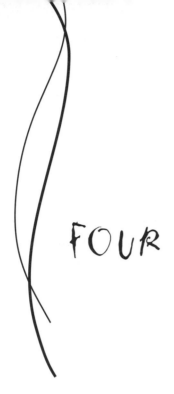

FOUR

*J*esus!" Rue said in a muffled voice as she breathed in and out of the lunch bag. There were greasy stains on it. "What is this?"

"Liverwurst and Miracle Whip," Murphy told her. "That's what he eats every other day. Liverwurst and Miracle Whip."

Rue looked at the way Murphy's partner bit into the sandwich and laughed. The bag expanded with the expulsion of air. She pulled the bag away from her face and wiped her eyes with her hands, smearing dark mascara under them; she looked like a raccoon. She felt the back of her head to make sure her braid was still clipped in place. Rue took her lit cigarette back from Murphy and puffed, trying to compose herself as much as a hooker can with two cops questioning her.

The owner of the lunch bag, Gabriel Nash, took another bite of his warm, aromatic sandwich. He had thirty years on the force and two clean kills; he'd been shot once himself, in the shoulder. Murphy trusted him with her life, but not with a hooker's feelings. She waved her partner over. They backed against the hood of Gabe's rusty Volvo station wagon, which was parked in front of an adult video store. For some reason, observed Murphy, the Volvo looked as if it belonged there.

"I told you not to yell at her," Murphy said.

"Big deal. I raised my voice. What the hell did she get so worked up for?" Gabe asked. He looked over at the hooker. She was sniffling and tugging nervously at her black shirt. The top was too tight and too short, and revealed a doughy, white expanse of midriff.

"I don't want to tell you how to do your job, Gabe, but you don't seem to get it," Murphy said in a low voice. "Rue needs a soft touch."

"Oh, pardon me. A sensitive hooker. That's a good one. What kind of name is Rue, anyway?'"

"Charlene cooked it up herself," said Murphy. "Sully told her she needed a street name, so she came up with Rue. It's French for street."

"Pretty fucking cute. What's up with the ratty hairpiece?"

"The braid? She got a couple of them from a garage sale," said Murphy. "When she wears them both at the same time she looks like Heidi. Maybe you should compliment her on it."

"Nah," said Gabe. "It looks like shit and it doesn't match the rest of her hair. Who the hell is Heidi?"

Murphy sighed.

One of Rue's Saturday regulars pulled up to the curb behind the Volvo. He was a fat man wearing a red polka-dot tie with a short-sleeved white shirt. The top of his head was bald and red from the sun, but gray hair the texture of steel wool stuck out at the sides. He was driving a yellow Cobra convertible, with the top down—like a circus clown who got lost looking for the Big Top.

"Hey, Charlene?" he yelled from the car. He was drunk and slurring his words. "Is this a fuckin' bakery line, or what?"

"Get lost, asshole." Gabe took another bite of his sandwich. The driver looked at him and rolled away.

Murphy pulled some tissues out of her shoulder bag and walked over to Rue. "Your mascara is all over the place, Charlene." The hooker threw down her cigarette and took the tissues, dabbing her eyes with them. "Okay, Charlene," said Murphy, "what were you saying about this yellow umbrella?"

Rue said nothing but continued fussing with her face. She extracted a small mirror and a mascara wand from the pocket of her skirt and applied a stroke or two of mascara to her eyelashes.

"Forget the umbrella!" said Gabe, his voice rising. He wiped his mouth with the sleeve of his sweatshirt and walked over to Murphy and Rue. "Did you recognize Finch's last trick? What kind of car was he driving?"

Rue opened her mouth to answer, but nothing came out. Her eyes were starting to tear up again. She dabbed at them with the tissue. Murphy gave Gabe the eye. "Okay, okay. I'm sorry I yelled," he said to Rue. "Now tell us about Finch and the goddamn umbrella."

"I didn't want her to get sick from the rain. We watched out for each other. We had the same birthday. Did ya know that? We were both born on Christmas Eve. I'm quite a few years older than Finch. I looked younger than her, though, 'cause I have such fine skin. Finch had pimples, poor darlin'. She wouldn't mind me tellin' ya that, God rest her soul." Rue quickly made the Sign of the Cross.

"Okay," said Murphy. "So the last time you saw Finch alive, she was standing alone in the rain on her usual corner . . ."

"*Our* usual corner," interrupted Rue.

"She was standing alone in the rain on the usual corner you two shared, and she was holding your yellow umbrella," Murphy continued. "Is that right?"

Rue nodded her head again.

"You didn't see her get in any car or go with any john?" Murphy asked. "Is that right?"

More nodding.

"All the other working gals had turned in for the evening?" asked Gabe.

"Except for me," said Rue.

"Do you remember about what time that was?" Murphy asked patiently, as if questioning a frightened child. "Was it nighttime? Was it dark out yet?"

"No, it was gettin' there, but it wasn't dark yet," said Rue. She pulled a cigarette from the pack stuffed in her shirt. "Now I told ya everythin' I know," she said, lighting up with shaking hands. "Can I go now? Please? It won't do my business no good if I'm seen talkin' to you two. No offense, darlin'."

Rue turned to walk away. "Charlene," said Gabe.

"Yes, Sergeant," she said, turning around.

"You dropped your hair," he said, pointing down. Rue bent over and picked the brown braid off the sidewalk. She clipped it back on and gave it a little tug to make sure it was secure. "It looks very nice on you," said Gabe.

Murphy usually worked alone because it was in her nature. She felt comfortable around men, but also felt hemmed in by them. She had grown up a middle child in a house with ten kids; she was the only daughter. Her parents owned a bar on the Mississippi that catered to barge workers. They made enough to pay the bills, but a big house was out of the question. The boys slept two or three to a bedroom. So she could have her own space, she dragged her mattress into the root cellar and claimed it as her room; her brothers called her "Potato Head." The day after she graduated from high school, she moved into an efficiency apartment. All through college at the University of Minnesota, she worked at two jobs so she could squeak by without a roommate. The solitude was glorious. Even during her marriage, she insisted that she have a room of her own—a small library filled with dozens of cookbooks.

As a patrol officer, she drove alone. As a vice cop, she walked among the hookers and johns by herself. Now as a homicide investigator, she almost always worked solo. The other cops thought she was spooky for wanting to work alone, but not Gabe. He'd known her half her life. He'd watched her handle rowdies at the family bar and talked her into police work. So when the head of homicide asked her to team up with somebody on this very visible case, she recruited Gabe.

What have we got? We've got a girl standing alone on a street corner in the rain," Gabe said as they drove back to the cop shop in Gabe's Volvo. The car was a wreck. The mustard yellow leather seats were grimy, apple cores and empty pop cans rolled around on the floor, and the air conditioning was out. It smelled of cigarette smoke. All the knobs for the radio were missing;

Gabe used a pair of pliers to work the controls. The front passenger seat leaned so far back, Murphy felt like she was in a reclining chair.

"We've got more than that," said Murphy, struggling to sit up straight despite the reclining seat. "We've got a girl standing alone on a street corner in the rain, holding a yellow umbrella."

"Jack shit," said Gabe, scratching his gray head. "And Jack hopped the last train outta town."

"Look, we didn't find the umbrella with the body. Right? So where is it? Find the yellow umbrella and maybe we have the killer."

"Yeah, and maybe we find the yellow umbrella and all we have is the yellow umbrella," said Gabe. "Maybe she dropped it on the street when he grabbed her, and somebody else picked it up." At a light, he reached into his pants pocket and pulled out some smokes.

"Thought you were trying to quit," Murphy said.

"Want to finish this pack," he said, lighting up. He took a long pull and blew it out the window.

Murphy opened her mouth for her "you're going to have a fucking heart attack" speech when her cell phone rang. She fished it out of her purse and leaned back to talk, abandoning her efforts to sit up in the broken seat. "Murphy . . . Yeah? Okay, we'll run over there. Ask Sister to keep an eye on him. He has a snake thing going on and if they start bugging him, he'll take off. Okay? . . . Yeah! . . . Snakes." She shoved the cell phone back in her purse.

"Snakes?" Gabe asked.

"Over to Sister Soup," she said.

"I am not a snake fan," he said.

Snaky Swanson was sitting alone at one end of a cafeteria table wolfing down a steaming plate of mashed potatoes and gravy. The potatoes were piled so high, they resembled a grade-school science project on volcanoes, with gravy lava running down the sides. Snaky looked like an end-up dust mop, with hair he kept tied into a ponytail with a shoestring. His jeans were filled with holes and he wore an army-surplus jacket with some other guy's name sewn on the front pocket. He kept his backpack on his lap under the table while he ate, occasionally touching the backpack with his free hand to make sure it was still there. He was twenty, but could have passed for fifty. His beard was streaked with gravy.

"Eats potatoes," said Sister Ella Marie DuBois, a petite black woman who met Gabe and Murphy at the door. She was wiping her hands on her white apron. It covered the simple navy blue, knee-length dress that served as her religious order's habit. Instead of a nun's veil, a cook's hair net covered her close-cropped gray-and-black hair.

"How's the snake situation?" asked Murphy.

"Under control," said DuBois, looking back at Swanson's table with her hands on her hips. "He's terrified this man is going to come after him."

"He taking his meds?" asked Murphy.

"Yes," said the nun. "I think he saw what he says he did."

"Thanks," Murphy said. The two detectives walked over to the table.

"I'm not going to go to jail, am I?" asked Swanson, looking up from his plate and wiping his mouth with his hand.

"Why the hell would you be going to jail?" asked Gabe, taking a seat on one side of Swanson. Gabe wrinkled his nose and leaned away from Swanson. He reeked of urine and mildew, like a parking-ramp stairwell. Murphy took a seat across from them.

"I didn't help her," Swanson muttered. "I didn't help her." He dropped his spoon and covered his face with his hands. DuBois walked over and put her hand on his shoulder.

"Samuel, you are not going to jail," said Murphy. "You couldn't have gotten to her in time to help her."

"I could have yelled," Swanson said, looking up. "I could have yelled. I could have yelled. I was afraid."

"That's cool, being afraid," Gabe said. "This freak *should've* scared you. He'd scare me."

"So, Samuel—what'd you see?" Murphy asked. "Was it only the one guy?"

"Yeah, one guy," Snaky said. "A white guy. Big. With blond hair."

"Long? Short? Curly?" asked Gabe.

"Short. Straight."

"Keep going," said Murphy.

"He drove a black car. One of those SUVs."

"Rust on the sides? Any big dings or dents? Busted lights? Busted-out windows?" Gabe asked.

"New," Snaky said positively. "Loaded."

"Did you see the license plate?" Murphy asked.

Swanson shook his mop head.

"Even a couple of letters or numbers?" she asked.

"I wasn't close enough, and it was getting dark."

"Anything weird about his face? Big nose, scar, anything?" she said.

"I told you!" Swanson said, anxious again. "I wasn't that close and . . ."

"Okay, okay," said Gabe.

"He had a jacket on, but he took it off."

"Color?" she asked.

"Light brown, beige, something like that."

"Good," said Murphy. "That's good. Any other details about the car or the man that you could see from the boat? Can you think of anything else that might help us find this bastard?"

Swanson frowned, concentrating. "Soccer. When this guy opened his Suburban, a bunch of soccer balls rolled out the back."

Here's what we've got," said Murphy, as she and Gabe drove to the cop shop. Gabe was steering with one hand and trying to adjust the car-radio volume with the other. The pliers kept slipping, causing the radio to suddenly blare or go silent. "Would you quit messing around with the radio and listen to me?"

He dropped the pliers.

"Here's what we've got," said Murphy. "A white guy who drives a black Suburban and coaches soccer. A family man. He probably makes a good living—Suburbans ain't cheap."

"Motive?" asked Gabe.

She thought for a moment. "He's crazier than shit?"

"Works for me," Gabe said.

Murphy's cell phone rang as they were pulling into the police headquarters parking lot. "Yeah, Murphy . . . Okay. We'll be waiting. I just pulled into the cop shop with Gabe . . . Yeah, he's still an asshole." Gabe gave the phone the finger. Murphy smiled and continued. ". . . I can't tonight. Let me take a rain check on that. Thanks. Later." Murphy shoved the cell phone back into her purse.

"Erik said Finch's hair was cut with a very sharp tool," Murphy said as they got out of the car. "He found a nick on the back of her neck near the hairline."

"So what are we dealing with? A mad barber? A crazed stylist?"

"Maybe not," said Murphy. "Erik said it was probably a scalpel."

"Good," said Gabe. "A whacked-out surgeon. I'd hate to think it was someone stupid who we could catch."

As they stood together in the dusty parking lot, the sound of weekend traffic droned from the nearby freeways. Gabe reached into his pocket and pulled out his pack of Winstons.

"How many left in that pack?" she asked.

"Not enough," he said.

"I've got three ideas on how we can find this guy," said Murphy, rummaging around in her purse for her car keys. When she didn't want to wear a belt or shoulder rig, the purse was also her holster, and carried a .40 caliber Glock Model 23 in a special sleeve.

"Number one, we might want to scope out the parking lot at a couple of soccer tournaments on this side of the Twin Cities," she said, pulling out her keys. "That is assuming the son-of-a-bitch is from around the East Metro area."

"Why do we think that?"

"Because only a local would be familiar with that isolated clearing in Lilydale."

"I'll do an Internet search for tourneys," offered Gabe. "Gotta be a state soccer association that keeps a schedule. Number two?"

"Well, number two is a long shot, but we should . . ."

"Check out Finch's funeral," said Gabe.

"You taught me that," said Murphy. The lesson was that sometimes a killer would go to the victim's service to observe his handiwork or, on rare occasions, to express remorse.

"What's three?"

"Well, I hate doing it and I'm a little old for this stuff, but I could spend a night out on the streets as a decoy. We might want to do it on a weeknight, since that's when he nailed Finch. It's another long shot."

"Your hubby sure as hell isn't going to like that idea." Gabe knew they were trying to get back together.

She remembered, looked at her watch. "Shit. I gotta go. I'll call you tomorrow morning after church."

She turned to go to her car, but Gabe grabbed her by the arm. "Hold on," he said. "What was that rain-check thing about with Mason?"

He pays attention to little things, thought Murphy. "Nothing," she said. "He wanted to get a drink. As friends. We're both running in the Twin Cities Marathon this fall."

"Hmmm."

"Oh, Gabe, come on," Murphy said. "Drinks."

"Yeah." He took one last drag and threw his cigarette on the ground. "Bullshit."

FIVE

*M*urphy stopped at a Lebanese grocery on the West Side, rifled around on the floor of the car and found an issue of *Bon Appétit*, and dashed into the small market. The place smelled of cumin and onions. Braids of garlic hung from the ceiling. Middle Eastern music twanged in the background, and Murphy immediately recognized it. Her mother played it, patiently translating the Arabic lyrics for Murphy or any other listener who didn't understand the language: "He loves Lebanon, even though the land is afire with war . . . She waits for him, but he has gone away, so she withers away in the cold winter . . . The moon is our neighbor and his house is behind our hills . . . A boy she knew was lost in battle . . . Even after we die, the flute continues to wail and cry." Murphy found it depressing; she preferred her father's Celtic tunes.

Standing in front of a mound of produce, Murphy flipped through the magazine. She needed pine nuts for a rice pilaf. The main course would be lamb kebabs with mint pesto. Instead of her usual standby salad of tabbouleh, she opted to try a cherry-tomato-and-artichoke salad. Jack would have to have her hummus, of course, and it was a simple enough recipe:

Six to eight cloves of garlic, peeled
One lemon, juiced
A half-teaspoon of salt
One fifteen-ounce can of garbanzo beans, drained but the liquid reserved
Two tablespoons of tahini (sesame seed paste)

Mix the garlic with the lemon juice and salt on high in the blender until white and foamy. Add the beans. If the mixture is too thick, add a little of the reserved liquid and keep blending. After a smooth paste forms, add the tahini and blend thoroughly. Chill and serve with Lebanese flatbread or pita.

Gonna be good, she thought.

"Larry, can you cube a couple of pounds of lamb for me?" Murphy asked the man stationed behind the meat counter.

"Sure, honey," he said, reaching into the glass cooler and pulling out a leg of lamb. He slapped it on a butcher-block table behind the counter and started carving. "Got a big date tonight?" he asked.

"Let me guess," said Murphy. "My mom and pop were in here."

"You got it," he said, laughing and encasing the lamb in white butcher's paper. "Got the latest news on your love life, hot off the presses."

On her way home, Murphy puzzled over how her folks had found out; she and Jack were trying especially hard to keep things under wraps this time. Jack hated it when her big, loud clan weighed in with marital advice. He was the only child of two university professors. Whenever she visited his folks' house in St. Anthony Park, she felt like she was in a library. When Jack joined her family for dinner, he had to shout to be heard over her brothers. "Your family wears me out," he told her more than once.

She pulled into the parking lot of her river neighborhood, with its assortment of houseboats tied up at the St. Paul Yacht Club across from downtown St. Paul. She was proud to be part of the odd collection of people living on the Mississippi. Her closest neighbors included a wildlife artist and his photographer wife, a dentist, a bartender and his teenage son, a psychic reader, an architect and a garage-door salesman who played the sax.

Each river residence was a miniature house, with a compact galley, small living room, bathroom with shower and one to three bedrooms depending upon the size of the craft. They even had washers, dryers and furnaces. In the winter, the exteriors were shrink-wrapped in plastic to keep out the cold. It looked goofy, but it worked. Most owned their houseboats and took great pride in them, keeping them well scrubbed and neatly painted. Murphy's needed some work. The outside paint job was peeling, the deck looked weathered and gray and sections of the deck railing were wobbly. She'd socked away some money for needed repairs, but had blown it all on upgrading the galley. She was content to live in a rickety houseboat as long as it had a great kitchen.

She spotted Jack's car in the parking lot. Great, she thought, the champagne should be chilling already.

She slid out of her cool car and into the stifling parking lot. Still well into the high eighties and humid. She wondered if this was the summer she would be forced to buy an air conditioner. Living on the river wasn't like living on a lake, with refreshing breezes coming off the water. As she walked toward her boat with a bag of groceries, she inhaled the Mississippi air and found it more putrid than usual. She nervously eyed the brown water around the dock. The last time it smelled this bad, there had been good reason. She'd found a rotting leg floating alongside her boat. Turned out it belonged to a towboat worker who'd fallen overboard and been run over by his own craft. The leg was late for its owner's funeral by a good two weeks.

Jack uncorked the champagne and poured them each a glass while she threaded the meat on long metal skewers. She carried the skewers out onto the deck.

"Gonna make some hummus?" Jack yelled from inside the boat. "Gotta have hummus if we're gonna have lamb."

"I'll make hummus," she yelled back.

"Make sure you put in enough garlic," he said. "Last batch was on the wimpy side."

"How did a white boy like you develop such a taste for garlic?" she asked.

He laughed and walked out with the drinks. "Here ya go, Potato Head." He handed her one glass and plopped into a chair with his.

Murphy slapped the meat on the grill, a shaky old Weber. One of these days she'd have to buy herself a new gas grill, she thought. Another item on the houseboat wish list.

The sound of a sax drifted from the water. Murphy turned and looked over her railing. Floyd Kvaal was in his canoe with his sax and his three-legged dog. Nearly every Saturday night in the summer he paddled up and down the shoreline, stopping to serenade whoever was out on their boat deck. Sometimes people tossed dollar bills into his boat. Sometimes they tossed him a beer and the dog a steak bone. The whole thing was weird, but Murphy thought everyone who lived on the river was a little warped and that's why she liked it.

"Hey, Paris, will play for food," said Kvaal. He set the sax down to paddle closer to her deck.

"Meat's not done yet," said Murphy, leaning on the railing. "How about some flat bread?" She tossed Kvaal a round loaf; he caught it, ripped it down the middle and gave half to the dog.

Jack stood up and peered over the railing.

"Oh, Jack. Hello. Didn't see you there," Kvaal said.

"I'll bet you didn't," Jack said. He sat back down with a frown. Kvaal saluted Murphy and continued his paddling, heading for the psychic reader who was also grilling on her deck.

"You could try being friendly," Murphy said to her husband.

"He's hitting on you," Jack said.

"He's being neighborly," she said.

"Bullshit."

"I'm ten years older than he is," she said.

"So what?"

"Jesus Christ. You think everyone is hitting on me," she said.

"I don't care for that mangy dog of his, either. Barks when I'm on the dock."

"Tripod's better than Brinks. That's his 'stranger on the dock' alarm. He knows you don't live here. He has other talents, too. He can pee against a tree while standing on two legs."

"Which two? Never mind. Don't want to know. Lamb's burning."

"No it isn't," she said. "It's perfect." She turned the skewers.

The meal was good and so was the lovemaking. She molded her back and bottom against his front as they rested on their sides and took in the night view from the bedroom windows. Across the river sparkled St. Paul City Hall and the Radisson Riverfront Hotel. The illuminated Wabasha Bridge looked decked out for Christmas. "I love it here," she whispered.

"So do I," he said, and curled tighter against her.

Sunday morning, she slipped out onto the deck, sat in one of the lawn chairs and deposited the newspaper on the seat of the other. The sun hadn't yet baked the mist off the Mississippi. She read the food section and came up with a new omelet to try on Jack.

"*Mmm.* Bacon," he said, shuffling down from the master cabin up in the boat's penthouse. He lowered himself into a chair at the kitchen table. Murphy poured him a cup of coffee. "I can at least pour my own java," he said with mild irritation. "Stop being such a good waitress, would you?"

After years of helping her mother cook for her father and brothers, and flipping burgers for barge workers at the family bar, Murphy couldn't break the habit of waiting on males at her table. It annoyed the hell out of Jack.

"Do you want to make the omelets, too?" she asked with a smirk. Jack couldn't cook.

"Never mind," he mumbled. She slapped a plate in front of him. He took a forkful. "Needs salt," he said. She put a plastic camel on the table with one hump containing a salt shaker and the other a pepper shaker. He raised his eyebrows. "This camel collection is getting out of hand. I counted six new brass ones in the living room."

"Shut up about my camels."

"You need to get in touch with your Irish roots. Why not leprechauns? Camels are so ugly."

"Are you trying to start a fight this morning?"

"How about a leprechaun riding a camel?"

She laughed and walked over to the refrigerator. The front of it was plastered with paperwork—bills, shopping lists, photos, postcards and reminders of medical and dental appointments—precariously held up by a variety of magnets. She scanned the mess and found the mass schedule she wanted under a magnet shaped like a miniature police badge. "How about the cathedral this morning?" she asked.

Murphy dipped her fingertips in the marble holy-water font inside the cathedral doors, made the Sign of the Cross and steered Jack toward the front of the church. Taking a pew up front was her habit. She was also one to enthusiastically participate in services, singing every hymn—albeit badly since she was tone deaf—and happily following along in the book. Her husband, on the other hand, had to work hard at keeping his place in the missal. He had been raised by parents who were lazy about religion. They went to mass on major holidays, but slept in most Sundays. Jack tried to do better to please Murphy, but his church attendance remained sporadic.

Before the mass began, Murphy drank in the lavish ornamentation of the cathedral—stone carvings, metal grillwork, imported marble. Massive statues of St. Mark, St. Luke, St. John, St. Matthew. Enormous, round stained-glass windows in a design reminiscent of a dial telephone. She never tired of the place. Every time she went to mass there, she discovered some detail she'd never noticed before. This time it was the words carved into the stone wall, over one of the cathedral's many doors:

"Conduct Me, O Lord, in Thy Way and I Will Walk in Thy Truth."

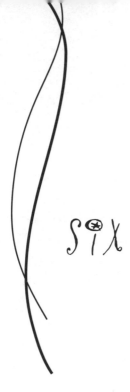

SIX

A mile away, in a smaller Catholic church, Michaels was also at morning mass. His attendance was better than sporadic, but his participation was cynical and self-serving. He took a pew in back and neither glanced at a missal nor sang the hymns. Sometimes he wondered what he was doing there. Church had provided comfort during the darkest periods of his life. The weeks following his mother's death, when he walked into his bedroom and thought for an instant he saw her sitting on his bed. "Come, Buzzy." The months watching powerlessly, a medical eunuch, while cancer shrank his father to a mumbling skeleton. The colors on the altar seemed more vivid, the ritual richer, coming on the heels of his personal dramas. As the pain and turmoil faded, so did his interest in the mass. He kept going anyway because he had been raised Catholic and believed in God and heaven and hell. He wasn't sure about the devil. Sunday services, he figured, were his insurance policy.

His mind drifted, but he was usually able to pull it back to catch some of the words floating from the front of the church. He often spent the hour glancing at the other parishioners and assessing them, measuring them. Sometimes it was a judgment based on their physical appearance, sometimes on their dress. Occasionally he found an especially attractive woman sitting near him, a woman with long hair, and spent the hour fantasizing.

This Sunday his mind was wrapped around Friday's poor outcome. That's what he decided to label this latest killing. Medical speak. Miss Poor Outcome. She was different from Miss Accident and Miss Incident. Something new was devouring his insides, setting fire to that knot in his stomach that could only be loosened with four or five or six glasses of Scotch. He couldn't put a name to it. Was it guilt or remorse? Was it the nagging fear of getting caught? He methodically dissected his emotions as he sat in back of the church. The words of the priest, the responses of the congregation, the hymns sung by the choir, and the incense carried by the altar boys all flowed ineffectually around him like muted music in a department store.

*M*y brothers and sisters, to prepare ourselves to celebrate the sacred mysteries, let us call to mind our sins."

*W*hat was bothering him? Was it fear of getting arrested?

He thought about the evidence he had left behind. First, there was the blanket. He realized Sunday morning it wasn't in the Suburban when he was rifling around in back for his windbreaker. He had remembered to grab the jacket off the picnic table, but he didn't recall picking the blanket up off the ground. Stupid mistake. Then there was the semen he'd left behind. He should have used a condom. Very stupid mistake. The police could use that, but they needed to match it with the DNA of a suspect. He was not a suspect. He had never been arrested for anything his entire life.

*M*ay almighty God have mercy on us, forgive us our sins and bring us to everlasting life."

Was he conscience stricken for killing her? Is that what was eating at him? Did he feel bad that he had killed her? Contrition was unnecessary, he reasoned. Miss Poor Outcome had been a prostitute—a whore who had forced his hand, made him lose his temper. He figured she shared the blame for her own death. Still, he couldn't deny there was something different about this one, this Finch. She'd prayed before he took her life, before he strangled it out of her. The others he had taken used their last breath to curse him, swear at him. Maybe killing a woman—even a hooker—with the Lord's Prayer on her lips was an abomination beyond simple rape and murder. Had he committed a sin for which there was no name? No forgiveness?

Suddenly the old man seated to his left thrust a basket in front of him. Already time for the collection. He reached into the right pocket of his windbreaker for his money clip, slipped out a folded bill, and tossed the money into the basket. He passed the basket on to the old woman seated to his right. When he shoved the money clip back into his pocket, he felt something else inside. A chain of some sort. Where had that come from?

Lord, I am not worthy to receive you, but only say the word and I shall be healed."

He pulled the chain out of his pocket and stared. How could this be possible? He didn't remember removing it. It wasn't even broken; it was still clasped shut. He would remember having slipped it over her head. He certainly would have remembered fumbling with such a tiny, cumbersome clasp if that was how he had taken it off the body. Why would he have wanted it in the first place? Jewelry wasn't his usual sort of souvenir. He felt the blood drain from his face. An icy sweat enveloped his body. The pounding in his head drowned out the background noise of the mass.

"Excuse me," someone said to him. They were lining up. Time for Communion. People were sliding past him in the pew to go up to the front of the church for the Eucharistic bread. He was motionless, ignoring them, as he stared into his right hand.

In his palm he cradled the murdered woman's crucifix.

He quickly shoved his hand back in his pocket, as if those around him would see the necklace and immediately know. He slipped out the back before the mass was over and ran to his car, pulling his jacket off as he went. He left the crucifix buried in the windbreaker and tossed it on the front passenger seat of the Suburban. During the drive home he kept glancing over at it, as if it were an unwanted rider in his car. He contemplated driving over the High Bridge and chucking the jacket out the window. He imagined it floating over the bridge railing and into the water, but that was dangerous. Someone could find it.

He pulled into his driveway. He left the jacket in the car and went into the house. He stayed inside with the shades down and the music turned up. The phone rang a couple of times. He didn't care if it was work or his wife or even his daughters calling from camp. He couldn't trust his own voice and what it might reveal in its unsteadiness. It took the entire day, but he calmed himself, kept the fly from busting out.

He swam laps in the basement pool until his arms and legs were numb. He walked naked through every room in the house, something he did when he was home alone. He forgot to eat, but he remembered to drink. By nightfall, Michaels had it all figured out. Wondered what he had gotten so worked up about. In his study, alone and in the dark, he stretched out naked on the couch. He loved the feel of soft Italian leather against his back and legs. He loved the smell of leather, the earthiness of it. From one of the surviving pheasant glasses, he sipped what remained of his fourth glass of twenty-five-year-old Glendronach. He rested the cool glass on his stomach, right over the spot that burned inside. He needed a game plan, he thought. What was tormenting him the most was not his fear of getting caught or guilt over her death. What was troubling him was the nagging possibility that he had committed a sin for which there was no absolution. Surely a priest—the right priest, at least—would offer him absolution in the confessional.

He needed to shop around, that's all. A suburban priest wouldn't do. They'd listened to too many boring confessions of working mothers guilty about swearing at their children. A guy like that might freak out. He couldn't go to a priest in his neighborhood; his voice might be recognized. Though what goes on in the confessional is secret, he still didn't want to take any chances. What he needed was a sophisticated city priest who'd handled a nice rich smorgasbord of sins. Adultery. Sodomy. Thievery. Incest. Rape. Hell, the right guy had probably dealt with a murder or two. Probably got a couple every year.

Confessions weren't generally heard Sunday nights and he didn't want to wait until the traditional Saturday afternoon. He might be able to find a church with weekday offerings of the sacrament. A church in Minneapolis.

There, he thought; it's all settled. He sat up on the couch, rejuvenated. He decided to go for an evening drive, cruise a bit with the windows down and the warm night air in his face. He pulled on the meticulously coordinated clothes—white silk boxers, taupe Egyptian-cotton slacks, ivory short-sleeved linen shirt and taupe Italian loafers—that he had deposited in a pile next to the couch earlier in the day. No socks. When he could get away with it, he went without socks. He liked the feel of leather against his feet.

As he slipped into the driver's seat of his Suburban he looked over at the windbreaker, a heap of nylon material on the front passenger seat. "Fuck you!" he said angrily. "I'm not afraid of you." He reached over and grabbed the jacket. Even though it was too warm for it, he slipped it on defiantly. He took the chain out of his jacket pocket, wiped the crucifix clean with the edge of his shirt and carefully put the necklace back in his jacket.

He glided down Summit toward the river and wondered when his wife would get home and ruin his fun. As far as he was concerned, she could spend her entire summer at the lake. God, he loved being alone in his house, without a nagging, nosy bitch yelling after him, "Where are you going now? Do you know what time it is?"

He laughed. That was such an inane question. He stopped at a light. "Do you know what time it is?" he said out loud in a high-pitched voice. "Do you know what time it is? Do you know what time it is?"

The light changed and he continued driving west and thinking about his wife. His Jennifer. Mrs. Perfect. He'd somehow ended up marrying a little mommy. Not his mommy. God knows his own mother never gave a damn how late he stayed out or where he went. How had he ended up with someone so sickeningly sweet and good when what he needed was someone as scarred as he? As a teenager he'd gravitated toward girls who were loose or damaged in some way. Girls who were not judgmental. His tastes for such women intensified after his mother's death with one additional requirement: They had to have long hair.

Jennifer's hair was what drew him to her in the first place. From across the campus mall he spotted her, so pale and petite and perfectly proportioned. She looked like a Barbie doll that had been left out in the sun. Her blond hair reached down to her butt.

He'd assumed too many things about Jennifer. While they were dating she'd have a glass of wine with dinner or a bottle of beer on the boat, so he thought she'd be okay with his drinking. Instead, she became a teetotaler with the birth of their children and ragged on him about his drinking. He'd carefully watched her with her father, saw the way he hugged her and kissed her on the corner of the mouth, and assumed incest. Whenever he saw parents kissing their kids a little too much or a little too close to the mouth, he assumed incest. Beyond a quick peck on the forehead, he rarely kissed his own daughters. He figured Jennifer would open up to him after they were married, spill all the sordid details. As it turned out, he was wrong about his wife's father. She came from a normal, loving family, and he resented her for it.

He reached the end of Summit and turned onto River Road.

At least her father had died of cancer the way his had, slowly and miserably. That offered Michaels some consolation.

SEVEN

"Paris, I don't think you're ready for a single."

"I can handle it."

"Why won't you ever listen?"

Jack and Murphy were inside the stucco boathouse of the Minnesota Boat Club on Raspberry Island, a sliver of land downstream from Murphy's houseboat and accessible from a bridge on the banks of the Mississippi. The Monday-morning sky was pink with dawn.

"Are you going to help me or not?" she asked.

"Do I have a choice?"

"Not if you want to get laid tonight." She reached for a twenty-six-foot boat.

"Jesus. Not that one," he said. "That's a racing shell. Here. Let's take this seventeen-footer." She took the bow and he the stern. They held the boat over their heads and walked the long, narrow craft out of the boat bay, down the ramp and onto the dock in front of the clubhouse. They gently flipped the boat into the water. Jack was a competitive rower and had belonged to the boat club since high school. After years of listening to him talk about "sculling" and "sweeping," Murphy had finally started a beginning-level rowing class and found she loved it.

"Why can't we do this after work?" he asked.

"I'm gonna be busier than hell today working Finch's murder. Might not get out in time." Murphy stepped into the hull, sat on the sliding seat and strapped her feet to a stationary platform. Jack looked down at her from the dock, frowning. She smiled at him. "I'll be fine."

"Let me take a boat out with you."

"No. I want to try this solo."

"Keep your hands . . ."

"I know, I know," she said. "Keep my hands on the oars at all times."

"They balance the boat and if you capsize, they'll keep you afloat," he said.

"I don't intend to capsize."

"Lots of people do their first time out in a single," he said. "Be careful of the barges and towboats. If they get too close . . ."

"I'll lift up my shirt and flash 'em."

"You're hilarious this morning. I'm so glad you dragged me out of bed for this."

"Look, this whole rowing thing was your idea," she said. "If you didn't hate running so much we could be pounding the pavement together right now. Safe and dry and on land."

"I thought this was something we could get into together. I didn't intend for you to take a single out by yourself after a couple of lessons. Can't ever do anything halfway, can you? Always out to prove something. This river isn't anything to mess with; it's a dangerous body of water."

"Stop worrying." She shoved off, smiling at him as she glided upstream toward the High Bridge.

"Stubborn," Jack mumbled.

She passed the Ramsey County Detention Center. The Science Museum. It was a good workout. She used the muscles of her legs as well as her arms and back to pull the oars. Her rowing instructor—a college kid with a tattoo on his shoulder of crossed oars—was surprised Murphy took to the oars as quickly as she did. She found it an easy movement that she could do with little thought. The river was quiet early in the morning. The solitude was even better than when she ran. No cars to dodge or pedestrians to step around. She had time to think about Jack and her marriage.

She wondered if they'd get anywhere this time, or if they'd follow their usual pattern. Jack called it the three F's—fucking, fighting, fleeing. She hoped she wouldn't be the one to blow it this time. She missed him, missed their marriage. No question they loved each other and wanted to be together, but they aggravated each other. It didn't help that their demanding jobs kept them flying out the door in different directions. She couldn't resent his work the way he hated hers. Jack was a top-notch E.R. doc at Regions. He'd led the push to make the hospital a Level-1 Trauma Center, so they'd be equipped to handle the worst of the critical-injury cases. Mangling car wrecks. Shootings. Stabbings. Sometimes, when she was accompanying a victim or a wounded suspect, their paths crossed in the emergency room. Jack always looked at her the same way, and she knew what he was thinking: "Paris, this could be you on the table."

"I'm careful," she told him. "I don't take chances."

"Bullshit," he said. "You're a gambler. You get high from taking risks."

He was right. He was the careful one. The methodical one. They were so different from each other, and those differences pulled them apart. Her father had called children the glue that keeps marriages together. Was it time for glue?

She set the thought aside and returned her attention to the river. After the High Bridge, the shores turned green and wild. It was a river view of Lilydale she rarely got to see. For a moment, she forgot it was where Finch had been murdered and simply thought of it as a wooded park along the Mississippi.

She turned around a short way into the park; she and Jack had to get to work. The return trip wasn't as peaceful. A barge. A wall of metal that towered over her in the water. It stayed in the middle of the river and she stuck close to shore. Murphy held her breath, clutched the ten-foot oars and steadied the bobbing boat as best she could. She exhaled as the barge cruised by her. "I did it," she said under her breath.

She was almost back at the dock when a speedboat, ignoring NO WAKE signs posted along the shore, zipped past her. The shell capsized and Murphy tumbled into the water.

"Dammit!" she sputtered, spitting out brown water and pushing her wet hair off her face. She looked toward the dock and saw Jack shaking his fist at the speedboater.

"You were right," she said as they walked the boat back into the bay. "I wasn't ready for a single."

"You were doing great until that asshole kicked up the water. You're a natural."

"I feel more natural on land," she said. "I'm gonna stick to running for a while. But thanks for not saying it."

"Saying what?"

"'I told you so.'"

"You will never hear those words from my mouth"—he looked at his watch—"this morning."

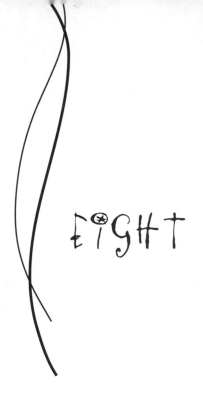

EIGHT

The cat got me," he told them when he arrived at the clinic Monday morning.

"A cat? I didn't know you had a cat," said one of the nurses. "What kind is it?"

"It's an alley cat; a red one," he told her, enjoying his private joke.

"Maybe I'll take it off your hands."

"You don't want her," Michaels said. He could win an Oscar. "She's a nasty stray I found on the street last Friday during the rainstorm. She's probably diseased. Let the Humane Society deal with her."

He walked toward Exam Room Three to look at another set of pendulous breasts. He did it all—rhinoplasty for those who wanted a new nose, mentoplasty for patients who desired a reshaped chin, blepharoplasty to fix baggy eyelids, otoplasty for protruding ears, chemical peels for superficial wrinkles and face lifts as the ultimate age eraser. Hair transplants were becoming more and more popular with men, and everyone was lining up for liposuctions and tummy tucks. He really shined with breasts. He could make a flat-chested woman look like a centerfold; and for women wanting to go in the other direction, from a bulbous DD to a perky B, there was reduction mammaplasty. Michaels loved the whole idea of carving up women and reassembling them to his own specifics.

One thing he wouldn't take was birth defects—cleft lips, cleft palates and the like. They weren't big moneymakers. He referred those cases to one of his do-gooder colleagues, claiming they had more expertise in that area. That was a lie, of course. No one had more expertise. No one. He was the absolute king of the hill. Over the years he'd been courted by several large practices and turned them all down; he liked being alone and in charge of his own show. In fact, he'd even thought about opening a couple of his own satellite offices around the Twin Cities, but he was already too busy.

He did manage to squeeze in some volunteer work. He didn't care about the pathetic indigents he dealt with—dumb women damaged by violent boyfriends and husbands—but donating his time polished his reputation. More important, that voyeuristic side of him, that little boy hiding behind the chair, was aroused by the stories of domestic abuse that accompanied these patients. He pushed them:

"How did he set fire to your nightgown? What did he use? A lighter? A candle?"

"Describe the knife he used to cut your face. Did he get it out of a kitchen drawer?"

"Did you cry when he broke your nose? Did you fight back?"

"Who started the argument? Were you drinking? Doing drugs?"

His curiosity was regularly rewarded; the details were delicious.

He had difficulty keeping his mind on his work this Monday, however. He was preoccupied with finding a priest to hear his confession. Michaels wanted reassurance, redemption, release from the nagging fear that he had paved his path to hell. He shut his office door during lunch and flipped through the Minneapolis yellow pages. He called a dozen Catholic churches until he found one that offered confession on Monday evenings.

Father Ambrose shifted his weight a bit and tried to find a comfortable position in his seat in the confessional. He was unsuccessful. He felt sore all over. What a great weekend he had had. Fishing at a parishioner's cabin all day Saturday and the better part of Sunday. Good steaks on the grill. Cold beer. All he had had to do was slip off the collar and slide into some shorts and a T-shirt and everyone relaxed, almost forgot he was a priest. He shouldn't have gone waterskiing, though. That was a mistake. He'd wanted one turn around the lake. It had been years since he'd been behind a boat and he wanted to see if he could still get up on one ski. He did, and now his hips were paying the price. He knew he would need hip-replacement surgery down the road. They'd been bothering him off and on since his football days at St. Thomas. Still, he'd waited this long and he could wait longer. He had plenty of time.

He sat in the dim, tiny room in back of the church and waited for his first penitent. The priest's portion of the confessional looked like a closet, with an out-swinging door and a chair inside. On either side of this tiny room was a booth, each with heavy maroon drapes hanging in the doorway serving as a privacy curtain for penitents. Inside each booth was a kneeler facing the priest's room, as well as a screen above the kneeler. The penitents knew it was their turn when the priest slid open a window covering the screen on their side.

Ambrose flexed his hands and examined his palms. They were sore from hanging on to the towrope. He smiled. Yes. It had been an outstanding weekend. He again tried adjusting his position a bit. No dice. His hips still ached. He knew he really needed to lose some weight, especially since his heart attack months ago. He wasn't terribly fat. He was husky. Defensive-lineman husky. Even dropping ten pounds would help. Then there was that ulcer of his. Perhaps the cook at the rectory could come up with a tasty low-fat, heart-healthy diet that was compatible with his ulcer. Lord, what a dismal thought. He'd be eating Cream of Wheat and applesauce all day.

He ran his fingers through his hair and rubbed his beard. So quiet in the shadowy, cool church. You'd think people would have a lot to confess following a weekend, but that apparently wasn't the case. Monday nights were frequently slow. Every time he tried to trim the confessional hours to only Saturdays, parishioners complained. People don't like change. Especially old Catholics. So set in their ways. Some were still whining about the nuns dumping the long habits. He was all for it. Nothing wrong with seeing a little leg.

"Time to get down to business," he said to himself. Ambrose reined in his mind from its wanderings as he prepared himself to hear the sins of the faithful. Someone stepped into the booth to his right. He slid open the window covering the screen on that side and tipped his ear toward the penitent. The screen allowed him to hear the sins but not clearly see the sinner. He waited. He heard paper shuffling. A child. Some kids scribbled their sins on bits of paper so they wouldn't forget.

"Bless me, Father, for I have sinned." A little boy. He sounded anxious. "It's been two months since my last confession."

A long pause. Ambrose heard more paper shuffling. A long silence. "Son? Are you still there?"

"Yes, Father. My sins are, I, umm. I yelled at my little sister. I called her a bad name."

"Yes, son."

"I yelled at my little sister. I called her a bad name."

"You already said that, son."

"I know, Father, I did it twice."

The boy had also pulled the cat's tail. Twice. Two seemed to be this kid's lucky number. For his penance, he assigned the lad two Our Fathers and two Hail Marys. "Be nicer to your sister, son, and leave the poor pussies alone."

The penitent immediately following the boy was undoubtedly the child's mother. She confessed to swearing at her son for swearing at his little sister. One of those "God dammit, stop swearing" moments parents have when they're losing it. Ambrose was bothered that she had booze on her breath. She wasn't drunk; after years of hearing people's voices but not seeing their faces, he could tell after listening less than a minute if someone needed a cab ride home. No, she wasn't drunk, but he could definitely smell the alcohol. She needed the drink either to deal with the kid or to muster up the courage to go to confession.

He wished people didn't dread confessions. Over years spent hearing them, Ambrose observed that an adult's trip to the booth had the same calming influence as a child's "time out" in a quiet corner. In both cases, it was a reflective time to examine one's conscience. Yet some people feared it so much, they went once a decade. Some even saved all the baggage until they got to the end of the road. He'd heard amazing things from the lips of dying people.

Healthy people weren't slackers, either.

The most memorable confessions involved sex. A bride-to-be asked for absolution on the eve of her wedding, after sleeping with her future father-in-law. A teenage boy asked for forgiveness after forcing himself on his sister, at knifepoint. A mother of five confessed to having an affair with one of her children's teachers, a woman. A farmer once drove an hour to the Minneapolis church to tell his sins to Father Ambrose. He didn't want to tell his own pastor that he'd been committing sexual assaults on a weekly basis, against his sheep.

Nothing surprised Ambrose anymore. After thousands of hours spent sliding that window open and shut and open again, hearing confessions had gotten tedious.

At least, up until that Monday night.

After a half dozen additional penitents—mostly lonely, elderly parishioners who seemed more in need of someone to talk to than a confessor to hear and absolve their sins—an extended silence enveloped the church. Perhaps that was it for the evening, thought Ambrose. He checked the luminescent face of his wristwatch, a recent gift from his parishioners in celebration of his thirty years in the priesthood. Five minutes remained of the scheduled half hour for penance. He stood up, shook each foot—the right one was growing numb—and sat down again.

He heard the heavy steps of a man. Someone entered the booth on his left. Ambrose slid open the window over the screen on that side.

"Bless me, Father, for I have sinned. It's been six weeks since my last confession."

Ambrose heard the penitent's breathing. Quick and shallow, as if the man had just finished running a race. He reeked of whiskey and perspiration, the sour-smelling sweat that comes from nerves and fear and guilt. A chill ran up the priest's spine. No minor offense, no venial sin, brought this man to the confessional. He was going to unload one of the big ones.

"I killed a woman, Father. A prostitute."

Ambrose gasped without realizing it.

"I strangled her. Raped her. Raped her twice, actually, if you count after she died. It wasn't entirely my fault, really. She made me mad, spit in my face. She shares responsibility for her own death."

The priest was stunned.

"One other thing, the thing that has really troubled me, kept me up at night . . ."

Good, thought the priest, perhaps now comes a sincere expression of sorrow.

"She was Catholic I think, and she started to say the Lord's Prayer while I was killing her, choking her, and I'm concerned this would somehow elevate the seriousness of this offense."

The man paused. The few seconds of quiet made Ambrose dizzy, as if the silence had somehow sucked all the oxygen out of the confessional. On his side of the wall, the priest's hands trembled and his legs felt wobbly. He didn't think he could stand if he had to. The weakness wasn't from fear, but horror. He wanted to listen and cover his ears at the same time, the way a passing motorist wants to at once gawk at a bloody accident and avert his eyes. His calling left him no choice, however; he had to minister to this man.

"Well, there, I've told you all there is to tell," said the man, breaking the silence. His voice had the casual relief of someone admitting to stealing a box of paper clips.

Ambrose struggled to deal with it; all this asshole wanted was reassurance he wasn't going to hell. "Recitation of one's sins is not enough to obtain for-giveness," Ambrose said. "Without sincere sorrow, confession accomplishes nothing. Nothing at all. Without sorrow for sin, there can be no forgiveness. No absolution. Surely you understand this. Are you not at all sorry that you killed her?"

"No, she was a whore," said the man, expressing it as flatly as someone stating a simple, widely understood fact. The sky is blue. The grass is green. She was a whore. "I realize and acknowledge it was a sin, as it's a sin to take the life of a dog or a bird or . . . a . . . cat."

The priest thought he heard snickering with that last word. This man was nuts. Had to be. "Son, give me permission to go to the authorities with this confession. In fact, let us together go to the police. You can begin your long walk down the road to forgiveness by offering amends to this girl's family and the greater society."

"No, Father. I will not turn myself in. That is not going to happen. Ever. I have too much to lose. Perhaps I'm not making myself clear, Father. She was a prostitute. A prostitute. A whore. I will not surrender my reputation, not to mention my freedom and my life—I have a good life, Father— because of a dead whore. Give me a penance, some prayers, and let me out of here."

"No. You've committed a mortal sin and a horrible crime. You must confess to the police."

"I'll fry in hell first—and drag you along with me!"

NINE

No way in hell I am gonna let you out of the house. You are not going to do this. Let someone else do it."

Murphy was dressed in a short, sleeveless black spandex dress that hugged her breasts, midriff and waist. It looked like a Speedo racing swimsuit with a tight skirt attached as an afterthought.

"You're chumming the water to attract a murderer, and you're the meat! This is pure fucking bullshit!"

"Stop yelling, Jack. I put a pan of lasagna in the oven for you and there's a loaf of rosemary bread baking in the bread machine on the galley counter. As soon as it beeps, take it out. You can eat in front of the television and watch Tuesday-night baseball or something. Aren't the Blue Jays playing at the Red Sox tonight? That should be a good game."

"Do the words 'Boston Massacre' mean anything to you?" he said.

"Yeah, sure," she said distractedly. "Whatever."

Murphy looked at herself in her bedroom dresser mirror. Jack was sitting on the edge of the bed, still dressed in his blue hospital scrubs. He had gotten off work as she was preparing to leave. While he fumed, she tugged on the dress. She'd be well dressed for a prostitute; most stick to blue jeans, T-shirts and sneakers. She needed to attract attention. At least the attention of this particular man, if he happened to be out.

"Look, I got full backup," Murphy said. "I'm gonna stop at the station and get wired, so Gabe can hear what's going on. There'll be unmarked cars up and down the street. It's all pretty safe."

"Safe my ass," Jack sputtered. "You can't predict what this maniac might do."

"Chances are we'll never see him," she said. "Hell, it was probably a one-time thing, and if he's smart, he won't be out trolling for hookers for a while. This is a shot in the dark. Nothing is going to happen. I'm sure of it."

Actually, she wasn't at all sure. She didn't tell him the Minneapolis cops had an unsolved murder with similar circumstances in the spring. A young woman, a regular at a Minneapolis S&M bar, was found beaten and strangled in a Hennepin County nature center. Her hair had been cut. Minneapolis homicide cops kept the haircut out of the news to preserve a detail only the killer would know. Murphy regretted letting Jack in on Finch's haircut. He'd keep it under wraps—they never violated each other's work confidences—but the twist to the case rattled him. Murphy could feel Jack glaring at her as she grabbed a brush from the top of her dresser and gave her hair a few strokes. She usually didn't wear it loose for work—she thought it looked too girlish and unprofessional—but she knew the hair might be a key. So did Jack. She clipped on some big rhinestone earrings shaped like butterflies.

"Are you listening to anything I'm saying?" he asked.

Impatiently, she kicked off the high-heeled sandals. "How the hell can I walk in these things?" she mumbled. She went down on her knees to rifle under the bed for another pair of shoes. Jack's legs were in the way and he wouldn't budge. "Move. I'm looking for something," she told him, trying to push his legs aside. He planted them farther apart to serve as an even bigger obstacle. She dove between them.

"Even from this angle, I can see your ass when you bend over. Do most prostitutes wear white Fruit of the Looms? Seriously, don't you have a longer dress? How about that blue one you wore to mass on Sunday?"

"I'm supposed to look like a hooker, not a church lady," she said, the sound of her voice muffled under the bed. She found the shoes, stood up and slipped them on. They were dusty. "Much better," she said, looking down at the black flats. "I can run in these."

"Run? What will you be running from? You shouldn't have to worry about running if you have good backup, right? What's this 'run' shit?"

"Jack."

"Don't tell me to fucking calm down!" He stood up, ran his fingers through his hair and paced once around the bedroom. "Don't do this, Paris. I mean it. I worry every damn day if you're going to come home from work in one piece. I can live with that if I have to because I know how much you love your job, but this is purposely putting yourself in harm's way. I have a hard time handling that."

"Jack, it's . . ."

"Stop telling me it's safe. I may be a civilian, but I'm not stupid. I've been sleeping with a homicide cop."

She smiled. "Jack, I love you, but I've got to do my . . ."

He stopped pacing and put up his hand to halt her words. They were standing in opposite corners of the bedroom. Her heart ached. She'd never felt closer to him than in these last few days. She'd even contemplated bringing up the subject of children.

"If you walk out that door, I won't be here when you get back. I mean it, Paris. This is my goddamn line in the sand. Do not walk out that door."

The hair on the back of her neck stood up and her eyes narrowed. If there was anything she resented, it was ultimatums. He knew that. She grabbed her purse and headed out. "Pound that line in the sand up your ass," she said over her shoulder.

$\int$o Jack was okay with this, Murphy?"

She didn't answer; she stared out the window with her arms folded. She and Gabe were in an unmarked department van, headed to the strip where Finch had last been seen alive. Gabe was driving, a Winston hanging out of his mouth. Murphy was in the passenger seat; she'd been wired. Not far behind them were two additional unmarked cars—Ford Crown Victorias—driven by Chuck Dubrowski and Max Castro, both veterans. They would visually track her and the johns. They carried Nikon F5s in case a particular man or car resembled the one involved in the killing. Gabe had his favorite country-western radio station turned low; Patsy Cline was falling to pieces. The humid city air smelled like rotten eggs.

"Murphy, what's wrong?" asked Gabe. "Talk to me. Come on." They stopped at a red light. He switched off the radio. "You had a fight over this decoy deal, right? I saw this coming a mile away. I knew this was going to be a problem. I predicted it, didn't I?"

The light turned green, but Gabe didn't budge the van. A car behind them honked twice and squealed around them.

"Drive," she told him. "The light isn't going to get any greener."

Gabe drove on, but kept talking: "It isn't too late. We can turn around and wire someone else. One of the women from Vice would love to get in on this. Go home and patch things up. Uncork a bottle of wine. Slide into something sexy. We can forget about . . ."

"Stop."

"Stop the van?"

"No, shut up. It's too late."

"What do you mean?"

"The fight's over, Gabe. The house lights are on. Jack has left the building."

"It's never too late to make nice, Murphy."

"Well, it's too late for at least tonight," she said. "Let's rock 'n' roll."

"Yeah, yeah. Let's rock 'n' roll," he said. He pulled over to let Murphy out on the strip. They looked like customer and client. "Just don't bend over," he said. He flicked his spent cigarette out the widow.

She hopped out with her purse, flipped him the bird and slammed the door.

There's an art to luring johns, thought Murphy. She strolled past a Burger King, then a bar with a neon sign on its roof that looked like a giant tilted highball glass. Next to that was a tattoo parlor with a hand-painted placard posted in the window: "Ask About Our Mother-Daughter Discount."

Enticing johns has nothing to do with clothing, jewelry or hairstyle. It doesn't have much to do with looks. It has absolutely everything to do with eye contact. When a woman standing alone on a sidewalk tries to make eye contact with every male driver or car passenger who passes on the street, she is effectively hanging out her hooker's shingle. Open for business. Come on in. Bring cash.

A husky, long-haired, bearded biker on a Harley drove right onto the sidewalk and stopped next to her. She knew this would freak out Gabe. "It's okay, guys. He's fine," she said under her breath. Still, she was ready to reach into her purse if necessary.

"Hey, mama, wanna get nasty?"

He was wearing so much black leather and silver it was hard to figure out where he left off and his hog began. "I only do it in cars, pal," she said, smiling sweetly. "Sorry."

He threw his shaggy blond head back and laughed. More silver inside his mouth. He was a big teddy bear. "I'll be back with my pink Cadillac," he said, winking at her. He rolled his bike off the sidewalk and went down the street.

There are horny idiots who will approach any woman standing on a street corner. Schoolgirls lugging backpacks are stopped. Mothers pushing strollers are propositioned. Elderly women carrying grocery bags are offered money.

A dumb shit waving his wallet at any and every female standing or walking on the sidewalk doesn't know what to look for, thought Murphy. He doesn't know how to shop. He wouldn't know a hooker if she sat on his lap and unzipped his pants. These are the obtuse fools who make life especially miserable for the people living in the neighborhoods haunted by prostitution traffic.

When she worked in Vice, Murphy once suggested, only half jokingly, that the morons arrested for propositioning respectable women should be forced to attend a class on identifying hookers. They could be shown flash cards. Hooker. Hooker. Woman carrying laundry. Hooker. Girl waiting for bus. Hooker. Lady walking her dog. Hooker. Hooker. Your grandma. Hooker.

A teenage boy in a metallic-green half-ton Chevy Silverado pickup truck pulled over to the curb. "How much for a knob job?"

Murphy looked through the window. God, was he even shaving yet? Why wasn't he off screwing teenage girls? Don't boys do that anymore? "Get lost, kid. You're jailbait!" she hollered and waved him off. "I don't need that kind of trouble."

"Hey, fuck you!" he yelled, and squealed away.

She took her time and looked at the cars as they passed under the streetlights. She looked particularly hard for black Suburbans, and studied blond men in any sort of car. After all, Finch's killer might be taking the wife's minivan out for a drive this evening and leaving his own vehicle in the garage. Was it a two-car garage in an upscale neighborhood in the city? Was it a three-car garage in some pricey suburb? What was his story? Why long hair? Why murder? Why a hooker?

What drives any man to pay for sex? Working in Vice, she'd heard every theory possible. One Vice cop told her the whole problem was that middle-aged wives wouldn't give blow jobs, so their husbands had to go out and pay for them. Another theory promoted by another Vice cop held that all men supplement the sex they get in marriage or dating. Most do it through masturbation, but those who aren't adept at jerking off get sex on the street or through extramarital affairs. She liked that second theory better than the first.

On Monday, Murphy had put word out on the street that the cops were going to be involved in a sting operation on the strip the following Tuesday night. Pros who wanted to avoid a night in a holding cell were advised to lie low. Murphy thought she had the avenue pretty much to herself. Then she saw a familiar figure sashaying toward her on the sidewalk. "Tia, get your sorry ass off the street," said Murphy.

"Wanna make sure you okay, baby," said the hooker. Tia was a friend of Rue's and looked like a Latina version of her. Fat. Tight skirt. Short top with a brown midriff bulging out. Lots of makeup. Tia's shoes were usually nicer than Rue's, and there was one other difference between the two hookers: Tia was a man.

"Why are you sticking that big nose where it doesn't belong?" asked Murphy.

"You mean this little button?"

"Go home," said Murphy. She noticed that Tia needed a shave.

"No place like home. No place like home. You like my new shoes?" Tia clicked the pumps together. "You ain't in Kansas anymore, Murphy."

Murphy looked down at the hooker's feet. Fire-engine red, with stiletto heels. "How the hell do you walk in those?" asked Murphy.

"They don't care if I can walk, baby. That's not why they pay me the big bucks."

Dubrowski pulled up and rolled down the passenger-side window. "Hey, Tia, how about I give you a ride to the station?" he yelled through the window. "Got a cell with your name on it, in two languages."

"I can take a hint; this munchkin going down the Yellow Brick Road," Tia said, and clacked down the sidewalk.

"Thanks, Chuck," Murphy said. Dubrowski pulled away from the curb.

Murphy stopped under the awning of a secondhand store. It had grand aspirations. ANTIQUE PARLOR said a sign in the shop's grimy window.

A dark sedan pulled up to the curb. A plastic statue of the Virgin Mary was stuck to the dashboard and a half dozen rosaries hung from the rearview mirror. Murphy recognized the car; it belonged to a priest from the neighborhood. He had helped close a strip club down the street by taking Polaroids of everyone entering and leaving the place and sticking the photos on the Web. Called it the Sodom and Gomorrah site.

She walked up to the car and poked her head in the passenger-side window. She saw him, a short, skinny fellow hardly visible above the steering wheel except for his black fedora.

"Sister, why are you selling your body? Are you familiar with the story of Mary Magdalene? It's not too late to save your soul," he said, holding up a Bible. "Jesus tells us . . ."

"Father, give it a rest. It's me," she said, smiling.

He squinted. "Murphy! What are you doing? Thought you'd left Vice for Homicide," he said.

"That's why I'm out here," she said.

"Oh, that prostitute's murder. Poor girl."

"Keep a lid on it, okay Father?"

"Gotcha, Murphy," he said. He reached over and opened his glove compartment and pulled out a religious medal on a chain. He tried to give it to Murphy.

"Father, it really doesn't go with the rest of my outfit," she said.

"I see what you mean. Incognito and all that." He made the Sign of the Cross. "Be careful, Daughter." He pulled away.

Murphy kept walking. She was getting warm in the close-fitting dress. She was glad she had gone bare legged; she would have died in panty hose. She stopped in front of a nail salon. FRENCH MANICURES said a sign in the window. She looked at her own short nails. Even in flats, her feet were starting to hurt. She slipped off her shoes and stood barefoot on the sidewalk; the pavement was still warm.

A skinny guy with curly black hair pulled over and honked. She stepped back into her shoes and walked over to the curb. At first glance, she couldn't tell if his hair was wet or greasy. After a closer look: definitely greasy. He was driving a pizza delivery car. He smelled like onions and sausage.

"Waddya charge for a full-fledged fuck, pretty woman?"

"I don't do guys in paper hats," she said.

He realized he was still wearing his work cap. "Aw, fuck!" he said. He ripped the cap off his head, threw it on the car floor and drove off.

So went the evening, with Murphy getting one offer after another, but clearly drawing no killer. They were almost ready to pull the plug on the operation and call it a night when Rue's clown customer from Saturday pulled over to the curb to make a bid for Murphy. "Nice hooters, baby. Will a couple o' twenties get me a peek and a feel?"

"Gabe," Murphy said under her breath. "Remember this guy? He doesn't know when to quit."

The fat guy in the yellow Cobra extracted himself from his convertible and stumbled drunkenly toward Murphy. He tripped on the curb, but steadied himself and managed to get up on the sidewalk without falling. This time he was dressed in orange Bermuda shorts and a yellow T-shirt. On his feet were yellow socks and black penny loafers. He practically glowed in the dark. The guy clearly needed to dry out—and get a clothing makeover.

"Gabe, get your ass over here," she whispered into her bosom.

The fat man was getting too close. "Come to Papa," he said, holding out his arms and belching. "I got the money you want and the meat you need."

"I don't think you can afford me, honey."

"Bulllllshit!" he said angrily, and reached for the wallet in his right shorts pocket. As he pulled it out, a pistol fell to the ground. Murphy recognized the small weapon immediately. Beretta Model 21. Nickel finish. Smooth walnut grip. Accurate as hell. When he bent over to pick it up, Murphy ran behind him and pushed his fat ass as hard as she could with her right foot. He fell flat on his face. She kicked the Beretta out of his reach and pulled her gun out of her purse.

"Don't move, sumo Romeo. I'm a cop and your ass is seriously busted."

Gratefully, she heard tires squealing. All three of the department cars. Dubrowski and Castro jumped the curb and blocked the sidewalk on either side of the drunk. Gabe double-parked with a screech next to the drunk's convertible, hopped out of the van.

"What the hell took you so long?"

Dubrowski helped the big man up and Castro cuffed him while Gabe retrieved the Beretta.

Murphy tucked her Glock back inside her purse and walked over to the yellow convertible. A half-empty Vodka bottle sat on the passenger-side seat. Murphy picked it up. "Buddy, you shouldn't be caught cruising around town with this loser friend of yours," she told the drunk as they eased him into the back of one of their unmarked squads.

"Well, I'm hungry," declared Murphy, standing in the middle of the sidewalk under a streetlight, her hands on her hips. She kicked off the shoes, pulled off the rhinestone earrings and marched barefoot toward the van. "Who wants to come over to my place for lasagna after we give our drunk pal a ride to the station house?"

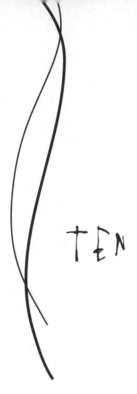

TEN

Murphy slid out of bed in the middle of the night and dumped two trays of ice cubes into a sheet-cake pan and set the pan in front of a fan. It didn't help. She moved the fan from the foot of her bed to the head, so it blew in her face. She rolled around trying to find a cool spot on the sheets.

At sunrise she got up and dragged herself down to the galley. Murphy opened a can of Diet Pepsi and sipped it while flipping through the newspaper looking for a sale on air conditioners. She couldn't find one. "To hell with it," she mumbled. She went back to her bedroom and pulled on some shorts and a T-shirt. The day was going to be another scorcher and she had to fit her run in before it got too hot.

She walked out onto the dock to do some limbering up. She felt stiff. She hadn't run for a few days and she didn't like that; running cleared her head and lifted her spirits. She stopped stretching suddenly when she heard something thumping against one of the piles beneath her. She walked toward the edge of the dock and looked down into the water. A huge, dead carp. A big chunk missing from its white middle. One milky eye. "Yuck," she muttered.

She got on her back and curled her knees to her chest. She heard howling and turned her head. Teenage boys on a pontoon.

"I'll help you exercise real good!" one of them hollered. His friends laughed.

She'd seen them on the river before, at all hours. She wondered if they ever went home. They gave her grief whenever they spotted her outside her boat. She usually ignored it, but she wasn't in the mood for their crap today. She flipped them the bird. They hooted even louder. "Little assholes," she mumbled to herself. She stood up and ran down the dock toward the road.

She wasn't fast—on her best days she did eight-minute miles—but she had endurance. She ran north up the Wabasha Bridge, glancing below at the Mississippi. A couple of paddleboats were docking along the riverfront across from downtown. In the summer, they made lunch and dinner cruises, and had Dixieland bands.

She passed the St. Paul City Hall and Ramsey County Courthouse. Two blocks later, Marshall Field's department store on one side of the street. Bald mannequins in pale dresses in the windows. On the other side of the street, a string of small shops. Nail salon. Comic-book store. Jewelry shop. Then a bagel bakery. Long line of office workers waiting inside. A deli and market. Signs promising cheap cigarettes. A tiny candy and popcorn shop. Women in brown aprons and hairnets scooping caramel corn into plastic bags. Children's Museum. Street-level storefront crammed with toys, games, puppets.

She ran across the bridge over Interstate 94 and crossed Twelfth Street. Wabasha ended at a grassy mall that led to the State Capitol Building. At the south end of the mall, where Wabasha came to a dead stop, were steps leading to the Peace Officers' Memorial. She wiped her face with the hem of her T-shirt and walked up the steps leading to the large black block that was the heart of the memorial. It sat in a pool, with water pouring from the top and down its sides. Engraved in the stone were words from Matthew 5:9—

Blessed are the peacemakers,
for they shall be called
the children of God.

She turned around and ran south down Wabasha. She thought about her husband. She thought about the case. The night before had done nothing to advance the murder investigation or her relationship with Jack. She needed to make headway in both areas. Time was slipping by quickly. The case was growing colder; so was her husband. By the time she got back to the house-boat, she'd made a decision: the job owned her ass during the day, but she needed to spend some evenings on her marriage. She would call Jack and apologize. Maybe a little candlelight dinner followed by a back rub.

The post-run shower was long, hot and relaxing. She heard muffled ring-ing as she was drying off. She grabbed the robe hanging from the master-bathroom door and padded into the bedroom. Where was that damn cell phone this time? She checked under the bed. Nope. In the nightstand drawer. No. She lifted up the pillows. "You bastard, where are you?" She found it buried in the bedsheets.

"Yeah, Paris Murphy."

Erik Mason.

"Paris. I hope I didn't wake you." He had a bedroom voice. Even in the morning, in the middle of the week.

"No, no, Erik. I was hopping out of the shower after a run," she said.

"Hey, we should run together sometime before the marathon," he said.

"I'd drag you down, Erik. I'm pretty slow."

"I like it slow," he said, laughing.

"So what's going on? Something with the case?"

"The autopsy didn't turn up anything unexpected. She was strangled and sexually assaulted—probably simultaneously. We found some blond pubic hairs on the blanket. We've got plenty for a DNA profile."

"Bet we don't get any hits out of the database," said Murphy. "I'll bet he's never been in the system."

"One more thing: Finch's parents and her pimp, Sully, say her necklace is missing. A gold crucifix on a chain. She kept it tucked under her top and never took it off. She'd been wearing it since Confirmation."

"I don't suppose anyone has a picture of Finch wearing it?"

"Her folks gave me a copy of her Confirmation portrait," he said. "She's wearing it against a light-colored blouse."

"I'll swing by this morning on my way in and pick it up."

"Better still, Paris, why not meet me for drinks after work and I'll hand it over then?"

"I don't know, Erik. I've got to . . ."

"Come on. Drinks. Besides, I'm busier than hell today. I've got to be in court in an hour."

Jack worked late Wednesday nights anyway, and it was just drinks. One drink. "I can't stay late," she said. "I've got some stuff to do."

That morning, at the cop shop, she picked up a bulletin from the Minneapolis Police Department about a black Suburban spotted leaving the scene of a bizarre crime Monday night. Someone had assaulted a priest, left him for dead on the floor of his church. The night janitor found him and called 911.

"Come on, Curtis! Why the hell did you guys sit on this Suburban for better than a day?" asked Murphy, yelling over the phone at one of the Minneapolis homicide investigators. Curtis Marx wasn't the best detective on the other side of the river, but he wasn't incompetent either. "You know we're looking for a black Suburb. What is this? Son of rim job?"

"We didn't get it until late last night. Honest to god, Murphy," said Marx. "The rectory housekeeper heard tires squealing Monday night and looked out a window in time to see the car tearing down the street," he said. "She didn't think anything of it. Thought it was another jerk burning rubber. She finished cleaning up and went home for the night."

"So . . . ," said Murphy.

"So when she got up in the morning and caught the television news, she flipped," said Marx. "She felt terrible about Father Ambrose—guilty that she hadn't run across the street to check on him. It took her a day to pull herself together. She's crying her eyes out."

"How's he doing?" asked Murphy.

"He's at Hennepin County Medical Center. Got a concussion, a busted hip. Looks like he was choked. He's pretty messed up, the poor guy, but he's gonna make it."

"I don't suppose the housekeeper got a license number," said Murphy. She didn't know why she even bothered asking.

"Shit no. Nothing."

"A look at the driver?"

"Nope."

"Figures. Anything else?"

"One little thing. We're keeping it out of the newspapers."

"Don't leave me in suspense, Curtis."

"It's probably nothing. A parishioner may have dropped it earlier. Chances are it has nothing to do with the assault. We're having trouble getting prints off it."

"A crucifix," Murphy said.

A moment of silence, then, "How'd you know that?"

She pulled out of the station-house parking lot and steered the Jeep onto the I-94 ramp headed west, for downtown Minneapolis. She needed to pry the crucifix out of the Minneapolis cops. It wouldn't be easy; it was their evidence and cops on both sides of the river were territorial. It didn't help that there was new bad blood between the two departments. In the spring, Minneapolis undercover had arranged a meeting with a low-level dealer in a St. Paul park, but they didn't flag St. Paul until an hour before the operation went down. The sting turned sour, ending in a shoot-out and a dead bystander. Lawsuits were still flying over that mess, and St. Paul cops looked as though they didn't know what was happening in their own city. From then on, Minneapolis P.D. called the mess in the park "the unfortunate miscommunication with St. Paul" and St. Paul cops called it "getting fucked in the ass by Minneapolis," or simply "the rim job."

Still, Marx sounded interested. She told him she suspected that the man who killed Finch had dropped the hooker's necklace while trying to murder Father Ambrose, and may also be the man responsible for their unsolved murder from the spring. Marx told her to drive over and pitch it to his boss.

Come on, Neal, don't you want to add a little more black to your board?" she said to the lieutenant in charge of Homicide. She was sitting under the white board he kept on his office wall. The solved cases were written in black and the unsolved in red. It was already shaping up to be a long, ugly summer in Minneapolis; there was a lot of red on the board.

Neal Olson grunted. He was a big, blond Swede with a whisk-broom moustache and long, yellow teeth.

"I'm not leaving without it," she said, folding her arms across her chest.

Marx, a tall, twitchy man with slick black hair, stood in the office doorway leaning against the frame with his hands shoved in his pockets. "It's not asking too much, Lieutenant," said Marx. "Shit, she's the one who put the pieces together on this thing."

"I'll take good care of the necklace," Murphy said.

Olson grunted again. "You'd better," he said. "Remember whose evidence it is. This is Minneapolis evidence. This is on loan to St. Paul. Fucking *on loan*."

"'On loan,'" she repeated.

"That means we get it back. Sooner than fucking later." He reached across his desk to hand her the white box. He stopped before dropping it into her palm. "When you gonna come work for me?" he asked.

She laughed, snatched the box from his hand and stuffed it in her purse. "Thank you," she said, and stood up to leave.

"You didn't answer me," Olson said.

"Thanks, Curtis," she whispered to Marx as he stepped out of the doorway to let her through. "Owe you one." He nodded.

"Think about it, Murphy," Olson yelled after her.

Murphy planned to take the crucifix to Finch's funeral for identification by the dead woman's parents, but she didn't want to upset them by showing them some stranger's trinket by mistake. Over drinks with Erik, she would compare the Minneapolis crucifix with the one in Finch's Confirmation portrait. If they looked similar, the necklace would be joining Murphy and Gabe on their road trip to a rural Wisconsin cemetery Thursday morning.

Why did the man who murdered a hooker also attack a priest? Why would a killer go to a priest? She had some theories. Maybe she'd bounce them off Erik. Over drinks. One drink.

Murphy walked into their meeting place, an Eastern European bar and restaurant down the street from the cathedral. When she entered, brass bells hanging from the top of the door announced her arrival. She stood at the hostess stand and scanned the room. To her right was an L-shaped bar with room enough for a half dozen bar stools. On shelves behind the bar was a wide array of vodka. Russian Prince, Polar Ice, Magic Crystal, Stolichnaya. Straight ahead was the restaurant. Modern-looking lights with wide shades hung from the ceiling by silver chains. A paisley fringe shawl covered each shade. The tables were draped with white linen and topped by lamps with red shades.

"Hello, Paris."

She started. He'd walked in right behind her. Erik was dressed in dark pants, a white shirt and a tie. He must have come right from court, she thought. The crispness of the dress shirt emphasized his broad shoulders. Unlike many male marathoners, he looked muscular instead of sticklike. Murphy guessed he supplemented the running with some serious time in the gym.

"Table for two?" asked the hostess, a compact woman with a Russian accent.

"We're not eating," stumbled Murphy. "We're here for . . ."

"Let's get a table," Erik said. The hostess led them to a table in a back corner. Ignoring her whispered protests, Erik guided Murphy by the elbow. "Thank you," he told the hostess. "This is perfect."

He pulled a chair out for Murphy.

"This was supposed to be drinks," she said, sitting down. "In fact, one drink. Period. I feel like I've been shanghaied, Erik. I'm busy. I don't have time for . . ."

"Make time," he said. He sat down across from her. "I know you and Jack have separated again."

"Well, yes," said Murphy, fumbling to form a complete sentence. "Yes, we have."

"I'd like to take you to dinner while the door is open," said Erik. "That's it. Dinner. Really. No need to be skittish."

"I'm not skittish; I'm a little surprised," she said defensively. She was still in her standard work outfit of jeans and a blouse. "I'm not dressed for a nice restaurant. This was supposed to be a work meeting over one . . ."

"I know—one drink. You look fine. Here. I'm not dressed either," he said, undoing his tie, slipping it off and dropping it on the table.

"Yeah. Right. That's much better," she said, laughing.

"The food here is great," he said. "I haven't eaten and you haven't either. I did bring that picture." He slipped Finch's eight-by-ten color photo out of a manila envelope as the waitress came by the table for drink orders. "Martinis are great here," said Erik. "Let me order one for you."

"Fine," she said, and reached across the table for the Confirmation portrait while he ordered.

The picture had been taken against one of those fake-looking nature screens used in department-store photo studios. This one had a spring scene with flowering apple trees. Except for the red hair framing her face, the girl in the foreground was nearly as pale as the blooms in the background. Finch was dressed in a cream-colored blouse with pearl buttons down the front and a prim lace collar. Against her blouse rested a crucifix, hanging from a gold chain.

Murphy set the small white box on the table and took the cover off. "You're not going to propose to me, are you?" asked Erik. She laughed.

"If the necklace inside this box matches the one in the portrait, we're in business," she said. She took the plastic bag out of the box, unsealed it and carefully extracted the gold chain. The crucifix sparkled in the soft glow of the table lamp. Murphy studied the portrait on the table in front of her and then scrutinized the crucifix, holding the chain a little closer to the lamp. "Bingo," Murphy said under her breath.

"Now explain," said Erik.

The drinks came; Murphy sipped.

"Vodka and Drambuie," he said.

"*Mmmm,*" she said. "Divine."

"Careful," he said, his eyes twinkling mischievously. "It's sweet, but strong."

"Please spare me." She laughed, almost choking on her drink.

"Tell me about the crucifix," he said.

She recounted the assault against the priest and offered her theory about the same man being responsible for both attacks, as well as a Minneapolis murder early in the spring.

Before she realized it, dinner had arrived. She was so busy talking, she didn't recall ordering. He must have done it for her. Again, his choice for her was wonderful: a Cornish game hen covered in a thyme-scented honey-wine sauce. He ate a bloody filet mignon smothered with mushrooms. Their conversation during the meal was comfortable. He switched from talking about work to discussing books and movies. She discovered he also liked to cook, and for some reason it didn't surprise her. He didn't ask her about her marriage, and she was glad. She wouldn't know what to say about it.

"Dessert?" he asked.

"No way," she said.

"One more martini?"

"God, no. You'd have to carry me home."

"That's entirely doable," he said. "I live a block from here."

"My home . . . not your home," said Murphy, again tripping over her words.

"We could do that, too," he said, reaching across the table and placing his right hand on top of her left. She quickly slipped it away.

"No. Really. I need to get home."

They strolled down the sidewalk to the parking lot on the side of the building. Night again failed to chase away the heat; warm air radiated up from the pavement.

"Tell me, Paris. Why did Finch's murderer go after a priest? What's your theory on that weirdness?"

"Are you Catholic?"

"No. I could convert."

She laughed. He was entertaining. "Catholics are suppose to go to confession on a fairly regular basis, but many don't. Either they think it's too intrusive or too scary, or they haven't committed any mortal sins and aren't worried about the venial ones."

"You lost me."

"Well, if I can remember the official definitions from my good ol' Baltimore Catechism, a venial sin doesn't deprive the soul completely of sanctifying grace. It's not as serious. Swearing would be a venial sin, for example."

"A mortal sin?"

"A mortal sin is a grievous offense against the law of God. It deprives the sinner of sanctifying grace. Basically, it's a one-way ticket to hell. Murdering someone would put you in the express lane."

They stopped at the Jeep and Paris fished her car keys out of her purse.

"So you think Finch's killer . . ."

". . . Is a practicing Catholic who went to Father Ambrose to obtain absolution, but something went wrong."

"Fascinating," said Erik. He suddenly flattened his body against hers, pinning her against the car, and kissed her on the mouth. His body felt good against hers; she enjoyed it long enough to feel guilty about it. "Would you call this a mortal sin or a venial sin?" he whispered in her ear.

She gently but firmly pushed him away with both hands. "I would call it a bad idea," she said. She opened the Jeep door and got in. "Good night, Erik."

"You don't know what you're missing," he said, leaning against the door. "I do a really good breakfast."

She smiled, shook her head and grabbed the door handle.

"Seriously. Don't write me off, Paris."

"Good night, Erik."

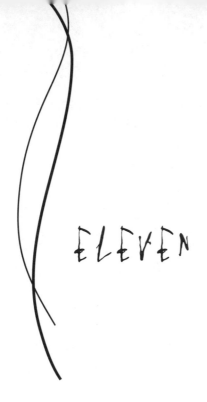

ELEVEN

*M*ichaels followed the news coverage about Finch's murder; but after the regrettable mishap in the confessional, he became preoccupied with the fate of the priest. Killing a whore—even a pious one—could be forgiven by some priest, somewhere, sometime. Murdering a man of the cloth was different.

"Sacrilege." That's what the priest had uttered before Michaels pushed the big man down and wrapped his hands around his throat. After fleeing the scene in a fright—he hoped to hell no one saw him—Michaels looked for a detailed definition of the word that same night.

"Sacrilege. Sacrilege. Where is *sacrilege*, dammit!" As he sucked down a couple of glasses of Scotch to calm his nerves, he frantically paged through a stack of religious reference books he'd pulled from the shelves of his home library and mounded on the coffee table in front of him. His clothes— windbreaker, slacks, shirt, shoes, boxers and socks—were in a heap on the couch next to him.

He lifted the enormous family Bible and immediately set it down again. Couldn't wade through that thing tonight. He picked up the compact Bible his daughters used for homework assigned by their Catholic school and opened it to the back. All he could find was a map index. "Just what I need—'The Division of Canaan' and 'Palestine in the Time of the Maccabees.' Useless." He threw it down.

He saw a slender book, a child's Catechism, and grabbed it from the heap on the table. He looked at the front cover a moment; it had a picture of Jesus holding up an opened book. Written inside the book was "I AM THE WAY AND THE TRUTH AND THE LIFE." He remembered it was his childhood Catechism. He turned it over and looked at the back cover. It had a picture of Jesus on the cross. Under it was written "LOOK AT A CRUCIFIX EVERY DAY. Ask yourself, If He loves me that much, what will I do for Him today? Start going to mass on weekdays? Spend more time in prayer?"

"Stop strangling priests?" he said to himself.

He scanned the index in back of the slender volume: "Revelation . . . revenge . . . reverence . . . right . . . rite . . . rosary . . . sacrament . . . sacramental character . . . sacramental confession . . . sacramentals . . . Sacred Scripture . . . sacrifice."

"Here it is," he announced to himself, taking another gulp of Scotch. "*Sacrilege:* the irreverent treatment, or mistreatment, of sacred persons, places, or things." A very serious offense—the kind that can send a man straight to hell.

"Son-of-a-bitch," he hissed under his breath. "Now I'm in some serious shit." Nothing he could do about it now, he thought. He threw the Catechism on the pile of books, polished off his drink and stood up. He walked back and forth in front of the couch. More immediate than his worries about his soul were his fears about getting caught. Had he left anything behind as he did with Miss Poor Outcome? Not that he recalled; he shouldn't have had so much to drink beforehand. He wondered what other evidence they could have on him. Fingerprints? No. He'd pulled his leather gloves on before opening the priest's side of the confessional. At least he had done that right. What if someone had seen him leaving the church, gotten a look at him or his license plate? It would be easy enough to claim mistaken identity. Suppose the police came knocking? What would they find in his home that would be difficult to explain, that could cause him problems?

He stopped pacing. The hair.

He ran up to the attic, pulled out the hatbox and ran back down to the library. He stood next to the built-in bookcase. It ran the length of the wall and reached to the ceiling. He pulled a shoulder-high shelf toward him, and a section of the bookcase swung open smoothly and noiselessly. The safe room. He reached to the right inside the room and flipped a light switch.

The ten-by-ten space was filled with furs, jewels, paintings and guns—a couple of rifles, but mostly handguns. A sweet little Russian PSM. A couple of Glocks. A collection of SIG-Sauers. A rare Civil War Union officer's sword hanging from one wall and a Picasso painting hanging from another. Michaels appreciated the room itself as much as what was in it. Behind the drywall, fastened directly onto the wall studs, was a system of heavy-gauge steel-mesh and bullet-resistant fiberglass panels. They could stop .44 magnum bullets. The door was similarly reinforced and could be barred from the inside. A cell phone, a radio and a small television allowed contact with the outside world. More than a safe room, it was a fortress, and he had designed it. His wife had argued against it, said it was overkill. He had told her she was naïve, that the world was a dangerous place, especially for the rich.

He walked to the small wall safe, set the hatbox down on the floor and paused, recalling the combination. The wall safe was a new addition to the room, and he hadn't used it much. His wife didn't know the combination and he would never give it to her; he intended to use it for things like this, like the hair. He turned the dial. Left forty. Right twenty-two. Left thirty-six. It clicked. He pulled it open. He felt around inside. Only a few legal documents. He picked up the hatbox and set it inside. He shut the wall safe and spun the dial around a couple of times.

He turned to walk out, but stopped to admire his wife's furs hanging in fluffy panels. He ran his fingers down the length of a Russian lynx stole. He stroked the white fox jacket hanging next to it. He'd lost count of how many minks he'd bought her. Only the best. God how he'd indulged her when they were first married, before he became bored with her, bored with their mundane and sporadic sex life. He slipped his naked body between a couple of long mahogany mink coats. Wonderful. He felt himself starting to get hard and laughed. His wife's coats—dead animals on hangers—turned him on more than she did. He buried his face in one of the coats, breathed into it. Almost as sensual as the hair, but not quite. He sighed and stepped out of the fur. No, it wasn't enough to get him off, but it wasn't too bad. He flicked off the light and walked out, shutting the door behind him.

Two days later, he read a story in the St. Paul paper that said the priest was hospitalized in serious condition. *Not dead.* Perhaps Michaels's soul wasn't entirely doomed. He still could make amends. His reputation could also remain intact. As with the whore's murder, the authorities had no suspects. Minneapolis police detectives were waiting for the priest to improve before interviewing him about the assault, according to the news account. This didn't worry him. Michaels assured himself that the priest's vow to keep confessions private would prevent the father from handing police a description of his assailant. Even if he opted to violate that confidence, he doubted that the priest had gotten a good look at him. The church was dim and it all had happened so very quickly, from what he could remember.

With the concern over the priest compartmentalized—placed in the "worry about it later" box—his thoughts returned to Miss Poor Outcome. He turned to the newspaper's obituary section.

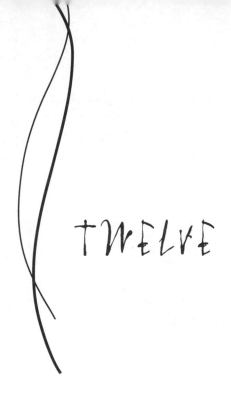

TWELVE

Murphy and Gabe took her Jeep, and she drove, taking the scenic route to Finch's funeral. Murphy had decided to keep the evening with Erik to herself. After all, it was just dinner and Gabe didn't need to know; she didn't want to listen to a lecture all the way to the funeral. Erik had rattled her, but also flattered her; she needed that. She was also attracted to him. It didn't help Jack's case that he wouldn't return her calls. Maybe he wasn't serious about getting back together except in the sack, the one place they never had any problems. Maybe it was all they had left in their marriage. Murphy didn't want to think about that.

She emptied her mind, letting the scenery wash over her as they passed one Wisconsin cornfield after another. "Knee-high by the Fourth of July," she mumbled.

"What?" asked Gabe.

"Haven't you heard that saying? Corn should be knee high by the Fourth of July. Or maybe it's corn as high as an elephant's eye. Something like that."

"It ain't the Fourth yet—and that corn looks crotch high to me," he said.

"How poetic is that?" She laughed. "Crotch high by the Fourth of July?"

"I never said it was poetic."

She laughed again and slipped a compact disc into the Jeep's CD player. He wanted country-western and she wanted rock. They compromised on jazz. The sound of a sax saturated the car, wafting through the interior. "Grover Washington, Junior," she said. "Live at the Bijou."

"Nice," said Gabe.

"Uh huh," she said.

He reached into his pocket and pulled out his Winstons. She gave him the eye.

"Fine," he said, putting them back. "I don't need it."

They drove through the town of Luck. A sign on the side of the road advertised the annual festival. "Lucky Days."

"Look, it says 'Pig Sale. Half Off.' Sounds like a good deal," said Gabe, pointing to a homemade sign stapled to a tree and decorated with balloons. "You suppose that means you get half a pig or . . ."

"I think it was meant to say 'Big Sale,' not 'Pig Sale,' Gabe," she said, smiling. "Part of the *B* fell off."

"Oh, yeah."

Outside of town, a herd of cattle stood in a pond, cooling off. While it wasn't yet noon, the temperature was already well into the eighties. They almost stopped at a roadside stand, where a man in bib overalls was selling enormous wooden sculptures carved with a chainsaw. Gabe eyed a six-foot-long rendition of a muskie.

"Seriously, Gabe. Where in the hell would you put something like that?"

"Yeah, you're right. Keep driving." They did. Cornfields. Farmhouses. Barns. Thick woods. Yellow road sign warning of deer crossing. More farms. Lutheran cemetery. John Deere dealership. Rows of green tractors. Another town. Liquor store. LOWEST BEER PRICES IN TOWN. Farther north, leafed trees giving way to pines. Three more deer crossings. Bigger town. Two liquor stores. LOWEST BEER PRICES ALLOWED BY LAW. COLDEST ICE IN TOWN. Another Lutheran cemetery.

Murphy noticed the dearth of Catholic churches and cemeteries. This hunk of Wisconsin was Lutheran country, with a heavy Scandinavian and German influence. Finch had been Irish Catholic. Her last name was Hennessy.

Murphy knew that. It turned out Finch wasn't her real name; it was Fionn. Her middle name was Clare. Murphy hadn't known any of that until Finch was dead. She wondered what the grave marker would read. Fionn Hennessy. Fionn Clare Hennessy. Daughter.

How sad to be ignorant of someone's full name until reading it on a death certificate. Still, a name, while an important detail, is not the full measure of a person, reasoned Murphy. Her mind wandered back to the necklace, now tucked away in her purse. The necklace was a detail. Like the yellow umbrella. Murphy had learned over the years that some details—seemingly innocuous, unimportant details—could make or break a case. Details like a strand of hair. A bit of fabric. A drop of blood. A noise down the street. A couple of gumdrops.

A few summers earlier, a Jane Doe was found murdered and dumped in a vacant city lot. She'd been beaten so badly her face was gone. The Ramsey County Medical Examiner found that she'd been drinking—and also found the remains of a few gumdrops in her stomach. Armed with that unusual detail, Murphy called a bartender. "Do any bars in town put gumdrops on the counter for customers to munch on?"

"No way."

"Are there any drinks served with gumdrops as a garnish?" asked Murphy.

"Anything is possible in the glamorous world of booze," he said. "Let me get my book . . . Yup. Here it is. It's called a gumdrop martini. It's got lemon-flavored rum, vodka, Southern Comfort, dry vermouth, lemon juice and—*taa daa!*—a lemon slice and gumdrops as garnish."

Murphy checked the bars, found one that served gumdrop martinis. After talking to the patrons and bartender on duty the night of the murder, she came up with the woman's identity and the name of the man seen bothering her. After his arrest, he confessed.

Some details were important.

We're here, Gabe. Wake up." She nudged him; he'd dozed off the last thirty minutes of the trip.

"Yeah, yeah. I'm up," he muttered.

He tightened his gray tie and smoothed his white dress shirt. Murphy wore a navy blue skirt and short-sleeved cotton blouse. Her hair was pulled back into a ponytail, held together with a plain navy blue ribbon.

Murphy turned into a tar parking lot off the road jammed with cars and pickup trucks. "Looks like Finch got a nice turnout," she said, pulling into a space at the corner of the lot. "I'm kind of surprised."

"How many hookers' funerals you been to?" he asked her.

"Umm. I think this is my first." She turned off the ignition.

"My fourth," he said. "No, wait. Fifth. Anyway, here's the deal." Gabe pulled down the visor and looked in the mirror. His tie was crooked and he tried straightening it as he talked. "Just because she was a hooker doesn't mean people won't turn out. In fact, I guarantee you some of them came *because* she was a hooker."

"Like going to a freak show?"

"Yeah." He continued struggling with the tie.

"That's horseshit," she said.

"That's life," he said. He turned and looked at her for help. She reached over and adjusted the tie.

"There," she said. "You look fine."

They worked up a slight sweat crossing the parking lot. The warm tar was soft under their shoes. "Pray for air conditioning," Gabe said as they climbed the sun-baked wooden steps leading to the church's door. Gabe's prayers were not answered. The church was an oven.

Murphy and Gabe walked to the front of the church, where a handful of Finch's family members gathered in a tight knot around a white coffin. Finch rested against a satin pillow. What remained of her red hair was artfully arranged around her face and neck so only her family—and Gabe and Murphy—would know that a lot of it was missing. A middle-aged couple stood at the head of the coffin. Both had red hair salted with gray. His was trimmed very short, almost Marinelike in its sharp angles. Hers was in a tight bun behind her head. Their son, Finch's younger brother by three years, sat alone in a pew in the middle of the church, his face in his hands. They were all dressed in black.

"Mr. and Mrs. Hennessy?"

"Yes?" said Finch's father. His voice was gravelly.

"I'm Sergeant Paris Murphy and this is Sergeant Gabriel Nash."

"We're very sorry for your loss," said Gabe.

"Thank you for coming," said Mrs. Hennessy. She was a tiny woman with skinny legs; she looked like a crow in her black dress. She took Gabe's right hand in both of hers and held it for a moment. Gabe nodded. Murphy thought he was far better at this sort of thing than she. She felt awkward trying to comfort grieving families; could never find words that sounded real.

"Hope my directions were okay," said Finch's father, shaking Murphy's hand.

"Real good directions," said Murphy. She noticed the farmer's palms had the texture of sandpaper, but his grip was weak. That surprised her because he was such a big man. His shirt collar was tight on his sunburned neck; his biceps looked one flex away from splitting the sleeves of his suit coat.

Husband and wife stood apart, facing the coffin and hardly looking at each other. Murphy sensed hostility between them. Maybe it was the grief. She'd seen it happen after other murders, survivors turning against each other. Murphy thought there was something else going on, however. Finch had never named who'd abused her as a kid. Murphy had assumed it was an uncle or neighbor because Finch had never said anything negative about her folks. Now Murphy wondered if it was the father.

"I have to apologize," said Murphy, pulling the small white box out of her purse. "This may be upsetting, but it's necessary." She feared they'd be even more distraught after the service, and didn't want to wait to show it to them. "I would like you to identify a piece of jewelry," she said, opening the box and removing the plastic bag.

Murphy drew the necklace out of the bag and held it up. Finch's mother gasped. She instinctively reached out for it, as if touching it would restore her daughter. "Fionn's Confirmation crucifix," she said. "You found it. Where? How? Can we have it back?"

"I'm sorry," said Gabe in the reassuring, gentle voice he reserved for crime victims and their families. "You will certainly get it back as soon as possible, but we really can't let you handle it right now. It's evidence in Fionn's case, and may also help solve a couple of Minneapolis crimes as well. You are sure this is her necklace? Take a good look."

Fionn Clare's parents stared at the tiny, gold chain and its crucifix. As Murphy held it in front of their faces, it swayed slightly in the warm breeze of the church fans. "Yes," said her father, his voice breaking. "That's our daughter's necklace. I remember the day I put it around her neck."

Murphy caught a glint of hate in the mother's eyes as he spoke. No, worse than hate. Repulsion. He was the abuser.

The church eventually filled to capacity, with some visitors forced to stand in back. So they could mingle more easily, Gabe and Murphy asked that the Hennessys not identify them as police investigators; and they asked that any strangers be pointed out. Gabe checked the parking lot for black Suburbans while Murphy watched the crowd, standing off to the side with some other women. In such situations, she wished she were shorter so she didn't stick out, so she could blend in easier. Such a hot box; she felt the perspiration collecting on her forehead and above her upper lip. She couldn't verbalize what she was looking for as she leaned against the wall and read the faces, concentrating on the blond men. He might appear guilty or remorseful, curious or smug. It could be some combination of those things—or something entirely different.

Is it you? she wondered, her eyes resting on one male face. No. He looked ready to nod off; his wife had probably dragged him here. What about you? No. He was relaxed as he whispered to a knot of other sunburned men. He was a farmer. You? No. Eyes too red and face too drawn. Probably a relative.

She prayed she would recognize the look.

As their eyes met and locked briefly, she thought she saw it.

He was standing in the back, behind some men in jeans. He wasn't overdressed. Gray trousers and a long-sleeved oxford shirt, with the top button undone. Everyone else in the room seemed a little uncomfortable in their church clothes, a little wrinkled and sweaty. He could have been standing under an air conditioner. His clothes were professionally pressed and looked expensive in their studied casualness. He was a big man, but not in the same way as Finch's father. He was tall and well proportioned, and handsome behind his thick, blond hair. Only his eyes betrayed his cruelty. His cool, gray eyes, at once savage and sad. She'd seen that same look in the eyes of pit bulls dragged away from dog fights.

Trying not to arouse his suspicions, she looked away after taking a mental photograph.

His eyes lingered on her quite a bit longer.

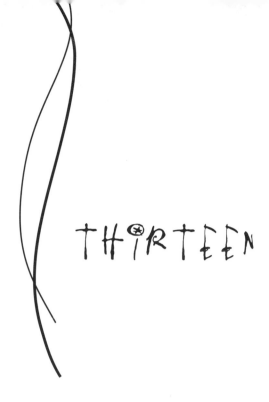

THIRTEEN

It never occurred to him that she was a cop. Not in his wildest, wettest dreams.

All he saw were full breasts straining against the white blouse, violet eyes and long, black hair confined by a band of ribbon. With her olive skin, she was more exotic-looking than the other women in the church. She was taller than he usually liked, but small boned with fine, fragile-looking wrists. Michaels wondered what she tasted like, how easily her lips would bruise under his mouth. He imagined undoing that ribbon and loosening her hair, running his hands through it. He was pleased that she had averted her eyes after he caught her staring at him. He found it submissive, and he adored that quality in a woman. She was obviously interested in him. If only he had the time, but this was a busy day. He had had his staff reschedule the morning appointments so he could make it to the service—he'd fed the nurses a story about a sick friend—but he needed to make it back to the clinic for his afternoon patients.

During the two-hour trip to the funeral—he took his gray Lexus sedan thinking it would be more discreet than his loaded Suburban—he'd contemplated what compelled him to attend. He thought back to his father's service. Brief. Formal. Little sentimentality. Pretty much summed up his father's personality when he wasn't drinking. His mother's service, like his mother, was another story. Friday-night wake with sobbing relatives. His mother inside the coffin, a rosary in her hands. Pink lipstick on her mouth. Michaels couldn't look at her without remembering the taste of her blood and lipstick. Saturday-morning funeral and burial that took hours. Flowers. Everywhere, flowers. Neighbors making pilgrimages to the house Sunday. Hot dishes and condolences. Michaels's father stopped drinking that weekend and Michaels started.

No. Michaels was not a big fan of funerals. More than once he almost changed his mind about Miss Poor Outcome's service, almost stopped the car and turned around. Now here he stood, in the back of a hot church in the middle of nowhere listening to the whore's weepy brother recite some shit by Oliver Wendell Holmes.

Her hands are cold; her face is white;
No more her pulses come and go;
Her eyes are shut to life and light;
Fold the white vesture, snow on snow,
And lay her where the violets blow.

This outing was a mistake, he thought. What had driven him here? What had lured him here? It had to be more than simple curiosity. Michaels thought back to the obituary notice sitting on the passenger seat of his car. During the drive over, he kept picking it up and looking at it whenever he came to a light. It had a small photo of the whore. It must have been taken years ago; she actually looked good in it. Almost beautiful. Almost. Those days were long gone by the time he'd gotten to her, which was unfortunate since he much preferred taking pretty women. Perhaps her funeral interested him because she had been pretty at one time.

He checked his watch. How much longer? He was suffocating. Haven't these hicks discovered air conditioning? Look at them all, dressed up with

their prissy wives on their arms. What a bunch of rubes. No wonder this
Finch fled to the city. Working as a hooker on the streets of St. Paul had to
beat shoveling cow shit out of a barn in the middle of Butt Fuck, Wisconsin.

Michaels sighed and looked at his watch again. He'd already lost an hour
of his life, an hour he'd never get back. Screw his curiosity. He contemplated
slipping out the door, but it was too crowded. He didn't want to attract
attention, although he was sure he was safe from any suspicion. If someone
inquired about his relationship to Miss Poor Outcome, he had a story ready.
He could say he had provided her with medical treatment as part of his volunteer work on that domestic-abuse program. What a lovely lie. He'd come
off looking like a saint. Brilliant. In fact, given an opportunity, he might
introduce himself to the whore's family as her bereaved physician. No. That
was too risky, and he needed to get the hell out of here as soon as the mass
was over. Still, what a delicious joke that would be, he mused. He covered his
mouth with his hand as he struggled to stifle a laugh. A woman in polyester
stretch pants standing next to him handed him a tissue and patted his arm.

"She's with God now," she whispered.

"Thank you," he said, and lifted the tissue to his mouth.

"Here, take this," she said. She tried to shove a plastic rosary into his
hands. This was too much. Any minute now he was going to lose it and
laugh out loud.

"No, thank you," he muttered through the tissue, and pushed her hands
away. She stared at him briefly and returned her attention to the front of the
church.

If any, born of kindlier blood,
Should ask, What maiden lies below?
Say only this: A tender bud,
That tried to blossom in the snow,
Lies withered where the violets blow.

She had only been a hooker. Hell, Michaels thought, she probably hadn't
even been good at hooking. Otherwise she would have been working for one
of those upscale escort services. Funerals gloss over the bad shit. Someone
should stand up and tell it like it is. What would he say? "She was a

mediocre prostitute who couldn't give a decent fuck if her life depended on it. Actually, her life had depended on it, and that's why she's dead." He forgot himself and smiled. A fat man with Frisbee-sized sweat stains under his arms glared at him. Michaels stopped smiling and glared back. He wanted to tell the fat turd to stop looking at him. Instead, he turned his face. He told himself to be more careful; sloppiness could get him in trouble.

Michaels checked his watch a third time. Why did the priest let the brother go on and on? This was a funeral, not a Romantic literature reading.

As he finished the poem, the brother broke down, sobbing. His father stepped up to the lectern, slipped an arm around his son's shoulders and helped him back to his seat. Finally, thought Michaels. Let's get on with it and get the hell out of this steam bath.

The mourners spilled out of the church and walked to the adjoining cemetery. Michaels intended to bolt right after the mass, but as he hurried down the church steps he noticed the black-haired woman standing in the grass, watching him. Who was that lout with her? Her father? An uncle? It couldn't possibly be her husband. She wanted him. No mistaking that gaze, so shy yet so intense.

He decided to stay for the burial.

"Gabe, I think that's him," Murphy whispered. She grabbed Gabe by the arm and they flowed with the crowd toward the cemetery, pallbearers leading the way with the casket.

"No Suburban! Not a single one," he said.

"I don't care about the car. He drove his wife's car or something."

"Why do you think?"

"Look at him."

"Yeah. Nice pants. He sticks out in this crowd. But I see a handful of other big blonds here who look capable."

"Watch them leave," she whispered. "Get their plates—especially the ones from Minnesota—and make sure you get that guy's car."

"Interesting bastard," Gabe said.

The family sat on folding chairs around the casket. They and the grave were shielded from the sun by a canopy erected over the site. The mourners clustered around the canopy while the priest prayed over the casket.

Grant this mercy, O Lord, we beseech Thee, to Thy servant Fionn Clare Hennessy, that she may not receive in punishment the requital of her deeds who in desire did keep Thy will, and as the true faith here united her to the company of the faithful, so may Thy mercy unite her above to the choirs of angels. Through Jesus Christ our Lord, Amen."

At the edge of the crowd stood Michaels. Now he realized why he had come, what had drawn him. This interment gave him a satisfying sense of completion. He could slide the cover over this compartment in his life. He smiled slightly.

The priest offered the final petition before the casket was lowered into the grave.

May her soul and the souls of all the faithful departed through the mercy of God rest in peace."

The doctor looked at his watch. Damn. He needed to hurry if he wanted to be back in time for his afternoon appointments. The dark-haired woman was gone. What a shame. Well, maybe some other time. He walked briskly to the parking lot and slipped into his car.

We can rule out your other big blonds," Murphy said. They stood beside the church, behind an evergreen. "Look at my guy's face."

"Motherfucker," Gabe said. "Kiss your ass if those aren't fingernail scratches."

FOURTEEN

As soon as she and Gabe returned to the station from Finch's funeral, Murphy hunkered down in front of a computer and started typing. She ran a check on the Lexus plates.

Dr. A. Romann Michaels.

"A doctor," she muttered.

His place of residence—a Summit Avenue address.

She was familiar with the stretch of homes in that section of Summit. While the entire avenue is gorgeous—called the best-preserved Victorian boulevard in America—the doctor's neighborhood was especially sumptuous. Meticulous lawns and lavish flower gardens protected by wrought-iron fences. Perfectly restored and maintained mansions listed on historic tours of the city. The wealthy who lived in these showplaces were the descendants of the lumber barons, railroad tycoons and politicians who had helped build the city and the state. His last name was also familiar. They were big-deal bankers. Could the murderer really be from the most respectable ranks of the community? Not any doctor, but a member of one of St. Paul's old, moneyed families? Or was she chasing the wrong man?

Murphy tried to brush aside a twinge of self-doubt. It wouldn't be the first time someone wealthy had gotten involved in something seedy. The city's history was peppered with such cases. Many years ago there was the department store heir who'd been sent to prison after paying someone to murder his wife and her lover. A few years back she'd busted a senior partner in of one of the oldest law firms in the city; she'd caught him at home as he was masturbating in a room filled with child porn. She'd heard that one high-society matron had been caught picking up male prostitutes in downtown Minneapolis last summer, but that had been kept pretty quiet.

Still, these cases were quite rare, thought Murphy. It's not that the wealthy have higher morals; they have better lawyers. They don't often do something wildly stupid or impulsive; they're too shrewd for that. It doesn't take brains to inherit a fortune and a place in society; however, it does take some intelligence to hang on to both for any length of time.

So what was he doing at Finch's funeral—with scratches on his face?

She did an Internet search using the doctor's name and discovered that his clinic had an impressive Web site. He was a plastic surgeon with an office in Edina. Of course, Murphy thought cynically. That's a suburb with a lot of disposable income for face lifts, tummy tucks and boob jobs. The Web site had some interesting pictures. It showed a drawing of a woman's silhouette before and after breast reduction. It had real photos—with the heads cropped off—of women's chests before and after breast augmentation. Murphy wondered why anyone would want bigger breasts. She found hers a handicap when she ran, and she resented the effort it took to find an adequate sports bra.

The clinic Web site had some personal information about Michaels. It said he was married and had two daughters. He was an avid swimmer and enjoyed sailing, alpine skiing, windsurfing and golf. "Weekend jock," she thought.

He also liked exotic-game hunting. Murphy wondered: "What the hell does he do—shoot elephants and rhinos in his off-hours?"

He had earned his medical degree from Northwestern University Medical School. He had completed residencies in general surgery and plastic and reconstructive surgery at Stanford University Hospital. He had capped his training off with a plastic surgery fellowship at the Mayo Clinic in Rochester. He was certified by the American Board of Facial Plastic and Reconstructive Surgery, was a fellow of the American College of Surgeons and a member of the Academy of Plastic Surgeons of Minnesota. The list of articles he'd written for professional journals was a mile long.

Something else in his background did give her pause. He'd received a prestigious humanitarian award for his work on a local domestic-abuse project. She was familiar with the program, an effort aimed at offering battered women free medical services—including plastic surgery to lessen the physical scars of their abuse. Jack and his colleagues in the E.R. were among the physicians who'd gotten the project off the ground a few years ago. It had received national attention and served as a model for other programs around the country.

Damn. Maybe she was mistaken about this man. But what about his presence at the funeral?

Gabe walked up behind her and handed her a Diet Pepsi. She popped it open and took a swig. "Thanks."

"What'd you come up with?"

"A. Romann Michaels, M.D."

"M.D.?"

"Yup," she said. She took another gulp of pop.

Gabe looked at her screen. "What's this?" he asked, pointing to a foreign phrase at the bottom of Michaels's bio.

Murphy rolled her eyes; she remembered it from her high-school days. "*Nulli secundus*," she said. "It's Latin."

"It means?"

"Second to none."

"You shittin' me?"

"I shit you not."

"Jesus. The guy's sure got a high opinion of himself," said Gabe, walking back to his desk.

"I'd say so," she replied. She clicked back to the home page and suddenly noticed the clinic's logo up in the corner. A bouquet of roses changing from buds to open flowers, and circled by the words: "Plastic surgery. Opening up a world of beautiful possibilities."

"Give me a break," she mumbled.

Amid the roses, a fly chased a bumblebee.

$\int$he wondered if Jack was familiar with this plastic surgeon. It would be a great excuse to call him, try to patch things up. Still, he hadn't returned any of her calls. Instead of applying pressure to the relationship—especially after that nasty fight—maybe it was best to step back a bit. Besides, she knew someone else who had helped launch that program—a guy who witnessed the final results of domestic abuse on the exam table of the M.E.'s office.

"Erik?"

"Paris. I was about to call you."

"Yeah. Right. That's what they all say."

He laughed. "No. Really. I snared a couple of Saints tickets for next month. They're playing the Sioux Falls Canaries. How about it?"

He had caught her off guard and stumbling for cover. "Well . . . I . . . I don't know Erik. We work together quite a bit and maybe we shouldn't . . ."

"As friends, then, Paris. Let's go as friends. I'll even let you pay for the beer and brats. How about it?"

"Yes, that sounds like fun, Erik. Sure. Why not?"

"Great. Let me grab the tickets and I'll give you the date so you can mark it on your . . ."

"Wait, Erik. Let's leave the logistics for later. This is a professional call."

"Sure. What's up?"

"Remember that tip you gave me about the scalpel cut on the back of Finch's head?"

"Yeah, I remember."

"You were right on the mark, Erik. I think her killer is a doctor. A plastic surgeon. I think this bastard who did Finch also assaulted the priest. This morning I showed Finch's parents the crucifix found outside the confessional and they positively identified it as their daughter's necklace. If all that isn't enough, Minneapolis has that unsolved murder I told you about with the same M.O."

"So who is he?" asked Erik. "Who is the murderer?"

"Romann Michaels."

"Whoa! Do you know who he is?"

"I know all about it."

"His uncles own half the politicians in town. He's got relatives up on the hill."

"Yeah, yeah."

"Are you sure about him, Paris? What's your evidence?"

"I don't want to talk about it," she said. "I'm not one-hundred-percent sure he's the one. So keep it quiet."

"Damn well make sure you got your ducks in a row before you go after him. He's very well respected, Paris. He's tops in his field—an artist. Won awards for his volunteer work. He's patched together battered women so they look even better than they did before they got beaten up."

"I wanted to ask you about that," she said. "You were involved in that program, right?"

"I still am, to an extent. So is your ex."

She didn't want to correct him. Jack was not her "ex" anything, at least not yet. "Did you work with this Michaels guy on that project? Can you tell me anything about him?"

"We were both presenters at a domestic-abuse conference held a couple of years ago for medical professionals in Chicago," Erik said. "He had a really slick show. He showed before-and-after slides of the battered women, but, uh, the only thing was, he . . . um . . ."

"Forget the tact, Erik," she said brusquely. "I'm a homicide cop, not a nun. Tell me."

"The thing about him was, he spent a lot of time on the 'before' photos, about the depth of the knife wounds or the severity of the burns, about the pain the women suffered, whether they were raped. He even talked about the genitalia injuries in detail. Way beyond what was necessary. He spent almost no time at all on the 'after' photos, which really showcased his work. He zipped right by them almost as if . . . well . . . like he was getting a hard-on talking about these women getting beaten," said Erik. "Like he was getting off on the abuse. At first I thought it was me. Then a couple of the conference attendees mentioned it, said they thought it was really weird. Sickening even."

Erik paused, thinking about what he had described to her.

"Shit, Paris. I don't know. Maybe you are on to something," he said. "He could be a nut case. I can tell you his conference presentation was disturbing."

"Anything else?" she asked.

"Yeah," said Erik. "The guy really likes his Scotch. The good stuff. Aged single-malt whiskey. He was really putting it away when I talked to him one night in the hotel bar."

"You had a couple of drinks with him?"

"Not really. I sat down at the bar and tried to strike up a conversation. He's a loner. He was more interested in his drink—and in watching the women in the bar."

"He liked the ladies?"

"Sort of."

"What does that mean?"

"He didn't say anything about them or try talking to any of them; he wasn't a pickup artist or anything like that," said Erik. "All he did was watch them."

"Creepy?"

"Yeah, a little."

"Exotic-game hunter," Murphy said softly, almost inaudibly.

"What did you say, Paris? What did you call him?"

"Never mind, Erik. I was thinking out loud."

His body was as lean as his office. He stood a ramrod-straight six feet, with a build that was muscular yet slender. His skin was tanned and leathery from his hours spent fishing. He tolerated golf and wasn't half bad at it, but he played only when he needed to bend the mayor's ear. His shirts were white, long sleeved and starched. His ties were dark. He wore a suit coat to work, though it was usually left hanging from the back of his chair. His thick gray-and-brown hair never deviated from a disciplined crewcut. His desk was not large—he had purchased it himself rather than make due with the standard-issue metal clunker—but it gave the impression of authority in its glossy oak finish and sharp edges. The desktop was bare except for a telephone, an eight-by-ten photograph of his three blond sons and a brass nameplate: CHIEF BENJAMIN THOMAS CHRISTIANSON III.

Murphy and Gabe had plenty of time to study the chief as they sat in chairs facing his desk late Thursday afternoon. Christianson was on the phone negotiating with the Minneapolis police chief. His voice was at once firm, smooth and convincing. He could have been a diplomat arranging a cease-fire between warring nations. Rumor had it he got the job because of family connections, but he clearly held on to it because of his own merits.

"Look, my people have made impressive headway, and clearly our investigation dovetails with your case involving the assault on the priest, as well as that homicide from the spring."

He paused, listening to his counterpart in Minneapolis.

"No problem there," he said. "I think we're both in agreement on that one."

Murphy briefly wondered what they were in agreement on; probably something in reference to the rim job. Then her mind wandered.

Sitting across from Christianson made her feel like she was back in high school, waiting to get chewed out for mouthing off or skipping class. Except for the lack of crucifixes on the walls, Murphy thought his office could pass for a Catholic school principal's office in its nearly spiritual devotion to simplicity. The walls were painted a flat white and were unadorned, save for a few photographs of the chief shaking hands with police officers receiving awards. Some were St. Paul cops and others wore uniforms from Des Moines, Christianson's hometown and where he'd served as chief before coming to Minnesota. A tall antique oak bookcase—another of the chief's personal furniture pieces—sat against one wall. The shelves were filled with books related to police work: *The Complete Guide to Compact Handguns. The International Biographical Dictionary of Law Enforcement. Homicide Investigation Techniques.* Behind his desk and off to one side, looking isolated and lonely on its own stand, was a computer. It was turned off. He used it only for word processing and e-mail. He viewed the Internet as the slacker's window to the world; he was suspicious of any cop who relied on it more heavily than old-fashioned footwork.

She remembered the last time she'd sat in this chair. She'd reamed out an assistant county attorney for refusing to prosecute one of her cases—her parting words to him were "Kiss my Lebanese ass"—and Christianson had called her in for a ten-minute lecture on cop etiquette. She'd listened to him, thinking he was a Puritan and a perfectionist. Then on her way out, he'd praised her for solving her latest case. She had to admit he did let her cut procedural corners when necessary. The only problem was they often disagreed on when it was necessary.

"Correct. That's all I'm saying," Christianson said into the phone, switching it from one ear to the other and swiveling his chair around to face the windows behind his desk.

Murphy sighed, leaned back in her chair and stretched her legs out in front of her. She hated this politicking and maneuvering; she just wanted to do her job. That's why she'd probably never get past sergeant, and that was fine with her. Sometimes Gabe chewed her out for her crappy attitude, but he wasn't exactly rocketing up the career ladder either.

"You have a talented bunch of detectives over there, but I know you're short on manpower and our load is lighter," Christianson said.

Gabe looked at her and rolled his eyes. She grinned back. The chief's a slick salesman, thought Murphy. That's what Gabe called Christianson behind his back—"Slick." The two men didn't like each other, but at least they had fishing in common. She had absolutely nothing to say to the chief that wasn't work related. Whenever she saw him stepping into an elevator, she took the stairs.

"That's right," Christianson said, swiveling his chair back around so that he faced the detectives. "So why not let my folks lead the investigation into all three cases?" He paused, listening again. He smiled at Gabe and Murphy and gave them the thumbs-up with his left hand while holding the phone with his right.

"Yes. Yes. I understand completely. Certainly. They will work with whoever you give them. We will keep you fully informed. Absolutely. Thank you. Give my best to Delores."

He hung up the phone, leaned over his desk and smiled at the detectives. "Well, we're in business," he said. "You two are running it. Minneapolis will throw a body your way if you need one. Let me know what you need from me and when you need it."

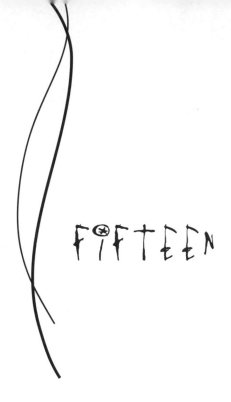

FIFTEEN

He used to look forward to certain Thursdays.

Every Thursday, a bar in Minneapolis hosted an S&M night. They called it "Pins and Needles." He didn't go every Thursday. He didn't want to become too familiar to the staff or the clientele, and he didn't want to become bored with it. So he indulged himself once every few weeks. Told his wife he was meeting old high-school buddies for drinks.

He decided to avoid the place after what had happened with Miss Accident in the spring; he'd picked her up at the bar.

After suffering through the whore's funeral and returning to a waiting room filled with pissed patients, Michaels decided it was time to treat himself.

He wore what everyone wore S&M night. Black. He slipped into a black T-shirt, black jeans and black shoes. He admired himself in the bedroom mirror before leaving the house. Black looked so good with blond hair. He drove the Suburban. More black. As he pulled out of the driveway, he slipped in a CD to get in the mood. Fine Young Cannibals seemed right.

"She Drives Me Crazy" rattled around inside the car. He shut off the air conditioner and rolled down all the windows; it was muggy out, but he didn't mind. He took Summit west almost to the river, hung a right on Cretin Avenue and took that to Interstate 94. He wished the drive were a little longer; anticipation was half the fun.

The night of Miss Accident, his drive to the bar had been in a drunken fog. Jennifer had called home. She'd lost the baby while up at the cabin with a friend. She'd delivered the bad news in a flat voice and hung up before he could ask any questions. He'd sat with the phone to his ear, listening to the dial tone and paging through the photo album that would never materialize. Cub Scout meetings. Baseball games. Sailing trips. Michaels had flung the phone across the bedroom and cried for the first time since his mother died. Then he'd grabbed his Scotch and his car keys and driven to the bar with the booze under the seat. He'd pulled the bottle out every third stoplight or so to take a swig. He'd never done that before, literally drinking and driving and drinking and driving.

He promised himself he'd stay sober and in control this visit. Keep the fly at bay.

He pulled into the club's parking lot. Crowded, but not full. By the end of the evening there would be cars parked on the grass. More and more people were discovering Thursday nights at this place; it was a dirty little secret that had grown large and not so secret.

The cold air hit him in the face as he walked into the club. The club's air conditioner was cranked. Then it was always cranked Thursday nights. It kept the women's nipples erect, gave the clothespins something to hang on to, and it hardened the hot wax more quickly. He looked around the warehouse-like room. There'd been a few decorating changes in his absence—he didn't remember that barbed wire along the balcony rails from before—but it was basically the same. Chain-link fencing here and there. Cages. Minimal lighting. Black-and-white posters from old prison flicks.

The real atmosphere was provided by the club patrons themselves. Many dressed as simply and conservatively as he, but others went all out. Women dressed in short, tight spandex dresses that showed every curve of their breasts. Some wore black slips and corsets. Gothics floated in wearing long dresses with black gloves up to their armpits. Lots and lots of leather. The vampire look was popular. He was surprised at how some men could wear a cape with a straight face. There were often surprises at the club from the costumes alone.

He tried not to look startled this particular night when a man walked out of the bathroom dressed in nothing but a white cloth diaper. That man was obviously a doer. There were two sorts of patrons S&M night. The doers and the watchers. Diaper man was a doer. Michaels was a watcher. He enjoyed watching, and thought it was more dignified.

He took a seat at the bar and watched the show onstage. A short, plump woman with spiked hair was dripping hot wax onto another woman's chest. The willing victim was tied to a pole, her wrists bound over her head with pantyhose. She wore a sheer blouse; the wax melted right through it. Next to this couple was a male-female team, with the man tied to the pole with a rope and the woman whipping him. Not too hard. Just hard enough.

"What can I get you?" asked the bartender. Her hair was oriental-looking—long, straight and blue-black. Her lips were painted black and so were her nails.

"Isn't it hard to keep those on all night?" he asked, eyeing the clothespins pinching her nipples under her thin tank top.

"Not at all. It turns me on," she said. She smiled. Black lipstick smudged her teeth. "What turns you on?"

"Don't ask," Michaels said. "You don't want to know." He scanned the greasy whiskey bottles behind her; their selection was usually lousy. "Got any decent Scotch?"

"All we have are blends," she said. "These twenty-somethings don't drink Scotch."

"Aren't you a twenty-something?" he said.

The flattery hit home. She reddened. "Don't ask," she said. "You don't want to know."

Michaels laughed. He liked her. She had big tits and a smart mouth. Her slightly lined neck showed her age. Necks were a dead giveaway, even more so than hands. He guessed she was in her late thirties. Most of the doers were in their twenties; the watchers were in their thirties and forties and fifties. She might be a doer in her off-hours.

"Johnny Walker neat," he said. "A double."

She set it down in front of him. He threw some bills on the bar, grabbed his drink and slid off the stool.

"Leaving so soon?" she asked.

"I'll be back," he said. "Wanna look around." He flashed her a smile. She was his for the taking. He wasn't sure if he was in the mood tonight. Besides, he had to be careful; he'd had enough problems lately. Didn't need to add to the list.

He walked to one of the side rooms, for the real action. For twenty dollars, you could watch while strangers strapped your date to a table and tormented him or her with clothespins, hot wax, whatever. That's where he'd met Miss Accident. Her date had been drunk and had run out of twenties. They'd kicked the loser out of the room. Michaels had stayed. He'd been only too happy to flip for a couple of treatments. She had had a high tolerance for pain.

Michaels pushed aside the velvet curtain hanging in the doorway of the first room and poked his head in. He wasn't interested. They were all too fat and ugly: the one on the table, the one doing the work and the one watching. The next room was empty. He checked his watch: only eleven o'clock, still early by S&M standards. The place didn't start hopping until midnight.

He headed back to the bar. Someone grabbed his arm. He turned.

"Hey, baby," said the woman at his elbow. "Need a slave? I've already been trained." She was tall and emaciated, with a chest as flat as a slab of marble. Her boyish hair was dyed the color of grape Kool-Aid and hugged her head like a purple bathing cap. Not his type. Not even close.

"Let go," he said, shoving her hand off his arm. "I don't want any."

"You sure?" she asked. Her fingers curled around his wrist like white snakes. She smiled; her teeth were gray stubs.

"Never been surer of anything in my life," he said, pulling his hand away. "Now get lost."

"Fuck you," she said. He watched her go. She crossed the room and wrapped her fingers around the arms of a man standing alone near the stage. She'd find some chump, maybe even a good-looking one. Thursday nights, even ugly women got lucky if they were willing to put out—and put up with some pain. She looked more than willing.

He returned to his seat at the bar. The bartender had her back turned to him. Her hair was a dark curtain down her tall, narrow frame. She was mixing a blender drink. She poured the pink slush into a couple of glasses and opened a fridge under the counter to retrieve something. Strawberries. She put one in each drink and took a bite out of a third.

"Don't tell on me," she said. She winked and tossed him one before sliding straws into the drinks. She walked to the other end of the bar and set the drinks on a waiter's tray. The waiter, a leather-clad kid who looked barely twenty, leaned over the bar and said something to her. She turned and looked at Michaels and then turned back to the waiter, nodding. Michaels figured she was telling the waiter she hoped to get laid after closing time.

She returned to Michaels's end of the bar with a big smile on her face. "So how's it look? Not much out there tonight?" she asked, wiping the countertop with a towel. "Or can't find what you need?"

"I don't know what I need tonight," he said. He tossed the strawberry stem into an ashtray and licked his fingers. He watched her watching him do it.

"Maybe I can help you out later," she said.

He studied her face. She wasn't very pretty. Her chin was too pointed, her nose too sharp and long; there was a big gap between her top front teeth. She had her hair going for her, though. Interesting, smooth hair.

"Maybe," he said, taking a drink of Scotch. "Later."

He met her outside after the club had closed. They both leaned against the side of the Suburban. The night air was hot and humid. She had a cigarette between her lips and was taking long, deep pulls. The clothespins were gone. Her nipples looked erect; he wondered if they were still sore.

"Which is your car?" he asked. There were two left in the parking lot, both of them beaters.

"Neither," she said. "I walk to work and mooch a ride home."

"Where's your ride tonight?" he asked.

"I'm looking at him," she said, smiling. He thought about it; he liked laying them on his own terms, and never in their own homes. Maybe it would be all right if he behaved himself, didn't let things get out of hand. Didn't let the fly cut loose.

She tossed the butt to the ground and stepped on it. "I know what you're thinking—that I'm some sleaze who might pull something. I'm really a nice, normal person," she said. "This bar scene is only for the summer. I'm an art teacher at a community college."

"Sure," he said. "Fine." He opened the passenger-side door for her. She hopped in and slammed it shut herself. A little too hard. This one was no frail flower. He slid behind the wheel and shut his door. "How do you know I'm not some maniac?" he asked, turning on the ignition.

She laughed. "Look at you," she said. "You're so clean-cut, it's pathetic."

He smiled but said nothing as he steered his SUV out of the parking lot.

High ceilings, tall windows, dark corners, bare brick walls, drafts everywhere. Typical warehouse apartment. Bad art hung from every bit of wall space and was propped up against half the furniture. The oil paintings were all swirls of pastel—pink, yellow, lavender, cream. The Easter Bunny's LSD trip. Nearly every flat surface—every table, chair and countertop—was covered with pink clay sculptures that looked like one sexual object or another. Breasts. Penises. Vaginas. Lots of vaginas. Some of them were crumbling. "Did all this yourself?" he asked.

"Yeah. What do you think?"

"Really interesting," he said. "Different. Lots of pink."

"Titty pink," she said, smiling. "It's my favorite color." She took a couple of paintings off the futon couch so he could sit down. "To be honest, I stink," she said. "I know I do. I still love it. It's a great release."

She disappeared behind a Japanese screen and reappeared with two glasses filled with Scotch. "Sorry. It's another cheap-ass blend," she said, handing him one of the glasses.

"It's fine," he said. He examined the glass; it had smudges on it and a chipped rim. He sipped hesitantly. She set her own glass down on a bare spot on the coffee table and sat down next to him. The hem of her short black skirt crawled up to her crotch. He studied her in the harsh light of the naked bulb hanging from the ceiling. Her hair. It didn't look quite right. Too shiny, too smooth. Much too perfect. "Your hair . . . ," he said, and reached out to touch it. She dodged his hand.

"Let's listen to some tunes," she said, sliding off the couch. She walked over to the CD player sitting on the floor across the room and popped in a disc.

The music was some screeching shit he didn't recognize. Irritating. She saw him frowning and turned down the volume, but not enough. He felt a headache coming on. He took another drink. This could be a mistake, he thought. Maybe he couldn't behave himself. He wondered if anyone had noticed her getting into his car. She'd probably told one of her friends in the club she was leaving with someone, a blond stranger she'd met at the bar. Control yourself. Control.

She walked toward him, smiling. The way her long hair swung was enticing, but not quite right. The ends were too even.

She sat back down and pulled the glass from his hand. "You didn't come for the booze anyway, did you, baby?" she said. She set his glass down, leaned over and kissed him. She smelled like cigarettes and tasted like whiskey and strawberries. She leaned over farther, pressing him back against the couch. Her tongue darted into his mouth, scraping against his teeth. Her right hand slid down to his crotch. "Baby, you are sooo big."

He grabbed her by the shoulders and pushed her away. "I like being the one in charge," he said.

She ignored him and fell against him, burying her mouth in the crook of his neck. She bit him.

"Dammit!" he said. He pushed her face away and felt his neck. She'd drawn blood.

"You crazy bitch!" he yelled. He shoved her off him. She landed on her ass, on the floor between the couch and the coffee table. He stood up to leave. That's when he noticed it. No wonder the hair looked wrong. He grabbed the top of it and pulled it off, throwing it on the floor. Underneath, her head was shaved and ringed by a black barbed-wire tattoo. Hideous. He stood over her, staring in disgust.

"What's your problem?" she said, grabbing the edge of the coffee table and standing up. "You some kind of tight ass? Can't handle something a little different? Afraid? Then what were you doing in the club?"

He wanted to hit her. He really did. Wanted to see her ugly egg head bounce against the wood floor. Wrap his hands around her chicken neck and squeeze. He knew the creepy cunt wasn't worth it, but he couldn't resist.

Couldn't hold back the buzzing. The fucking buzzing. He clenched his fists and took a step toward her.

The door opened and the young waiter in black leather walked in. "Hey, teach," the kid said. He shut the door behind him, walked over to the bald woman and stood behind her, gnawing on her shoulder. He had to be fifteen years her junior.

"Hey, lover," she said. "What kept you?"

The kid pulled his mouth off her shoulder. "Some ass wipe poured hot wax on the urinals, plugged 'em real good. Had to stay and scrape it off." He looked at Michaels. "Did we find a new student?"

"What the hell is going on here?" asked Michaels. "Who is this?" He took a couple of steps back; the kid was skinny but taller than he was. His head was shaved and ringed by barbed wire, too. Multiple hoops in both ears and in his nose.

"Josh here is in my art class," she said, smiling at the doctor. "Beginning Oil Painting."

"She's teaching me a few other things, too," the kid said. He reached around from behind and cupped her breasts with his hands. He had crude homemade tattoos on his fingers.

"Josh wanted a classmate," she said. "You looked brave enough, healthy enough."

"It'll be tasty," the kid said. He smiled and then licked his lips, so Michaels could see the silver studs dotting the tip of his tongue.

"Come on," she said. "Don't let the wig thing bum you out. Bet you never had a man and a woman at the same time."

Michaels strained to listen; he could barely hear her above the buzzing. Buzzing. Buzzing.

The woman untangled herself from the boy's arms and walked over to Michaels. She peeled off her shirt and dropped it on the floor at Michaels's feet. The barbed-wire tattoo circled each of her breasts and silver rings pierced each of her nipples. Michaels reached out his right hand and, with his fingertips, traced one of the hoops. He grabbed the ring between his thumb and index finger and pulled. She smiled, creepy cunt. She liked it.

She slipped her arms around his neck and arched her back, grinding her crotch into his. "That's it, Mr. Clean. Give it a try. Get a little dirty."

He was getting hard, but something was wrong. The buzzing was erratic, as if the fly had hit a window. This won't work, thought Michaels. Not two at once. Not a bald woman and a tattooed boy.

Michaels wrapped a hand around each of her bony wrists, peeled her arms off him and backed away. He felt something under his shoe and looked down. The wig. An ugly mound of fake hair.

"Freaks," Michaels growled, and kicked the wig. It slid across the floor like a mad black cat and slammed into the stereo. He yanked open the door and walked out.

"Pussy!" the boy hollered after him.

The bald woman laughed.

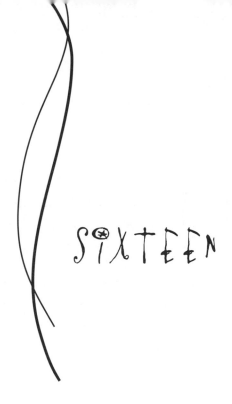

SIXTEEN

re you nuts, Paris? Do you know who he is?"

Friday's telephone conversation with Jack did nothing to validate Murphy's intention to pursue the plastic surgeon. She had called Jack hoping he could offer some insight into Michaels's background. She also prayed they could get their reconciliation efforts back on track. Instead, Jack lost it.

"You're ready to accuse him of killing another woman in Minneapolis? Let's not even talk about the assault on a priest. He's on the parish council of the oldest Catholic church in town. He's a family man; he's got a wife and two daughters. Babe, you are way off base. You are not even in the right fucking ballpark. How can you do this?"

"I'm not doing shit yet," she said. "I've got a lot of legwork to do, but he's a suspect, and I want you to keep that under your hat."

"No need to worry about that. This is absurd."

"No, it's not—the fact is, you don't know what the hell you're talking about, and I do. I saw him there at Finch's service, with scratches on his face.

So did Gabe. Can you tell me why he'd attend a hooker's funeral, one—two hours away in Wisconsin?"

"Maybe she was one of his patients," said Jack. "Ever think of that? Maybe he knew her from his volunteer work."

"I checked with Finch's family—both the one on the street and the one on the farm. They've never laid eyes on Michaels. Finch hadn't seen a doctor for years, and her pimp never beat her badly enough to leave scars. He's far too clever for that. Maybe she knew Michaels. We'll check, but I don't think so . . ."

"Here's a brilliant idea, hot-shit detective. Why don't you call Michaels and ask him why he was there and where he got the scratches?"

"'Cause he'd bullshit me," she said. "But hey, thanks for telling me how to do my job."

"Fuck your shit job. I can't tell you how nuts this seems."

"Erik Mason doesn't think so," she said.

"What'd he say?"

"He said Michaels gave a pretty disturbing presentation at a domestic-abuse conference for medical professionals."

"I remember the conference. Two years ago, at the Drake. I didn't make it to that particular talk. What was disturbing about it? Wait. Don't even bother answering that question. I don't give a shit what Erik Mason thinks. He's got his head way up his ass on this one and so have you."

"Listen . . ."

"I don't want to listen to any more of this bullshit," he said curtly. "I've got to get dressed and go to the hospital. If I allow myself enough time, maybe I can murder a hooker or two on my way to work."

"Jack . . ."

He hung up on her.

The doctor isn't in. If you need to schedule a plastic surgery consultation, I can transfer you to the appointment desk."

"I'm not a patient. I'm a rep for Texas Surgicare. You guys use our sutures, and we've got some new surgical tape we'd like him to try."

"Maybe you should talk to our office manager, then. Why don't I put you into her voice mail?"

"That's okay. I'd really rather talk to Dr. Michaels. Will he be in later?"

"He's gone for the day. He had a weekend soccer tournament in Wisconsin. May I take a message? Would you like to leave your name and phone number?"

"No, I'm traveling. I'll give him a try next week."

"That's fine."

"Thanks for your help. Have a nice day." Gabe hung up and winked at Murphy, who was sitting on the edge of his desk sipping a Diet Pepsi. On his desktop, ringed with coffee stains in its service as a temporary coaster for his mug, was a printout from a state soccer association Web site. It listed all the teams, their coaches and game dates. A weekend youth tournament was set to start that Friday night across the border in Hudson. Snaky Swanson's tip about the soccer balls had proved invaluable. Michaels was indeed a coach, and his team—one made up of girls ages twelve and thirteen—was scheduled to compete.

Gabe popped the last of his liverwurst and Miracle Whip sandwich into his mouth, chewed twice, swallowed and asked, "How was that?" He wiped his chin with a sheet of computer paper. "Did I sound like a medical-supply salesman?"

"No," said Murphy, sliding off his desk and tossing her pop can into his wastebasket. "You sounded like a used-car salesman. Next time, skip that 'Have a nice day' stuff. I hate people who say that."

"I'll make a note of that," he said.

"So, feel like watching a little soccer tonight?" she asked.

"You betcha."

They were in Murphy's Jeep, but she'd let Gabe drive, an agreeable compromise. Murphy wished she and Jack could work things out in their marriage as effortlessly as she and Gabe did on the job. As they crossed the bridge over the St. Croix River, they looked down at the dozens of boats dotting the water. The early-evening sky above the sails was darkening with storm clouds. The sign at the end of the bridge said WISCONSIN WELCOMES YOU, and bragged about the state's troika of activities: INDUSTRY. AGRICULTURE. RECREATION.

"It should say, 'Cheese. Cows. Beer,'" said Gabe, chuckling at his own joke.

"I'm not exactly sure how to get there," said Murphy, wrestling with a road map. "Maybe we should stop at a gas station and ask directions. I have my cell phone in my purse. I could call . . ."

"I have a pretty good idea where we're going," Gabe said. "Sit back and enjoy the ride." Gabe took Exit 2 and found the soccer fields north of Interstate 94, down the road from Hudson. Eight of them, like checkerboards in the cornfields. They parked between two minivans with soccer stickers plastered to their windows and stepped out of the Jeep.

The outside smelled like approaching rain and freshly mowed grass. A game official went by in a golf cart; girls dressed in matching yellow soccer uniforms followed him, giggling and squirting each other with their water bottles. A teenage boy carrying an armload of black-and-white soccer balls went the other way. Every few feet he dropped one and picked it up again, cursing each time it happened. The back of his shirt read: "If I Am Not A Courteous Player, Please Let Me Know. Call 1-800-EAT-DIRT." The sound of cheering spectators and yelling coaches filled the air.

Gabe looked wistfully in the direction of the snack bar at the edge of the parking lot.

"Now what?" he asked.

"Did you bring that printout?" asked Murphy. "It lists the teams and the field numbers."

"Shit," said Gabe. "I forgot it. It's sitting on my desk under some other crap."

"God dammit. All right, you check the fields and see if you can find him. I'll snoop around the parking lot and look for his truck."

As Gabe wandered off, mostly in the direction of a hot-dog stand, Murphy walked down the rows of cars, looking for a loaded black Suburban or a gray Lexus sedan. She figured he hadn't driven his sports car because it would seem so ostentatious and out of place in the sea of middle-class minivans and station wagons. Dressed in cutoffs, sneakers and a T-shirt, she looked like all the other soccer fans sitting on blankets and in folding chairs along the sidelines.

"Lose your car?" asked a woman cutting through the parking lot with a sleeping toddler in her arms.

"Yeah," said Murphy. "I can *never* remember where I park."

A heavy man in a sweat-stained muscle shirt grunted past her, carrying a cooler filled with bottles of Gatorade. He set it down on the gravel-covered lot for a few seconds, caught his breath and picked it up again. Six boys in matching royal blue soccer uniforms ran past her, heading toward the snack bar. A few drops of rain splattered her arms and spotted her T-shirt. From what Murphy remembered of the tournament printout sitting back on Gabe's desk, the games would not be called because of rain, but would be shut down immediately if there was lightning. She looked up at the slate-colored clouds, but saw no flashes.

She continued her tour. Minivans, especially of the forest green variety, were everywhere. Minivan. Minivan. Minivan. Station wagon. Minivan. Station wagon. Minivan. Minivan. Whoa. Here's a rebel—a full-size conversion van, and painted eggplant purple, no less. She wondered how that one had slipped past the soccer fashion police.

Then a new black Suburban, sharp-edged in the green meadow of gently curving minivans. She reached into her purse for the list of plates, and slipped between the Suburban and a minivan parked next to it. The plates were right. She knew they'd be. She crammed the paper back into her purse.

As the rain grew heavier, fans began running to their cars for umbrellas and slickers. Murphy heard someone crunching on the gravel toward her row of cars. She didn't want to be seen by Michaels, so she ducked to the other side of the green minivan, crouched and adjusted the side-view mirror of the van so she could watch the black Suburban through the van windows.

There he was. Michaels was dressed in khaki slacks and a white polo shirt. His shoulders were broad, and his arms were tan and sinewy. His hands were large. She hadn't noticed that at the church. She assumed surgeons—especially those doing such delicate work as plastic surgery—had small, nimble hands. Not this one. He opened the rear passenger-side door of the Suburban, rummaged inside it, tossed an empty pop can to the ground.

A litterbug, Murphy thought.

"Where the hell is it?" she heard him mutter to himself. "I know I saw the damn thing." More digging and cursing. "There you are," he said. He pulled something out of the car, slammed the door shut and sprinted across the parking lot, heading back toward the fields.

Murphy stood up and poked her head around the corner of the minivan to watch him. Halfway across the lot, Michaels popped open a yellow umbrella. Even through the downpour, Murphy could see. Finch was calling from the grave.

"Son-of-a-bitch," Murphy whispered. "There it is."

SEVENTEEN

He couldn't remember where it had come from. As Michaels slid into the driver's seat of his Suburban after work, he'd noticed it on the floor behind the front passenger seat and was grateful for it. The darkening sky above the interstate signaled the little umbrella might come in handy. He would have preferred his oversized golf umbrella, but he hadn't been able to find it when he was leaving for the clinic that morning. God knows where his wife had stashed it. Hell, she probably gave it to the Salvation Army. She was always giving shit away. She had absolutely no respect for his stuff.

His wife. He briefly wondered when she was returning home with the queen mother. He thought about his daughters and how they might be doing at the camp. He hadn't received a call from them in better than a week. He shuffled the fleeting concerns to the back compartment of his mind as he tried to concentrate on the Wisconsin soccer tournament.

He wanted a drink, but didn't have the time. Too bad. Booze made the tiresome games more tolerable. His assistant coach wouldn't be there. He was vacationing up north. Fishing. What a stupid sport. Regardless, Michaels would have to run the entire show by himself. He especially hated taking charge of the line changes. Parents who thought their precious daughters weren't getting enough time on the field were quick to buttonhole him on the sidelines. They were all a bunch of whiners, but the mothers infinitely more so than the fathers. If the fathers didn't like something, they stood grim-faced and silent with their hands buried in their pockets. They might approach him after the game, mumble something, but the mothers couldn't wait. They practically ran to him during the game to complain. He frequently fantasized about lining them up in a row and slapping each and every one of them right across the face. That one in particular—a tiny, full-lipped brunette with big tits and an even bigger mouth. He'd love to slap her good and hard, leave some red marks on her face. He'd love to make her weep. She probably wouldn't be much of a challenge. Her spoiled crybaby daughter was one to burst into tears at every opportunity; he wished he could really give her something to cry about.

He deeply regretted having gotten suckered into coaching this year's soccer team, especially since his daughters were missing part of the season. On top of everything else, the team was having a lousy year and he would undoubtedly be blamed. Admittedly, some of his extracurricular activities after work had caused him to miss some games and practices. They were a crappy bunch of players anyway, and no amount of drilling and training and scrimmaging would elevate their level of play. He had to admit that even his own daughters were mediocre. If he had boys, that would be different; they would be fine soccer players. Wishing for a son was pointless, of course. The miscarriage had ended that dream.

He turned into the tournament parking lot and pulled into the first space he could find. He sighed as he stepped out of the car and walked to the back of the SUV. He opened the gate and dug out a couple of soccer balls, the water bottles, the goalie jersey and his coach's clipboard. The board was blank. He knew he should have planned his lineup and a couple of plays, but screw it. He'd wing it. The dumb little shits didn't listen to him most of the time anyway. He slammed the gate shut and looked up at the sky. "Come on, God," he thought as he scrutinized the dark expanse over his head. "Give me a break."

His bad luck; all he got was rain. His arms were too full to grab the umbrella on his first trip between the car and the field. The game hadn't started yet and he figured he still had time to retrieve it. He bounded across the parking lot for his second trip to the car and was drenched by the time he reached it. It took some digging around—it had rolled under the back passenger's seat—but he found it. As he ran across the parking lot on his way back to the soccer fields, he opened the umbrella.

"Piece of shit," he mumbled at the tangle of yellow nylon and flimsy spokes. "Don't tell me you're broken, you worthless thing." To hell with it. He'd mooch an umbrella off one of the parents. Maybe that mouthy little brunette would share a corner of hers if he smiled nicely and put her clumsy daughter in as the starting goalie. Anything was better than this defective scrap of metal and material. Where in the world had it come from? He'd never have bought anything so inferior. Disgusted, he tossed it into a muddy puddle at the far end of the parking lot and continued his sprint back to the soccer fields, silently cursing the summer storm that brought torrential rain but no lightning.

Murphy had been following him from a distance by dashing and ducking between cars. Checking to make sure Michaels was well out of sight, she emerged from her hiding place between two minivans. She carefully picked up the soggy umbrella by the edge of the cloth. "Hello, my precious," Murphy cooed at the dripping mess. She ran back to her Jeep with it. Even if no useable prints could be pulled off the thing, it was still valuable evidence. Rue could testify that the yellow umbrella had been in Finch's hands the night she disappeared. Finch had undoubtedly left it in Michaels's car after he picked her up.

After sticking the umbrella in the Jeep, Murphy retrieved her own umbrella from under a pile of magazines and popped it open. Time to watch a little soccer, she thought.

Sara, get back in the net! You're playing too far out of the goal! They'll get around you! Get back!"

The goalie ran back toward the net in the driving rain, slipped and fell face forward into the wet grass inside the white lines of the goalie box. The left forward for Minneapolis shot from the side and scored the first goal of the game against Michaels's St. Paul team.

"Dammit!" Michaels yelled. "I told you to get back. You can't play that far out!" The goalie slowly rose from her prone position in the grass and promptly dissolved into tears. Bits of dirt speckled her wet face. "Perfect," Michaels mumbled. "Goalie sub!" Michaels yelled and waved the goalie over to the sidelines. "Should I pull you out of the net? There are three girls behind you ready to take your place. I don't have time for bawling," Michaels told her, his right hand gripping her left shoulder. He towered above her. Even in the pouring rain, the girl could see the veins standing out on his forehead. His hand was squeezing her shoulder, hurting it, but she was afraid to say anything or push it away. "Answer me, Sara. Are you up for this or not? Do you want to sit on the bench? Should I put in one of the subs?"

"No," she said, wiping her nose with the back of her right goalie glove. "I'm sorry they got past me. I thought I could get back in time."

"Well, I guess you thought wrong," he said. "Maybe next time you'll listen to me."

The ref blew his whistle. "Are you going to sub or not? Put someone in the net and let's get going!" he yelled. Michaels let Sara back into the goal. The game resumed in the rain, which slowed but remained steady. The frustrated surgeon, soaked to the skin, stood glowering along the sidelines with his arms folded across his chest. He braced himself, waiting for the mouthy brunette to pounce and bitch at him for yelling at her princess.

"Would you like to share my umbrella?"

He turned toward the husky female voice on his right and smiled broadly. He couldn't believe his good fortune. Finally things were going his way. He ducked under her black umbrella. "Thank you," he said. He ran his fingers through his wet hair. "What I really need at this point is a towel."

"I recognized you from the funeral," said the black-haired woman.

Her wet shirt was matted to her skin. He could make out her nipples under her bra. She was even more enticing than when he'd seen her from a distance, inside that country church. Her long hair was unfettered this time and hung in a thick, damp sheet around her face. What a face. Smooth.

Flawless. He couldn't improve a single feature. Not one. "Yes, I saw you at the service," he said. "I remember you. Vividly."

"So sad," said Murphy.

"Yes," he said. "Sad."

"The service was nice, didn't you think?"

"Very nice," Michaels said. With a small smile, he added: "Especially the brother's reading."

"I hope they catch whoever did it," she said. She watched his face and listened to his voice for a reaction.

"I'm sure they will," he said evenly.

Not a muscle on his face twitched; he's a cool one, she thought. "How did you know Fionn?" she asked.

"She was a patient of mine," he said, relieved that he had fabricated that story earlier so it quickly popped out of his mouth. "I'm a surgeon," he continued. "I met her through my volunteer work with abuse victims."

"How admirable," said Murphy, impressed with how quickly and easily the lies rolled off his tongue.

One of his players fell. He stepped toward the field to yell: "Come on, ref. Tripping!" The ref shook his head. "Horseshit, ref," he said under his breath. He returned to his spot under the umbrella.

"What about you?" he asked. "Were you related to the poor girl?"

"I'm a friend of the family," said Murphy.

"Oh, I see," he said. "How coincidental bumping into you here. Do you have someone in this tournament?"

"Yes . . . I have a couple of nieces playing for Hudson," said Murphy. "I was on my way back from the car with my umbrella when I saw you."

"Is your father here with you? At least, I assumed that was your father with you at the funeral."

Murphy smiled, amused by the thought of Gabe as her father. "He's here with me, but he's not my father," she said. "He's an old friend."

"It sounds like you have lots of friends," he said, smiling and stepping closer to her under the umbrella. "Any husbands?"

"Not as many husbands as friends," she said. They both laughed.

"What about you?" Murphy asked. She could smell his cologne through the rain. Obsession for Men, a scent she adored but could never get Jack to wear. "Are you attached? You must have children on this team."

"My two daughters. They're in Europe right now."

"You're their coach?"

"Yes. I really enjoy it," he said.

"You must be so busy, being a doctor and all. I suppose your wife helps with the team."

"Their mother and I are . . . no longer together," he said, glad he had removed his wedding band.

"That's too bad," Murphy said. She wondered if he was telling the truth; she couldn't see his ring finger and his face was hard to read.

"Not at all. We're much happier apart," Michaels said.

The parents on his side of the field started yelling over a slide tackle made by the other team. "I do need to get back to the game," he said, stepping even closer to her. He could smell her hair, fragrant from an herbal shampoo. "I'd like to talk with you later, so don't wander too far. I don't even know your name."

A cheer erupted from Michaels's side of the field. His team had scored. He stepped out from under the umbrella, turned toward the field and clapped. "All right!" he hollered. "Way to go, Lauren! Nice goal! How about a couple more of those?"

Murphy stepped back from the sidelines and almost tripped over Gabe. "What in the hell are you doing?" Gabe hissed into her ear. He grabbed her arm. "Have you lost your mind? Have you completely lost it? What are you doing with Dr. Demented?"

"Figuring him out," she whispered. She yanked her arm away from Gabe and continued eyeing Michaels.

"Too fucking dangerous, Murphy," Gabe said. His face was a knot of concern.

"He had the umbrella," she said, stepping farther away from Michaels's field and closing her own umbrella. The rain had stopped.

"What?" said Gabe, looking at the dripping umbrella she had just folded shut. "What are you talking about?"

"Not this one," said Murphy. "He had the yellow umbrella, the one Rue loaned to Finch the night she was killed."

"What do you mean by 'had'?"

"He threw it away and I picked it up," she said. "It's sitting on the floor of my car."

"You have it?" he asked.

Murphy nodded her head, watching Michaels's back as he yelled directions to his players. He wouldn't win any popularity contests.

"First step," Murphy said.

"I'm afraid to ask what your second step might be," said Gabe.

"Get him alone in a quiet place—but a public one. Maybe a restaurant or a bar," she said. "It sounds like he's a big drinker. Maybe I can loosen him up."

"Bullshit," said Gabe. "It's too dangerous. I won't let you do it. No way in hell."

Her eyes narrowed and seemed to change color, going from violet to black. He knew the look. "Fine," he said. "I am going to be there—along with my good friend Mr. Glock."

"You can't," she said. "He remembers seeing both of us at the funeral. I told him we're friends of Finch's family and that you and I are . . . chums."

"Oh, we're chummy, are we? Well chums don't let chums drink alone with murdering rapists," Gabe growled.

She recognized that tone of voice. She wasn't going to change his mind, and he wasn't going to change hers. "Okay, then you'll have to wear a disguise," she said. "Dust off that wig."

"Fine with me. As long as I'm there."

At the game's halftime, Michaels chewed out his team for letting go of a three-point lead. "You're benched for the rest of the game," he told the sniffling Sara. "You're a sieve tonight. I'm going to put Debbie in net."

The mouthy brunette stepped into the team huddle. "Dr. Michaels, I do not like the way you're treating my . . ."

At his sides, Michaels's hands tightened into fists. "Don't tell me how to coach," he told her. "Go sit down with the other parents or you can stay home the next game. You and Sara both." Her face reddened. She shut her mouth and went back to the sidelines. Michaels relaxed his hands. Embarrassing her wasn't as good as hitting her, but it wasn't bad.

He turned around to look for the woman with the black hair. She was standing several yards away, chatting with that friend of hers, but she turned her head and their eyes met. Michaels stepped out of the huddle and walked toward her while her cloddish friend ambled off with a cigarette between his fingers. "Drinks Monday night? How about the bar at the St. Paul Hotel?"

"I know the place," she said. "Very nice."

"Your name?"

Murphy flashed him a smile. "Let's save some surprises for later," she said.

He laughed. "I like that," he said. "I like that a lot. You've got style. Okay, let's trade the formalities over a glass of single-malt whiskey."

"Only if they pour Lagavulin," Murphy said.

"A Scotch connoisseur, too," he said. "Perfect." The ref blew his whistle. The game was resuming. "I'll meet you there at eight o'clock Monday," he said, and ran back to the field.

Gabe came up behind Murphy. "Eight o'clock Monday at the St. Paul Hotel bar," she said.

"We'll be there," Gabe said, as he patted the gun holstered under his sweatshirt.

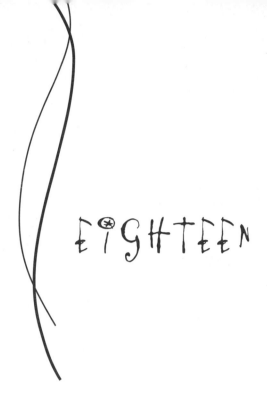

EIGHTEEN

"Paris, I hate to say it, but Gabe is right. This is too dangerous. He's a head case, and you can't predict what he'll do."

"Gabe will be in the bar."

"For some reason that does not make me feel better about this whole scheme."

"Come on, Erik. I know you aren't exactly president of the Gabriel Nash fan club, but he isn't called 'Nasty Nash' because he's a pushover. Give him some credit."

Murphy and Erik were talking as they ran along Lilydale Road Saturday morning. Murphy usually ran alone, preferring to set her own pace and use the quiet time for sorting out problems or simply emptying her mind, but Erik had called first thing in the morning and asked to join her.

The day was going to be hot and muggy following Friday-night's rainstorms. They ran past Harriet Island, which was already filling with picnickers staking out claims to tables. From the running trail atop an embankment, overlooking the park and the river, they could see a Mexican family hanging a piñata from a tree. Salsa music wafted from a tape player. Closer to the river, they could see several blond children, already pink from the morning sun, climbing all over an enormous ship's anchor assigned permanent shore duty as a park decoration. After the neatly mowed Harriet Island came the disheveled Lilydale Regional Park. The steep bluffs and paved road were to their left. To the right of the running path were thick woods and then the Mississippi River flowing parallel to the road.

Murphy thought about Finch. She wondered whether they should go to the clearing where her body was found. "Why don't we run over to . . ."

"Let's not go there, Paris."

"What are you talking about?" she said. "You don't know what I was going to say."

He didn't answer and kept running a few steps ahead of her. The hum of insects filled the long, silent pause. She could feel him waiting for her to capitulate.

"Okay," she said. "I thought . . ."

"You think too much," he said shortly. "Run . . . Don't think . . . Run."

He was pressing her to do eight-minute miles. Erik was a strong runner; she knew he was holding back so she could keep up. She appreciated his patience. On the rare occasions when she ran with other women, she was usually the fast one and grew frustrated trying to match a slower pace. They ran under the railroad bridge that gently curved through the park—the same bridge that looked over the clearing where Finch's body was found. Graffiti was spray-painted all over the bridge's supports, including words that had been there since Murphy was a kid: THE RIVER RATS RULE. A short distance past the bridge, they turned around and doubled back for the return trip to Murphy's houseboat.

They pounded down the dock. Tripod ran out and barked from his owner's deck. Erik stopped and laughed. "Goofy-looking pooch."

"Tripod."

"How'd he lose his leg?"

"A car, when he was a puppy," she said. "You like dogs?"

"Dogs. Cats. Kids. Like 'em all," he said, smiling at her. "What about you?"

"Take cats off the list."

He laughed and wiped his wet face with the bottom of his T-shirt. They talked and slowly walked the rest of the way to her boat.

"Why didn't you and Jack ever . . ."

"We could never agree on a breed."

Erik looked at her. She smiled. "Sorry," he said. "I was stupid for asking. If you don't want to talk about it, that's fine. It's really none of my business."

"You're right; it is none of your business. I'll tell you anyway. The timing was never right, that's all. We're both perfectly healthy and all that, and we both love kids. But we could never agree on when to start a family. Whenever it was right for one of us, it was wrong for the other. There. Now I've told you twice as much as I've ever told my mother."

She and Erik tripped sweaty and tired into the galley. Erik looked into her living room. "Camels," he said, laughing.

"Like them?"

"Yeah. Camels are cool. I see you have both the one-humped and the two-humped variety."

"I don't discriminate," she said.

He walked to the sink, turned on the tap and stuck his mouth under the faucet.

"God, don't drink that," she said. "It's St. Paul water. I've got some bottled stuff in the fridge."

"Why does everyone piss all over St. Paul water?" he asked in between gulps. "It's fine."

"*Piss* is the operative word here," she said. She walked over to the fridge to get some water and was not surprised to find a note from two of her older brothers, Patrick and Ryan, taped to the handle. "Potato Head: Stopped by with the new boat. Sorry we missed you. Look for us upriver." The message was scrawled on a sheet of stationery from the orthopedic surgery practice they shared.

"Something wrong?" asked Erik, leaning against the kitchen counter with one hand and wiping perspiration off his neck with the other.

"My overachieving brothers swung by with their latest toy," she said, crumpling the note. "We missed them, thank God." She and Jack had been frequently surprised at their Dutch Colonial. Once Jack was standing naked in front of the refrigerator gulping milk when Murphy's mother walked into the kitchen. Jack used the milk carton to cover his crotch. "Shame on you," said the tiny, dark-haired woman, shaking her finger at him. "Go get a glass."

Murphy grew sad thinking about Jack. She contemplated calling him. Maybe making good on that promise of a romantic dinner followed by a back rub could lure him back to her riverfront home. Of course, if he heard about her plan to meet Michaels for drinks Monday night, that could ignite another huge fight.

She was startled from her thoughts when she felt Erik's arms wrapping around her waist from behind. "Got anything going on the rest of the day?" he asked.

"What?"

"I have some ideas about how you could fill your weekend," he whispered in her ear. "Why don't we start with a hot, soapy shower after our run and see where that takes us?"

"No, Erik. I was thinking I should . . ."

"As I said earlier, you think too damn much, woman," he said, nibbling on her neck. "Don't think."

"I thought we were going to be friends," she said, trying to push his arms off her waist.

"Friends can make wonderful lovers," he said softly.

He was hard. She felt him through his thin running shorts as he pressed against the small of her back. He smelled of perspiration and the outdoors; she liked the salty-fresh combination.

"Come on, Paris. Relax. Let it happen," he said. He pressed his body against her back. He slid his right hand up under her sweat-dampened bra and T-shirt and cupped her right breast.

"Do you want me to stop?" he asked. "Say if you want me to stop."

She inhaled sharply. "Stop," she breathed, and pushed his arms off her. She took a step away from him but kept her back to him. "You'd better leave," she said.

"Look at me," he said.

"No."

He stepped in front of her and took her face in his hands. Her eyes were down; all he saw were dark lashes. "You can't, can you? You can't look at me. You want me and you're afraid."

"It's not about being afraid," she said. She pushed his hands away from her face and raised her eyes. "It's about my marriage."

"You've split."

"We're working on it."

"If it takes too much work, maybe it isn't there," Erik said. "You should move on."

"Go," she said. "Go home."

She took a long shower, as hot as she could stand. She wanted to scald the memory of Erik's hands off her. Jack would never sleep with another woman, even when they were separated. He was as consistent and steady in his marriage as he was in his professional life. So was she, up until Erik. She'd never come so close to giving in. Why now? Could it be the physical attraction alone? Was she that weak?

The questions and the guilt burned her worse than the water.

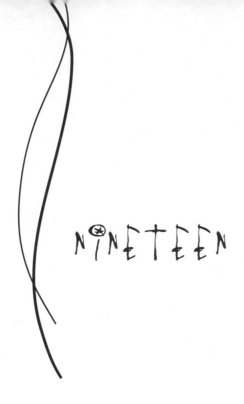

NINETEEN

That weekend, the good doctor also contemplated the cheating heart—his wife's.

Michaels had tried the cabin's telephone over the weekend, starting with a call late Friday night after the dismal soccer game. He'd called again in between the two equally pathetic tournament games on Saturday. When he got home Sunday afternoon from the fourth and final game—at last, a win—he tried yet again. No response, only Jennifer's cloying recorded message: "Ahoy, landlubbers! We can't answer your distress signal right now. We're riding the waves of Lake Superior. If you'd like to flag down the captain or his first mate, please leave a message at the sound of the foghorn!" God, he hated that message. He slammed the phone down and paced around the master bedroom.

"Where the fuck are you? Are you banging someone else? Where are you?" he muttered. He took off his clothes, threw them in a corner and fell back on the bed, a mahogany four-poster that matched the Victorian armoire with the carved door panels and the marble-topped mahogany nightstands on either side of the bed. He appreciated that there was nothing delicate or modest about the room, a cavernous space filled with dark, massive furniture that had been in his family for generations. As much as he loved the bedroom, his wife hated it. Perfectly symbolic of their marriage, thought Michaels.

After an hour, Michaels got up from the bed, walked across the floor to the armoire and threw open one of the tall doors. The inside of the nineteenth-century antique had been retrofitted with an entertainment center that included a television and a stereo system. He slipped a disc into the CD player and turned up the volume on his favorite selection from Dylan's *Blood on the Tracks*.

Bobbing his head to "Tangled Up in Blue," Michaels made his way to the dresser and, from the top drawer, pulled out an old key with a hair ribbon looped through one end. He walked to his nightstand, carefully inserted the key into the lock on the drawer and slowly turned to the left. The drawer was fussy and frequently stuck, but this time it opened with ease. He reached in and pulled out a bottle of Scotch—a twenty-five-year-old limited-edition Tomatin. Next he pulled out a painted pheasant glass, set it on the marble top and filled it with Scotch, well past the cock in flight.

He set the bottle of Scotch down and reached into the deep nightstand drawer to retrieve his oldest memento—a long braid of auburn hair he'd retrieved from the hatbox earlier that weekend. He'd thought about returning it to its hiding place in the safe room, in case his wife returned from the cabin unannounced. He'd decided to enjoy it a bit longer . . .

The twist of hair was held together at each end with a rubber band. He buried his nose in the braid. She'd used a fruit-scented hair spray. He loved it that years later, he could still smell traces of it. He draped the braid over his neck like a scarf and pulled down the comforter so he could rest on the ivory satin sheets, the only furnishing he'd allowed his wife to select for the room. With a sigh, he stretched out on the bed again. Next to him on the sheets, he laid out the braid. He handled it gently; it was his first and his favorite.

He gazed up at the bedroom ceiling. If Jennifer was sleeping around on him, where was her mother? Maybe she was out getting some action as well. He laughed at the prospect of his mother-in-law rolling around under the covers with some poor gigolo. Then he swiftly dismissed the disturbing image. "You probably forgot how to do it, you dried-up old bitch," he said out loud. He laughed again, and turned on his side to reach for the Scotch glass. He emptied it and poured himself another tall one, spilling a bit on the nightstand and spotting the sheets. "Where are you, you two bitches?" he said, loudly. He took another long drink, enjoying the warmth trickling from his throat down to his belly. A few drops splashed on his chest, hitting the few blond curls and turning them wet and golden. The scent of his cologne mixed with the smell of the booze, and he liked it.

He scratched his testicles with his left hand and thought about another bitch. A delicious one. That black-haired woman with the flawless skin and full, round breasts. He switched the drinking glass to his left hand, freeing his right hand to wrap around his stiffening cock.

If it appeared that his wife wasn't going to be home Monday night, perhaps he could bring the mystery woman back with him and do her right here, in his bedroom. Then he could fuck his cheating wife on the same sheets when she finally got her whore ass home. That would be sweet revenge. No. It would be satisfying, but far too dangerous. He didn't want to betray too much of himself to the woman. A room at the hotel. Yes.

He continued stroking himself with his right hand. With his left hand, he set the Scotch down and reached for the braid. His soft, compliant lover. The throbbing beat of the music bounced off the walls of the bedroom. The amber liquid in the glass atop his nightstand rippled slightly, like a puddle trembling before an approaching thunderstorm.

The St. Paul was an old hotel with thick walls. No one would hear her screams. He wouldn't hurt her too badly. He didn't need to add to his growing list of mortal sins. He'd keep it to a light beating followed by some vigorous sex. She'd enjoy it. He only hoped she was a good fighter. She'd already displayed some spunk in refusing to disclose her name. Perhaps he should encourage that little game, insist they maintain their anonymity, or exchange first names. He'd make one up. He hated his first name; it was his father's. He didn't like his father.

He'd loved his mother. Bee.

He stroked his hard cock with his right hand. With his left, he caressed the braid, bunched it up, and rubbed it against his testicles. Wonderful.

Silkier than the sheets. He shut his eyes and imagined the hair belonged to a woman, a beautiful woman who did what he told her to do. Exactly. "That's it, baby," he whispered. "Like that." He slowed his stroking; he didn't want to come too soon.

Perhaps he could reach his apex with that black-haired woman, finally feed the fly's gnawing hunger that seemed to be occupying more and more of his waking moments and even invading his dreams. Since his return from the cabin, he was finding it increasingly difficult to sleep straight through the night. He would sit bolt upright at two or three in morning, his head filled with the buzzing. Fucking buzzing. Sometimes it took almost half a bottle of Scotch to lull him into a stupor that resembled sleep.

This woman with the violet eyes and succulent breasts and long hair could finally satiate him. Then maybe he'd make her his last. He needed to wind down his activities. He'd been making too many mistakes, too many bad judgment calls. Look at the mess Thursday night. Yes, maybe he'd make her his last. The fly's last. She'd be a magnificent finish. "Yes, you could be the one," he whispered, picturing her under him, frightened and squirming.

What about the hair? He killed them when he took the hair, and he wanted her hair. He thought about her hair.

Emitting a moan and clutching the auburn braid, he ejaculated.

TWENTY

*M*urphy stared at her computer screen Monday morning, studying the e-mail that had arrived shortly after she'd gotten to the station house. On an intellectual level, it was rewarding, because it confirmed her suspicions and validated her investigative instincts. She was absolutely correct about this gifted surgeon, respected community member, killer. On an emotional level, however, the information in the electronic message disheartened her and it troubled her that she felt this way. As she sat still and silent in front of the screen, she tried to dispassionately analyze why she was so disillusioned despite having been proved right.

Why am I feeling this way? she wondered. I can't possibly empathize with this bastard. We have absolutely nothing in common. Economically and socially, we come from opposite sides of the tracks. We grew up on opposite sides of the river. Literally. Why do I care? She decided it was his looks. The face. The hair. The body. The whole package was so attractive and hid so much evil. Her job was easier when the bad guys looked the part. Scummy and ugly and capable of doing wrong.

These were shallow, surface observations. She was afraid to probe too deeply into her own psyche for fear she might find the common ground she shared with Michaels. All her adult life, she'd denied those impulses.

During college, she'd found herself gravitating toward athletic partners. She told herself that was what she wanted in bed. Athleticism. Still, they usually disappointed. They were too tentative and gentle, and far too self-conscious. On the rare occasions when she found a man who satisfied her, she never had to tell him what she wanted. He knew. Perhaps it was the way she fought back in bed. Perhaps it was the hoarseness in her voice or the catch in her breath. Maybe it was how she behaved outside the bedroom. How she carried herself. She didn't act like a timid person.

She could never name what she wanted. It scared her that roughness might appeal to her.

Was that what drew her to Michaels, and why he frightened her?

Murphy, what are you reading so intently? You look like you're going to pop a vein in your eyeball."

Gabe's words jarred her out of her trance. He came up behind her and handed her a cup of coffee.

"I got an e-mail from the Rochester P.D. They have an unsolved murder from several years ago with the same M.O. as our friendly doctor."

"No shit," said Gabe.

"No shit," she said. "A nurse who moonlighted as a stripper was found in a farmer's field—raped, beaten and strangled."

"What makes you think the doc did her?"

"She had this long, auburn hair—I'm talking down to her knees. Sort of a gimmick for her act. She was pretty well known for it around the strip-club circuit."

"So?" said Gabe.

"So someone gave her a sloppy haircut the night she died," said Murphy.

"He's twisted," Gabe said.

"He did her while he was at the Mayo Clinic, for his fellowship," said Murphy. "The years match up."

"So what's wrong? You read Dr. Demented like a large-print book."

"Nothing's wrong," she said. "Sometimes when I expect the worst from people, I wish to hell they'd disappoint me."

"Almost never happens, kid. Expect the worst and . . ."

"Hope for the best?" she said.

"No, hope the shit doesn't hit the fan," he said. Then: "Hey, has Mason come up with anything more for us?"

"No," Murphy said curtly, and quickly switched subjects.

"I'm going to give Rochester Homicide a call," she said, picking up the telephone. "I might want to go down there and see what they've got in their files. Do you want to go down there with me? How about tomorrow? We can leave first thing in the morning and be back by dinner."

"Uh, I've got some legwork to do before we talk to Ambrose," said Gabe.

"Forgot. That's right," she said. She was secretly pleased that she could drive her car and play her own music for a change. "Never mind. I'll make a quick trip of it." She started punching Rochester's number, but Gabe took the receiver out of her hand and put it down.

"That can wait," he said, sitting on the edge of her desk. "We need to talk about tonight."

Gabe wasn't a pedantic tutor. He stood vigilantly but quietly in the wings, waiting for his protege to ask for direction. He believed it was best to learn by mistakes, as long as the errors were not life threatening or embarrassingly stupid. When Murphy needed help, she'd ask for it. He remembered when she'd been in Vice and struggling with her first big case. A john was robbing the hookers, and had shot one in the thigh. Still, the hookers refused to cooperate. They gave vague descriptions of the perpetrator and were afraid to say too much.

"I don't know," Murphy had said. "Maybe they don't know me well enough yet to trust me." She had been ready to hit the streets as a decoy, but Gabe steered her in another direction.

"Look, Murphy. Some asshole is dipping into the till at the goody store, right?" he'd told her. "Who do you think really gives a shit? The cashiers at the goody store or the owner of the goody store?"

She'd talked to the pimps and solved the case in no time. "Thanks for your help," she'd told Gabe afterward.

"Thanks for asking for it," he'd said, and he meant it.

What about tonight?" asked Murphy.

They were in a long, narrow conference room with the door shut. Gabe had insisted their conversation be private. From the bank of tall windows that stretched against one wall, they could see the tangle of freeways that bordered the north side of the cop shop. Gabe took a chair at one end of the long, lacquered conference table. Murphy sat a few chairs away from him, sipping her coffee. She leaned back in her seat and stretched her long legs out to prop her feet atop the table's edge.

"Let's shit-can the entire operation," Gabe said. "Forget about the bar."

She opened her mouth to react, but Gabe kept talking. Quickly. An appliance salesman making another frantic pitch. "This is a bad idea, Paris. Michaels is unpredictable as hell. He's on the soccer field one minute and murdering hookers the next. He's got this weird hair fetish going on. Forget about it. Don't show up at the bar. Okay? Let's forget the whole damn idea."

"Jesus Christ, Gabe! Where did this come from?" She pulled her legs off the table and sat up.

"I'm worried about you."

"He won't try anything," she said adamantly. "It's a public place. I can handle myself."

"You're too sure of yourself," said Gabe. "You've usually shown a little common sense. I haven't seen that here."

Murphy jumped out of the chair and started pacing along the windowed wall. "What in the hell are you talking about? Huh?"

"I'm talking about the unnecessary risks you've been taking to get close to this guy. I'm talking about the unnecessary risks you've been taking in your personal life. I'm talking about you and Mason."

She stopped pacing and took a deep breath. She turned away from Gabe to look outside, resting both hands against the waist-high window ledge. She saw the busy stream of cars crisscrossing the highways at the edge of downtown and longed to be in one of those cars, heading north to the woods and lakes, or east to the forests of Wisconsin. Anywhere but here, in this office, having this conversation.

She turned her head to look at Gabe, but kept her hands against the ledge. Suddenly, he looked old and tired to her. There were deep lines in his face she had never noticed before. Even his hands looked old and wrinkled. Maybe it was the harsh ceiling lights in this room, or maybe she was seeing her mentor through more seasoned eyes. A wave of sadness mixed with nostalgia threatened to wash over her, but she pushed it back. She took her hands off the ledge and stood straight, squaring her shoulders.

"Fuck you on the Mason thing," she said. "And this isn't different from any other undercover gig."

"Bullshit, Paris, you . . ."

"Meet me at my place at about seven," she said, pushing her hands into the pockets of her jeans. "Don't forget your trusty wig and beard. Okay?" He sat in the chair looking at her, his coffee cup between his hands. She was suddenly torn. She wanted to win this one. For some reason, maybe to reassure herself he wasn't getting old, she also wanted him to first resist her a little more. Put up more of a fight.

"Okay," he said, sighing.

She didn't want him to see her face, her disappointment. "I've got to call Rochester," she said. She quickly turned her back on him, opened the door and walked out of the conference room, leaving him sitting alone at the end of the long table.

Murphy helped Gabe into his disguise before dressing herself. She brushed his gray hair and pulled it all back into a ponytail held together with a flat barrette. She used a bunch of bobby pins to secure the ends of the ponytail to the top of his head and slipped the blond wig securely over the whole mess. The wig was even longer than Gabe's natural hair and more neatly trimmed. A few gray strands stuck out along his forehead; she tucked them in. She walked around him and studied his head from all angles as he sat in a kitchen chair in the galley. "It's crooked," she said. She tugged it to one side and then the other.

"Ouch."

"Sorry." She stepped back to look at him. "Good," she declared. "Nice and straight. There's no gray hair peeking out from underneath."

She used spirit gum to attach the short, blond beard to his face.

"How do I look?" he asked.

"Like a well-groomed Dead Head," she said, laughing.

"That's cool," said Gabe. "Jerry Garcia is my hero."

"I thought you only liked country-western," she said.

"There's a lot you don't know about me," said Gabe, grinning and inspecting the beard with his fingers. "I'm actually a very complex person. A Renaissance man." He started humming "Truckin'" and tapping his feet to the beat.

"Well, as long as we're onto a Grateful Dead theme, why don't we take it all the way," said Murphy. She ran up to her bedroom and came down with a couple of ties draped over each forearm. "Official Jerry Garcia–label ties," she said. "Pick one, Mr. Renaissance Man."

"Mason's ties?" Gabe asked suspiciously, his eyes narrowing.

"Jack's ties," said Murphy. "Erik won't be leaving any ties here."

"Good," said Gabe, smiling and pointing to the brightest of the collection.

Murphy started to help him secure the tie around the collar of his white dress shirt, but he stood up and brushed her hands away impatiently. "I've been dressing myself for better than fifty years," he said. He got out of the chair and went into the guest bathroom to look in the mirror while he worked. After knotting the tie, he loosened the belt on his navy blue dress pants. "Gotta drop some pounds," he muttered to himself, pinching his waist.

"Start getting dressed, my sugar magnolia," he yelled from the bathroom.

Murphy ran back up to her bedroom. She scanned her small closet, searching for something in particular. She saw it. She pulled out a simple black slip dress and threw it on the bed. Fishing through her dresser drawers, she found an unopened package of panty hose she had stashed in there for some occasion or another. She ripped open the package, pulled out the hosiery and threw both on the bed next to the dress. She disrobed, tossing her clothes in a pile on the floor, and grabbed the hosiery. "Whoever invented these obviously hated women," she grumbled, tugging one leg on up to her thigh and then the other before pulling the panty portion over her hips and waist.

She lifted a strapless bra out of a drawer. It looked like a giant bandage. She could hardly breathe when she wore the thing, and it crawled down her chest. She tossed it back in the drawer. She slipped the dress over her head. It slid silkily into place. Did she need to shave her armpits? She looked in the mirror and lifted up her arms. No dark shadows. Good. From under the bed, she retrieved a pair of dusty black pumps. She wiped them off with a wad of Kleenex and stepped into them.

She surveyed herself critically in the bedroom-dresser mirror. She frowned and reached behind her head to unfetter her hair. Michaels liked his women with long locks and she needed to show off hers. She shook her hair out and grabbed a brush to give it a few strokes. After she put down the brush, she studied her face in the mirror, searching for the same signs of age she'd spotted in Gabe's. She saw a couple of fine lines around her mouth. No crow's-feet or gray hair. Yet. She touched her face with her fingertips. "Tick tock, tick tock," she muttered into the mirror.

She reached into her top dresser drawer and dug around for some lipstick. She hadn't worn any in ages. She pulled out a tube and read the label: "Killer Coral." She smiled. "That's appropriate," she thought. She leaned closer to the mirror and applied a couple of strokes to her lips.

"How you doing up there?" Gabe yelled.

"Come on up, Jerry," she said. As he came up the stairs, she admired how his conservative slacks and crisp shirt nicely complemented his contemporary hair and tie. Over his arm was draped a dark blazer, a necessary item of clothing to hide the holstered gun hanging from his shoulder rig. Maybe he didn't look so old and tired after all. "You clean up real good, partner," she said, smiling.

He laughed and blushed. "Yeah, right. Tell it to my ex-wives."

"Really. You look very nice," she said. She walked over to straighten his tie; this time he didn't push her hands away. "You look like a music company executive or something."

"You look pretty hot yourself," he said. He noticed her lipstick, and that she wasn't wearing a bra. "A little too hot as a matter of fact. Murphy, are you sure you don't want to . . ."

"Stop, Gabe. We had this conversation."

"Okay, okay," he said, throwing up his hands. "I give up."

"Ready to rock?" she asked.

"Let's rock," he said.

TWENTY-ONE

Back and forth. Back and forth. Michaels stopped counting after fifty laps. A good workout, the best he'd had in some time. He started with the breaststroke, broke it up with the crawl and then returned to the breast-stroke. He ended with the butterfly; all he could manage was a few laps, and he thought that was pathetic. It used to be his signature stroke in high school, what had earned him two state trophies. He'd have to work on that. After the last lap he stretched out on his back and floated for a while. The long, white-tiled room was dim, with most of the illumination provided by the lights lining the walls of the pool.

When he was a kid, the basement pool was a great refuge when he wanted a break from the screaming and chaos in the rest of the house; water is wonderful for muffling the senses. When she was in town, his favorite cousin joined him. They'd float on their backs for what seemed like hours, silent and naked, stretching out their arms to touch fingertips. They didn't need to talk; they were partners in purgatory. Her parents were crazy, rich drunks, too.

He finally rolled over, swam lazily to the ladder and climbed out of the

water. He pulled a robe over his nude body, slipped his feet into some sandals and walked up two flights.

He dropped the robe on the master-bath floor, kicked off the sandals
and, with a sigh, eased his frame into the bubbling Jacuzzi. He leaned back
and shut his eyes. He was glad he'd had the time to exercise before the big
night; it rejuvenated him and helped him order his thoughts. He had once
again packed away his questions about his wife's whereabouts to make mental room for his fascination with the mystery woman. He was so looking
forward to meeting her that night at the bar—and possibly taking her up to
a room at the hotel—that he had barely been able to concentrate on his
patients during the day. He'd left work early, leaving his nurses to offer
excuses to the patients remaining in the waiting room.

On his bed he had laid out his clothing for the evening—Italian-made
charcoal gabardine trousers and jacket, midnight blue dress shirt with
mother-of-pearl buttons, dark blue Hermès silk tie with black diagonal
stripes, black Italian loafers, dark dress socks and gray silk boxers. He was
taking a chance by going with a more formal look, but he wanted to impress
this woman, sweep her off her feet. He looked good in his Wop outfit.

He stepped out of the tub and toweled off. He stood back and inspected
his body in the mirror. Broad chest and well-defined shoulders. He still had
a swimmer's shoulders. Flat stomach. Strong thighs. Nice, big cock—that
crazy barbed-wire bitch from the club had been right about that. He turned
sideways. Hard, round ass. He flexed his biceps, felt them with his hands.
Not too bad. He needed to hit the weights and the pool a little more regularly. Otherwise, she'd have nothing to complain about tonight. Not one
damn thing.

He wrapped the towel around his waist and walked into the bedroom.
With the remote-control pad, he flicked on the television in the armoire. He
tossed the remote onto the bed, dropped the towel to the floor and started
to dress.

A stiff-haired male anchor from one of the local evening news programs
was on, giving a promo for the ten o'clock news. "An Apple Valley man leads
police on a wild high-speed chase, injuring two pedestrians and another
motorist before his car careens into the side of a town house. Legal troubles
and criminal charges continue to mount for a Twin Cities psychologist and

father of four accused of fondling his female patients. Dutch elm disease makes a comeback in the metro area. Will your favorite shade tree be the next to go?"

After stepping into his boxers, Michaels reached for the remote to change channels. There had to be something else on.

"Tune in at ten for an update on the Minneapolis priest who was brutally assaulted and left for dead in his own church a week ago. What do authorities hope to discover when they question him from his hospital bed this week?"

Michaels froze. The crammed "worry about it later" compartment of his life suddenly burst open, spilling out its unsettling contents.

He waited to hear more from the television news anchor, but the promo ended and a commercial for a fast-food joint paraded some burgers across the screen. He spent half an hour surfing the local stations, anxiously searching for similar promos from the other television news programs. "Will a man of the cloth help police identify his attacker?" asked a breathy female anchor giving a teaser for another news station. "Or does his vow to keep confessions confidential seal his lips? Watch us at ten to learn more about this priestly dilemma."

All the news stations had it. He flicked off the television and angrily hurled the remote across the room. It shattered against the wall, scattering batteries and broken plastic pieces on the carpet and wood floor. "Son-of-a-bitch!" What if the priest did describe him?

He stomped past his wife's dresser, the marble top loaded with perfume bottles, religious statues and silver-handled hairbrushes. In one fluid and rage-filled motion, he knocked it all off with a swipe of his arm. The delicate bottles exploded, releasing a riot of fumes into the air.

He spotted the lone object left standing on his wife's dresser—a small statue of St. Jude, patron saint of hopeless cases. St. Jude was his wife's favorite saint, the one she'd prayed to while her father was dying of cancer. He would hear her whispering in the middle of the night, when worry stole her sleep: "Pray for me, I am so helpless and alone. Make use, I implore you, of that particular privilege given to you, to bring visible and speedy help where help is almost despaired of."

He picked up the small statue, no bigger than his hand, and glared at it contemptuously. At that instant, it represented the crippling emotions that threatened to weaken him and bring his world cascading down around him—the nagging guilt for his mortal offenses, the terrifying fear of landing in prison or hell, and the anxious dread that he was losing control of his life. "When am I going to get this Catholic monkey off my back?" he growled, and slammed it against the dresser top. The statue crumbled, all but disintegrating in a dusty cloud of clay.

He needed a plan, but there wasn't time to think about that now. He looked at the clock. "God dammit to hell," he said, running his fingers through his hair. He needed to finish dressing and get to the bar. Didn't want to keep the mystery lady waiting.

As he hurried east down Summit Avenue toward downtown, his knuckles turned white from the grip he had on the steering wheel of his Porsche. He didn't bother turning on the radio or slipping in a CD. He cursed every red light. The top was down, but the rush of summer air against his face did nothing to cool his temper, or drown out the buzzing in his head.

He picked a dark booth huddled against the wall opposite the bar and sharply ordered the waitress to bring him a double of the twenty-two-year-old Craigellachie, neat.

"Can I get you anything else?" she asked.

She was a tall brunette with short hair, a flat chest and no visible hips. The long black skirt and unfitted white blouse did her boyish figure no favors, he observed, but at least she looked professional.

"Would you like a glass of water on the side?" she asked.

"Surprise me," he said dryly.

She returned with a snifter containing the Scotch and a tall glass tinkling with ice water. "Shall I start a tab?" she asked.

He didn't answer immediately; he was staring straight ahead, lost in thought.

"Sir? A tab?"

"Yes, yes!" he snapped. "Start a tab." He picked up the snifter.

"Enjoy," she said, smiling, and walked away.

He sipped, luxuriating in the gentle burn that trickled from his mouth down to his gut. He drank again. He was starting to feel better. Much better. The fly was settling down.

He scanned the long, narrow room. A quiet night, as he would expect of a Monday evening at any establishment in town. Two fat, bald businessmen in white dress shirts sat bellies up to the bar, one at each end, resting their wide bottoms on tall wooden stools with ladder backs and black leather seats. Their suit jackets were draped over the backs of the stools. One of them puffed on a cigar purchased from the small glass humidor kept behind the bar.

Two male bartenders in white shirts, black trousers and dark ties busied themselves behind the bar polishing martini glasses and wine goblets. They could have passed for twins. Both wore their blond hair slicked back with some kind of gel, giving them a retro look consistent with their vintage surroundings.

The dark bar itself was an impressive slab of L-shaped wood furniture, running half the length of the room and curving around the back wall. It boasted a top that was glasslike in its high-gloss finish. The shiny counter surface was softly illuminated by a couple of green-shaded library lamps sitting on the bar top, one at each end. Behind the bar were glass shelves stacked six high and mounted against mirrored walls, giving the illusion of depth. The shelves were stocked with a mind-numbing array of liquor, but Scotch clearly ruled the day. Auchentoshan, Bladnoch and Glenkinchie from the Lowlands. Clynelish, Glenmorangie, Oban and Tomatin from the Highlands. Speyside in the north was well represented by Cragganmore, Glenfiddich, Inchgower, Mortlach. From the windswept isle of Islay came Bowmore, Bunnahabhain and Lagavulin. That's what the mystery lady had asked for. Lagavulin. Not a bad choice, thought Michaels. It has a powerful, peaty taste and smell accented by sweet undertones. He favored it after a heavy dinner, with a good cigar.

Where was she? He checked his wristwatch. Still early. He took a couple of slow, calming breaths and settled in to enjoy the view from his dark nook, with its glove-soft leather upholstery. Against the opposite wall and close to the bar's entryway from the hotel lobby was a blackboard with the quote of the day scribbled across it in white chalk. Today's offering was from Hemingway's *The Sun Also Rises*. He smiled as he read it, appreciating its slam against sentimentality: "This wine is too good for toast-drinking, my dear. You don't want to mix emotions up with a wine like that. You lose the taste."

He watched a chesty young woman sashay in wearing a short, black leather skirt, tight taupe sweater and black pumps with clear acrylic stiletto heels. The nice Catholic boys at the prep school he'd attended called those kinds of pumps "Come fuck me" shoes. From her forearm dangled a handbag covered with fake leopard fur. Her short, curly hair was bleached and dyed a hideous shade of platinum. Her makeup looked as though it had been applied with a trowel. She was a cheap piece of work, barely one step up from the whores he found on the street corners.

She hopped onto a bar stool next to one of the fat businessmen and started chattering. He ignored her. She kept yammering. He threw some bills on the bar, slid off the stool, grabbed his coat and left. She moved on to the man at the other end, the one with the cigar. He nodded his head a couple of times and then took the cigar out of his mouth to study the damp end, apparently finding it more interesting than the woman. He put it back in his mouth and pointedly turned his head away from her to watch the baseball game on the television mounted from ceiling brackets above the bar.

One of the bartenders leaned over the counter and said something to her in a low voice. She responded, shaking her blond head vigorously. The other bartender looked at her and put his hand on the phone behind the counter. "Fuck you," she sputtered. "I'm outta here." She hopped off the bar stool, turned on her heel and clicked out. Unruffled, the two bartenders returned to polishing glasses.

Michaels eyed her spiteful retreat. She had fat thighs, he thought, and she was stupid. Everyone in town knew that this bar—and the hotel, for that matter—threw hookers out on their asses. This fact was so well known and obvious Michaels was surprised there wasn't some sort of permanent sign posted at the hotel's glass front doors, right next to the stickers welcoming Visa and American Express. The unwritten law of the land was that this particular bar was a club for gentlemen and their invited ladies. No whores allowed. Michaels agreed with that. Some places had to be off limits. Everyone knew that. Everyone except this ditsy blonde.

As she left, another blond ambled in from the hotel lobby—a man with long hair and a beard. Long locks aside, he looked like a businessman in his white shirt, dark slacks and blazer. The tie was a bit much, however. He was probably involved in the arts in some way. The new arrival took a booth near the door, along the same wall as the bar. Something about the man's barrel body was familiar, but Michaels brushed the thought aside.

He took another sip of Scotch, rolled it around in his mouth and swallowed. A few more minutes went by. He glanced up at the television screen. The Tigers were winning at St. Louis. He was about to check his watch again when he saw her glide in from the lobby, and she was exquisite.

Her black hair hung like a velvet curtain around her swanlike neck. The black slip dress draped temptingly from her smooth, olive shoulders by two thin spaghetti straps. Those straps would be so easy to snap, he thought. The lustrous material glided over her breasts and hips, describing the smooth lines of an athletic but feminine woman. The hem fell above the knee. Hard, well-defined calves detailed her long legs. She must be a runner, he thought, and that bodes well for her endurance in the bedroom. At the same time, her small wrists and ankles told him she would not be too difficult to contain. That's what he wanted—a woman who could put up a lively fight, but would succumb when he desired.

He smiled to himself, pleased he had reserved a room at the hotel. He had used an alias and planned to pay in cash. In case things got a bit out of hand, as they had been wont to do lately. If that happened, she would be the last. The fly could be put to rest. That's what he told himself.

Good enough to eat, he thought, his eyes caressing her up and down. Good enough to eat, but easy enough to beat.

TWENTY-TWO

*M*urphy surveyed the room, noting the big man seated at the bar as well as the waitress and the two bartenders. Otherwise, the place appeared empty of civilians. That was good, she thought. She didn't want to run across anyone who recognized her. On any other night of the week, there was the possibility of bumping into a familiar judge or lawyer who might greet her by name or rank. A Monday in a downtown bar should be pretty quiet. She glanced briefly at Gabe, who had a clear view of the entire room from his seat near the door. He pushed back his blazer slightly. Murphy welcomed the private and reassuring peek at the holstered gun hanging from his shoulder rig.

On the wall above her partner's booth were several framed black-and-white photographs of the glitterati who had visited the bar or hotel, or worked at the establishment before they became famous. F. Scott Fitzgerald, Hubert H. Humphrey, Judy Garland, women's golf pioneer Patty Berg and railroad giant James J. Hill. Despite the bow to a couple of female notables, it was a very male establishment, reeking of cigar smoke, expensive Scotch and Italian leather. She'd always felt very comfortable in the place.

Murphy saw Michaels stand up. She hadn't noticed him there when she first set foot in the bar; she was being too slow or inattentive or both. She needed to be at the top of her game tonight. She quickly plastered a smile across her face, taking in his figure as he strolled across the bar's wood floor. He had a deliberate, graceful gait. He was handsome in his almost mono-chromatic attire, but even those dark blues and rich blacks couldn't coax any warm color from his cold, gray eyes. If you feel yourself wavering, she told herself, simply look into those heartless, soulless orbs. They were probably the last things Finch saw before she took her final breath. The last things the priest saw before he nearly died on the floor of his own church. The last things uncounted other victims saw as the life was strangled from their bod-ies. Remember Finch, she told herself. Remember Fionn Clare Hennessy, buried in a country cemetery.

"Hello, lady," he said. "You look beautiful. Absolutely stunning."

"Thank you," she said, smiling. "I guess we both like black."

"Black is the color of seduction," he said. "I'm sure you know that already." He extended his right hand. She reached out and took it. Such soft, smooth skin, he thought. He walked her over to his booth against the wall. She slid into it so she faced the lobby door. He sat down across from her. He longed for the feel of her legs pressed against his, but he initially kept his distance fearing such immediate closeness would make her uncomfortable. He had to move quickly but carefully this evening, he thought. She wasn't going to be one of his usual conquests.

The skinny waitress walked over. "What can I get for you?" she asked Murphy.

"The lady will have a Lagavulin," he said. "Neat."

The waitress looked at Murphy, who nodded. This man was used to barking out orders and seeing them followed, Murphy thought.

"Would you like another, sir?" the waitress asked, picking up his empty snifter.

"Yes," he said curtly, and turned his head away from the waitress to stare into Murphy's eyes. Then his gaze moved lower. He could make out the points of her nipples under the dress. She wasn't wearing a bra, and he liked that. What magnificent breasts, he thought.

"Thank you, miss," Murphy said. "Please bring me a tall glass of ice water like the gentleman's."

He is no gentleman, thought Murphy. He's rude, accustomed to treating others like servants. Having money shouldn't preclude politeness. Of course, she couldn't remember the last time she'd come across a well-mannered maniac.

The waitress quickly returned with their drinks. "Let me know if you need anything else," said the young woman. "I'll be back in a bit to see how you're doing."

"Thank you," said Murphy. She looked at Gabe seated near the door. His beer sat untouched in front of him, but he was smoking like crazy. His eyes were glued to the booth she shared with Michaels. The doctor didn't notice because he was too busy studying her breasts; she wished she'd worn the strapless bra.

"Tell me about yourself," he said to Murphy. He took a deep drink of Scotch.

"You go first," she said, smiling coyly. He laughed.

"Why don't we keep names out of it," he said. "I rather enjoy this game."

"Fine," said Murphy. "Then tell me as much as you can about yourself without name-dropping."

"I like that," he said, smiling. "Another rule for the game. Now let me think." He took a long drink and paused, staring up at the ceiling. He drummed his fingers on the table. "I need a cigar in my hands for these deep thoughts," he said. "Do you mind if I grab one? I won't light up yet."

"Please go right ahead. I like a good cigar myself once in a while."

Michaels slid out of the booth, walked up to the bar and pointed to the humidor. The bartender pulled out a fat cigar and showed it to him. The doctor examined the band, shook his head and pointed to another one. He held up two fingers. The bartender handed him a pair of slender cigars. Michaels examined the bands, sniffed them and nodded. He slipped them into the inside breast pocket of his jacket. He's a fussy bastard, she thought.

Michaels was all smiles walking back to the booth. "I got us both a treat for later," he said, and he slid into the booth next to her. She could feel his legs against hers. "Back to our game. I'm a doctor," he said. "I think I can tell you that without giving away too much."

"A gynecologist?" she asked.

He laughed. She felt his left hand on her left shoulder, softly stroking and rubbing her bare skin. She looked over at Gabe. His eyes were wide; he looked ready to jump out of his seat.

"You are naughty," he said. "No, a plastic surgeon. Now your turn."

"I work with food," she said, deciding to invent a career involving something familiar.

"You're a waitress?" he asked, sounding a little disappointed.

"No, a gourmet chef," she said. "I cater private affairs."

"Wonderful," he said. "Tell me about some of your favorite dishes."

He's testing me to see if I'm telling the truth, she thought. "Well, it's hard to pick one or two favorites," she said. "If you're talking appetizers, I prepare a wonderful olive-and-artichoke tapenade. For the main course, I would have to go with my roast leg of lamb with lemon-coriander crust. To accompany that, I might pick grilled asparagus with gorgonzola butter and spring greens with candied walnuts tossed in a raspberry vinaigrette."

"Dessert," he said, picking up his snifter to take a deep drink. "Let's not forget dessert."

"Life would be boring without dessert," she said. "How about a caramel flan?"

"Marvelous," he said, clearly impressed. After putting down his snifter, he rested his right hand on her thigh, only removing it to lift the glass to his lips.

"Are you a gourmet? You obviously know your Scotches and cigars," she said. "Tell me about your other interests, your extracurricular activities." Yes, she thought, describe those special hobbies of yours—rape and murder.

"Golf. Can't be a doctor unless you play golf. I love the water. Swimming. My favorite is sailing," he said. "We . . . I mean, um I . . . I have a cabin and boat on Lake Superior."

"You said 'we' at first," Murphy said, taking a dainty sip of Scotch and following it with a gulp of water.

She is way too observant, he thought. "I owned the boat and the cabin with my wife," he said. He took a long drink of Scotch before continuing. "We've been divorced for some time," he said. "She let me keep both. She isn't much of a sailor." That last part is the god's honest truth, he thought sourly.

That first part is a lie, thought Murphy, who detected the telltale white tan line around his left ring finger. She also noticed how his voice caught in his throat when he said the word "wife." He must despise her, she thought.

"What about you? Hobbies?"

"I run," she said, then decided to throw out another teaser. "I hunt. Small game. Pheasant and grouse mostly."

"How unusual. A woman who knows her Scotches, smokes cigars and hunts."

"I grew up in a houseful of males," she said.

He nodded, finding that believable.

"Do you hunt at all?" she asked. He smiled but didn't answer. Murphy decided not to push the question; she didn't want to make him suspicious.

He emptied his snifter and snapped his fingers to attract the attention of the waitress. He noticed Murphy had hardly touched her Scotch. "Is there something wrong with your drink?" he asked.

"Not at all," said Murphy, taking a longer drink to appease him. She felt a rush of warmth from the alcohol. "What else? Where were you born?"

"Well, I was born in St. Paul but I'm a product of the Minneapolis Catholic school system," he said. "The discipline was actually fine preparation for medical school. Would you like me to dazzle you with a little Latin?"

The waitress brought him another snifter. He took it from her hands before she set it down. He lifted it as if toasting. *"In vino veritas,"* he said, and nearly drained the snifter.

"In wine there is truth," Murphy said.

"Very good," he said.

"How about this one?" she asked. *"Facilis descensus Averno."*

"The descent to hell is easy," he said. For a moment, the drunken smile faded from his face.

"A favorite of my high-school religion teacher," she said. "A kick-ass Christian Brother."

"Aha! You went to Catholic school as well," he said. The smile returned. He laughed and raised his glass to her. "A toast to our shared misery." He emptied it.

Murphy saw it took quite a few drinks to get him to this stage. He's a heavy drinker.

"They're wrong, you know," he said, running his index finger along the edge of the empty glass. "The descent is anything but easy."

"What do you mean?"

"Are you as tormented by Catholic guilt as I am?" he asked. "What is it about us that drives us to beat ourselves up over normal, human failings?"

"What sorts of human failings do you consider normal?" she asked. Here we go, thought Murphy. This should be as interesting as hell.

He leaned conspiratorially into her ear, nearly putting his mouth on it, and whispered: "How do you like your sex?"

"Straight up and neat," she whispered back. He threw his head back and laughed so loudly the man at the bar and the two bartenders turned around. Gabe stared at them.

"I like mine with an extra twist—a rough one," he said. "Is that so decadent? Is that so sinful? Why do I have to beat myself up over that?"

"You don't have to beat yourself up," she offered, again pushing his hand off her thigh. "Isn't that what confession and penance are for?"

He shook his head. She didn't say anything. She waited for him to say more. She thought he was close to handing her something useful and revealing, something incriminating about his most recent trip to the confessional.

"Tell me," he said, looking into her eyes. "When was the last time you went to confession? Things have changed. Priests aren't what they used to be. They aren't content with laying a few rosary beads on you. They want you to do all sorts of shit."

"Well, the penance depends upon the seriousness of the offense," she said, realizing Father Ambrose must have asked too much from this man. Perhaps he even demanded he turn himself in to the police. "Some things require more than prayer," she said evenly, trying to sound reasonable. "Some sins require . . ." She wanted him to fill in the blank.

"Require what?" he asked, an edge of bitterness in his voice.

"Restitution?" she said.

"Bullshit. Remorse should be enough. Simple remorse."

Keep going, she thought. He stopped talking and stared straight ahead; he seemed to be studying the air itself.

"Enough small talk," he said, sliding out of the booth. "Let's go out in the hotel garden and admire the stars. It should be dark enough by now. We can have a smoke out there."

He threw a wad of cash on the table and held out his hand, but Murphy ignored it. She wiggled out of the booth and walked out with him. When she passed Gabe's table, she tried not to meet his eyes. Her partner wouldn't be liking this at all.

"Great," Gabe muttered. He crushed his cigarette butt in the ashtray, threw some crumpled bills on the table and got up. Carefully staying several paces behind, he followed them into the lobby and out of the hotel. He stopped outside the double glass doors of the hotel entrance, standing nonchalantly next to the doorman.

A black limo pulled into the circular drive at the hotel entrance, spilling out a drunken man in a rumpled gray suit and a sober, somber woman in a blue dress. The doorman, a young man dressed in a period costume, held the door open while the man tripped in ahead of the woman. She stomped after him.

On either side of the circular drive were elaborate English gardens decorating the front of the hotel. The one on the north end of the building was the smaller, less lavish of the two. The larger garden on the south end seemed to grow more elaborate every year, even within its confined urban space. This summer, walking paths wound their way under metal arbors and snaked through patches of yellow snapdragons and peach day lilies. White clusters of sweet alyssum scented the air. Rabbits hopped among the plants.

A tall, black wrought-iron fence separated the gardens from the sidewalk. On the street beyond, a couple of cabs were parked in front of the hotel. The cabbies were leaning against the sides of their cars, having a smoke and talking. One had his radio tuned to the game. Otherwise, it was quiet.

Gabe watched his partner and Michaels walk to the far end of the larger garden. He lost sight of them. He didn't want to get too close, for fear of tipping Michaels off. He pulled out his pack of Winstons. Empty. He strolled down the drive between the two gardens to the sidewalk, giving a sideways glance to see if he could spot Murphy and Michaels from that angle. They were sitting on a bench that backed into some tall evergreens planted against the side of the hotel. He looked straight ahead and recognized the cabbies; he bummed a cigarette off one of them. A large group of people walked through the hotel doors. The cabbies tossed down their smokes and got in their cars, pulling up the circular drive for the fares. Gabe stood alone on the sidewalk for a minute and then walked back to the hotel entrance. He stayed there, one hand shoved resentfully in his pants pocket and the other occupied with a smoke. Under his blazer, his Glock was ready.

After the two taxis pulled away, the only sound was that of an occasional car passing on the street. The night air had turned cool. Murphy shivered. Michaels slipped his left arm around her and rubbed her bare shoulder. "We should go back inside, where it's warmer," she said.

He took off his jacket and draped it over her shoulders. "I almost forgot our treat," he said. He slipped his hand inside the coat to pull out the two cigars, brushing her left breast as he did so. He felt his pants pocket. "No matches. Stay right here." He stood up and walked through the garden to the lobby doors. "Got a light?" he asked the doorman.

The doorman reached into his pants pocket and pulled out a book of hotel matches. "There you go, sir."

Michaels started to leave, but eyed Gabe for several seconds. Gabe stared back, puffing on his cigarette. Michaels thought he looked very familiar, but couldn't place him. "Do I know you?" Michaels asked.

"Don't think so," Gabe said, then turned around to stroll through the smaller garden.

Michaels went back to the bench. Gabe took a hard pull on his cigarette and watched the doctor disappear into the garden; he gritted his teeth. "Bastard," Gabe whispered.

Michaels sat down and tried to give Murphy one of the cigars. She shook her head and pushed his hand away. "Let's smoke them inside," she said. She felt in control since he was drunk and she was sober. Still, this garden spot was far too dark and private. She took off his jacket and handed it to him.

"That bar is dreary," he said. He slipped the cigars back in the jacket pocket, threw the jacket over the back of the bench and leaned toward her. "We could get a room," he said softly.

"You've got to be kidding," she said. She stood up to leave. "I don't even know your name, let alone . . ."

He grabbed her by the arm and yanked her back down to the bench. He pulled her toward him and kissed her hard on the mouth. His left hand cradled the back of her head, his fingers entwined in her hair.

"Stop," she said when he lifted his mouth off hers for an instant.

He didn't respond; he was listening to the buzzing. He pulled her off the bench and onto the ground.

She felt some sort of fragrant ground cover beneath her. His body was flat on top of hers. Through her thin dress, she could feel he was hard. For an instant—one out-of-control instant—she was aroused. Then she was terrified. "Don't," she said.

"I'll take it slow," he whispered. "Slow, but rough. A woman like you, I'll bet you like it rough." He again sealed his lips firmly over hers. He tasted sharply of Scotch. His right hand cupped her left breast. He squeezed hard, his hand slipping a bit on the satiny dress.

She struggled to push against his chest with both hands, but he was too strong and heavy. She tried to scream, but couldn't with his mouth over hers. His right hand moved from her breast to the strap of her dress. He slipped the strap off her shoulder and pulled down the bodice. His mouth moved from her lips to her breast. She emitted a squeak that was the very beginning of a scream, but he quickly covered her mouth with his left hand. With his right hand he grabbed her left wrist and pinned it down on the ground, close to her side. He peeled his mouth off her breast and put his lips close to her ear:

"The fly shall marry the bumblebee," he breathed.

His words made no sense to her, and that frightened her as much as his actions. He was nuts. Her head was spinning. Was she going to be raped by a crazy man in front of this hotel, in the middle of downtown, with her partner yards away? After all the jams she'd gotten out of over the years, was she finally going to be finished by one of her own making? Hell no, she thought. This is not going to happen. She pushed against his chest with her free right hand and bit the meaty palm covering her mouth. He didn't budge. She bore down as hard as she could with her teeth, grinding. He pulled his hand away with a yelp. "You bitch!" he snarled, letting go of her wrist to slap her.

He lifted his body slightly off hers, resting on his right elbow and shaking his left hand in pain. That gave her the maneuvering room she needed. She bent her right leg and kneed him in the groin. He grunted and started to roll off her, but she grabbed him by the shoulders for leverage and kneed him again, even harder. He tumbled off her, rolled into a ball and clutched his crotch.

She scrambled out of the garden, fixing her dress strap as she ran. She almost knocked Gabe over on the sidewalk in front of the hotel. He threw down his cigarette. "What the fuck is going on?" he asked, gaping at her disheveled state. Bits of greenery were tangled in her hair, her dress was askew and she was panting. He saw a red mark on her face; the bastard had hit her. "Did he . . ."

"No, he didn't get that far," she whispered frantically. "Now shut up and get me the hell out of here before he catches his breath. My cover is still good and I don't want to blow it."

"Bullshit," hissed Gabe, looking toward the garden while reaching under his blazer for his gun.

She stopped him, resting her trembling hand on his arm. The doorman eyed them nervously, but became distracted when a taxi pulled up, disgorging two women loaded with shopping bags from the Mall of America. The doorman took a couple of the bags and held the door open for them before following them inside with their purchases.

Murphy pulled Gabe into the smaller garden. "We can get the son-of-a-bitch for assaulting a cop right now," said Gabe. She couldn't see his face in the dark, but she could tell from his voice that it was red with rage.

"It's his word against mine," she said. "He's got all the money in the world to fight it. We need hard evidence on these murders."

"How about I stroll over there and beat the living shit out of him?" said Gabe. "At least let me make that small contribution."

"I'd like to kick the warped bastard's ass myself," she said, struggling to steady her quavering voice. "Right now, as far as he's concerned, I'm just the one who got away. Let's keep it that way. Besides, he didn't get off scot-free."

"What did you do to him?" asked Gabe.

"Let's say he won't be walking upright for a while," she said.

Should we stop at the hospital and get you checked?" asked Gabe as they trotted toward Murphy's Jeep, parked on a downtown side street.

"No. I'm fine," she said. "I'm just a little shaky. You drive, okay? You've got the keys in your pocket anyway."

They stopped next to the Jeep. "Go ahead and get it over with, Gabe," Murphy said as her partner fished the keys out of his pants pocket. "Say it." She leaned against the car with one hand while he fumbled with the door lock, taking what seemed like forever to finally open it. She was still trembling like a kicked puppy; her face still burned where Michaels had struck her.

"What are you talking about?" he asked as they slid into the car.

"Say it. I deserve it. I want you to say it. Really. I do!" she said, shouting without realizing it.

"What, Murphy? Say what?" he yelled back.

"Oh, fuck you," she said, slamming the passenger-side door shut.

"Okay," said Gabe, slamming the driver's-side door. "I told you so! I fucking told you so! There. Are you happy? Are you?"

"Yes," she said softly. She touched her sore cheek. "Now don't say another goddamn word about it for the rest of the night."

TWENTY-THREE

She drove alone down to Rochester Tuesday morning. All the windows of the Jeep down. The radio blaring. Tina Turner. "I Might Have Been Queen."

I might have been dead meat, mused Murphy, thinking back to the previous night and the near catastrophe in the dark hotel garden. At a light, she looked in the rearview mirror and checked the small, pale bruise on her face where he'd struck her. She'd covered it with some makeup; it would be gone in a day or two. She knew his words would stay with her longer.

"I'll bet you like it rough."

His words bothered her because she worried that they were true. She wasn't delicate; she was drawn to coarse and primitive things. Even mean things. Did that make her coarse and primitive? Mean? She adored the abrasive nature of police work, with its intimate exposure to the violence of the streets and the rawness of people's emotions. She loved living on the urban shores of the unpolished Mississippi. She enjoyed the rowdiness of her family's riverfront bar, with its clientele of barge workers.

When she was in her early twenties and pouring drinks at the bar one summer night, she slipped out for a stroll along the Mississippi with a Cajun towboat pilot fresh from New Orleans. He had a strangely musical accent that was at once French, Canadian and southern. He was a head taller than she and a decade older, with massive arms, jet-black hair and piercing green eyes. They went to his cabin aboard the boat, got drunk on Southern Comfort and fell into his bed. He was very rough, holding her wrists tight during their lovemaking, grabbing her hair in his fists. It frightened her and, though she would never admit it, excited her.

She didn't tell anyone about that night along the river. Not even Jack. Especially not Jack.

Of course, she didn't want it as rough as rape. No woman did. She had thought she could manage the situation at the hotel, but it had all boiled over into a wretched mess. Why had she fooled herself into thinking she was in control of a clearly uncontrollable situation? Had she been asking for trouble, for rape? No. She had endangered herself and the case with her arrogant overconfidence.

For all her trouble, what had she learned about Michaels? He was a high-class alcoholic who liked his Scotch expensive, neat and in great quantities. He was a womanizing control freak who quickly evolved into a masochistic rapist with the help of his booze. He was a tormented Catholic who felt enough guilt to go to confession, but had assaulted the priest when the penance proved threatening. He was an unfaithful husband who hated his wife. She had managed to assemble a pretty complete profile of the guy in one evening, but almost at the cost of her life. His rape victims didn't live to tell about it.

One thing in the picture didn't fit: his nonsensical words. "The fly shall marry the bumblebee." It sounded like a child's song. She'd have to do an Internet search and see what that pulled up.

Unlike the drive to western Wisconsin, this trip had few stretches of woods and forests breaking up the monotony of farmland. She passed one cornfield and peeling red barn after another, interrupted only by meadows covered by bales of hay rolled up like giant pieces of Shredded Wheat. At least it was a short trip.

ROCHESTER WELCOMES YOU and MAYO MEDICAL CENTER EXIT 4 MILES read two signs at the city limits. From the highway, Murphy could see a cluster of red buildings up on a hill that represented a fraction of the sprawling medical campus. She took the hospital exit and wound her way around the campus until she found the coffee shop where she was meeting a Rochester homicide investigator. She preferred buttonholing colleagues away from their station houses. She found fellow detectives more relaxed and open when they were off site, freed of the distraction of ringing phones and bellowing superiors.

"Sergeant Paris Murphy," she said, smiling and offering her hand.

"Sergeant Daniel Klassen," he said, sliding out of his seat at the coffee shop to stand and introduce himself. He was Murphy's height and in his mid-fifties, with short gray hair and a neatly trimmed moustache. Gold wire-rimmed glasses framed his eyes. A slight paunch pushed out his white dress shirt and draped over his navy blue trousers. He waited until she took a seat at the table before sitting down himself.

The waitress, an older woman with hair drawn back in a bun behind her head, brought grease-stained breakfast menus to the table. She wore a yellow dress covered by a white apron, also grease stained. "How ya doin' there, Sergeant Dan?" she asked Klassen.

"I'm doin' fine, pretty lady," he said, grinning and not bothering to glance at the menu. "What kinda pie we got today?"

"We got apple, strawberry-rhubarb, lemon chiffon, banana cream, cherry, Mississippi mud and chocolate silk," she said. "I put aside a piece of your favorite, in case you came in today. Which you did."

"Which I did," he said, smiling. "Bring on that peach pie, then. Don't forget the java."

"What can we get for you, sweetie?" she asked Murphy.

"Coffee is fine, thanks," Murphy said. "Black."

After the waitress left, Klassen slid a manila file folder across the table. "Here's what I can give you," he said. "You can keep it. It's all photocopies."

The tab of the folder carried the victim's name, last name first. "Magnuson,

Roxanne E." A person never wants her name on the tab of a file folder, thought Murphy. It's rarely for a happy reason. "I hope you don't mind if I poke around your case," she said, rifling through the file.

The waitress set down two coffee cups and what looked like half a peach pie, à la mode.

"Hell. If you think you can crack it after better than a dozen years, more power to you," he said, digging into the pie and vanilla ice cream. "We thought some out-of-towner probably did it and then took off," he said in between bites. "When I heard you guys had a case with the same M.O., especially with the weird hair thing, I thought I'd better flag you. Figured after all these years, maybe the son-of-a-bitch resurfaced up in St. Paul. Maybe he got hungry for some city meat."

"I appreciate that," she said, smiling.

"Yeah, but when you called me yesterday afternoon and told me who you were looking at, well, I have to tell you, it's hard as hell to believe one of our doctors did this," he said, wiping ice cream off his moustache. He took a sip of coffee and gave her a tight smile.

"Our doctors." Rochester took care of its own.

"It's just a theory I have," she said, still smiling and taking a sip of coffee. "Do you have any suggestions regarding folks I could reinterview? Any loose ends I could reexamine?"

"Not really," he said. He looked up from his pie; the smile was gone from his face. "We interviewed and reinterviewed everybody and his goddamn uncle."

Murphy realized she'd pissed him off with the suggestion that there were loose ends. A couple of male uniformed officers walked through the café door. Klassen nodded at them. Murphy suspected he would rather be sitting with them than an uppity female cop from the Twin Cities. She wasn't going to get very far asking this guy for help. "Well, thanks much," she said, sliding out of her chair. She reached into her purse to throw some cash on the table.

"Don't worry about it," he said, waving away the money. "Good luck."

"I'll give you a call if we find anything," she said.

"Yeah, you do that," he said. He didn't try to mask the skepticism in his voice.

"Thank you very much," she said again, and left. As she walked down the sidewalk to her car, she could see through the coffee-shop window that he had wasted no time in joining his colleagues at their table—and ordering more pie.

Murphy drove to a lake in the middle of Rochester, parked her Jeep in a lot overlooking the water and studied the file. She rolled down the car windows to enjoy the meager breeze off the lake. Warm, but overcast. The beach off the parking lot was void of swimmers but filled with fat Canada geese; their droppings littered the sand. Several of the big birds waddled up to her car, looking for a handout.

Everything seemed to be in order in the file. The autopsy report found that Roxanne E. Magnuson had been beaten and raped, but no semen was found. The suspect had apparently used a condom. That bit of information made Murphy doubt the rapist was a spontaneous stranger. "Out-of-towner my ass," she mumbled, flipping through the police report. The cause of death was strangulation. The report also made a reference to the section of missing auburn hair. As with Finch, the victim had a nick on the back of her neck, probably from the sharp object used to shear off her hair.

The murder victim's housemate, another nurse named Marcia Colvin, told officers her friend had been seeing a married man on the sly. Colvin didn't know the man's name; Magnuson had been very secretive about the relationship. Colvin claimed she saw him parked outside the house one night, dropping her friend off. Colvin happened to be up studying for a medical school entrance exam, having aspirations beyond nursing. The rental house was on an unlit country road and Colvin had been unable to see the car clearly. When Magnuson opened the car door to get out, triggering the car's interior light, Colvin was able to get a good look at the man behind the wheel. Her description was detailed enough to result in a police composite sketch.

Murphy pulled the drawing out of the file and held it up. These things are always so generic-looking, Murphy thought as she studied the sketch. It could be the doctor or any other big, blond guy in Minnesota, a heavily Scandinavian state brimming with big, blond guys.

None of the victim's other friends or co-workers—at the hospital or on the strip circuit—knew anything about Magnuson having a regular beau, married or not. The woman slept around quite a bit—and probably did a little hooking on the side—and was seen in bars around town with lots of different escorts. For those reasons, it seemed investigators eventually discounted the theory that a boyfriend had committed the crime. They decided Magnuson must have fabricated the story about the steady man in her life, perhaps as a cover for the stream of johns and one-night stands.

Murphy read the written report of Colvin's description. She said the man in the car that night was handsome. Strikingly handsome.

That composite sketch didn't do him justice. He was so handsome, almost beautiful. Do you know what I mean?"

Murphy stood on the front porch of a newer house on the outskirts of Rochester. It looked pretty much like the other enormous single-family homes in the upper-middle-class development. They were all painted taupe, beige or a close cousin. They all boasted three-car garages. The lawns were trimmed and fertilized so meticulously they looked like golf-course greens. White petunias filled every white window box. The entire neighborhood was a suffocating tribute to beige and all other things bland.

The stripper's housemate had stayed in town, and Murphy was easily able to track her down. She was married and had two kids—they kept tugging at their mother's pants leg as Murphy tried to interview the woman—but Marcia Colvin kept her maiden name.

"Poor Roxy," Colvin mumbled as she studied the composite sketch. "How long has it been?" She answered her own question, sounding sadly retrospective. "It's been at least twelve or thirteen years I think. Maybe more," she said. "I can't believe how time flies. We're all getting older, aren't we? I know she wasn't exactly a nun, but Roxy had a good heart. Then don't we all when we're stupid young women?"

Colvin was close to Murphy's age but a few inches shorter, plump and tired-looking. Her brown hair was in the close-cropped, efficient style of a frantic mother. Gray was starting to creep into it, but she was probably too busy even to think about coloring it. The toddlers, two girls, kept her running. Her medical-school plans had fizzled. She was still a nurse and worked at the hospital five days a week, mostly nights. Her husband was an accountant at the hospital with day hours. They took different shifts to avoid putting their kids in day care.

"I'm pretty sure I could still point him out if I saw him in the flesh," she said. "I'm sorry I can't say I'm one-hundred percent sure. I guess too many years have gone by for me to swear on a stack of Bibles, but if I saw him in person, I think I could identify him with ninety-nine percent certainty. He was gorgeous."

Ninety-nine percent isn't too bad, Murphy thought gleefully. "Did your housemate ever drop any names?" Murphy asked. "Even a first name or some dumb pet name she had for the guy?"

"No," said Colvin, shaking her head. "All she ever told me is he was a married man, and that's why they both kept it under wraps. I think the police thought Roxy was fantasizing by telling me she had someone steady, but I believed her, and I did see this guy that night."

"I'll be getting back to you," said Murphy, reaching into her purse. "In the meantime, do me a favor. If anything comes to mind that might help me out—something about the man or his car or something Roxy said—please give me a call. Here's my card. Please don't share anything we discussed. Not even with your husband."

"Son-of-a-gun," the woman said, taking the card and handing the composite sketch back to Murphy. "Imagine catching the guy after all these years. Wouldn't that be a kicker? Son-of-a-gun."

"Thanks for your time," said Murphy. "I'll let you get back to your kids." One of the chubby-cheeked toddlers clutched what looked like the remains of a peanut-butter-and-jelly sandwich. The other one had a fistful of spaghetti noodles and a face stained with red sauce. They were still in their sleepers.

Murphy started to step off the porch and then stopped and turned around. "Hey," she said. "You've got kids so maybe this sounds familiar. 'The fly shall marry the bumblebee.' "

"It's a line from a nursery rhyme. Mother Goose," said Colvin. "What does that have to do with this?"

"Rather not say right now. Can you recite the whole thing?"

"Wait a minute. I've got a book." Colvin disappeared into the house for a minute. The two toddlers stood on the porch staring up at Murphy. The one with the squished sandwich held it up to her. Murphy laughed and shook her head.

"No, thank you."

Colvin reappeared, flipped through the book and opened it to a page with a picture of a fly and a bee standing atop a wedding cake. Murphy took the book and read the rhyme:

"Fiddle-de-dee, fiddle-de-dee,
The fly shall marry the bumblebee.
They went to church and married was she.
The fly has married the bumblebee.

"What in the world can that mean?" Murphy mumbled to herself. She handed the book back to Colvin.

"Who is this guy, anyway?" asked Colvin.

"We think he's a surgeon," Murphy said.

"Plastic?"

"Why?"

"That could explain it," Colvin said.

"Explain what?" asked Murphy.

"Well, Roxy made pretty good money between nursing and dancing and whatever," said Colvin.

"Yeah, I'm sure the 'whatever' paid especially well," said Murphy, smiling a little.

"Look, I never gave a darn as long as she came up with her half of the rent and didn't bring anyone home," Colvin said defensively.

"Sorry," said Murphy. "Her lifestyle wasn't your responsibility."

"Well, anyway, she made decent scratch but not enough for something like that," said Colvin.

"Something like what?" Murphy blurted. "What are you talking about?"

"Well, she had this tattoo on her shoulder," said Colvin. "She got it in high school. A red heart with an old boyfriend's name in it. Ed was his name. I joked with her that she should find a guy named Fred or Ned or Ted. Then all she needed to do was add a letter or two."

Murphy laughed.

"Anyway, she talked about getting it removed, but she made some calls and found out it would be expensive," said Colvin. "It could be done in a doctor's office, but it would take several clinic visits."

"So," said Murphy.

"So suddenly Roxy starts getting the treatments—over weekends," said Colvin. "I asked her about it and she didn't want to talk about it."

"He must have given her a freebie in his office after hours," said Murphy. She didn't share with Colvin her suspicion that it also could have been in trade for Roxy's services.

"That is very good information." Murphy scratched in her notebook.

"Well, good luck trying to nail him, my dear," said Colvin, offering Murphy a firm handshake.

"Thank you."

"Let me know what I can do to help," said Colvin as Murphy stepped off the porch. "Go carefully, Detective. You know, some people think doctors are gods and can do no wrong. That's doubly true for surgeons."

"You sound like someone who knows better," said Murphy.

"Darn right I know better," said the woman, picking up one of the fussy toddlers. "I'm a nurse."

Victorious but drained, Murphy drove straight home from Rochester.

Her heart fluttered when she turned into the parking lot of her riverfront neighborhood. "Great," she mumbled to herself. "What is this about?" Jack's silver BMW was there. She was at once excited and apprehensive. She questioned what brought him to her houseboat after a week of ignoring her calls.

One word came to mind: Gabe. She wondered exactly how much her partner had shared with her husband about the last several days, and then decided it was irrelevant because all of it was bad. Some of it was just worse for her marriage. She pulled her key out of the ignition, but sat in the Jeep for a couple of minutes. She drummed the steering wheel with her fingers. She considered starting up the car again and pulling out, going to the cop shop. She had plenty of paperwork she could do. If she stayed away long enough, maybe he'd leave. She pushed the key back in the ignition, but didn't turn it.

Don't be such a chicken shit, she said to herself. She pulled the key out again, shoved it in her purse and slid out of her car. She stopped to take a breath, slammed the car door and walked down the dock and into the houseboat.

She found him sitting in the galley, dressed in jeans and a white T-shirt. He had set the kitchen table with a white tablecloth, china, silverware, candles and a bouquet of Sweetheart roses. She loved Sweetheart roses; he had given them to her when they were dating.

"I'm sorry," he said, getting up and lighting the candles.

"What?" she said, dropping her purse on the floor.

"I apologize for my behavior of the last several days," he said, walking to her and wrapping his arms around her. "I've been a world-class prick."

"I guess we make a great pair," she said. "Who the hell else would put up with our garbage?"

Gabe must have told him about her dangerous encounter with Michaels, but not about Erik. She would have to confess to him sometime, but not now.

"So this asshole is actually a sick pervert who rapes and murders women and then takes their hair as some kind of war trophy. He nearly added my wife to his list of victims."

"He didn't get very far," she said. "He still doesn't know I'm a cop. He assumes I'm some woman he picked up, mauled and let get away. We need to keep him thinking that way. There'll be plenty of opportunity to kick his ass in court, after we nail him on these murders."

"Are you really all right? Gabe said you were okay. You should have let him take you to the hospital to get checked over."

Jack was stroking her hair and she wanted to push his hands away. She felt guilty, like she didn't deserve him. "I'm okay," she said. "Stupid of me to think I could control that situation, manipulate it. Gabe tried to talk me out of the whole dumb operation. He really did."

"The stubborn Irish completely ignored him."

"Why is it stubborn Irish? Why isn't it stubborn Lebanese?" she asked.

"I think the Lebanese in you kicked Michaels in the nuts," he said. "Twice."

"The first hit was a grounder," she said. "The second one was out of the ballpark."

He laughed and then grew serious. "I am so very sorry I doubted you," he said.

"What have you done to my kitchen?" she asked, suddenly noticing the pile of pots and pans in the sink. "What is that awful smell?"

"Um, that was going to be dinner," he said.

"You can't cook," she said, slipping out of his arms and walking over to the sink to investigate the black mess inside the pots. She saw the charred remains of a chicken or some other bird in one pan and burned rice in another.

"I am well aware I can't cook," he said, sounding a little sheepish. "I reaffirmed that this afternoon, with a vengeance. I wanted to surprise you."

"You sure did," she said, picking up one of the pans by the handle and staring inside.

"Maybe this will make up for it," he said. He walked over to the refrigerator, opened the door and pulled out a bottle. He showed it to her.

"Dom Pérignon!" she gasped. "You can't cook, but you sure know how to chill a good bottle of champagne."

He set it on the table and pulled two frosty champagne glasses from the freezer.

"What next?" she asked.

He pulled a box of takeout food from the refrigerator and, with great ceremony, set it down on the linen-covered table.

"Oh no!" she said. "Jack. Honest to god! With Dom Pérignon? The wine police will break down our door."

"Look, I know it's not coq au vin, but what the hell, it's still good food, right?" he said, pulling a chair out for her and motioning for her to take a seat. *"Madame, pour vous."*

"I love you," she said as he took a seat across from her.

"I love you, too," he said, a catch in his voice. "Now tell me," he said, clearing his throat, "do you want regular or extra crispy? Stop eyeballing those drumsticks, wife. I call first dibs on those puppies."

The sound of a New Orleans–style band floated down the Mississippi from a riverboat carrying revelers on a moonlight party cruise. The enormous stern-wheeler sliced a tame wake through the water, gently rocking

Murphy's compact houseboat. "Do you hear?" she asked, pausing with dirty dishes in her hands. "Louisiana Two-Step" drifted through the open houseboat windows. "Remember the music coming out of the open doors of the clubs along Bourbon Street? We should do that trip again. Listen to that." She swayed back and forth.

"I can't hear anything but your voice," he said, grabbing her from behind and wrapping his arms around her waist. "Put the plates down and come to bed, babe. We can clean up in the morning."

He was shirtless and shoeless, dressed only in his jeans. She had discarded her slacks and shoes and was clothed only in panties and a blouse. He pulled the china out of her hands and set the pieces down on the kitchen counter. Facing her, he clamped a hand on each of her shoulders and pulled her toward him. He kissed her hard on the mouth, his tongue pushing past her teeth. She arched her back, pressing her body into his, and moaned softly. She scraped her teeth against his tongue as he pulled it out.

"I want to make love," he whispered in her ear.

"I think I'd enjoy that, horny wench that I am," she said, smiling and reaching behind him to push his buttocks into her hips.

He pulled her blouse over her head, not bothering with the buttons. She clawed at the zipper on his jeans. They made love on the living-room floor. He was on top because that's how she liked it. No discussion. He knew what his wife wanted before she did.

"That's what you want, isn't it, babe?" he breathed in her ear as he entered her. She groaned and clutched his buttocks, grating her pelvis against him. "It's what you need," he said hoarsely. "Isn't it?"

"Yes," she whispered.

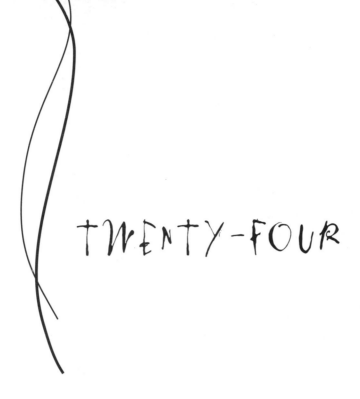

TWENTY-FOUR

*R*oom One. Rhinoplasty.

"Don't expect instant results, Mrs. Merrill," Michaels said to the woman sitting on the exam table. "This isn't one of those soap operas where the surgeon removes the bandages and you're suddenly a beauty queen."

"I understand."

"You will wear a splint for several days after the surgery," he said. He sat across from her in a high-backed leather office chair.

"Yes," she said, nodding her head. "A splint."

"There will be swelling on the inside and outside of your nose," he said.

"Yes," she said. "Swelling. I understand."

"Your eyes will turn black and blue because of bruising of the loose tissues around the eyelids; it'll look like someone punched you. This is perfectly normal and not a cause for concern," he continued. "The whites of your eyes may even turn red, but this shouldn't alarm you, either. In most cases, it clears up in a couple of weeks or so."

"I understand."

He was dutifully giving her the same lecture he gave his other rhinoplasty patients, but Mrs. Merrill, dressed in a cream-colored Liz Claiborne slacks ensemble, wasn't paying too much attention. Michaels guessed she was stoned on some prescription drug, probably Valium. Her high-heel-shod feet were dangling off the edge of the exam table and she was studying her cream-colored shoes. A black scuff on one of the toes apparently troubled her more than the predicted aftereffects of her upcoming surgery. She reached down and rubbed the scuff with her thumb.

"Please realize, Mrs. Merrill, that it may take as long as a year for the final appearance of your nose to become apparent," he said. "That's because normal healing takes place quite gradually."

"I understand," she said. "As long as a year."

"If we don't achieve the results you want, we can make some minor adjustments down the road, a little fine-tuning," Michaels told her. "I doubt that will be necessary. I get it right the first time and rarely have to go back for revisions."

"Scarring?" she asked.

He couldn't believe she had asked a question. "Inside the nose," he said. "It's not visible."

She nodded. She was in her late fifties and still dyed her hair bright red. With her thin frame covered in cream and her fiery shock of hair, Michaels thought she looked like a lit wooden matchstick. She was bored and stoned, and probably depressed because she was getting older. Michaels had already given her a breast lift. Now the nose job. Her husband didn't care, kept forking over the money for the operations. He told Michaels he'd do anything to keep her happy and out of his hair. Michaels figured what she really needed was to get off her ass and get out of the house, find a constructive activity, something other than shopping and surgery. He could probably tell that to half his patients, but he wouldn't make any money that way.

"Here's a brochure," he said, shoving a pamphlet into her hands. "Please read it. A nurse will contact you before your surgery date to provide you with additional instructions."

"Yes, Doctor," she said.

He left the room and headed down the hall.

The last place Michaels wanted to be on Tuesday was trapped in his clinic measuring the pendulous breasts and massive snouts of doped-up matrons. He had a nagging headache. His muscles ached. His left hand was sore from that black-haired woman's bite. His mind was still trying to get a grip on Monday night's fiasco. How had she beaten him? She was stronger than he'd expected, and more coolheaded than he liked. He shouldn't have picked such a tall woman. The small ones were better; they were easier to subdue and seemed to panic and lose control quicker. Would she be able to find him and press charges? He hadn't left anything behind that would identify him. He'd paid for everything in cash. Remembered to grab his jacket off the garden bench. The two of them had never exchanged names.

On the other hand, he decided he had no reason to worry. He could rightfully claim she'd consented and then freaked out when things got a little rough. Hell, he could accuse her of assault. It had taken him what seemed like an eternity to uncurl his body. Fortunately no one saw him stumble out of the garden and wobble to his car. That doorman with the black top hat was preoccupied with late-arriving hotel guests.

Then there was that other side of him, the side that still desired her. Perhaps even more than before, now that he had tasted her mouth and breasts and run his hands over her skin. Now that he had experienced her squirming under him, struggling for release. If he had the opportunity, he would try to take her again. Next time, he'd know what to expect from her and he'd come prepared. Next time, she wouldn't get away from the fly.

Room Two. Reduction mammaplasty.

Clutching the chart, he rapped on the door once with his knuckles and walked in.

"How are you doing, Mrs. Townsend?" he asked the plump blond woman. She'd gone from a sagging 40DD to a perky B in a three-hour operation the month before.

"Well, I'm still a little sore," she said. She was dressed in a blue paper robe and had her chubby arms folded protectively over her chest. She was modest to the point of ridiculousness, despite her forty-five years of age and five children.

"Please open the front of your gown," he said. She didn't budge. "Mrs. Townsend?"

"Can't we skip that part?"

"Mrs. Townsend, I don't have X-ray vision," he said impatiently. "I need to have a look at them." He untangled her arms; their pink flabbiness repulsed him. "I think they're coming along quite well," he said, examining the scars that ran under her breasts. They were thin and would fade even more with time. He was a fucking artist.

"The area around your nipples also looks excellent," he said as much to himself as to his patient. "Yes. Marvelous outcome around the nipples." She was blushing. He imagined screaming the word "nipple" until she collapsed in an embarrassed, jiggling heap on the exam table. "Nipple! Nipple! Nipple!"

"Why don't you try going without a bra for a while longer?" he told her. "The rubbing could irritate your nipples."

"Thank you, Doctor," she said, quickly rewrapping herself in the paper robe.

"Hold off on the jogging for a bit longer, all right?" he said.

"Oh, I don't jog, Doctor," she said, smiling.

She didn't get the joke.

"Should I try vitamin E? My sister-in-law said it works wonders on . . ."

"Is your sister-in-law a plastic surgeon?"

"No."

"I guessed not. Some people believe vitamin E hastens healing and lessens scarring, but there is no solid medical evidence to back that up."

"So should I use it?"

"Do as you please," he said tiredly. "Come back and see me in two months and, again, don't irritate those nipples."

Then there was that other issue involving the priest. He needed to silence the man, one way or another.

To hell with organized religion and all its trappings, he thought bitterly.

He'd been a good Catholic all his life, serving as an altar boy, attending Catholic school, marrying a Catholic girl in a Catholic church, making it to mass on a fairly regular basis and even serving on the parish committee. He'd baptized his daughters and sent them to Catholic school as well. He'd donated enough money to the archdiocese over the years to build his own cathedral. Yet the one time he needs some big-time forgiveness, he's told to chuck everything he's worked for and turn himself in to the authorities. Bullshit, he thought.

All he had to show for his devotion to the faith was angst-filled Catholic guilt—and that had done nothing but cause him grief.

He wondered how differently his life would have turned out if he had been born a Lutheran.

*R*oom Three. Tattoo removal.

These were becoming increasingly popular as teenage decisions haunted people into adulthood. A yellow rose that looks appealing on a pert eighteen-year-old butt looks bad on the flaccid ass of a middle-aged woman.

This patient happened to be a man, however, and his skin art was a recent acquisition. He wanted a large tattoo removed from the area over his right shoulder blade. "Let's get a look at what we're tackling here, Mr. Smith."

Michaels pushed aside the paper robe covering the thirty-five-year-old man's back. The patient was a tall, thin, pale man with wispy black hair and faded blue eyes. Michaels took one look at the tattoo and immediately wondered how many drinks had been needed to convince Mr. Smith that getting this masterpiece was a perfectly sound idea. The coffin was about seven inches long and deep purple in color. The casket lid was slightly askew, revealing a smiling gray skeleton inside. The skeleton's eye sockets were red, its teeth were yellow and it had one bony hand raised, flipping the bird. This had to be a six-drink tattoo, thought Michaels. Maybe even seven. Seven tall ones.

"Out of curiosity, Mr. Smith, what is your profession?"

The patient cleared his throat. "Umm. I'm a . . . umm . . . funeral home director."

"I see," Michaels said dryly. "I have to be honest with you, Mr. Smith. Tattoos are tough to take off, and yours covers quite a large area. There are several removal methods, but they all leave some scarring. People should think about that before they . . ."

"Spare me the lecture," said the patient. "I've already heard it in spades from my wife. Get the thing off. I'd rather have the scar."

"I would suggest a series of laser treatments."

"Great. Let's do it." He pulled the paper robe back over his shoulders and hopped off the table.

"Certainly," said Michaels. "I'll send a nurse in and she can set you up with a treatment schedule."

Driving home after work, he decided he would pay a visit to the hospital later that night, before the police did. There were elegantly simple ways to make it look like an accident.

As he pulled into his driveway, he noticed his next-door neighbor sipping iced tea on her front porch. A sense of urgency enveloped him. He needed to make a dash for the house before she collared him.

He got to the side door off the driveway before she intercepted him. "How are you, stranger?" she chirped. She'd materialized at his elbow.

"Hello, Elaine," he said, setting his briefcase and lab coat down on the steps leading to the side entrance of his home. "What are you up to?" About two hundred pounds, he thought cynically. He found everything about Elaine Roth simply too large and blocky. She was a tall woman, easily matching his height. She was also big boned, with wide wrists and hands. Her long, brown, frizzy hair was streaked with gray and kept back from her face with two large tortoiseshell combs. She dressed like a clerk in a food co-op—long, gauzy skirt the color of mud with a white peasant top and leather sandals with white ankle socks. Elaine was divorced; he decided it had to be because she'd switched teams, turned into a lesbian.

"So where's your better half?" Elaine asked.

"Huh?"

"Your wife. My partner in crime. Where is she? I haven't seen her in ages. Where are you hiding her? Is Jennifer locked in the attic, or what?"

"She's still up at the cabin with her mother," he said.

"Really? We were supposed to go to the Man Ray photo exhibit at the Walker tonight," she said, frowning. "We've been talking about it forever."

"I don't know what to tell you, Elaine," he said, shrugging his shoulders. "She's still at the lake. I've been having trouble getting in touch with her myself. She doesn't seem interested in answering my calls."

"Well, that's odd," said Elaine, winding a frizzy strand of hair around her plump finger.

Elaine probably knows all about it, Michaels thought; she was more up to speed on the state of his marriage than he. Elaine had been the one at the cabin when Jennifer lost the baby. Elaine was the one Jennifer ran to with gripes about him. The two women spent many summer evenings walking and talking, undoubtedly spilling their guts to each other. They made an odd-looking couple—his tiny, slender wife and this tall, imposing woman—as they strolled up the grassy parkway that ran down the middle of Summit Avenue. He once asked Jennifer if Elaine had ever tried to get her in bed; Jennifer told him he was a pig. He wasn't sure if that was a "yes" or a "no."

"Look, Elaine, I'm in a bit of a rush and I don't have time to chat," he said. He picked up his lab coat and briefcase and put one foot on the first step. Without warning, the big woman reached up to touch his left cheek. He started and shoved her hand away from his face.

"What happened there?" she asked, staring at the fading but still visible red lines left over from his encounter with the redheaded hooker.

"Cat scratched me," he said. He brushed past her, ran up the steps and went into the house, slamming the door behind him.

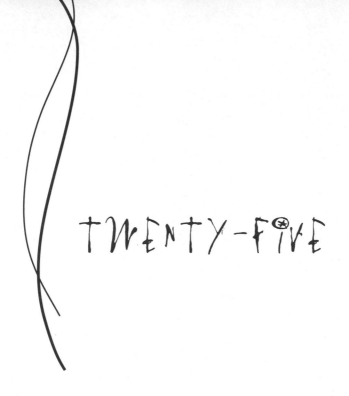

TWENTY-FIVE

*M*ichaels stepped off the elevator and looked to his right and left, scanning both ends of the hallway. He smiled. Quiet and empty, as he knew it would be.

Late at night, hospital hallways become tomblike in their silence, disturbed only by the occasional squeak from a nurse's shoe or the rattle of a lab cart. Sometimes a restless patient hollers for more pain pills or ice chips. Maybe a midnight emergency funnels doctors and nurses into an individual room. Chatter from the nurses' station might carry down the hall a bit. Mostly they are quiet and empty.

He walked down the corridor, looking at the room numbers on the doors. He was praying Ambrose had a private room; a roommate would complicate things. In a room with an open door, an old man groaned loudly and rolled over to face the hallway. Michaels walked past quickly, making sure his head was turned the other way. He was dressed in his lab coat and had a stethoscope draped around his neck. He had altered his name tag, in case he was stopped. Tonight, he was DR. HAEL. He'd thought about removing it entirely, but that could flag an attentive nurse or security guard.

His nerves were steadied by a decent amount of Scotch. Not enough to make him drunk; he needed sufficient sobriety to get the job done. There could be no mistakes. No screwups. This one had to be quick and clean. The fly had to stay out of the picture.

He'd mentally walked himself through the evening several times and could see a couple of instances where there'd be a danger of leaving prints, so he wore surgical gloves. He kept his hands shoved in his coat pockets, again to avoid attracting attention; doctors didn't generally run around at all hours wearing surgical gloves. In his right coat pocket he had his fist wrapped around his most essential tool, other than his nerves: a syringe filled with a killing quantity of potassium chloride. Such a delicate thing, the chemistry of the human body. Too much or too little of a seemingly unimportant element can kill rapidly and efficiently, often leaving no visible evidence behind.

In his hospital bed late Tuesday night, Father Ambrose slept uneasily in his medication-induced stupor.

His room was small and faced the freeway, but he was as happy as hell it was private. No hacking, wheezing roommate to keep him up at night. The window ledge was jammed with flowers and cards. The children from Vacation Bible School had made a banner that hung on the wall opposite his bed. The kids had used finger paints to put their handprints on it and then each signed it. He could tell which students were suffering through Mrs. White's class during the school year; she really hammered them on their handwriting. Behind her back, he and the school principal called her the "cursive Nazi." Men from the parish council had hand-delivered ceramic mallards filled with green ferns and ivy. The liturgical-music director had surprised him with a planter shaped like an open hymnal. Hokey, but well-meaning.

Boxes of chocolates were stacked on his nightstand. When he was bored, he tortured himself by staring at them. His ulcer was acting up, and he couldn't eat them. He was on blood thinners after his hip replacement to avoid blood clots, a common by-product of inactivity, and the blood thinner was making his ulcer bleed. He was nauseated and couldn't eat in the days following the surgery anyway, so he was on intravenous feeding. He was also on a heart monitor, something doctors considered a wise precaution given his heart attack several months earlier.

His sister had visited him over the weekend. "Jesus Christ," she'd blurted out, staring at all the tubes and wires. "You're all fucked up."

He was, and in ways she couldn't see or understand.

He stirred in his sleep, pushing the covers off his arms. Doubts filled his dreams.

It had been eight days since the attack. In the week following it, he had recovered from near strangulation, a serious concussion and hip-replacement surgery. Ambrose had hoped the police would wait to question him in the comfort of his rectory after his release from the hospital, but they were persistent; they were scheduled to visit him Wednesday in his room. Tuesday night he'd fallen asleep still sorting out in his mind what he should do.

He could say to hell with it, dump the priesthood and tell the cops everything, including that the maniac had confessed to killing a prostitute. He wondered if that was more moral than following the rules dictated by his collar.

Plenty of times, he'd had second thoughts about his choice of profession. Once or twice it was the sight of a beautiful woman sitting in the front pew during mass; the long-legged ones captured his attention. He questioned himself again after he'd failed to save a favorite parishioner's marriage. Then he couldn't talk his own sister out of getting her teenage daughter an abortion. "Mind your own business," she'd snapped. "You don't have kids. What do you know?"

What *do* I know? he'd wonder. Then he'd tell himself: I know I'm a horseshit priest. He'd open up the jobs section of the want ads. He'd manage to snap out of it, regain his footing. Sometimes through prayer. Sometimes with a stiff drink. It wouldn't be so easy this time; nothing had challenged him as much as this mess.

If he stuck by his calling, anything his assailant had revealed in the confessional was off limits. Every priest knew the drill. He could not divulge the sins uttered to him to save his own life or even spare the life of another.

He could not reveal them in the name of justice or to avoid a public calamity. No law, no officer, no courtroom could compel him to disclose the secrets of the confessional. The only possible release from this obligation of secrecy would be if the penitent himself granted the priest permission to speak. Ambrose was sure that permission was not forthcoming, especially given the crazy asshole's violent reaction when the priest had said going to the police would be part of his penance.

Maybe he could satisfy his calling and his conscience: Ambrose was certain he wouldn't be violating the Seal of Confession by giving the detectives a description of the penitent—but not his sins—as the man who had nearly strangled him to death on the floor outside the confessional. Father Ambrose had gotten a good look at the mean S.O.B.

His cold, gray eyes were not easily forgotten.

Michaels slipped unnoticed into the priest's room. As he had hoped, the man was sedated and tethered to an IV, but the heart monitor took him by surprise. Damn. He should have thought of that. The old boy was fat and undoubtedly had at least one heart attack under his belt already. The monitor would trigger an alarm when the priest's heart was in distress, alerting the nurses' station. That might give them an opportunity to save the priest.

Worse yet, the EKG on the monitor would show spikes pointing to high levels of potassium. He had no idea if the priest had already given the cops a description of his assailant for a composite sketch. The elevated potassium could point to sabotage by a medical professional, and that might be enough to narrow the focus dangerously close to him.

Still, he had to make sure this priest never made it to the witness stand. Doubts could be raised about a composite sketch, but live testimony would hang him. He had to get rid of this pain-in-the-ass priest and it had to look like a natural event. Like an act of God.

Michaels took the syringe out of his lab coat and gently pushed the tip of the needle into one of the ports in the IV line. He pushed down on the plunger, sending the potassium into the priest's body. It would take about thirty minutes for the potassium to send the father's heart into an unwieldy rhythm.

He checked his watch. He wanted to give the potassium time to do its work before he made his next move.

He studied the five round patches taped to the man's chest, each a different color and each with wires leading to the heart monitor. He looked for the wire from the green patch. This was the ground lead. Unsnapping it would send a low-level alarm to the nurses' station indicating the leads to the monitor had somehow come undone. It would also mask the alarm indicating his heart was in distress.

They would eventually come to the priest's bedside to snap the errant wires back on, but they wouldn't rush. It wouldn't be considered a life-threatening emergency. By the time they got around to it, they would find the priest clinging to life, call a code and start working on him. Hopefully, they would forget about the monitor. They would have no EKG record pointing to a spike in the level of potassium.

Michaels checked his watch again. He needed to wait a bit longer. He didn't want to unsnap the green lead too soon. He was perspiring under the lab coat; he could feel the sweat trickling down his back. He wiped his damp brow with the sleeve of the coat. He wanted to do this and get out of here. He walked to the door and poked his head into the hallway. He scanned both ends. Still empty and quiet. Good. He walked back to the priest's bed.

He had an excuse ready should he be caught in the room—he had been checking on one of his own patients on another floor and decided to look in on the priest, an old friend of the family. He knew it was a flimsy story, and full of holes. He didn't even have surgical privileges at Hennepin County Medical, let alone a recovering patient. If they woke Ambrose to confirm the story, he'd be shit out of luck.

He studied the small room, indirectly illuminated from the freeway lights outside the window. GET WELL SOON, FATHER AMBROSE! read a banner stretched across one wall. The sign was decorated with children's handprints. How saccharine, thought Michaels. There were so many bouquets in the room, it smelled like a funeral parlor. Father Ambrose would be seeing the inside of one of those soon enough, he thought, smiling.

Michaels checked his watch again. Hallelujah. Time to do it. He looked down at the sleeping priest. "Hope you said your bedtime prayers," he whispered. Without hesitation, he unsnapped the green lead and strolled out of the small, dim room.

He walked calmly but quickly down the hall toward the elevators. He pushed the down button and paced in front of the door, waiting for it to open, willing it to open. The thing was taking too long. Maybe there was somebody on it. A late-arriving patient. He scanned the hallway for exit signs. Where were the stairs?

"Can I help you?"

Shit, he thought. He shoved his hands in his pockets and turned toward the inquisitive female voice. She was a nurse—a thin reed with stringy black hair.

"No thank you," he said evenly. "I was checking on a patient on another floor and thought I'd stop here to look in on a friend." The elevator doors opened and he stepped on.

"At this hour?" she blurted out.

The elevator doors closed before he was forced to concoct a response. He breathed a sigh of relief. He looked at his hands. They were shaking. With his trembling right hand, he gripped the railing along the elevator wall, steadying himself during the trip down.

Ah, shit," said Libby Delmont. "It looks like the leads in twenty-six are screwed up."

"That would be Father Ambrose's room," said Phyllis Jared, a tall woman with short, gray hair.

The two nurses stared at the bank of monitors resembling a stack of miniature computer screens, each bearing a room number. "Where's Tess?" asked Delmont. "The poor bastard is the space cadet's patient tonight."

"She's checking on thirty-two," said Jared.

"Flip ya for it," said Delmont.

"Naah. I'll take it," said Jared. She sighed and stood up. "I need the exercise."

Jared liked Father Ambrose. He was a flirt. She saw him checking out her ass once while she was opening his window blinds. Plus he was an angler, so they had a little something in common. At one time she could have talked religion with him, but she'd quit the Catholic Church years ago. She told him she saw too much misery to believe there was a god. Ambrose didn't try to pull her back into the fold. Instead, they had friendly, invigorating debates about the role suffering and death played in life.

When she walked into his room, she found him struggling for breath, fighting for life. "Father Ambrose," Jared said into his ear, trying to get a response. She couldn't find his pulse. "God dammit to hell!" she muttered.

"Libby! He's in v-tach!" she yelled down the hall, using the shorthand term for ventricular tachycardia, a fast heart rhythm. "Call a code! He's unresponsive!"

"Son-of-a-bitch!" said Jared, looking down at the priest.

TWENTY-SIX

T hat murdering bastard. He did it, Gabe. I know he did," Murphy whispered into her cell phone as she sat nude on the edge of her bed early Wednesday morning. She didn't want to disturb the man sprawled naked next to her.

She held the phone to her ear with her right hand and, with her left, grabbed her robe off the edge of the bed. She tiptoed into the bathroom, gently shutting the door behind her. "Wait a minute, Gabe," she said in a low voice, and set the phone down on the bathroom counter so she could slip into the robe. The morning was cool for a change.

"He's going to be all right, isn't he? Ambrose?"

"Yeah, the code team got to him in time," said Gabe, who was calling from the nurses' station down the hall from the priest's room. "They've stabilized him and shipped him over to the ICU. We won't be able to talk to him today; that's for sure."

"He's lucky to be alive," she said.

"Luck had nothing to do with it," said Gabe. He winked at nurse Jared, who was standing at his elbow. She smiled at him and handed him a cup of coffee. He already had her phone number stuffed in his pants pocket.

"So the blood work confirms someone loaded him up with potassium, huh?" Murphy said.

"Sure as shit looks like it," said Gabe. "Then they unsnapped the heart monitor to cover their tracks. Who'd know to do that?"

"A doctor."

"Bet your ass a doctor," he said. "We were idiots. We should have put someone outside his room."

"Yeah, well, that's Monday-morning quarterbacking," she said. "What do we do now?"

"We need to show that it wasn't some medical screwup," he said.

"Right," she said. "That would be the obvious defense—that the hospital screwed up. Did anyone see him? Patients? Nurses? The shift hasn't changed on that floor yet, has it?"

"No, but you'd better get your butt over here pretty soon if you want to talk to them," said Gabe.

"What happened?" asked Jack, shuffling into the bathroom.

"Someone tried to off that poor priest last night," she said, wrestling her hair into a ponytail behind her head.

"No shit?" asked Jack, stepping back to give her room before he got a faceful of black hair.

"I shit you not," she said. She dropped her robe to the floor.

"How?" He picked up her robe and hung it on the bathroom door hook.

"Potassium," she said. She opened the medicine cabinet, grabbed the deodorant off the bathroom shelf and rolled it under her arms.

"You're sure some nurse didn't mess up and give it to him by mistake?" he asked. He squeezed past her and lifted up the toilet seat to pee.

"Tell me something, Jack," said Murphy. She closed the cabinet and looked at him, smirking while she took a good-natured jab. "Why are doctors so quick to blame the nurses?"

"Why are nurses so quick to blame the doctors?" asked Jack.

"In this case, I know it was a doctor," said Murphy. "A particular doctor."

*W*ith the car windows rolled down and the wind in her face, she navigated her Jeep onto westbound I-94. The early rush-hour traffic was fairly light on the St. Paul side of the river, but she hit a snarl at the city limits. "Great," she muttered. A logjam around the University of Minnesota exit. "Damn students should take the bus." The tangle loosened, she wove around a slow-moving semi truck, and breathed easier as she took a downtown Minneapolis exit and made her way to the hospital parking ramp.

I saw a guy by the elevators last night," said Tess Clayton, nodding her dark head. Clayton took a sip of coffee from a Styrofoam cup. In between sips, she picked at the rim of the cup. She was a skinny, nervous type, and needed to keep her hands in motion. "He was gorgeous," she said. "He was tall. I swear to god he had shoulders out to here." She stretched her arms out. "He looked like a model or something. Blond hair. Gray eyes. Icy gray. He looked like a soap opera guy."

Murphy and Gabe had gathered the night nurses together in their break room to ask if they had spotted anyone suspicious roaming their floor Tuesday evening. They sat at a sticky round Formica table marked with brown rings from coffee cups and Coke cans. The room smelled like old coffee, burned popcorn and melted cheese. The nurses kept looking at their watches; their shift was long over.

"Was he dressed like a doc?" asked Murphy. She was scratching notes in a pad.

"He had on a white lab coat and a stethoscope," said Clayton.

"A badge? Some kind of ID?" asked Murphy.

"A name tag. Wait. I'm not sure about the name tag. If he had one, I guess I didn't really look at it."

"Christ," Jared said, rolling her eyes.

"He looked lost or something. He looked like he didn't belong here," said Clayton. "That's why I stopped and asked him if he needed help."

"What did he say to you?" asked Gabe.

"He said he was visiting someone on our floor after checking on a patient of his on another floor," Clayton said. "That sounded like a bullshit story to me. Who visits at that hour of the night? Then he got on the elevator and was gone."

"You didn't report this to anyone?" asked Gabe.

"No," said Clayton, pausing to take another sip of coffee. "I didn't report it."

"Earth to Tess," said Delmont.

"Go to hell," Clayton said. "What was I suppose to do? Tackle him before he got on the elevator?"

"Okay, okay, let's not lose it here," said Gabe.

"Anything else weird about him?" asked Murphy. "Think."

Clayton chewed her bottom lip and peeled another half inch off the rim of her coffee cup.

"This is painful," said Delmont.

"Yeah," Clayton said suddenly. "Yeah. He had surgical gloves on. Why would he need those if he was visiting, right?"

"Right," said Murphy. Across the table, she and Gabe exchanged glances.

"So you know who this guy is?" asked Jared. "Is he a doctor? Are you going to arrest his ass?"

"We're gonna talk about it," said Gabe. "Please don't discuss anything you've heard here. What was said in this room stays in this room, ladies. Got it?"

Surgical gloves," Murphy said as she and Gabe walked to their cars. "Michaels is getting slyer by the second."

"Guess we can kiss the possibility of prints good-bye," he said.

"Speaking of kiss—you got her phone number?" Murphy asked.

"I got her phone number," he said. "She likes to fish."

"You don't give a damn that she can bait her own hook," Murphy said.

"What do you mean by that?"

"You know what they say about nurses and sex?" asked Murphy.

"No, what do they say?" asked Gabe, perking up.

"I don't know," said Murphy. "I thought you knew."

They stopped in front of Murphy's Jeep, parked a couple of spaces away from Gabe's Volvo, and she took the car keys out of her purse. "We'd better get together with the chief to go over what we have," she said.

Gabe grumbled.

"Look, he's been pretty decent so far," she said. "He's cut us a lot of slack. We haven't been pulled away to work on any pissant stuff and he sent a uniform over to watch Ambrose."

"Yeah, yeah," said Gabe. "He's my new best friend."

"I'll meet you at the cop shop," Murphy said.

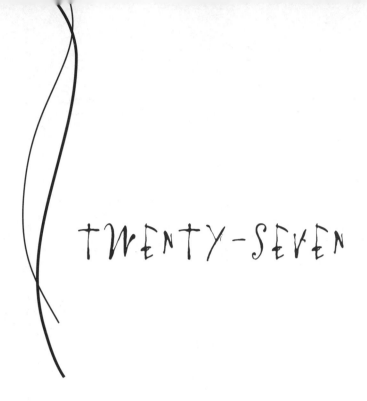

TWENTY-SEVEN

$\mathcal{G}$abe sat back in his chair while Murphy did the shouting. He wasn't surprised by what Slick had to say. It's all circumstantial and we can't arrest someone for appearing guilty. Blah. Blah. Blah. We need more before we can haul him in because this isn't a police state you know. Blah. Blah. Blah. The county attorney will throw it back in our faces without something resembling a smoking gun. Blah. Blah and still more blah.

"What the hell do you mean?" Murphy asked. "We have more than enough. This is bullshit!" Murphy paced back and forth across the carpeted floor of the chief's office, behind Gabe's chair.

Gabe was enjoying the whole show.

"Murphy, sit down," said Christianson.

"I will not sit down," said Murphy.

"If this guy was Mr. Joe Fucking Average . . ."

The *F* word. She hadn't used that in front of the chief in weeks.

"Murphy . . ."

"If this was Mr. Joe Fucking Average, we'd have yanked him off the street with half this evidence. You're only saying we don't have enough because he's a surgeon and because his family is . . ."

Christianson's back stiffened in his chair. "This has nothing to do with his family," he said.

"This has everything to do with his family!" she yelled.

"Calm down," Christianson said.

"I will not calm down!"

"Paris, please," Christianson said, quickly switching to the friendly, first-name approach.

"Don't patronize me!" she said, her eyes narrowing. She looked at Gabe. "Say something, will you? Help me out here!"

"Murphy . . . ," the chief continued.

"Chief, maybe I didn't make clear everything we have on this creep," she said. "Let's go over all of it one more time."

"Oh no, let's not," pleaded Gabe, rubbing his forehead. "Please, let's not."

She shot her partner a threatening look, and he clamped his mouth shut.

"Number one," she said. She saw Gabe cringe and stopped pacing. "What is your problem?" she asked, glaring at him.

"I have no problem," he said, raising both palms defensively. "No problem at all."

"Good," she said. "Now where was I?"

"A," said Gabe, trying not to smile. "I believe you were on A."

"Thank you," she said, and resumed her pacing. "A. We have the yellow umbrella. Charlene Rue, a working girl, is ready to testify the yellow umbrella discarded by Michaels is the same umbrella she handed to Finch— I mean Fionn Hennessy—the night she was raped and murdered."

"We don't have good prints on the yellow umbrella," Christianson said.

"No," said Murphy. "We don't. I saw him remove it from his black Suburban and throw it away."

"Okay," said the chief. "He can say he found it somewhere, picked it up. What else?"

"B. We have a witness who saw Hennessy beaten by a blond man driving a loaded black Suburban," said Murphy. "A Suburban filled with soccer balls. Michaels drives a black Suburban and is a soccer coach."

"Our witness wasn't close enough to see the killer's face or get a license plate, and, unfortunately, happens to be schizophrenic," said Christianson.

"He was on his meds and perfectly sane when he saw the murder," offered Gabe.

"That's all fine and dandy," said the chief. "But you both know the defense attorneys will chew him up."

"We have Sister Ella Marie willing and ready to testify that Snaky—I mean Swanson—was taking his Risperdal at the time and was mentally healthy when he witnessed the killing from the boat porthole," said Murphy. "I'd like to see them poke holes in a nun's testimony."

"Then I suppose we should pray for an all-Catholic jury," said the chief, smiling. "What else have we got, detectives?"

"Three is the necklace," said Murphy.

"Ah yes," said the chief. "The well-traveled crucifix."

"The killer removed it from Hennessy's neck and later dropped it while assaulting Father Ambrose," said Murphy. "It ties the same man to both crimes."

"This assumes the murder victim's crucifix and the one found outside the confessional are indeed the same necklace," said Christianson.

"Her parents will take the stand to identify it as their daughter's keepsake," said Murphy. "If we get hard up, we could even haul in her pimp to confirm it is Hennessy's necklace. He'll testify that she never took it off."

"Wouldn't defense attorneys have a good time taking shots at Sully's credibility?" said the chief. "How long is Mr. LePlante's rap sheet?"

"Pretty fucking long," Gabe said.

Murphy glared at him but continued talking and pacing. "Four, Gabe and I saw Michaels slinking around Hennessy's funeral service, with scratches on his face. Tell me that is not incriminating behavior."

"As I pointed out earlier in our conversation, the scratches could have come from anywhere," said Christianson, leaning back in his chair and rolling a pencil between his palms. "Michaels offered an explanation for his presence at the funeral, did he not?"

"That was a load of crap," sputtered Gabe. "Finch was never his patient."

"We don't know that for certain," said the chief. "All we have to base that on is the dubious word of her pimp and her prostitute friends."

"Her family also said she was never—" said Murphy.

"A family that hadn't seen her in how long?" interrupted Christianson. "Michaels could easily claim that she was a patient and then refuse to offer anything more detailed, citing patient privacy. I think it's quite believable that he treated her, given his volunteer work with that domestic-abuse program."

"What about Father Ambrose?" she said.

"What about him?" Christianson said with a dismissive wave of his hand. "We haven't even interviewed him yet. We have no idea what he brings to the table. Can he positively identify Michaels as the man who assaulted him? How much is he willing to say about what was revealed to him in the confessional? My understanding is priests are obligated to maintain confidentiality in much the same way a doctor is required to keep patient information private."

"The assault took place outside the confessional," said Murphy. "Therefore, that should be fair game."

"Maybe," said the chief, tapping the eraser end of the pencil on his desk.

"As far as what was said inside the confessional itself, well, you might be right," said Murphy, sounding discouraged. "We might be screwed there."

"Speaking of the priest, we have a witness who saw a black Suburban leaving the scene of the assault at the church," said Gabe, trying to bolster his partner's position. "We have a nurse who can testify that she saw Michaels on her floor the night someone tried to finish off Father Ambrose."

"Being a medical professional, he could offer a reasonable explanation for being in the hospital that night," said Christianson. "Even if it's a bogus excuse, like the one he gave the night nurse, a jury might buy it. He could even claim it was a case of mistaken identity, that it wasn't him at all on the floor that night. Do we have any prints from Ambrose's room?"

"No," said Murphy.

"How's that possible if Michaels is your man?" asked Christianson.

"He was wearing surgical gloves," she said.

"Clever bastard," Christianson said in a low voice.

"What about his connection to previous murders—the ones in Rochester and Minneapolis?" asked Gabe. "They had the same M.O. as with Finch. The killer strangled them and cut their long hair with a sharp tool, possibly a surgical instrument. Murphy even got the Rochester victim's housemate identifying Michaels as the dead stripper's married boyfriend."

"The Rochester murder took place years ago," said Christianson. "The defense will take apart the housemate. More important, where is the hair? We don't have it."

"Let's get a search warrant for his house," said Murphy, who stopped pacing and stood in front of the chief's desk, her arms folded across her chest. "Let's demand a genetic sample from him to compare with the semen found on Hennessy's body and the skin under her nails."

"Not yet," said the chief. "That would be tipping our hand too soon."

Murphy fleetingly wondered if she should tell the chief about that night at the hotel, but quickly brushed aside the dangerous thought. She and Gabe had agreed it was best to keep the entire unsanctioned and ill-advised operation from their superiors.

"You've done some good work here and you've accumulated an impressive amount of evidence," said the chief. "But . . ." His voice trailed off. He put down the pencil and swiveled his high-backed leather chair around to stare outside the row of windows behind his desk. He released a barely audible sigh and turned his chair back to face Murphy and her partner. Murphy thought Christianson seemed depressed and distracted, like after the Minneapolis mess.

"But what, Chief?" asked Murphy. Christianson wasn't looking at them anymore; he was staring at the photo of his sons on his desk. "Chief?" said Murphy, returning to her seat to look Christianson squarely in the eye.

"His family's got deep pockets and lots of friends," Christianson said. "We need more than we've got." The chief spun his chair around again to face the windows. He didn't say anything for several seconds. Then: "Keep working the case," he said tiredly. The two detectives sat motionless, anticipating something more. "That's all," Christianson said without facing them.

Gabe and Murphy looked at each other and got up from their chairs. Christianson continued staring out the windows. Gabe held the door open for Murphy. Before she walked through, she looked at the chief's back and then at her partner, raising her eyebrows. They walked down the hall.

"Christ, what was that all about?" asked Murphy. She stopped at a water fountain in the hallway to drink. She suddenly felt thirsty and tired.

"I knew it wasn't going to be a slam dunk," said Gabe. "I never thought I'd say it, but Slick is probably on target with this thing. Ramsey County doesn't want to screw up its felony conviction rate by prosecuting cases it might not win. He's also right about this guy and his family having the bucks to fight this."

"That's not what I'm talking about," she said, wiping her mouth with her hand. "Who do you think is riding the chief's ass on this case? He sounded whipped."

"Yeah, I noticed that," said Gabe. "Well, it's high profile. The media are doing a number on him. The mayor. Who knows? Probably wishes he was back in Iowa."

The pair walked into Homicide's office and past Dubrowski and Castro, each seated at a desk piled with paperwork, newspapers, old lunch bags and dirty Styrofoam cups. Even though one was of Polish descent and the other Mexican, they had worked together so long they looked alike—curly gray hair, big arms, bushy eyebrows, red necks. They wore identical wire-rimmed glasses and the same brand of jeans. Dubrowski's gut was a little flabbier.

"Congratulations," Murphy told them. They got a conviction.

"Thanks," said Dubrowski.

"How's your case shaping up?" asked Castro.

"Gabe and I are on our way to the conference room to talk about that," she said.

"We are?" asked Gabe. "Oh yeah, we are."

Dubrowski and Castro laughed as Murphy and Gabe walked into the long, narrow room and shut the door behind them. Gabe took a seat at the head of the table while Murphy sat on the edge of the table and planted her feet on the seat of a chair.

"What would happen if we did connect some of the dots for the press, without naming Michaels as a suspect?" she asked. "Let's play that out. What would it do for us if we simply went public with the theory that the three murders—in St. Paul, Minneapolis and Rochester—were committed by the same person, by someone we haven't yet identified? We don't even have to say why we think they're related or reveal anything about the hair jobs. That way we don't tip our hand too much."

"What about Ambrose?" asked Gabe. "What do we say about him?"

"We also leave out the connection between Finch's murder and Father Ambrose," she said. "That way we protect him. Michaels disconnected that lead off the heart monitor to cover his tracks. Let's make him think he was successful. If anyone asks how Ambrose is doing, we simply say he had a heart-related setback in the hospital."

"So Michaels thinks he got away with his second attempt on the priest's life," said Gabe, scratching his chin.

"In fact, let's tell the reporters that before Ambrose had his setback, he met with us and refused to discuss the assault in his church because of the Seal of Confession," she said.

Murphy slid off the table and walked to the other end of the room, where a white, erasable board hung from the wall. She picked up a marker and drew a vertical line down the middle of the board. On one side she wrote the word "PROS" and on the other she scribbled "CONS."

"On the pro side, we might scare up some new witnesses to the crimes," said Gabe. "We could get some new leads."

Murphy nodded and scribbled "New Witnesses" and "New Leads" under "PROS."

"On the con side, we would tip Michaels off," said Murphy. "He might lawyer up. Worse yet, he could skip town."

She wrote "Doc Gets Lawyer" and "Doc Flees" in the "CONS" column.

"On the other hand, he might get smug and comfortable if he thinks we're clueless when it comes to naming a suspect," said Gabe. "He could make some mistakes, mess up big time and really hand us the case."

"Or he might get so rattled that he messes up," said Murphy. "We could lay a real head game on him by running a composite sketch. We'll make it close to his likeness, but not identical."

Gabe laughed. "I like that idea a lot," he said. "That gets my vote."

Under "PROS" Murphy scribbled "Doc gets nervous/comfortable—screws up."

"Then let's watch our suspect," said Murphy. "Let's put him under surveillance, at least for the first few days after the press conference, to see what he does."

"Okay," said Gabe. "Slick might go for that."

"Now wait a minute," said Gabe, standing up and pacing the width of the room with his hands shoved in his pockets.

"What's wrong?" asked Murphy. She stopped writing and turned to face him, the marker still in her hand.

"For us to run a composite sketch, someone has to give us a description of Dr. Demented," Gabe said.

Murphy paused and frowned. She walked over to the conference-room windows and glanced outside as she tried to think the problem through. She tapped on the ledge with the butt of the marker and looked at the traffic below, with cars crawling along the freeway. "We'll say a passing motorist saw him pick up Finch," she said, pointing the marker out the window. "Then we can even run a description of his Suburban."

"That's good," said Gabe, smiling. "A passing motorist. That could be anybody."

"Here's one more for the pro side," said Gabe. "Going public with some of this also takes some pressure off the department. Not that I give a shit about Slick."

Murphy walked back to the board and scribbled "Good P.R." under "PROS."

"I didn't call it P.R.," said Gabe. "That sounds so phony and calculating."

"Well, that's what it is, good public relations," she said. "Really, this whole damn scheme is phony and calculating. So what? Let's make those media dogs help us out for a change."

"Yeah, I guess you're right," he said.

They stopped talking and stared at the blue scrawls on the white board. "Well, it looks like the pros have it," said Murphy. "Let's call a press conference tomorrow, in time for the lunchtime news. They'll replay it for the six o'clock and the ten o'clock. The papers will follow along."

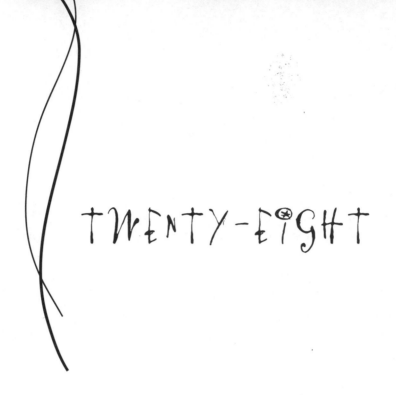

TWENTY-EIGHT

*M*ichaels was suffocating, suspended facedown in a sea of hair. Fragrant, radiant hair. Red hair flaming like a bonfire. Brown hair the color of walnuts. Blue-black hair as dark and glossy as a crow's feathers. Gold hair, braided like his mother's.

Somewhere in the distance, surrounded by the hair, was his wife. She held a baby in her arms, a boy. He started to cry. Jennifer held the wailing infant out to him and laughed. Then she reached up and grabbed a length of white hair. It turned into a rope like the rigging from their sailboat. She wrapped the rope around herself and the baby until he couldn't see them anymore; all he saw was a coil of rigging. The rigging turned into a snake, its head at the very top of the coil. He heard screaming and crying and knew it was his wife and the baby, even though he couldn't see them. An arm poked out from the coil and he saw it was Jennifer's; he recognized the diamond wedding ring on her finger. Another arm poked out; it was a chubby baby arm. The snake reached down and bit off each of the arms. It spat out the finger with the wedding ring still on it. It wasn't Jennifer's ring anymore; it had turned into his gold band, and the amputated finger was his own.

Michaels looked at his hands. His ring finger was gone. He tried to swim toward the amputated finger, struggling to maneuver his naked body. Ribbons of hair twined around his arms and legs and waist, pulling him down, down, down. The hair had a will of its own and had a mind to kill him. It promised to be a soft death. He forgot about his wife and the baby and the snake and the missing finger. He stopped struggling. He surrendered and relaxed his limbs, letting the locks pull him deep into an abyss. The pit didn't have a name, but he knew it was hell, and he didn't care.

Then panic replaced submission. He twisted and turned as he fought the tangle of hair. The bands only tightened their grip. He felt a swatch of hair tighten around his penis and another wrap around his throat. He tried to scream, but all that came out was a buzzing noise.

Michaels woke facedown in his pillows. He rolled over and sat upright in his bed. The sheets were tangled around his legs. He kicked them off. His head burned and throbbed like an open wound. His damp body shivered uncontrollably. He covered his face with his hands and released sobs that rocked his shoulders. His breakdown lasted a few minutes. Then he wiped his face with the corner of the top sheet and angrily punched the mattress with his fist. "I'm weak. I'm a coward," he said.

In the dark, he fumbled around but couldn't find what he needed. He pulled the chain on the lamp atop his nightstand. The lampshade's colored glass cast a comforting glow. He yanked the bottle of Scotch off his nightstand and poured a modest amount. With great effort, he wrapped his shaking right hand around the glass and lifted it to his lips. He drank until the glass was empty. The heat trickling from his throat to his gut smoothed his nerves. He poured himself another, taller drink and finished it as quickly as the first.

He sat on the bed, his knees pulled up to his chest, his arms wrapped around his knees. He thought about the priest and wondered if he was dead; he'd heard nothing on the news about him. He thought about the nurse who'd spotted him by the elevators; he hoped she'd bought the story he fed her. He thought about his unreachable wife; he made a mental list of the men who could be fucking her at the cabin. He thought about the black-haired woman; he silently berated himself for letting her get away.

He checked the clock next to the lamp. 11:22 P.M., but he briefly forgot what day it was. He thought hard. Wednesday. 11:22 P.M. Wednesday.

"I can't even remember what day it is anymore," he whispered. He stretched out flat on his back, grabbed a pillow to hug to his chest and stared up at the ceiling. His compartmentalized existence was collapsing around him. The killer and the doctor, the husband and the rapist, the Catholic and the heretic were coalescing like a palette of watercolors left in the rain.

"I have to remember who I am," he said. He knew what that meant: no more holding back the fly.

He threw off the pillow and jumped out of bed. He yanked on his boxers, jeans and a polo shirt. He slid his bare feet into his loafers. He was still damp and shivering, so he put on a summer blazer. He sifted through the car keys piled on top of his bedroom dresser and selected the set for his Porsche. He shoved the keys into his right blazer pocket. He opened the top drawer of his dresser and retrieved his driving gloves. Before he slipped them on, he looked at his fingers and laughed. Of course they were all still there. He pulled on the gloves, wiggling his fingers a bit and enjoying the tightness of the leather. From under a stack of clothing in the same drawer he extracted a little kit he hadn't used in a while: a scalpel and a plastic bag. He wrapped the bag around the surgical tool and shoved the package into his left blazer pocket.

The top was down on the Porsche. He inhaled the night air as he shifted gears. He needed to do a little shopping, and what he craved couldn't be found along the well-lit highway. Being in a convertible made him more exposed, vulnerable. Under the driver's seat he kept a handgun, a 9mm SIG-Sauer. Black matte finish. Trigger with a click as smooth as that of a Minolta camera. He took a roundabout route to his final destination so he could cruise down University Avenue in a calming exercise before the chase. On University Avenue you could have your palms read, buy a used pinball machine, fix a flat tire and find a decent bottle of Scotch. Even in the middle of the week, on a Wednesday night, there were things to see and do on University Avenue.

He stopped at a red light and looked to his right. Several well-dressed people were spilling out of a nightclub. They were laughing. A couple of the men in the group were weaving drunkenly as they walked along the sidewalk.

The light changed. He drove on.

Another traffic light. He looked to his left, at an all-night convenience store. Teenage girls were clustered around a pay phone at the edge of the store's nearly empty parking lot. Two teenage boys were skateboarding in the middle of the parking lot, probably hoping to attract the attention of the girls, but the pay phone apparently had more magnetism. Such lovely girls. One turned her head, looked admiringly at his car and then at him. She smiled and he smiled back. Such beautiful, long, blond hair. So like his daughters' soft locks. He felt an ache in his crotch, a catch in his throat. He'd never taken such a young thing before. Her body would be so firm, her breasts so fresh. She'd be so tight, maybe even still a virgin. She wanted him; he was sure of it. He could tell by the way she looked at him. Perhaps . . .

The light changed. He hesitated, wondering what would happen if he took a left into the store parking lot. A car behind him honked. He drove on, reluctantly.

Enough sightseeing, he thought. He glanced to the right at the Porsche's clock. Midnight. He piloted the car to the fringes of town, to a stretch of avenue with boarded-up storefronts, fast-food joints, bars and video shops offering hard-core porn. "Sex and the Single Clown" read a poster in the filmy window of one adult-video store. It depicted a white-faced, red-nosed clown in a circus costume with his arms wrapped around a woman. Another poster displayed nothing but a woman's feet, with red-painted toenails. "Toe Job" was the title. Michaels laughed and shook his head as he drove past the shop. Some people have such strange fetishes, he thought smugly.

He surveyed the sidewalks on both sides of the street. The pickings were slim late at night in the middle of the week. Across the street, on his left, he saw a fat blonde dressed in tight white shorts and an equally snug white T-shirt. The car in front of him—a blue Ford station wagon sporting a bumper sticker that read, "Driver Carries Less Than $20 Cash. He Has Teenagers"—made a frantic U-turn and stopped at the curb next to the woman. She walked over to the car and leaned into the open front passenger-side window. She and the driver exchanged words. She nodded her head and got in, slamming the door hard. At the next intersection, the car took a right turn. They were headed to a dark side street, where she could give the family man a blow job in the front seat of his station wagon. He apparently carried enough cash for that. Or maybe he only had enough for a toe job, Michaels thought wryly.

The doctor drove on, hungry and hunting. He found himself driving toward the corner where he'd picked up that little redheaded whore, the source of all his recent problems.

There, on that very same corner, was a prospect. Standing under a street-light with a cigarette hanging out of her mouth. She was short but heavier than he usually liked. Her tight jean skirt stretched across her wide hips and seemed on the verge of separating at the seams. Her close-fitting tank top accented the roundness of her doughy shoulders. While it was difficult to see clearly in the yellowish haze cast by the streetlight, she at least seemed to have a nice creamy complexion. He guessed she was in her late twenties or early thirties.

He almost kept driving when he got to her hair, noticing how short and lackluster it appeared. Then he spotted the thick braid in back of her head. "She'll do," he muttered to himself.

He pulled over and she strolled over to the Porsche, doing nothing to hide her childlike admiration for the car. "Nice ride," she said, running her fingers across the red finish. She smiled at him. "Lookin' for a date?"

"Get in," he said, leaning over the passenger's seat to open the door for her from the inside. She dropped her cigarette into the gutter, slid in and gently closed the door. How unusual, observed Michaels. A thoughtful whore. "Let's talk business," he said, pulling away from the curb. "What do you charge?"

"Well, darlin', that depends on what you want," she said, inspecting the Porsche's instruments with her fingertips.

"What if I want a full fuck?" he asked coarsely. She seemed to cringe at the word *fuck*. A thoughtful, sensitive whore.

"We need to go to a particular motel for that," she said. "I provide the protection and you pay for the room, as well as for my services. If you don't want to use a rubber, you're gonna have to pay more."

"How much for your services, with a condom?"

She opened her mouth to answer and he cut her off. "It doesn't matter what you charge. I'll pay for it. Okay? Tell me where to turn."

"A man who knows what he wants," she said, smiling. "It sounds like you done this before, darlin'."

He threw his head back and laughed. He felt good. Very good. Very much in control. Something he hadn't felt in a while. "Is it down this street?" he asked.

"The next one," she said.

"What's your name?" he asked. "I like my *dates* to have a name." He turned right and headed down the dark road that led to the motel.

"Call me Miss Rue," she said. "That's French for street, you know."

He steered the car around the potholes in the motel parking lot and parked the Porsche at the far end. Rue had turned down the visor over the passenger's seat and was checking her makeup in the mirror. She wrestled a mascara wand out of her skirt pocket and applied a few strokes to the upper lashes of each eye. She snapped the lid back on and returned the wand to her pocket. She reached in back of her head and felt her braid, turning her head a little to look in the mirror.

He was impatient. "You look fine, Miss Rue," he said. "At least for my purposes."

"What's that supposed to mean?" she asked, looking at him quizzically.

"Never mind," he said. He threw a couple of twenties into her lap. "Go pay for the room," he said, nodding toward the motel office at the opposite end of the lot. "I've got to raise the top on the convertible."

She stepped out of the car, and with an exaggerated sway of her hips, walked toward the office. The shack was detached from the motel but a few steps from the closest rooms. "Be sure to get a room at this end," he said after her. "I want some privacy."

"You betcha, darlin'," she said over her shoulder. "I'll bring back the change."

I'll bet you will, thought Michaels, shaking his head. He wondered how someone so childlike had lasted so long on the street.

The Magnolia Manor was a dreary, dirty place and exactly what he'd expected. The building was two stories high and covered with pink aluminum siding. At one time it had probably been a bright pink, but it had long ago faded into something resembling a pale flesh tone. A set of rickety wooden stairs at the end closest to the motel office provided access to the rooms on the second floor. Black wrought-iron fencing provided a railing for the rooms on the second story. A black coach lamp was mounted next to each door of the dozen motel rooms, but only a couple of them worked. No attempt had been made to match the A-frame office to the motel. It had the long, steep roof and tall windows of a typical A-frame building. Faux stone covered the sides of the office, giving the building a north-woods look. This was furthered by the sickly pine trees planted on the sides of the building.

The only other vehicles in the tar lot were a beat-up Honda motorcycle— probably belonging to the innkeeper—and a Chevy Nova with busted-out windows and four flat tires. Both were parked outside the motel office. After raising the top on the Porsche, Michaels moved the car to the side of the motel, next to a stand of birch trees and overgrown bushes. The street traffic was thin at that hour, but he didn't want to take any chances.

In a feeble and condescending tribute to decorating, a poster for *Gone With the Wind* hung on the wall above the bed's brass headboard. It was mounted in a black plastic frame and was covered by scratched acrylic. It showed Scarlett O'Hara in the arms of Rhett Butler while Atlanta burned behind them. "That's my favorite movie," said Miss Rue, as she entered the motel room ahead of Michaels.

"Figures," Michaels said.

She stood studying the poster for a moment while Michaels shut the door behind them and locked it. He slid the security chain in place as well. "If I seen it once I seen it a hundred times," she said wistfully, as much to herself as to Michaels.

With his black driving gloves still on, he fiddled with the clock radio on the nightstand next to the bed, finding an agreeable rock station. He stopped when he hit some Tom Petty and the Heartbreakers. "Even the Losers."

Rue walked into the bathroom and checked her face in the mirror. She pulled a tube out of her skirt pocket and applied a stroke of pink to her lips. "Jesus Christ," Michaels said, watching her through the doorway. "I want to fuck you, not marry you."

"You're a strange one," she said. He laughed and walked over to the bed and sat down on the edge.

She turned and checked her braid in the mirror. Satisfied, she walked out of the bathroom. She looked around the room; it wasn't her usual. She took her johns to the room closest to the office. She sat down on a metal folding chair—the only other furniture besides the bed and nightstand—and peeled off her shirt. Michaels leaned back against the headboard and watched. "Why ain't you undressin'?" she asked as she stood up to wiggle out of her tight skirt. "It takes two to tango, darlin'." She folded her clothes and set them on the seat of the chair.

He stood up, removed his blazer and laid it on the end of the bed. He walked to the nightstand and turned up the volume on the radio.

It wasn't as loud as the buzzing in his head.

"Tell me," said Michaels, stepping toward her, "do you like the way Rhett sweeps Scarlett off her feet?" Before she could answer, he grabbed her by the shoulders and pulled her toward him. He pushed her backward onto the bed and fell heavily on top of her soft form. Her eyes were wide but calm. She'd had rough johns before.

Not this rough.

He wrapped his gloved left hand around her throat and squeezed. With his right, he grabbed a fistful of hair on the back of her head. Suddenly his face contorted in a mixture of confusion and rage. "What the hell!" he yelled. From behind her head, he pulled the brown braid. He held it for a moment, staring at it in the gloved palm of his right hand. It looked like a dead animal.

"You bitch!" he snarled, looking down at her frightened face.

"What?" she squeaked. She was clawing his left arm with her fingers in an attempt to dislodge his left hand from her throat. She tried to raise her knees against him and push him off, but she couldn't; he was too heavy.

He dropped the braid on the floor and released his grip on her throat. He rolled off her and slid off the mattress, standing on the floor next to the bed. He looked down at the whore gasping for air. Brown mascara mixed with tears ran down her cheeks. All the fury and frustration of the previous two weeks bubbled to the surface, spilling out onto the writhing female figure sprawled out on the dirty bedspread. He drew his arm back and punched her in the stomach. She wheezed sharply and curled into a ball. With his left hand, he pulled her to a sitting position on the bed by the top of her hair. He swung his right arm back and slapped her face hard, all the while keeping a tight clamp on her hair. He slapped her until his hand hurt.

Blood oozed out of her nostrils. She fought for breath to scream or cry, but found she had none. She scratched at his left arm with the fingernails of her right hand in a weak attempt to release his hold on her hair. She raised her left arm in front of her face to try to fend off his blows.

He let go of her hair. She fell back on the bed, panting and sobbing. He fell on top of her again and wrapped both hands around her throat. She pulled at his shirt and then used her chubby fists to beat at his back. He laughed at her.

Her eyes rolled to the back of her head as she slipped into unconsciousness.

He didn't rape her. He decided Miss Rue, a hideous fraud, wasn't worth it. He peeled himself off her sweaty body and walked to the end of the bed. From the pocket of his blazer he withdrew the plastic bag and scalpel. He unwrapped the scalpel and laid the plastic bag on the nightstand. He bent over her and grabbed the top of her hair with one hand. In the other, he held the scalpel. Her eyes fluttered open. He looked down at her and smiled. Amazingly, she smiled back, weakly. He put his mouth to her ear and whispered: "The fly shall marry the bumblebee."

He slit her throat in a single, deep stroke. He wiped the blade on the bedspread and shoved it back in his jacket. He inspected his gloved hand, the one he had used to strike her and then slit her throat. "Disgusting," he said, and wiped his glove on the bedspread. The leather was smeared with her pink lipstick and blood.

Pink lipstick and blood. For an instant, he saw his mother sitting on the bed, patting the mattress. "Come, Buzzy."

"No," he said. "No, Bee." He blinked and his mother was gone. The buzzing was fading; he could hear the radio again.

He looked around on the floor. Where did it go? He found it; he'd accidentally kicked it under the bed. He picked it up and dropped it into the plastic bag. He would keep the braid—not as a valuable souvenir, but as a reminder of his own stupidity.

He would call this one Miss Mistake.

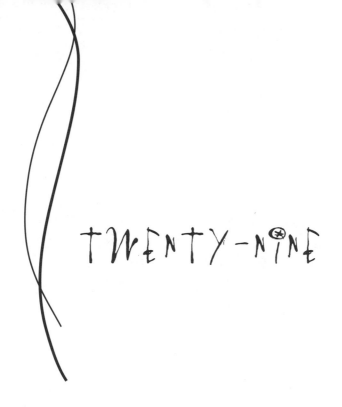

TWENTY-NINE

A row of reporters and photographers assembled like a firing squad in front of Christianson's desk Thursday morning. Before the press conference, Christianson had set down some ground rules for the reporters: he would take a limited number of questions after reading a prepared statement; only he could be quoted directly; the two detectives could provide background, but couldn't be named or pictured in the print or television news accounts.

Murphy and Gabe stood in the back while the chief gave a statement outlining the theory that the three murders were connected. A couple of the reporters' mouths dropped open, but they kept scribbling in their notebooks. The bored-looking newspaper photographers stood straighter and snapped pictures. A routine press conference had turned into a good story.

"We are asking the public to assist us in solving these crimes," said Christianson. "If anyone has spotted this man, we're asking them to call us here at the station. He may be driving a newer, black Chevrolet Suburban."

The chief's public-information officer, a nervous bald man with a wispy moustache, handed out composite sketches of the suspect. The reporters nearly ripped the sheets of paper out of his hands.

"Is he armed?" asked Glory Harding, a bug-eyed public-radio reporter who looked as though she'd come straight out of college. "Should he be considered dangerous?"

"No, you should invite him over for dinner," Gabe whispered to Murphy. She smiled and rolled her eyes.

"His weapon is chiefly his hands," said Christianson. "Each victim was strangled and beaten. As far as being dangerous? I'd say so."

"Chief Christianson, who provided you with a description of the suspect?" asked Cody, elbowing his way to the front. "How do you know he drives a black Suburban?"

"Sergeant Murphy, Sergeant Nash. Would either one of you like to answer that question?" said the chief.

Murphy stepped forward, but stayed behind the cameras. "A passing motorist saw Fionn Hennessy get into this man's car shortly before she was killed," she said.

"Can we have the name of the witness, get a few quotes?" asked Cody.

"Not a chance in hell," said Gabe. "You know that."

"A guy's gotta try," said Cody.

"Is he a john?" asked Foster Jones, the *Minneapolis Tribune* reporter, a black, salt-and-pepper-haired veteran with a big gut. He and Gabe were fishing buddies.

"Is the passing motorist a john?" asked Gabe, trying not to grin.

"No, no," said Jones, laughing. He knew Gabe was pulling his leg. "I'm wondering if the killer is a john. Well, I suppose the motorist could be a john as well. My question is . . ."

"I know what you're asking, Foster," said Murphy, smiling. "We don't know if this man was one of Fionn's tricks. It's certainly possible."

"Why do you think these murders are related?" asked Cody. "Beyond the strangulation thing, what else about the killer's M.O. connects the three of them?"

"We can't discuss that," said Christianson.

"As long as we're all standing here, how about an update on Father Ambrose?" asked Jones. "Is he talking about his assault?"

"Father Ambrose is unable to help us at this time," said Gabe. "He had a setback in the hospital. Some kind of heart trouble."

"I still don't understand why St. Paul P.D. is taking charge of a Minneapolis case," said Mimi Englund, an A.P. reporter. "Is this some sort of weird payback for that Minneapolis shoot-out in St. Paul? What do you guys call it?"

"The rim job," offered Foster, grinning.

"Ouch," Murphy whispered to Gabe. "That one had to piss off the chief."

Christianson didn't blink. "We've already explained we're not in charge," he said. "We're simply lending a hand to our overloaded colleagues across the river."

"That sounds a little too warm and fuzzy to be the whole story," said Englund, planting her hands on her hips. "Is there a St. Paul angle to the case you're not sharing with us?"

"No. That's all for today, ladies and gentlemen," said the chief. "We'll keep you apprised as more information becomes available."

"That went okay," said Gabe as he and Murphy left the chief's office. The public-information officer herded the media pack down the hall to the elevators.

"I guess," said Murphy. "Do me a favor, though. The next time you and Foster are out in the boat, watch what you say in front of him as far as work goes."

"What do you mean?"

"Rim job."

"Oh yeah," Gabe said. They both laughed as they walked into homicide.

"I hate to wreck your jolly mood," said Castro, putting down his telephone. "One of your witnesses turned up dead in a cheesy motel."

Ah, man," said Murphy as she parked across the street from the Magnolia Manor. "What a crappy place to die."

"What the hell were you expecting?" asked Gabe.

"The Hilton!" Murphy snapped. She turned off the ignition and threw open the car door. "I figured Rue was going to get croaked at the Hilton."

Yellow police tape blocked the entrance to the motel parking lot, which was dotted with a half dozen marked and unmarked squad cars. Tia and a couple of other pros stood outside the tape, craning their necks to see what was happening. A group of neighborhood kids on bicycles pulled up next to the hookers. "You get the bastard who done Charlene! You hear me?" screamed Tia as Murphy and Gabe ducked under the tape. "You assholes fuckin' do your job!"

Some of the kids laughed. "Fuckin' do your job!" one of them repeated. They all picked up on it and chanted: "Do your job! Do your job! Do your job!" More laughter. Murphy and Gabe kept walking across the parking lot.

Murphy stepped into the motel room ahead of Gabe and immediately noticed how the hooker looked more elegant in death than she ever had in life. She was flat on her back, making the curve of her stomach appear gentle rather than bulging. Her limbs looked smooth, pale and graceful in their final repose. Her head was thrown back against the bed, as if in some fanciful pose struck for a painter.

Her face and throat told the true story. Dried blood snaked out of her nose and crusted her nostrils. Her cheeks were battered and streaked with mascara. Her lips were split and pink lipstick was smeared around them as if from a sloppy kiss. Her throat was a congealing, red smear. A large, dark stain started at the pillow under her head and spread under her in a large, elliptical shape.

The crime-scene photographer had come and gone. Murphy and Gabe chased the uniformed officers outside; it was so crowded in the motel room they could hardly turn around. The radio was blaring. "That was on when we got here," said a young patrolman, one of the last uniforms to leave. "We didn't touch it. We didn't touch anything."

"Good," said Gabe, holding the door open for him. "Now take a hike."

"He probably cranked it to cover the noise," Murphy said.

They stood at the side of the bed, looking down at Rue's nude body. "Murphy, this really doesn't fit," said Gabe.

"It can't be a coincidence," she said, shaking her head. "It would be too convenient for him, too lucky."

For different but closely related reasons, both detectives were apprehensive upon finding Erik Mason at the scene as the investigator for the medical examiner's office. "Paris, I have to agree with Gabe," said Erik, standing at the foot of the bed.

"Pinch me," Gabe said. "I must be dreaming."

Erik flipped him the bird and continued. "This isn't Michaels's M.O. He likes a nice, clean strangulation and this is a bloody mess. He goes for women with long hair and you said yourself that Rue kept her hair short. We'll do a workup, but so far it doesn't even appear she had sex with whoever did this to her."

"You know how the Doc favors some sex mixed with his murder," added Gabe. "I mean, that's what floats his boat."

"I know, I know," said Murphy. "With the coup de grâce being a crappy haircut for the victim."

"Rue's clothes are even neatly folded on that chair over there," Erik said. "It really looks like this was some customer gone sour. Nothing more."

"A customer gone sour? Nothing more?" Murphy sputtered. "Whoever it was beat the hell out of her and then sliced her throat. Even if this isn't the work of our doctor pal, it's pretty horrible stuff. Whoever did this is an impressive maniac in his own right."

"Yes, yes," said Erik. "I wasn't trying to make light of what happened here. I was . . ."

"Never mind," she said, rubbing her forehead. "I know what you were saying. I'm saying . . . I don't know what I'm saying. I'm a bitch today, okay?"

Murphy and Gabe stepped away from the bed while the two somber-faced men from the medical examiner's office loaded Rue into a body bag. Murphy studied the dead woman's hair until the zipper finally made its way to the top, sealing in the battered face. In the recesses of her mind, she could see Rue alive and laughing, tugging on a skirt that was always too short and too tight, fussing with her makeup. Something about her hair. Something recent. A blurry image. Murphy struggled but couldn't bring it into focus. "Something is wrong with this picture," said Murphy. "When you mentioned Rue's short hair, something clicked."

"What?" asked Erik.

"I don't know," she said distractedly as she watched the men lift the bag onto a stretcher.

"How do we find her people?" asked Gabe, stepping to the side as they wheeled her out. "Have we got phone numbers for them down south?"

"What do you mean, 'down south'? She's from northeast Minneapolis," said Murphy.

"Really? What was that half-baked accent about?" said Gabe. "You know, all that 'darlin'' stuff."

"Rue wanted to be someone else," said Murphy.

"You mean she didn't want to be a prostitute?" asked Erik.

"She wanted to be a more glamorous one," said Murphy as she stared out the motel windows and watched Rue's body being loaded into the medical examiner's hearse. "She picked up that silly southern accent because she thought it made her sound exotic."

The hearse pulled out of the parking lot. As it did, Murphy saw Tia collapse sobbing into the arms of the other prostitutes. The neighborhood children pedaled off on their bicycles, laughing as they chased the hearse down the street. One threw a rock at it.

"How sad to have no greater goal in life than to be a more alluring hooker," said Erik.

"Yeah," said Murphy. She turned and looked at Erik. "Sad."

"Hey, Paris, how about drinks tonight?" asked Erik as he and the two investigators stood in the motel parking lot. "We still need to firm up stuff on that Saints game."

Murphy gave Gabe the eye. He raised his eyebrows but said nothing as he took the hint and walked toward their car. He smiled to himself. After the way Murphy had snapped at Erik in the motel room, Gabe was confident she wasn't going to be too long. Still, he wanted to keep an eye on things. He crossed the street to the car and leaned against the side of it, turning the driver's-side mirror out a bit so he could watch what was happening in the parking lot without being obvious. He took a pack of Winstons out of his pocket, peeled off the cellophane top and pulled out a smoke.

"Erik, I'm back with my husband," said Murphy. "I'm sorry. I should have called you."

"I'm a patient man," Erik said. "You two have tried this before." Erik looked across the street to make sure Gabe wasn't watching them. He stepped closer to Murphy, grabbed her by the arm and pulled her toward him. "I know what you like, maybe even better than Jack does," he whispered into her ear. "You'll be back."

Murphy looked up at him and started to say something in response. Instead, she shoved his hand off her arm, turned on her heel and walked away. She ducked under the police tape and saw that only Tia was left standing in the street. The other hookers had returned to their corners. "Want a ride?" Murphy asked.

"No," said Tia. "I want Charlene back."

"Me, too," Murphy said tiredly, and crossed the street to Gabe. He was standing outside the car, leaning against the driver's-side door with a cigarette between his fingers. She fished the key out of her purse and tossed them to him. "Your turn to drive," she said.

Gabe didn't look at her as he got behind the wheel with the cigarette between his lips. "Thought you were gonna quit after you finished that last pack," she said.

"This is the same pack. Got a couple left," he said.

"Yeah. Right. Roll down your window. I don't want to smell that shit."

He rolled down the driver's-side window.

"Better straighten out that side mirror," Murphy said.

"Huh?"

"Don't pull that innocent crap on me," she said.

"Jesus Christ," Gabe said. He pulled the cigarette out of his mouth and flicked it outside. "What is your problem this morning?"

She didn't answer. As they pulled away, Murphy looked into the rearview mirror and saw Tia still standing alone behind the police tape, staring at the motel.

Murphy braced herself for questions about Erik and was grateful that Gabe instead held his tongue. They said nothing to each other as they headed back to the station. Murphy closed her eyes and rested her head against the car window. Her mind shuffled back and forth between Rue's body sprawled on the bed and her own body under Michaels's. In the background, she could hear Tia's words mockingly repeated by the neighborhood children. "Do your job. Do your job."

THIRTY

She was on her back in bed, but couldn't feel any support beneath her. The room was too bright, as if the sun had come indoors. Still, she couldn't make out his face when he came to her. He flashed a long knife in front of her face. With her fingertips, she felt along the blade and recognized it as one of her own kitchen carving knives. He pushed her hand away and slipped the tip of the knife under the bodice of her nightgown. With one pass, he slit the gown down the middle and it fell off her body. She shivered and he crawled on top of her. He was fully dressed, but suddenly his clothes melted away and she felt his warm nakedness against her own. He stretched out so his body rested flat against her body. His legs on top of her legs. His stomach against her stomach. He didn't move for a while. He rested. At first he felt light, but he grew heavier. She sensed his chest rise and fall with his every breath; she felt the beating of his heart. Somehow she knew he was Jack, and that made her comfortable. She strained to see his face, but it was turned away from her and buried in her hair.

"Look at me," she said. Her lips didn't move, but she could hear her own words. They echoed, as if coming from inside a cave. "Look at me. Look at me." The face buried in her hair laughed, and she knew it wasn't her husband. Instead she wrapped her legs around him and clawed at his back. His skin came off in her hands. It felt dry and lifeless, like parchment paper. She bunched it up in her fists and released it. The flesh fluttered into the light, turning into a swarm of bees. Hundreds and hundreds of bees.

"I really hate you," she heard herself say. "Hate you. Hate you."

"Then you love me," he said. His breath burned her ear and the white walls turned red. He lifted his face off her hair and looked at her with his gray eyes. Michaels.

She screamed.

Paris. It's okay. Paris."

She opened her eyes and shuddered. She turned her head and looked at the clock on her nightstand: 3:07 A.M. She pulled the covers up around her neck, even though it was warm in her bedroom. For a moment, she was afraid to turn her head to see who was in bed with her, consoling her. She did turn her head, and was relieved. Jack. Of course.

"Must have been quite a dream," he said. He rolled over onto his side and rested on his elbow as he talked to her in the dark. She stayed flat on her back, clutching the sheets with clammy hands. "Do you remember what it was about?"

"No," she said, lying. "Why?"

"You were yelling in your sleep," he said.

"What did I say?" she asked.

"You said, 'I hate you. I hate you.' Pretty weird."

"Yeah," she said. "Weird."

He fell back asleep, but she stayed awake another hour, staring at the ceiling. She finally shut her eyes and went back to sleep after the lights from a passing barge cut across her bedroom walls, reassuring her that she was safe in her bed and not lost in another bad dream.

Potato Head, wake up."

Murphy rolled over onto her side. Morning already, and she was wiped out. Jack shoved a phone into her hands. "It's your mother," he whispered. "I picked up your cell phone by mistake. I guess we're busted."

"Never mind," Murphy mumbled, struggling to sit up in bed while Jack flipped onto his stomach.

"What did you say, honey?" Amira asked on the other end of the phone.

"Nothing, Imma," said Murphy, using the Lebanese term of endearment for mother. "What's up?" Murphy glanced at the clock. Not yet seven. Instinctively, she covered her naked top with her pillow and pulled the edge of the bedsheet over Jack's bare bottom, as if her mother could see them through the cell phone.

"You take such a nice picture, honey," said her mother.

"Thanks, Ma."

"I wish you would do something with your hair."

"Yeah, Ma."

"Otherwise, the photo in this morning's *Pioneer Press* looks lovely. I sent Papa out to buy some extra copies. I'll save one for you."

"Thanks, Ma." Murphy paused for a moment, then realized what her mother had said.

"Shit!" Murphy said. "Shit, shit, shit!"

"Watch your language, young lady," said her mother.

"Sorry, Ma."

"I'll bet your mother told you to watch your language, didn't she, young lady?" Jack muttered into his pillow.

"It's . . . those lizards!" Murphy said angrily, running her fingers through her hair.

"What lizards?" asked her mother, alarmed. "Do you have lizards on your boat, honey? I told you not to live on that filthy river."

"Ma."

"What, honey?"

"Can I call you back later?"

"Sure, honey. Kiss Jack for me. Tell him to put some clothes on before going into the kitchen. He could catch a cold."

"Okay, Ma. I'll tell him."

"Please. Think about doing something with your hair, Potato Head."

"Okay, Ma. I will."

"You can't keep pulling it into a ponytail. You're not a twelve-year-old tomboy anymore."

"Okay, Ma."

"I love you, honey."

"I love you, too. Bye." Murphy put down the cell phone, not knowing whether to laugh or scream. She released some visceral combination of the two. *"Aaahhh!"*

"What happened?" asked Jack, rolling over onto his back.

*C*ody, you bastard! I thought I could trust you!"

"What did I do, Murphy? What in the hell are you talking about?"

"You know damn well what I'm talking about, you lying piece of garbage," Murphy shouted into the phone. "You ran my photo and name in the paper today, asshole. That's what I'm talking about. You're going to ruin this entire investigation."

"I don't know what you're talking about," Cody sputtered. "Let me get a copy of the city edition."

She heard paper shuffling. While she was on the phone, her partner walked over to her desk and dropped his copy of the *Pioneer Press* on her desk. He looked grim faced.

"Shit," said Cody, back on the phone. "You know, this isn't even my story. It's a wire story we picked up from the Associated Press. It's got Mimi Englund's byline on it and it's not about the murders. It's a short update on the priest based on what you and Nash said yesterday. Our copy desk must have pulled a file photo of you to run with the wire story. Shit. I'm sorry."

"Gabe and I were not supposed to be quoted directly about anything we said during that press conference," she said. "The chief made that clear."

"Well, I'm not defending what Englund did," he said. "I think there was some misunderstanding. I suspect she thought you couldn't be quoted about anything related to the murders. You've been quoted before about the priest's case."

"Yeah, but I was never pictured," she said. "Today you used my name and my photo, making it crystal clear who I am and sending up flares for the killer."

"You know who he is, don't you?" asked Cody.

"Don't change the subject," she said angrily. "Even if it's not your story, you ran it. With my photo. Did the *Tribune* run the A.P. story, too?"

"Yeah, but they buried it on the inside and didn't run a head shot of you," said Cody.

"I suppose TV is going to pick it up, too," she said.

"I doubt it," said Cody. "Not enough visuals."

"Did the photo make it into your on-line publication?" she asked.

"Probably not. Let me check," Cody said.

Gabe sat down at his terminal and also logged on to the Internet. She heard Cody and her partner both typing frantically on their keyboards. Gabe looked over at her and shook his head.

"No, we didn't run a photo on line," Cody said.

"Well, that's something," she said.

"You know, we only ran the photo and story in the city edition," Cody said, trying to reassure her. "If he doesn't live in the city, maybe he didn't see it."

She didn't respond.

"He does live in the city," said Cody. "You do know who it is! Come on, Murphy. Give me something."

"Drop dead, Cody," she said, and slammed the phone down. Murphy picked up the paper and frowned at her photo on the front page of the metro section. Gabe walked over to her desk and sat on the edge of it.

"You know, to be fair, Slick should have made the ground rules a littler clearer," he said.

"Since when are you the great defender of the Fourth Estate?"

"All I'm saying is . . ."

"Well, it's neither here nor there now," she said with a dismissive wave of her hand. She threw the newspaper in the wastebasket. "Our friendly plastic surgeon knows who I am, and I'm sure who you are as well," she said. "We really need to pull that surveillance operation together pronto. God dammit!"

Her phone rang. Erik:

"I think I have some good news for you. At least, I think it's good news. Relatively speaking. Why don't you get Gabe and come on over?"

The public face of the Ramsey County M.E.'s office was a neat, modern, bright conference room off the front entrance. Erik was waiting there with a plastic bag. "That's what I couldn't remember," said Murphy, grabbing the bag containing a brown braid. "Rue did have long hair recently—when she wore those secondhand hairpieces."

"When that Puerto Rican friend of hers came by to identify the body . . ."

"Tia," said Murphy.

"Yeah, Tia told me about them," said Erik. "Rue had two of them. Sometimes she wore pigtails. Usually, when she did wear the hairpieces . . ."

". . . It was clipped to the back of her head," finished Gabe. "Now I remember, too. One fell off while we were interviewing her."

"I had Tia come back with this one," said Erik, pointing to the braid in the bag. "She wore the other one the night she was killed. It's missing."

"I know exactly where it is," said Murphy, taking a seat at the conference table and putting the bag down in front of her. "It's in Michaels's trophy case. I was right, wasn't I? He did do poor Rue."

"The wound across her throat was made with a very sharp tool," said Erik.

"A scalpel," said Gabe, sitting next to Murphy.

"I don't understand why he changed his M.O.," said Erik, pacing the width of the room as he talked. "He doesn't strangle her. He slashes her throat. He beats her, but he doesn't rape her. Instead of finishing off with his signature haircut, he takes home a ratty braid."

"That might be why he did Rue differently," said Murphy. "He only gets his rocks off on longhaired women. Maybe he didn't know it was a hairpiece until he got her inside the motel room."

"After he discovered the hair was fake, he couldn't rape her because he couldn't get it up," said Gabe. "All he could do was slit her throat."

"The braid must have really pissed him off," said Murphy.

"Then why did he take it with him?" asked Erik, who stopped pacing and took a seat across the table from the two detectives.

"Who knows? I'm not a psychologist," said Murphy. She stared at the braid. "Maybe he couldn't stand leaving empty-handed. He had to take some sort of souvenir with him, even if it was a lousy braid."

"What do we tell the press about Rue?" asked Gabe. "Should we connect the dots for them on this one?"

"Forget it. I'm out of the dot-connecting business," said Murphy. "Let them figure it out for themselves or make up whatever they want."

"We can't say much official anyway because this is all conjecture," said Erik. "We didn't find anything in the autopsy that you didn't see in the motel."

"Of course not," Murphy said. "That's how this entire case has been going! It's not that he's a brilliant professional killer, but he *is* very careful. I'll give him that. No one noticed him or his car at the motel that night. He had Rue go to the office to pay for the room. He didn't leave a weapon and probably left no prints. The thing is, he's also very, very lucky."

"Tough to fight," Gabe said. He stood up to leave, but Murphy stayed in her seat, looking down at the braid in the bag.

"Rue told me she talked the woman down to five dollars for both."

"What?" asked Erik.

"The woman running the garage sale wanted five dollars for each and Rue got her down to five dollars for the pair," said Murphy. "Charlene was pretty proud of that bit of bargaining." She slid the plastic bag across the table to Erik and stood up. "It really sucks to think a life can turn on a two-for-one hairpiece, doesn't it?" she said.

THIRTY-ONE

*M*ichaels was trapped in surgery the better part of Friday with one breast reduction after another. The last one went badly because of excessive bleeding. Hester Hanson had disobeyed his orders to stay away from alcohol and garlic for two weeks prior to her operation. In fact, she'd had enough wine that she'd thinned her blood so it wouldn't clot properly. To make matters worse, she took aspirin the morning after her drinking for her hangover. This had happened before with other patients, though not to this extreme. Most denied the transgression. In this case, however, her husband, Zachary, claimed they'd never received such preoperative instructions from him.

"Doctor, I swear we never heard any such thing," said Zachary Hanson as he and Michaels argued outside Hester's room. "Why would we ignore something so important? Do you think my wife wanted to bleed to death so she could have a couple of glasses of wine and some chip dip?"

Michaels knew it wasn't a couple glasses of wine. A bottle perhaps. "Mr. Hanson, I assure you the situation was not that dire," said Michaels. "She did not come close to bleeding to death."

He didn't like the Hansons. They were nouveau riche ex-farmers who made money by selling their farm parcels on the southern edge of the Twin Cities. They still dressed and talked like farmers. Every time he saw Zachary Hanson, he was in the same flannel shirt and baggy-ass blue jeans. Like he had just stepped off the soybean field.

"I also want to assure you, Mr. Hanson, that I did indeed give you instructions warning against the consumption of alcohol, garlic and aspirin in the weeks prior to surgery," Michaels continued, his face reddening in contained anger. "Your wife set a new standard among my patients. She managed to use all three!"

"Bullshit!" said Hanson. "That is a crock! You didn't warn us about jack shit!"

Michaels was tired. He had a headache. He wanted to go home to a hot bath, a cold steak sandwich and some good Scotch, in precisely that order. "Look, Mr. Hanson, I tell all my surgical patients this personally and I have my staff pass along written instructions as well. I know I told your wife. Positively no alcohol, garlic or aspirin for two . . ."

"You're covering your ass," snarled Hanson, sticking a fat, ruddy finger in Michaels's face. Two surgical nurses walked past them in the hospital hallway, still dressed in their scrubs. They looked back as Hanson's voice continued to rise. "You're one lucky son-of-a-bitch that she made it through the surgery. Here everyone says you're the top tit man in town. I'm still waiting to be impressed. That's for damn straight!"

The doctor felt the muscles around his jaw tighten. No one questioned his skills, his talents, his gifts. Especially not some ignorant rube riding high on his newfound wealth. He grabbed Hanson by his shirt collar and shoved him flat against the wall. "Look, you hick jerk," he growled lowly. "I *am* the best in town. In the country, for that matter, and don't you forget it! It's not my fault your dopey wife can't follow some simple instructions."

The two nurses stopped at the end of the hall and turned around wide-eyed to watch. Michaels released Hanson, who looked genuinely frightened. "The nurse will send you home with some post-op instructions tomorrow," Michaels continued. "If there are any problems this evening—and I'm sure there will be none—they will page me. Is all that clear?"

Hanson nodded but said nothing.

"Now why don't you go down to the cafeteria and have a cup of coffee?" Michaels said evenly.

The smaller man nodded, turned and walked quickly down the corridor, brushing past the two nurses. The pair watched him step onto an elevator. As the doors closed behind the startled man, the two women turned and stared at Michaels. The taller of the two leaned toward the other and whispered something. The shorter one nodded. Michaels glared at them. "Nosey cunts," he hissed under his breath.

He didn't get to the newspaper until Friday night, as he was stretched out naked on the bed with a glass of Scotch on the nightstand.

He inhaled sharply when he unfolded the A section and read the headline stripped across the top of the front page: MAN SOUGHT IN THREE MURDERS. Police had made the connection between the murder of the redheaded whore and the deaths of women in Minneapolis and Rochester. How did they find out about the one from his fellowship? How? Miss Incident was years ago. He fought to control his trembling hands as he held the newspaper. With great effort, he forced himself to read slowly and carefully, even though his frantic eyes demanded he skip ahead to find anything that clearly pointed a finger at him. His hands dampened the edges of the newspaper as he held it. He turned to the continuation of the story on page three. A composite sketch—of him!

The buzzing. Not now. He dropped the newspaper and covered his ears with his hands. "Calm down," he told himself. "Fucking calm down." He shut his eyes and took deep breaths, and it stopped. He opened his eyes and lowered his hands from his ears. Good. The fly was back in the jar.

He picked up the newspaper again and studied the sketch carefully. It could be anyone, he told himself. Anyone. The police chief was asking for the public's help, according to the story. Anyone seeing the man in the sketch—possibly driving a newer black Chevy Suburban—was asked to call authorities. Shit. They had the color and make and model of his car! How? He kept reading.

Supposedly, someone saw the whore get into his car. Bullshit! The streets were empty that rainy night. He remembered that clearly. This was conjecture on the part of the police. Nothing in the story revealed why they thought the three cases were related. Nothing. The news account also failed to make the connection between the murder of the whore and the assault on the priest. It had no mention of his most recent and disappointing outing. Didn't the fat whore make it into the paper at all? Surely someone had found Miss Mistake's body by now.

He threw the A section to the floor and grabbed the Metro section, quickly flipping through it until he found a short story on the back page about a woman's nude body found in a motel room. Her name was being withheld pending notification of relatives. That was it on Miss Mistake. No cause of death. No mention of whether the police were looking for anyone.

On the surface, the police appeared stumped. They had bits and pieces, but they didn't have the entire puzzle assembled. Very far from it.

He wasn't so naive. He suspected they knew much more about him than they were letting on. Perhaps they even knew his name. So why were they claiming they needed the public's help? They were tormenting him, challenging him. He was sure of it.

How had they gotten the information they did have?

He dropped the Metro section on the bed and reached over to his nightstand to grab his Scotch glass when a photograph on the front of the section caught his eye. He picked the section up again and nervously unfolded it.

He was stunned. "God dammit," he said. "You had me."

That evening rendezvous with her, with this Detective Paris Murphy—finally a name to the beautiful face—had been a net cast for him. He knew he should be furious, but instead he was pleased.

He took a sip of Scotch and mulled over what he had said to her that night; it was hazy. He had had too much to drink, but he hadn't said anything that implicated him in any of the murders or the assault on the priest on the floor of the confessional. He was safe there. Something else about that evening, something that had nagged him that night at the hotel. What was it? He took another drink and it came to him. That familiar-looking man on the hotel steps, the one with the long hair and the beard. He was part of the scam. Now Michaels remembered where he'd spotted that barrel figure and Cro-Magnon posture before. He was that so-called friend of hers from the funeral and soccer tournament, dressed in a lame disguise. Must be her cop partner.

"Such a cool liar," he said. He studied the photo. So professional, with her dark hair pulled back sternly from her face. She had high cheekbones; he hadn't noticed that before for some reason. Those eyes. He lost himself in those eyes. He stroked the photo with his fingertips and smiled. That night in the hotel bar and garden had been a trap set for him, but she was the one who was almost snared. She yielded for an instant. He felt it as his lips sealed over hers, as his mouth tasted her breast. She could have surrendered. She would surrender if he had an opportunity to be alone with her again.

He read the story under the photo. A short update on Ambrose. The priest had refused to talk to the police because of the Seal of Confession. It also referred to a heart problem the father was suffering from in the hospital. Was it possible he had managed to slip the potassium into the old boy without anyone spotting it? No. He would have to be incredibly stupid to believe that. The police knew about it.

They were baiting him with these stories filled with half-truths, teasing him, hoping he would make a revealing mistake. They were buying time. They needed more evidence before they brought him in, especially with his family's influence around town. That's what all this was about. His father's youngest brother, a downtown developer, had bankrolled the mayor's reelection campaign and another uncle, a downtown banker, had the governor's ear. Cousins in the legislature. So many powerful, moneyed cousins. Blood ties and wealth. Unbeatable. His relatives would come through for him. Most liked him. The ones that didn't like him wouldn't want the family name dirtied.

He grabbed his cell phone off his nightstand and held it for a moment, debating which uncle to tap for help. Maybe he'd start with another relative. Someone especially well positioned to help him. Someone who'd take his side no matter what. He punched in the number. She answered.

"Hello, cuz," he said into the phone. He lay back against the pillows. "It's been too long."

Michaels set down the phone and smiled. The relative front was in order. He hopped out of bed and paced across the floor. Now he needed to get out of town for a while, let things settle down. A trip to the cabin would be good.

He'd leave in the morning. He needed to talk to his wife, anyway; time for some serious ass kicking. Maybe he'd spend a week or two up north. Screw work. He could have his staff reschedule his appointments and surgeries.

He wanted to pay someone a visit before he left town. He wanted her to know he was on to her little scheme. He wanted her to know he still desired her. Most important, he wanted her to know he was fully aware that she desired him.

He ran down to his home office and logged on to the *Pioneer Planet,* the on-line news publication of the *Pioneer Press.* He went into the newspaper archives and did a search using her name. He came up with dozens of hits. It seemed Detective Paris Murphy was an investigative star of sorts. She got all the tough cases. A satisfied smile stretched across his face. "I suppose I should be flattered you're pursuing me," Michaels muttered. He pulled up one police story after another, but what he needed was some personal information.

Here it is, he thought. A recent profile from the newspaper's feature pages. He rolled his eyes at the title: "Murphy's Law." "Who writes this shit?" he grumbled. He quickly scanned the piece.

She usually preferred working without a partner, but sometimes teamed up with a veteran detective, Sergeant Gabriel Nash. "So that's the ugly fuck's name," Michaels said to himself. She came from a large Catholic family and had attended Catholic schools. Her hobbies included running and cooking. "So you didn't lie about everything," Michaels said in a low voice. He found no mention of hunting and he clearly remembered her asking him if he liked to hunt. That was obviously a ploy to pull something out of him about his favorite pursuit. Michaels was pleased to read she was separated from her husband, an emergency-room doctor. The newspaper story didn't name him. She lived in a houseboat on the river.

That last bit of information was what he needed, and he knew exactly where that floating neighborhood was docked. He went back upstairs, opened a dresser drawer and pulled out some clothes.

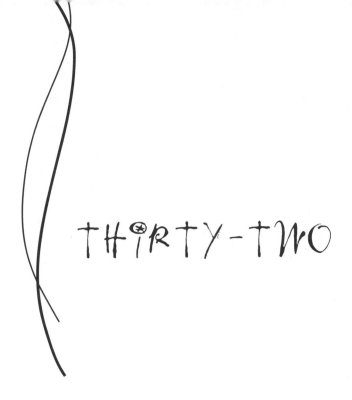

THIRTY-TWO

Tell her it's him all right," Castro said, peering through his binoculars. "He's leaving by the side door and walking down the driveway toward his garage."

"Actually, it's a carriage house, converted into a garage," Dubrowski said, correcting his partner.

"Fucking excuse me," Castro said. "Then tell her he's walking down the fucking driveway toward his fucking carriage house, converted into a fucking garage." Castro sat behind the wheel of the unmarked squad car—a dark blue Crown Victoria—parked across the street from Michaels's house on Summit Avenue on Friday. In the passenger seat next to him, Dubrowski was on a cell phone speaking to Murphy. She had asked them to call her at home that evening if the surgeon left his house during their surveillance.

"What a long driveway," Castro mumbled. "I'd hate to shovel that puppy in the winter."

"What did he say?" Murphy asked Dubrowski. "Michaels has a shovel?"

"No, no. He said he'd hate to shovel that driveway."

"He's opening the garage door," Castro said, picking up his burger to take another bite but still watching through the binoculars.

"He's opening the garage door," Dubrowski repeated to Murphy.

He paused in his narration to pick up his fish sandwich and finish it off. He wiped his mouth with a paper napkin and started sucking on his shake. The front seat of the car—littered with crumpled paper napkins, empty paper bags and paper cups—looked like the tabletop of a fast-food restaurant. The floor of the backseat was covered with newspapers and pop cans. Sitting on top of the backseat was a cardboard box across which was scrawled in black marker: "Detectives—Clean up after yourselves, assholes. Dump trash in here." The inside of the box was the cleanest spot in the car.

"Now what's he doing?" asked Dubrowski.

"I don't know," said Castro. He popped the last wedge of burger into his mouth and wiped his hand on his pants while continuing to look through the binoculars held in his other hand. "I don't have a clear view because part of the garage is tucked behind that big mother house. He's probably in there choking the bishop. Actually, I'm pretty sure he's . . . Whoa! Wait a minute. Wait a minute. Yup. Here we go!"

He threw down the binoculars. "Gentlemen, start your engines," Castro said with a grin, turning on the ignition.

Michaels rolled out of the driveway and sped down Summit. The Crown Victoria pulled away from the curb and went after him, keeping a discreet distance. "He's headed east toward downtown," Dubrowski said into the phone.

"Stay with him," Murphy said.

"He doesn't have a private plane at the downtown airport, does he?" Dubrowski asked Murphy.

"No, he doesn't," she said.

Castro saw Michaels look in his rearview mirror. The Suburban stopped at a light. Castro slowed and let another car cut between the squad and the Suburban before he stopped.

"What the hell are you doing?" asked Dubrowski.

"I don't want to ride his ass the whole time," said Castro. "He'll get wise to us."

"We're gonna lose him."

"The hell we are. How long have I been doing this? I ever lose anybody?"

"What's going on?" asked Murphy.

The light changed. The car ahead of Castro took a turn and the squad was again behind the Suburban.

"Castro almost lost him, but now we're okay," Dubrowski said into the phone. Castro flipped his partner the bird.

They followed the Suburban through downtown St. Paul. "He's headed toward the Wabasha Bridge," Dubrowski said into the phone.

"The West Side isn't his usual hunting ground," said Murphy.

As if dropped from the sky, a white limo cut sharply in front of the Crown Victoria and Castro hit the brakes. "Shit," he muttered.

Up ahead, the Suburban turned south onto the bridge.

"Now we're going to lose him for real!" Castro said. He honked at the crawling limo. A black airport van pulled up next to the limo. Both lanes were blocked. He couldn't pull around both the van and the limo with opposing traffic zooming by. "Oh great! Fucking great!" said Castro, pounding the steering wheel with his fist.

"Can you still see Michaels's Suburb?" she asked.

"No, but I'm sure he's over the bridge by now," Dubrowski said into the cell phone.

"Where is he going?" Murphy wondered aloud. Suddenly it occurred to her. She inhaled sharply.

"Murphy, what's wrong?" Dubrowski asked. He heard only her breathing. "Murphy, what is it?"

Then it also occurred to him. "We gotta get to Murphy!" Dubrowski said.

"Get out of there!" he yelled into the cell phone. "Get out of there now!"

The silence on the other end of the phone made him fear it had gone dead. He held the cell phone tight to one ear and plugged the other so he could hear more clearly.

The airport van pulled up. Castro squealed around the limo and took a right onto the bridge.

"Murphy! Murphy!" Dubrowski yelled. "We're coming. We're on the bridge."

A long silence.

"It's too late," she said. She heard a car pull up and then Tripod barking wildly. Stranger on the dock. "He's here." She stood in her living room, with the sliding glass door leading to the deck wide open. Beyond the deck was the Mississippi. She stared at the flat, brown water and tried to draw a sense of calm from it.

"I'm going to radio some backup for you," Dubrowski said. "I'm calling Gabe."

"Hurry," she said. She switched the phone to her left hand and with her right pulled her gun from her purse. "Don't come in too soon. I want to hear what he has to say. Stay in the parking lot."

"Murphy, there is no way I am going to leave you alone with that head case," he said.

"It'll be okay," she said.

"Hello, Paris." She turned around and looked into his face. She pulled the cell phone from her ear, but continued gripping it tightly. She stood in the living room, behind the counter that separated it from the galley. He stood on the other side of the counter in the galley.

"Are you going to kiss me or kill me?" he asked coolly.

"Neither," she said evenly.

"Your neighbor, the amazingly untalented sax player, was kind enough to direct me to the right houseboat after his mutt tried to take my arm off," he said. He scrutinized the galley and living room. "Nice place you have here. Just like you."

"I'll take that as a compliment," she said.

"I meant it as one," he said. "How big is it? How many bedrooms?"

"One," she said.

"*Hmmm.* How about a little tour?"

"No," she said flatly. "What the hell do you want, Michaels?"

"Please call me Romann," he said. "I think we know each other well enough, especially after our intimacy in the hotel garden."

"Fine," she said. "What the hell do you want, Romann?"

"You're not a gracious host," he said. "Aren't you going to offer me a drink?"

"I'm fresh out of Scotch."

"The wine will work," he said, crossing the galley's wooden floor; he took a bottle of Cabernet Sauvignon from the wine rack. He studied the label, frowned and slipped it back into the rack. "Not nearly complex enough."

"I'll bet you've got some nice Chardonnay chilled," he said, and walked to the refrigerator. He eyed the collage of bills, postcards and photos plastered to the front of the appliance. "It's such a Catholic thing," he said, surveying the mess. "We have this need to cover the entire front of our refrigerators with scraps, as if we're trying to re-create those paper stained-glass windows we made in grade school." He yanked open the refrigerator, stuck his head inside and rummaged around. He emerged with a bottle of white wine. He slammed the door shut and set the bottle on the counter. He grabbed two wineglasses off the open kitchen shelf next to the wine rack. He held them up to the ceiling light to inspect them for spots. Finding them satisfactory, he set them down on the counter next to the bottle of Chardonnay. He pulled open a couple of kitchen drawers, but couldn't find what he needed. "Do you want me to open it with my teeth?"

Still keeping the gun and her eyes on him, she set down the phone, opened a drawer under her side of the counter and fished out a corkscrew. She threw it to him and he caught it. With great finesse, he opened the bottle, sniffed the cork and poured each of them a glass. He carefully recorked the bottle and returned it to the refrigerator. He noticed he had spilled a drop of wine on the counter. He grabbed a sponge from the sink and wiped it up.

"Are you always so careful about cleaning up after yourself?" she asked slyly.

He looked at her but said nothing as he tossed the sponge back in the sink.

"Why don't we enjoy this with a river view?" he said, a stem in each hand.

"After you," she said, nodding toward the deck. He acquiesced, walking around the counter and across the living-room floor. He stepped through the open sliding glass doors that led outside. She followed him.

"Quite a view," he said, scanning the riverfront. On the shore across the river, a crane groomed itself from its perch on a rock. A pair of ducks bobbed on the water a yard from her boat. The sky was purple and the air was warm and dead still. He handed her a glass. She took it with her left hand. In her right, she continued holding the Glock. "Can't we sit down?" he asked, nodding toward the deck chairs.

"Fine," she said.

"Ladies first," he said. She slowly lowered herself into one chair and he sat down in the other.

He took a sip of wine. "Nice," he said, smiling. "It's a low-end California, but nice."

She studied his face. His gray eyes. His broad shoulders. The muscled expanse of chest. Fleetingly, she wondered why the most venomous snakes were also among the most dazzling.

"That was an interesting game you played with me," he said, smiling and taking another sip of wine. "You had me fooled, but in the end, you only fooled yourself. Don't you agree?"

"Why?" she asked warily.

"We're so much alike, you and I," he said.

She laughed dryly. She took a drink of wine—her nerves needed it—and set the glass down on the deck.

"I'm serious," he said. "You lied to yourself. You told yourself you were doing your job, pursuing a suspect. What you really wanted—and what you almost had—was a soul mate."

"That's ludicrous," she snapped.

"Hear me out," he said. He paused and took a sip of wine. He frowned thoughtfully, staring at the liquid in the glass. He sloshed it around a bit, admiring the way it lightly coated the sides of the goblet. "We're both loners by choice, you and I," he said softly, his eyes still trained on the wine. "We're both ambitious and headstrong, which adds to our sense of isolation. Then there's that whole Catholic guilt trip that colors everything we say and do and think. It's like this additional, hovering presence in our lives, constantly watching us and waiting for a misstep so it can judge us. It's almost like our third parent. A mean, suffocating parent."

As reluctant as she was to give any weight to his words, she couldn't deny the slivers of truth in them.

"We both value a sense of control over our lives. 'I have everything under control.' How many times do we say that to ourselves? It's almost our mantra, isn't it?" he continued. "We're not in complete control, are we? We both suffer this uncontrollable thirst. There's a yearning inside of us, a nagging hunger we can't identify or put a name to. It comes from this shadowy, passionate corner deep inside of us. We're genuinely afraid to go there."

She felt as if she was looking into a cracked mirror. Her reflection was looking back at her through him, but she hated what she saw: something ugly and splintered.

"We almost went to that place together, that night, in that hotel garden," he said, his eyes leaving the wineglass to take in her face and read her eyes. "I felt it. I felt you soften. You came so close to giving in."

"No."

"Yes," he said. "I could have given you something you've never had before. I could still. Right now. Let's go back inside. You can keep the gun on me. I find that exciting."

She shook her head again.

"I know you want it," he whispered.

"No," she said. "No, I don't."

"Oh yes you do," he said in a low voice. "You're getting weak and your head is spinning thinking about it."

"No," she breathed.

"Come on, Paris," he whispered, leaning toward her intimately. Conspiratorially. "No one has to know. It will be our filthy little secret."

"Stop," she said sharply, raising the gun barrel. "I know what you're trying to do, you sick son-of-a-bitch." She stood up. She felt dizzy and momentarily grabbed the back of the deck chair for support. The wine. "Is this how you did it? Is it? Was the poetry this pretty? What did you say to Rue before you beat the hell out of her and slit her throat?"

His eyes widened.

"I know about Rue," she said, still pointing the barrel at him. "I know about Finch and Roxanne and that woman from the club in Minneapolis."

He stood up. "Sit your ass down!" she barked. "I'm not through with you yet."

He hesitated, staring at her face and then the gun, wondering whether she would really shoot him. He looked at her face again and lowered himself back into the chair.

"Tell me about the hair," she purred, walking back and forth across the deck in front of him. "Why is it so important to you? Why do you have to take it? Is there a name for that sort of fetish?"

"I don't know what you're talking about," he said, lowering his eyes and staring into his wineglass.

"Oh, sure you do," she said. She slipped the ribbon off her ponytail, threw it into his face and shook her hair free.

He stared at her but said nothing. He took a long drink of wine, finishing the glass. He fingered the ribbon as he held it in his lap and wondered if he could overpower her. Raping her would be satisfying; he started to harden thinking about it. His hand tightened around the ribbon.

"What do you like about long hair? Do you play with it at night, roll around naked in it?" she asked tauntingly, running the fingers of her free hand through her own hair. "Where do you keep all that hair you've so carefully collected? Under your pillow? Maybe you suck your thumb while you're holding it, like a baby and his blanket."

"That's enough," he snapped.

"Oh, no. I'm just getting started," she said. "Bet it really pissed you off when you discovered Rue's hair wasn't real. Did that make you angry? Is that why you did her differently from the others? Is that why you didn't rape her? I suppose you can't get your rocks off with fake hair."

He bolted out of his chair. She took one last poke at him: "'Fiddle-de-dee, fiddle-de-dee. The fly shall marry the bumblebee.' What does that mean, Michaels? Are you the fly or the bumblebee?"

His face turned ashen. "Do I look like a fucking bug?" he asked. He angrily threw his glass overboard, but he held on to the ribbon. "I'm leaving now," he said, his eyes angry slits.

"Don't break my heart," she said, a small smile on her face. Though she had failed to extract anything resembling a confession from him, though she had learned nothing new in the case, she'd won. He'd barged into her home to rattle her and he was the one leaving in an emotional tangle.

"This isn't over, Paris," he said, his eyes locked on hers, his fist wrapped around her hair ribbon. "We still have some things to resolve, you and I. I will be back."

Murphy heard Tripod barking again.

"Paris!" bellowed a male voice from inside the houseboat.

"Out here," she yelled.

Gabe ran through the doors onto the deck with his gun drawn. Behind him were Castro and Dubrowski. Gabe reached for his cuffs. "No," Murphy said, putting her hand on Gabe's arm. "Let him go."

Gabe looked at Michaels's face; Michaels stared back in disdain. "Are you sure you don't want me to fuck him up a little?" Gabe asked. "That pretty mouth is begging to get busted."

"Sign me up for a piece of that," said Dubrowski.

"No," Murphy said. "I just want him out of here."

Gabe stepped out of Michaels's way. Michaels walked through the open patio door past the other two detectives. Castro pursed his lips in a mock kiss as Michaels went by. They heard Tripod barking and then Michaels's SUV squealing out of the parking lot.

"You okay, Murphy?" asked Dubrowski.

"Fine," she said. "Thanks, you guys. Thanks a lot." He and Castro holstered their guns and went back outside.

"What happened in here?" asked Gabe.

Murphy stuffed her gun in the waistband of her jeans and sat in one of the deck chairs. "Nothing happened," she said, shutting her eyes and breathing in the river air.

"Did he give up anything?"

"Jack shit," she said, opening her eyes again.

"Want me to hang around for a while?" asked Gabe. He shoved his gun back in his holster.

"Nah. I'm okay. That asshole won't be back." She noticed her wineglass at her feet. She picked it up and took a long drink. "A low-end California."

"What?"

"Nothing," she said, and emptied the glass.

THIRTY-THREE

Michaels drove home and, after pounding down a couple of tall Scotches, collapsed exhausted into bed. He slept fitfully. He found himself getting progressively less sleep every day. The worries were piling up on him like bricks, and it was taking more and more energy to keep the fly tucked away.

He woke well before dawn with his face buried in his pillow and his sheets kicked into a heap at the foot of the bed. He was still tired. He checked the clock on his nightstand and saw her hair ribbon next to it. He grabbed the ribbon and flopped over on his back. He tried to go back to sleep with the ribbon bunched in his right fist, but instead he stared at the ceiling for twenty minutes. He rolled out of bed, threw the ribbon back on the nightstand and ran down to the basement. He lost track of how many laps he did; he swam until his legs and arms ached and his eyes stung from the chlorine. He went back upstairs, took a long, hot soak and pulled on some clothes. While he was dressing, he glanced out the bedroom window that faced Summit Avenue.

There they were, parked across the street from his house. They were wedged between a couple of other cars, but not hiding themselves. He probably should have expected some sort of tail. Fuck them, he thought angrily. The getaway up north was more and more appealing. Let them tail him all the way to Duluth and beyond. What did he give a shit? Nothing for the cops to see at his lake home, except for his whore wife and her witch mother—and for all he knew they were on the sailboat, tied off somewhere along shore. He still couldn't reach them by phone, or his daughters at camp for that matter.

He called his office and left a message on the machine for his staff, curtly ordering them to reschedule his appointments and surgeries for the next several days. A death in the family, he said; he didn't try for a neat excuse.

From his closet he grabbed a black leather bomber jacket. It got cold around the lake. He walked over to his dresser for his car keys and caught his reflection in the mirror. His eyes were bloodshot and there were dark, puffy rings under them. He resolved to take better care of himself. He'd been denying the fly what it needed and was losing sleep as a result. Now he was nothing but a knot of tired, frustrated nerves. He shut his eyes and deliberately conjured up a satisfying image. "I can still make it happen," he said to himself. "I will make it happen." He opened his eyes, scanned the collection of car keys on his dresser top and scooped up the set for the Porsche. Might as well let them get an unobstructed view. He'd ride with the top down. He wanted to look them straight in the eye and make them fully aware that he could also see them. He pulled open the top dresser drawer, took out a pair of black driving gloves and shoved them into the jacket pockets. From his nightstand, he took her ribbon. He sniffed it; it smelled like her herbal shampoo. He smiled, curled it into a neat circle in the palm of his hand and slipped it into his pants pocket.

He ran to the library for one last essential. He pulled open the bookshelf and walked into the safe room, flipping on the light switch. He wanted a second gun in addition to the Sig, for insurance. He popped open a gun case, eyed his Browning automatic but instead picked out his Smith & Wesson, shoving it in his pocket. He turned around to shut off the lights but before he did, he looked back at the wall safe. He'd stashed the scalpel in there after its last use. He thought about taking it and the hatbox with him.

He walked over to the wall safe, opened it and pulled out the hatbox. He lifted off the cover. The ugly brown braid and the scalpel were both sitting on top, each in its own plastic bag. How had Paris Murphy connected him to Miss Mistake and to the others? She was taunting him. Teasing him. If she had some hard evidence on him, she wouldn't have let him walk away. What he had in his hands would qualify as hard evidence. If the cops ever found the hatbox and its contents, he'd be in some serious shit. An army of uncles and cousins couldn't save his ass then. No. Better to leave the souvenirs home, where they'd be hidden and secure. He reached into his pants pocket, pulled out the circle of hair ribbon and set it on top of his collection. He looked at the ribbon. A taste of things to come. He put the cover back on the box and set the box back in the wall safe. He shut the safe, gave the knob a couple of spins, turned out the lights and shut the door.

He walked to the middle of the library and turned around to study the bookcase. There were no major gaps between the shelves; there was no unevenness in the woodwork. Nothing gave it away, especially if you weren't looking for it. It would take the cops forever to find it. His valuables would stay well hidden. He turned around and left.

Evans Bergen and Pete Sandeen had been parked in front of Michaels's house since five in the morning, relieving the surveillance team that watched the house all through the night and into the early-morning hours. On the seat of the car were an empty doughnut box, crushed juice cartons and balled-up paper napkins smeared with chocolate glaze.

"I can't believe the union isn't gonna fight the chief's bullshit plan," said Bergen, licking glaze off his thumb.

"Which bullshit plan would that be?" asked Sandeen, a union steward. He was a head taller than Bergen, twenty years older, and had a thick head of white hair. "There's so many you've got to be more specific."

"That crap where he's eliminating the lieutenants and captains and replacing them with a handful of commanders. There's no place to advance after you make sergeant. What's the point of bustin' your ass?"

"We filed a grievance," said Sandeen, bumping off his coffee and tossing the empty Styrofoam cup on the seat of the car.

"I know the commanders get paid a hell of a lot more than the lieutenants did, but you can't make it unless you kiss the chief's ass," said Bergen.

"Quit pissing and moaning and join the grievance committee if you want something done," said Sandeen. "Otherwise shut the hell up and let the thing wind its way through the process."

Bergen grumbled.

"What time is it?" asked Sandeen. He was behind the wheel. He punched the dashboard clock with his fist. "I swear to God the clock on every fleet car is busted."

Bergen checked his Dick Tracy wristwatch. "It's almost seven," he said, yawning. "Time flies when you're having fun, don't it?"

"Whoa—that's him!" said Sandeen. They saw Michaels exit his house through the side door and walk calmly but purposefully to his garage. Sandeen turned on the ignition. "The horses are out of the gate," he said as the Porsche darted out of the driveway, heading east down Summit Avenue.

"Nice wheels," said Bergen as the Crown Victoria followed. "What do you suppose those go for?"

"Too much," said Sandeen.

At a stoplight, Michaels turned his head and looked behind him. He made eye contact with Sandeen, gave him a little smile and a wave. He turned back around and slipped on his sunglasses. "He knows we're on his tail," said Sandeen. "Arrogant bastard."

"Big deal," said Bergen.

The light changed and the Porsche pulled away, with the Crown Victoria close behind. "You'd better wake Murphy and Gabe," Sandeen said.

Bergen sifted through the pile of debris on the seat and pulled out the cell phone. "Hope he ain't going far," he said as he punched Murphy's home number.

"Who the hell knows?" said Sandeen. "Life is one long orgy for this guy. Maybe he got a bead on some new whorehouse specializing in longhaired hookers."

"Do you suppose there is such a thing?" asked Bergen.

"Somewhere—probably in L.A.," Sandeen said wisely.

"Yeah, in L.A.," said Bergen, nodding in agreement as he waited for Murphy to answer her phone.

"There's no answer at Murphy's or at Gabe's," he said.

"It's early, but they might be at the cop shop already," said Sandeen. "Give them a try there."

Gabe picked up the call from Bergen; his partner was on her line talking to Michaels's neighbor, Elaine Roth.

"I really should have called yesterday when I saw that composite sketch in the newspaper; it's hard to believe someone you know could do something like that," said Roth. "He looks exactly like that man, and he drives a black Suburban, like the story said."

"We appreciate the tip, Ms. Roth," said Murphy.

"On top of all that, I remembered those scratches I saw on his cheek when I talked to him earlier this week," Roth said in a breathy voice. "He said a cat scratched him. I know for a fact they don't own a cat. The girls are allergic. I started to put two and two together. Then when I heard him tearing out of his driveway early this morning, I knew I couldn't wait any longer."

"Has his behavior been unusual in any other way lately?" asked Murphy. "Have any of his family members or other neighbors mentioned anything to you?"

"He has two daughters and they're both at a soccer camp in Europe," said Roth. "His wife . . ."

"His wife?" said Murphy. "Isn't he separated or divorced?"

"No, no," said Roth. "Although she really should dump him. He drinks like a fish and he's so verbally abusive. They're forever fighting and have nothing in common but their children, and sometimes he seems barely able to tolerate his own daughters. He wanted sons, you know, but she was glad they had girls. She was afraid the boys would turn out like him. That's why she . . ."

Roth hesitated.

"Why she what?" asked Murphy.

"Nothing. Never mind."

"You were saying something about his wife's whereabouts."

"She's still up at their cabin with her mother," Roth said.

"Have you ever been there?" Murphy asked. "Can you tell me where it is?"

"Sure," said Roth. "Jennifer and I have had a couple of good weekends up there."

While Murphy jotted the directions to the cabin in her notebook, Gabe leaned over her desk, scribbled a note on some scrap paper and shoved it in front of her face:

"THE DOC IS ON THE RUN."

"Thanks, Ms. Roth," Murphy said quickly. "We'll call you if we need anything more. Good-bye."

$\int$o where is this place?" asked Gabe after they hit the highway.

"It's outside of a North Shore town called Castle Danger," she said, studying her notebook containing the directions Elaine Roth gave her.

"Castle Danger?"

"Roth said it's named after the formations along the shore and a ship named *Castle* that sank on the rocks."

"But Jesus. Castle Danger?"

"Look, it could be worse."

"How?"

"We could be headed to Climax."

Her cell phone rang. She fished it out of her purse, assuming it was Jack or her mother, and quickly answered it. "Paris Murphy here," she said.

"Hello, lover."

She shivered. "How did you get my phone number?"

"You really shouldn't leave your bills out for anyone to see," he said, his voice dripping with smug pleasure at catching her off guard. "Someone could steal your charge-account numbers."

"I'll be more careful next time," she said. "Won't let any scum into my kitchen."

He laughed. "I miss you already, and we've only been apart twelve hours."

"Then why don't you stop and turn around, save us all a long road trip?"

"Can't do that," Michaels said. "I'm tempted to slow down so you can catch up. On the other hand, I don't want to make this too easy."

"Easy would be boring," she said.

"I assume you're already on the interstate," he said.

"Yeah. Coming up," she said.

"I'll put the coffee on," he said, and hung up.

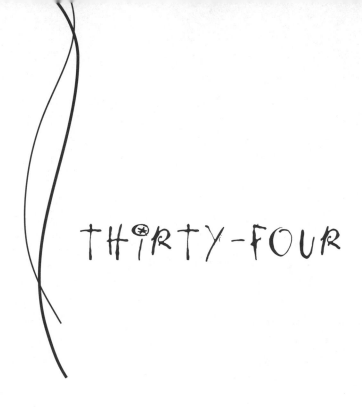

THIRTY-FOUR

The bright Saturday-morning sun quickly burned off the gray mist. Michaels looked below to his right as he entered Duluth from Interstate 35, taking in the city's industrial area and the harbor beyond it: massive ships coming and going with their cargo. Grain elevators. Railroad tracks. Steam pouring from factory stacks. Small, working-class homes in muted colors huddled under towering power lines. Out of Duluth, the highway hugged the Lake Superior shoreline, crossing the rivers running down to the lake. Hardwoods and pines punctuated the shore and the adjacent ridgeline.

He pulled into the marina before stopping at the cabin; his sailboat was still there. It didn't look like it had been taken out since he'd last used it and that angered him. If they weren't out on the boat, why the hell weren't they answering the phone?

The cabin was forty miles north of Duluth outside Castle Danger. The summer home sat atop a hill overlooking the lake. Michaels pulled the Porsche down the driveway; his mother-in-law's silver Mercedes sat the end of the drive. They must be home. He parked behind the Mercedes, yanked off his sunglasses and stepped out of the car.

"Would you look at this shit!" he said aloud. The grounds were low-maintenance by design. Giant hosta lined either side of the driveway with clumps of orange daylilies and yellow black-eyed Susans. Native evergreen and oak trees required nothing in the way of attention. The only real maintenance necessary was lawn care. Rather than hire a garden service, Jennifer insisted they pay some neighbor boys to cut the grass. Apparently she hadn't bothered calling them. The lawn hadn't been touched since he'd left two weeks earlier.

He thought back to that week he had spent at the cabin with his wife and her mother. He'd drunk too much—parts of it were completely obliterated from his memory. He could summon blurry images and faint words to fill in a few of the blanks. He and his wife had had a fight his last night at the cabin. A big one. It started in the house, spilled out into the yard and ended up in the carriage house. Her mother walked in on it. Then the three of them were yelling. What was it about? Something about a bill. He remembered holding it in his hand. A fight over a bill sounded reasonable. She was always spending too much. There was something else, wasn't there?

The front door was unlocked and slightly ajar. That didn't feel right. He pulled the gun out of his pocket, pushed the door open and walked into the house. He stood still in the foyer, listening. Silence. He called out their names. Nothing. He walked through the house filled with arts-and-crafts pieces from the early 1900s. The thump of his shoes on the wood floors seemed amplified by the emptiness of the cabin and stark simplicity of the furniture. He made his way from one room to another.

Almost unconsciously, he ran his hand across the top of an oak sideboard in the dining room. All the dust on his fingers. Strange. Not like his wife to let the housekeeping go like this.

In the study, he critically eyed the surface of a desk that sat under an open window. The early-furniture piece was made of quarter-sawn oak and was one of his favorites, but now the top was marred with water stains. It had rained up at the cabin in the last two weeks and no one had bothered shutting the windows. A breeze pushed out the curtains, made them billow over the desk. He walked over to close the window and looked through it to the water. Whitecaps. A rough day on the lake. He walked into the kitchen. Everything clean, no food left out. He checked the sink. One glass. He picked it up. A Scotch glass, his. Was there any booze left in the cabin? No, he'd finished it all that last night. He set the glass back in the sink and walked out of the kitchen.

His survey of the first floor found nothing missing; there had been no burglars or robbers or other intruders. He slipped the gun back into his pocket and walked upstairs, each footstep producing a creak with its own unique sound. When he reached the top of the stairs, he stopped and again called out their names. No one answered. He inhaled deeply and exhaled slowly. His mind was starting to clear. He continued his solemn inventory of the house, knowing he would not find them but still hoping they were there.

He looked inside his younger daughter's room, her bed mounded with stuffed animals. Children. That struck a cord. The fight had had something to do with children. Had it had to do with his daughters, perhaps some spending on their account? No. That wasn't it.

He walked into the hallway bathroom. Nothing amiss. He pulled back the shower curtain and looked into the stall. Bone-dry, with a spider crawling around a web in one corner. He reached up and swiped it with his hand. They'd been gone long enough for a spider to spin a web. How long does that take? He felt sweat collecting on his forehead. He grabbed some toilet paper and wiped his brow and the back of his neck. He caught his reflection in the mirror. He looked like a lunatic; a lunatic worried about spiders' webs. He dropped the tissue on the counter and quickly walked out of the bathroom, shutting the door behind him.

He poked his head inside each of the other bedrooms. Nothing seemed out of place. All the beds were made. Jennifer did the beds herself, as soon as everyone was up. She said she felt her home was in order if the beds were all made, and they had to have hospital corners.

Hospital. The argument had something to do with a hospital. Was he spending too much time at the clinic? No, she didn't give a shit about that. Something else. It would come to him.

He stopped in the doorway of the master bedroom. Out of the corner of his eye he saw Bee sitting on the edge of the mattress, waiting for him. "Come," she said through her mouth painted with pink lipstick and blood. "Come, Buzzy." He turned his head quickly and she was gone from the bed.

"Leave me alone, Mom," he said tiredly. "Fucking leave me alone." He turned away from the bedroom and went back downstairs.

As he walked through the kitchen toward the back door, a piece of paper caught his eye. A bill or statement sitting on the library table by the back door. He reached for it and paused briefly before picking it up. He knew what it was now; it was a bill from a medical clinic. The fight came back.

It wasn't a miscarriage. His wife had aborted their third child, his son, at a Duluth clinic during a vacation at the cabin with Elaine. She had planned to intercept the bill when it arrived in the cabin mail, but he found it first.

"I'm forty," she said. "I'm too old to have another baby."

"I'm tired," she said. "You're never around to help."

Finally it came out: "I don't want to bring another like you into this world."

That's when he slapped her. She ran from the yard into the carriage house and he followed, drunk and hurt and angry. Behind him ran her hysterical mother, horrified at what her daughter had done, terrified of what he might do in retribution.

Clutching the bill in his right hand, he walked out the back door of the cabin and crossed the yard to the carriage house. He hesitated, and then pushed open the heavy oak side door of the windowless building and stepped inside the blackness. The odor turned his stomach.

He ran back outside, slamming the door shut behind him. He fell to his knees in the overgrown grass and vomited. The acid from his stomach burned his throat on the way up. He continued retching after there was nothing left to bring up, his body vibrating with dry heaves. He didn't bother going back inside the carriage house. He knew they were both dead—his wife and her mother. He had strangled his wife with his bare hands and caved her mother's head in with a shovel as she crouched crying over her daughter's body.

Still kneeling, he dropped his face into the sheet of white paper that had ignited his rampage and wept. He cried not for his loss, for even now he could not pretend he had ever loved her. He cried not for the aborted son, for the child was an abstract thought or dream fragment, and not an infant he had held and loved. He wept only for his own lost body and soul. He was doomed to life in prison and an eternity in hell. It was one thing to kill a collection of whores and sluts and leave their bodies in anonymous public places; that left open the possibility that the acts could be blamed on random strangers. But in his murderous rage, he had sloppily killed his wife and her mother and left them to rot under his own roof. In his intoxicated state, he had even cut his wife's blond hair as a souvenir, adding it to the collection of hair he had tucked away in the hatbox. The evidence against him would be overwhelming. He had handed the cops everything they needed to lock him away forever. He was a drunken idiot and a weakling.

"Stupid! Stupid! Stupid!" he chanted through his sobs.

In his mind, the buzzing drowned out his own cries.

*M*inutes passed. He wiped his eyes with the sleeves of his shirt and slowly rose to a standing position. He dropped the balled-up medical bill into the tall grass. He heard the crashing swells of the lake, and it beat back the buzzing in his head. He shut his eyes and listened, deliberately slowing his panic-stricken breathing to match the calmer pace of the pulsating surf. "I can still do it," he whispered.

He opened his eyes again and started pacing. "Okay. What are my options?" he muttered. "What? What? What?" He paced until he left a flat rectangle in the tall grass. He briefly considered burying the bodies or dumping them in some isolated area in the surrounding woods for the animals to finish. How about the lake? The cold, deep lake. He concluded that he couldn't bring himself to touch the decomposing corpses. Besides, there would be other evidence not so easily disposed of, such as the blood on the floor of the carriage house. From what he could recall, his mother-in-law hadn't died easily.

He remembered the gun. He pulled it out of his pocket and looked at it, running his fingers along the barrel. One pull on the trigger and it was over. Maybe it was the only way they'd ever stop hounding him, the only way to finally silence the fly. Still, it would be an even bigger sin than the one he had committed here, and where would it leave his daughters? He didn't have the stomach for it; he loved his life too much. No. It wasn't an option, now or ever. He shoved the gun back in his pocket.

He had his wealth and his medical talent. He could fight it or flee, or do both. His relatives could help, and his daughters would forgive him in time. They didn't need to know everything anyway. He could tell them it had been an accident or the work of a burglar. How could he explain away the hair collection? Given enough time, could the cops or someone else find it? No. Impossible. Still, he shouldn't have left it behind.

He checked his watch. He'd wasted valuable minutes stewing over his own stupidity. Now there was simply no time to cover his tracks. They'd be here soon. He didn't bother locking up the house. He didn't give one look back to the carriage house as he rolled the Porsche out of the driveway.

THIRTY-FIVE

There it is," Murphy said.

"Got it."

The Crown Victoria pulled up behind the silver Mercedes. "Fuckin' quiet," Gabe said.

Michaels was dead meat: while Murphy and Gabe were on the road, Dubrowski and Castro were conducting an early-morning interview. Although he refused to release details of Michaels's confession, Ambrose was able to identify the man who had assaulted him outside the confessional. The chief had given them the green light to pick up Michaels.

"This isn't his," Murphy said, studying the Mercedes as she stepped out of the car. She peered through the windows. Nothing inside. She touched the hood, ran her fingers over it. "Covered with dust. Dammit! He could be on his way to Canada for all we know."

"Easy," Gabe said. "Let's look around, okay?" He moved a bit stiffly as he stepped out of the car. It had been a long, tense drive, with Murphy vocally second-guessing herself the entire way. Gabe had never seen her this edgy.

"Grass hasn't been cut in a while," Murphy said as they walked toward the house with weapons drawn.

"Some cabin," said Gabe, walking a few steps ahead of her. "Where in the hell is the outhouse? I say it ain't a cabin unless there's an outhouse."

"I see a carriage house," she said.

"That doesn't count."

They reached the top of the front steps and saw that the front door was ajar. Murphy raised her eyebrows and looked at Gabe. He gently pushed it open farther with his left hand and walked through. "We don't have a search warrant," Murphy said under her breath, at the same time stepping in directly behind him.

"Fuck the search warrant," whispered Gabe, looking to his left and right as he went inside. "He invited us."

"Yeah, right. For coffee," Murphy said dryly.

"Nice cabin furniture," said Gabe, surveying the dining room.

Both stopped walking and listened. All they heard was the churning lake. Murphy nodded toward the ceiling, indicating that she planned to look around upstairs. Gabe lifted a hand and they split up.

Murphy went up the stairs and methodically walked through the second floor. The door to each bedroom was wide open. No dresser drawers were pulled open. Nothing seemed out of place. Even the beds were all made. Only one door upstairs was shut; she figured it was the bathroom. She put her ear to the door, held her breath and listened. Not a sound. She gently pushed the door open, walked in and looked around. No one inside. She spotted a wad of tissue on the bathroom counter. She picked it up by the edge. Still damp. She sniffed. His sweat and cologne.

"He was here all right," she told Gabe, who was waiting at the bottom of the stairs.

"He must have left in quite a hurry," said Gabe, returning his gun to its holster. "He didn't even take time to lock up."

"Let's quick check out the carriage house," Murphy said. She slipped her Glock back in her purse.

They walked through the kitchen, out the back door and across the yard. On their way to the carriage house, Murphy noticed a flattened strip of grass and a ball of paper in the middle of it. She bent over and picked it up.

She unfolded it and studied it as they continued walking to the side door of the carriage house.

"Do you think his wife and his mother-in-law are on the run with him?" asked Gabe as he pushed open the heavy oak door. The overpowering stench on the other side of the door hit them in the face.

"No," Murphy said.

Gabe pulled the collar of his shirt over his nose. Murphy dug a kerchief out of her purse and held it to her face. She felt a chill as she worked her flashlight around the room. "Dammit!" she gasped. "All four of them."

"Bastard!" Gabe growled.

"His daughters," Murphy said. Her light rested on two small figures sprawled next to each other, blond hair matted with dried blood. "He even did his daughters."

Cops and sheriff's deputies were crawling all over the cabin and woods by the time he called. This time, she knew who it was when she answered her cell phone. "Hello, lover," he said smoothly.

She resisted the urge to rip into him, played it as cool as he. "I thought you'd *be* here," she said. "I might go dance with someone else."

Michaels laughed.

Gabe was inside the carriage house with the Lake County coroner and his staff. She was outside the side door, standing in the tall grass with the medical statement in her left hand and the phone in her right. "Quite a mess you left here," she said. "It's so out of character for you not to tidy up after yourself."

"What are you talking about?" he asked.

"Come on," she said. "Don't bullshit me. We looked in the carriage house. I got a whiff of your cologne in the cabin."

"Obsession for Men. Like it?"

"I used to," she said.

He laughed again.

"You must have been very hurt, very angry, when you found the clinic bill," Murphy said, trying to muster a sympathetic tone.

"Now you're patronizing me, Paris," he said.

"No, I mean it," said Murphy. She shoved the medical statement into the pocket of her jeans and tromped a path through the tangled grass as she walked back and forth outside the carriage house. She plugged her left ear so she could better hear from her right above the sound of the crashing waves and the television news helicopters overhead. "I don't have kids of my own, so I can only imagine how it would feel to lose a baby. You deserved better." She stopped talking. She heard his breathing. It sounded slightly labored. She deliberated, and then tossed one last piece of well-chosen chum into the water.

"Was it a baby girl?" she asked. "Or was it a boy?"

"A son," he said. "That's why she did it. She didn't want a boy because she knew I did. For years I wanted one. She said she never wanted to bring another like me into the world."

He stopped talking for several seconds and Murphy didn't attempt to fill the silence. She wanted him to do it.

"I hoped to continue the family name," he said. "Wanted someone to share my interests, my life."

"Why did you stay married to her for as long as you did?" she asked.

"It wasn't easy," he said in a low voice. "We stuck it out for Stephanie and Alexandra."

"Your daughters?" she asked.

"Yes," he said. "I'll admit to being a horse-shit husband, but I am not a bad father. I love my daughters . . ."

His voice trailed off with the word *daughters*, as if he were falling asleep midsentence. Murphy thought he sounded tired, genuinely anguished and confused. Very confused. The self-assured sexual demon was slowly slipping beneath the surface, being replaced by a weary, lonely man. "Why don't we meet and talk?" she offered. "How about it? The two of us, over that coffee you promised me."

"Talk about what?" he asked warily.

She took a chance, risked having him hang up on her: "Romann, what does that rhyme mean? Who is the fly and who is the bumblebee?"

His answer was barely audible: "My mother read that rhyme to me."

"Your mother is . . ."

". . . Dead. Killed herself. A long time ago. She was the bee. I pretended she was the bee."

"And you were the fly."

"Yes."

"I'm sorry." Murphy stopped talking for several seconds. Something more had happened between mother and son. Murphy didn't want to probe any deeper. He was already on the edge. She switched gears: "Aren't you tired of all this? Aren't you tired of the sleeping around and paying for sex, the killing and the lying and . . ."

"I want you to know something, Paris," he said, interrupting her. "I want you to know I never meant to . . ."

She pressed the phone hard to her ear. She thought he was going to utter something resembling a confession or an expression of remorse, but he abruptly stopped himself.

"I didn't do it," he said. "I didn't kill them. Someone, a burglar probably, killed the two of them sometime after I left the cabin to go back to . . ."

"Killed the *two* of them?" she asked.

"Yes, dammit! I didn't do it. I don't give a shit if you believe me or not. You don't have anything on me. Nothing."

"We'll see," she said. "We're searching your house back in St. Paul right now."

"I think it's safe to say you won't find a thing," he said.

"What about the hair?" she asked.

He paused, then laughed. "As I said, it's safe to say you'll come up empty-handed."

"We'll catch up with you eventually," she said. "You can't run forever."

"I don't plan to," he said.

"Romann . . ."

"Don't try to find me, Paris," he said. "I'm leaving the country. Remember, *vita brevis, ars longa.*"

"What the hell does that mean?" she asked.

He hung up.

Gabe came out of the carriage house and ran to her side.

"Him?" he asked.

"Who else?" she said.

"We'll trace it," he said.

"He's on his way to Canada," she said. "I know he is." She slipped the cell phone back in her purse.

"We've got checkpoints set up all along the highway," Gabe said. "The sheriff sent deputies to the marina, in case he slips past them to get to his sailboat. We're bringing in some dogs."

"He's smart," she said. "He'll get across and disappear."

"We've alerted the border cops," Gabe said. "We'll get him."

"We're gonna lose him," she said. "We've already lost him."

"Murphy . . ."

"Another thing," she said. "I think he's completely lost it. Completely."

"Shit. What makes you say that? The pile of bodies he left behind?"

"I don't think he has a handle on exactly what went on here," she said, nodding toward the carriage house.

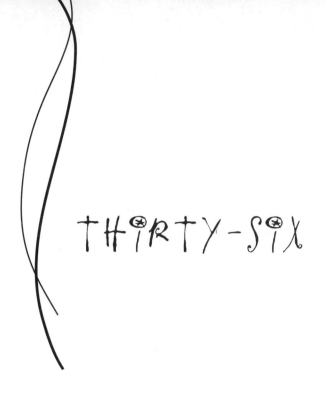

THIRTY-SIX

The phone call was traced to International Falls; Murphy figured he was well into Canada by that night. Dogs. Helicopters. State troopers up and down the highway. Border checks. All turned up nothing. Over Murphy's protests, Christianson told the two detectives to forgo a trip to the border and stay in the Duluth area to help the local cops process the murder scene.

Murphy and Gabe trudged soaked and exhausted up the steps of their cabin at eleven o'clock Sunday, their second night in Castle Danger. The temperature had dropped and the wind had picked up. The drizzle had matured into a steady rain. The cabin was one of six that sat atop a steep hill at the water's edge. The collection of log homes was the only tourist accommodation in Castle Danger. Gabe and Murphy had an end cabin, with the woods on one side of them. By the time they'd come in for the night, the interiors of all the other cabins were dark.

The instant she flicked on the lights her cell phone rang; she started and looked at Gabe. "Want me to take it?" he asked, holding out his hand.

She shook her head and reached into her purse for the phone.

Christianson: "You two pull up stakes and come back in the morning," he said.

"Chief?"

"Michaels is long gone and there's no point in you and Gabe hanging around," Christianson said. "The Lake County sheriff can wrap up without you." Murphy thought he sounded exhausted and stressed-out.

"What about Canada?" she asked.

"The authorities there have a handle on it," he said.

"The hell they do," she said. "Let me and Gabe go up."

"Forget about it. I want the two of you back at the station."

"Chief . . ."

"You've got plenty to keep you busy right here," he said. He hung up.

"Fuck," she said. She shoved the phone back in her purse and threw it on a couch. She plopped down next to it and put her face in her hands.

"Murphy?"

"He wants us back in St. Paul," she said through her fingers.

"You okay?"

She lifted her face out of her hands and nodded. "Yeah. Just tired." She rubbed her arms. "Jesus, it's freezing in here. What do you say we start a fire and warm the place up?" She stood up and shuffled over to the stone fireplace along the front-room wall. She pulled some dried, split logs and old newspapers from the wicker basket next to the fireplace. She stacked the logs in the hearth, shoved some newsprint in between a couple of them and struck a match to the paper. "I don't get him," she said as she kneeled in front of the fire.

"Who?"

"Christianson."

"Let it go," Gabe said as he rubbed his wet head with a kitchen towel.

"He's acting like a dick in the biggest case we've ever had, and I'm supposed to let it go."

"Let it go for tonight. We've got a roof over our heads, a roaring fire and a six-pack of beer. What else do we need? I suppose I could have picked up another six-pack, but I figured you weren't a big beer drinker so . . ."

"Gabe, never mind the beer," she said, grabbing a poker out of the basket to jab the logs. "We forgot the food. I don't know about you, but I haven't eaten all day. I'm starving."

"I'm kind of hungry, too," he said, tossing the towel in the sink. "I'll run out for pizza." He grumbled as he checked his pants pockets for the keys to the Crown Victoria. "I suppose I should fill up the tank while I'm in town, too." He walked through the kitchen.

"If you smoke in the car, roll down the windows," she yelled after him.

"It's raining out," he said.

"Fine," she said. "Go." She waved him away. He exited out the cabin door, shutting it tightly behind him.

She propped the poker against the wall and stayed kneeling in front of the fire. She shut her eyes and listened to the surf as the blaze baked her face. She concentrated, trying to read the lake's rhythm. It seemed every seventh wave was a big one that dashed against the bedrock beneath the cabin. She counted again. Yes. Every seventh one. Then she heard a splash that seemed out of sync. Perhaps she only imagined there was a pattern. She started counting again. On the fifth wave, she heard the door in the cabin's kitchen open. Against her back, she felt a chilly gust from the outside. "What did you forget now, Gabe?" she asked tiredly without opening her eyes.

From behind, a large hand clamped over her mouth and a muscular arm snaked tightly around her waist. She opened her eyes wide and pulled frantically at the arm as she felt herself being yanked quickly to her feet. "Hello, lover," he whispered into her ear. "I dropped by for a visit on my way back home."

He pushed her against the cabin wall next to the fireplace, flattening his body against her back. He bit hard on her neck while she struggled, her angry protests muffled by his left hand.

"Are you cold?" he breathed. "Why not let me warm you from the inside out." He forcefully ground his pelvis into her back. His right hand reached around from behind, slipped under her shirt and bra, and roughly cupped her right breast. "Your nipples are hard, lover," he murmured. "Could it be I excite you?"

She turned her head. He'd colored his hair brown. She writhed and he crushed her even harder against the cabin wall. She felt as if all the oxygen was being pressed out of her body. His breath, reeking of whiskey, made her sick to her stomach. She tried to bite his hand; he was wearing leather gloves. He laughed. "I'm ready for your bullshit this time, Paris," he said hoarsely. "It's useless." He groaned as he rhythmically rubbed his pelvis against her. He released her breast and slipped his right hand into the front of her pants. She felt his fingers under her panties, against her skin. Into her ear he whispered those words. Strange words. "The fly shall marry the bumblebee." She knew he was about to move in for the kill.

He eased his body off hers slightly, giving him more maneuvering space. She discovered that her left arm was loose, no longer pinned tightly against the cabin wall. She reached over with outstretched fingers and snatched the fireplace poker resting against the wall next to their bodies. Gripping it tightly in her fist, she jammed it down as hard as she could into his instep. She felt it hit pay dirt through his athletic shoes.

"Bitch!" he snarled. He released her and stumbled backward. She whirled around, grabbed the poker with both hands and swung, catching the side of his head. He grunted and fell flat on his back.

She raised the poker to stab him in the chest as he was sprawled on the floor, but he wrapped both hands around the tip and yanked it away from her. It clattered to the floor next to him. She tried to run past him, but he rolled onto his stomach and lunged for her ankles. She fell flat on her face with his arms locked around her legs. She extracted one foot and slammed the bottom of her shoe into his face. He howled and grabbed his nose.

She scrambled to her feet, ran through the kitchen and threw open the cabin door. She tripped down the wet, wooden cabin steps and fled through the dark, with the rain cutting her face and the waves roaring in her ears. She ran toward the neighboring cabin, setting her sights on the light cast by a wall sconce mounted next to its door.

He was on her heels. He tackled her and they both tumbled down the rocky hill to the icy water's edge.

He stood up, blood oozing out of his nose. She rose to her knees and tried to stand in the surf, but stumbled. She felt something warm and wet trickling down her forehead. He grabbed her by her hair and pulled her to a standing position, only to slap her hard across the face and knock her back down onto the rocky shore. "Get up, bitch, so I can hit you again!" he hollered above the waves.

"Are you crazy?" she screamed.

"Fuck yeah!" he yelled, and pulled something out of his jacket pocket. Over the sound of the waves, she heard a crack. In the glow cast by a yard light outside her own cabin, Murphy could make out what was in his hands. Her heart sank. A gun.

He fired another shot over her head. "Don't!" she screamed. "Don't shoot!" She managed to get up on all fours on the shore while he stood over her at the water's edge, his back to the lake. Her feet and hands were growing numb.

"Come on," he growled as he pointed the pistol toward her head. "You can do better than this!"

Count the waves, she told herself. Count the waves.

"You disappoint me! This is way too easy."

That was five, she thought.

"I like you like this, on the ground, like a dog! Maybe we should do it doggie style."

That was six, she thought.

"Or maybe I should blow your fucking brains out!"

She paused patiently. Now! she told herself. She charged forward like a linebacker and rammed him hard below the knees as the seventh wave roared up on shore behind him. Between the force of the wave and her hit, he lost his footing and toppled down into the water. She heard a thud and hoped his head had hit a rock. She sprinted away as the surf boiled over him.

As she crawled up the rocky hill in the rain, blood dripping from a gash in her forehead, Murphy prayed that Michaels had drowned.

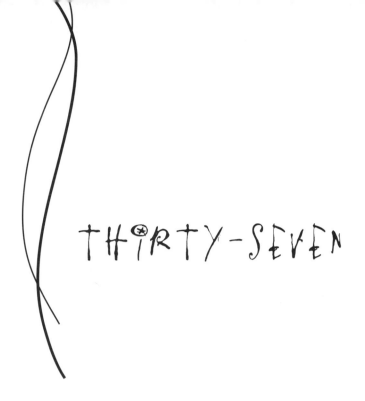

THIRTY-SEVEN

They found a beat-up truck down the road from the log-cabin resort. Michaels had driven up to International Falls after fleeing Castle Danger, and then swung back down through the Iron Range, trading in the Porsche along the way. Murphy and Gabe couldn't figure out why he'd returned, other than for revenge.

She was at work by Thursday, with stitches in her forehead.

"Nothing," Murphy said, hanging up the phone.

"That's not a surprise," Gabe said. "Superior doesn't burp up bodies until it's good and ready. Don't worry. Lake County said they'd call us and they will."

She stood up and walked to Gabe's desk. The dark rings under her eyes troubled him. "You came back too soon," he told her.

"I'm fine, really."

"Still having nightmares?" he asked in a low voice.

"No," she said.

"He's gone, Murphy. You have to believe that."

"He's resourceful," she said.

"He's dead," Gabe said.

"He knows the North Shore," she said. "He knows how to swim."

"He knows. He knows. He knows. Now all Michaels knows is the bottom of the lake." Gabe stood up, grabbed her by the elbow and pulled her toward the conference room. Castro and Dubrowski, both standing by the water cooler, watched them go.

"She's losing it, I tell ya," Castro said, shaking his head.

"Paranoid," said Dubrowski.

Gabe steered her into the conference room ahead of him. He saw Castro and Dubrowski staring and whispering. He flipped them the bird and shut the door.

"Why won't you believe?" Gabe asked.

"He could be hiding," she said.

"We looked, the cops up there looked," he said.

"So where's the body?" she asked. She folded her arms across her chest. "Show me the body."

"He's fish food," Gabe said. He sighed and sat down on one of the chairs. He shut his eyes and ran his fingers through his hair. "You're giving him way too much credit. He wasn't sane enough to save himself. He was flipped out. All that fly and bee bullshit."

"Crazy people can't swim?" she said, and walked over to the windows to look outside at the morning sun ricocheting off the cars on the freeways.

"You need some time off; you need a vacation," Gabe said. "Why don't you and Jack take a little trip? You've been talking about going back to New Orleans. Throw some shit into a suitcase and go."

"Louisiana in June?"

"Okay. Bad idea this time of year." He looked at her back, expecting her to turn around and say something. She stood staring out the windows. "How about you two driving to my fishing shack in Hayward and kicking back on the lake for a week?" he offered. "I've got electricity up there now. Television. VCR."

She didn't answer.

"You and your hubby could rent some porn flicks and screw your brains out."

No response.

"Paris!"

"Huh? What did you say?"

"Might as well use some of that comp time you've got on the books before Slick gets on your ass about it," he said. "How many weeks have you got?"

A knock at the door. "Yeah?" Gabe yelled.

Castro opened it a crack and poked his head into the room. "Chief wants you guys. Pronto."

"Speak of the devil," Gabe said, getting up from the chair. "Murphy . . ."

"Coming," she said, turning around and following him out.

Wrongful death?" Gabe sputtered. "You have fucking got to be kidding!"

"We knew this lawsuit was coming," said Christianson. "They're trying to clear up the family name."

"What about the family he slaughtered?" asked Gabe. "What about his wife and her mother and those little girls?"

"Michaels's relatives are claiming we got it all wrong, that someone else killed them. A burglar or whatever," said Christianson. "They're launching their own investigation."

Murphy laughed. "Their *own* investigation?" she said. "That'd be hilarious if it wasn't so disgusting. They're buying Michaels an alibi. Postmortem. I could puke."

Gabe stood up and walked back and forth in front of Christianson's desk. "Don't let them near the house," he said.

"It's still sealed tight," said Christianson. "I just wish we'd found more inside. We can certainly pin the priest's assault on Michaels, and of course the attack on Murphy. The deaths in Castle Danger are not our problem."

"'Not our problem,'" Gabe said dryly.

"You heard me correctly, Nash. *Not our problem!*" Christianson snapped. "We needed more to tie Michaels to the murders here and across the river."

"What about Finch's crucifix?" asked Gabe. "What about . . ."

"The hair," said Murphy. "We needed the hair, and we didn't find it."

"No question the hair would have clinched it," said Christianson.

Christianson's secretary knocked once and opened the door. "Your wife's on line two. Says it's urgent."

Christianson frowned and put his hand on his phone. "I have to take this," he said to Gabe and Murphy. "We'll talk more later."

Murphy and Gabe walked out of the chief's office. "You're right about one thing," Gabe grumbled in the hallway.

"That one thing would be?"

"Slick acting like a dick on this case. It's way more than his usual dick behavior. 'You heard me correctly, Nash.' Fuck him."

"Who died?" asked Castro as they walked into Homicide. Gabe ignored him and sat down at his desk.

"Too many loose ends," mumbled Murphy as she sat down at hers. "Too many holes." She grabbed the file, staring at the tab before opening it. Michaels, A. Romann. She flipped it open and shuffled through the mound of paper inside of it. She found a scrap of paper and puzzled over it. Four words. It suddenly came to her when she'd scribbled them. She picked up the phone and punched in a number.

"Sister Ella Marie?"

"How are you feeling, Paris?"

"Fine. Better," Murphy said. "Sister, how's your Latin these days?"

"You should know better than to ask that of an old school nun," DuBois said, laughing.

"Well, mine's a little rusty," Murphy said. She struggled to read her own handwriting. "What does *vita brevis ars* . . ."

"*Vita brevis, ars longa,*" said DuBois.

"That's it," Murphy said.

"Life is short, art is long," said DuBois.

"What the hell does that mean?" Murphy asked.

"Pardon?" said DuBois.

"Sorry, Sister. Does that phrase have some deeper meaning?"

"It means what it implies," DuBois said. "That art outlives humanity."

"Art outlives humanity," Murphy repeated.

"What's this all about?"

"Tell you later. It has to do with a case."

"Sounds interesting."

"That's one word for it. Well, thanks, Sister."

"Take care, dear," DuBois said. "Stop by and see me sometime."

"I will. 'Bye," Murphy said, hanging up the phone.

"Art, art, art," Murphy repeated, tapping a pencil on her desk as she stared at the piece of paper cradled in her other hand.

"Hey, Gabe, Murphy, wanna get some lunch?" asked Castro as he headed for the door.

"There's a new Coney Dog joint down the street," said Dubrowski behind him.

Gabe stood up to join them. Murphy waved them off. "Not hungry," she said. "Thanks anyway." She tucked the slip of paper back in Michaels's file and continued paging through the folder. The three men walked out, leaving her alone.

She took the file home with her.

"How's your head doing?" asked Jack.

"Stop asking, would you?" she said. "It's fine."

Murphy and Jack sat on her houseboat deck. Though early evening, it was still warm out. The mosquitoes were thick. A citronella candle burned on the table between their chairs. Murphy grabbed the can of insect repellant and sprayed her legs and arms.

Jack set his beer bottle down on the deck and leaned over from his chair to kiss her. She stiffened. "Baby, what's wrong?" he asked. She didn't answer, didn't look at him, sipped her wine. "It's those dreams, isn't it?" he asked. "You're still having them."

"I wish you didn't have to go out of town," she said.

"You know I can't get out of this conference," he said. "I'll be back in time for the Fourth."

"Yeah, yeah," she said, finishing her wine.

"Want me to pour you another glass?" he asked.

"You think getting drunk might help?" she asked.

"Can't hurt," he said.

"Then bring it on," she said, lifting her glass.

He poured her another, set down the wine bottle and stood up. "I'm sorry, baby. Gotta go," he said. He bent over and kissed her on the cheek. "If it's a horseshit conference, I'll slide out and take an early flight back."

"Fat chance," she said. He turned and left. She heard his car pull out of the parking lot, and the sound depressed her.

She sipped the wine and watched the river. A party barge floated by. The railing along the deck was strung with blinking white lights. The sound of laughter and music drifted across the water. She kept swatting; the repellant wasn't doing much. "Damn skeeters," she mumbled. She blew out the candle, stood up and went inside with her wine.

She took a long shower, scrubbing hard to get the oily bug dope off her skin. She rested one hand against the shower stall, enjoying the hot water running down her hair and face and body. She thought about picking up the phone and calling him, to talk. She chastised herself for thinking about him. She stood in the shower until the water turned cold. She turned it off, toweled dry and wrapped herself in her robe. She walked over to the phone on her nightstand. She hesitated for an instant and then picked it up. Punched in his number.

"Paris. I was thinking about you. Are you alone?"

"Yes."

"Where's Jack?" asked Erik.

"Chicago. Medical conference."

"He shouldn't leave you alone," he said.

"I'm fine," she said. "He's got a life."

"Do you want me to come over?"

She paused. So tempting. She was lonely and more nervous about the night than she wanted to admit. It would be her first night alone since getting back from Castle Danger.

"Why don't I come get you, if you don't feel right about me spending time there."

"No," she said.

"Then what do you want me to do?" he asked. "Tell me."

She wanted his company but felt guilty, and at the same time resented the guilt itself.

"Paris?"

"Come over." She hung up and tossed the phone at the foot of the bed.

He pushed her down onto the bed and peeled her clothes off so quickly, she didn't have time to help. She took it slower, moving her hands up his chest as she slipped off his T-shirt. She gasped the first time he entered her. "You are so tight," he said appreciatively.

It had been a long time since she had made love to anyone other than Jack; Erik's body seemed so foreign to her, and that made it exciting. They were both athletic, a tangle of tanned and sinewy arms and legs and backs. He lost his hands in her hair. She ran her hands over his back and shoulders. Muscular and smooth.

Her mind was empty and clear as long as they were in motion. When they were finished, it all came rushing back. Fears about Michaels. Fears about her marriage. A new layer of guilt over what she'd just done. She stared at the ceiling as if she were watching some movie only she could see.

"He really did a number on your head, that bastard," Erik said. He was on his side, staring at her troubled face. Her clock radio was turned low, to a jazz station. The sax was barely audible, competing with the sound of a speedboat cruising down the river.

"I'm fine," she said. Her voice was emotionless. She rolled away from him to face the patio window.

"Stop saying that," Erik said. "You sound like a busted tape recording. 'I'm fine. I'm fine. I'm fine.' You aren't fine. Your head is all messed up."

"Nothing's wrong with my head," she said, still facing the window.

"Great. You invite me over, we screw and then I have a conversation with your back. Forget this shit. I don't need this." He sat up and swung his feet over the edge of the bed.

She turned her head. "Where are you going?" she asked, immediately hating how needy that question sounded.

"I think I should leave you and Michaels alone to work out your differences," he said.

"What do you want me to do?" she asked angrily. She sat up in bed.

"Talk about it," he said, swinging his legs back on top of the bed and turning to face her. "Look at me and talk about it. Talk to me."

"Okay, Mr. Therapist. You want to hear it?" she said. She grabbed the pillow from his side of the bed and hugged it in front of her. "I haven't slept well since I got on this case. I wake up in the morning dead tired. When I do sleep, I have these weird-ass dreams. They started even before Castle Danger. Now I have them twice a night, sometimes more. Twisted dreams. He's on top of me, raping me. Did I share enough, or do you want more?"

She tossed the pillow on the floor, swung her legs over the bed and hopped out. She ran into the bathroom and turned on the faucet. She splashed cold water on her face until it felt numb, and then scooped water into her mouth until she felt full. He walked up behind her and slipped his arms around her waist. She resisted the urge to shove his arms off her.

"I'm sorry," he said, his face buried in her neck. "I didn't mean to push you. You're acting so strange, so distracted. I'm worried about you."

She clutched the edge of the bathroom sink to steady herself. "You're right," she said lowly. "I'm not fine, but I don't know how to fix it. I mean, I'm so obsessed I brought the file home. Tell me that isn't sick."

"All right. Then let's use that. Let's sit down and go through the file together," said Erik. "He's not a demon, but you've made him out to be one. Let's pick him apart."

"An autopsy," she said.

He opened a beer and she poured herself another glass of wine. They sat on the bedroom floor—he in his boxers and she in her robe—and rifled through the thick file. Each took possession of a stack of paperwork. For several minutes neither said a word. The patio doors leading to the deck were open. No breeze blew in, but the mosquitoes had thinned out. A motorboat sped by and then another. A busy night on the river.

"Jennifer," said Erik, breaking the silence between them. He took a sip of beer as he held up the sheet of paper.

"What?" asked Murphy. She put down some crime-scene photos.

"I didn't know his wife's name," he said.

"Yeah. Jennifer," she said, grabbing a forensic report.

"His daughters?" he asked.

"Stephanie and Alexandra."

"Oh yeah, here they are," he said, picking up two photos, their most recent school portraits. "Pretty blond girls." He set them down and held up a yellowed newspaper clipping.

"What's this?"

"We have a file on his mother. Found dead in the swimming pool."

"You don't think he killed her, too?"

"No, no. Suicide."

Murphy picked up the wrinkled scrap of paper with the Latin scribbled on it, set it down on the floor in front of her and smoothed it out with her hands. *"Vita brevis, ars longa,"* she mumbled, taking a sip of wine.

"Arthur," Erik said, holding up a copy of Michaels's driver's license.

"What did you say?" she asked.

"Romann was his middle name. His first name was Arthur. Didn't you know that?"

"Yeah. I never gave it much thought. He used the initial. Lot's of people go by their middle names because they hate their first."

"All the kids at school would have called him Art the fart," Erik said, chuckling.

"Art," she repeated. She stared at the scrap of paper in front of her and smiled a tight, thin smile. "Life is short, art is long."

"What?" Erik asked.

"He's still alive," she said. "Michaels is still alive."

"Paris?"

"When I talked to him over the phone, after we found the bodies in the carriage house, he told me to remember *'Vita brevis, ars longa.'* That's what he said."

"Forgive me; my high school didn't offer Latin," Erik said. He stared at her.

"It means art outlives us," she said. "Only he didn't mean sculptures and paintings. He meant Art with a capital *A*."

"Paris. Come on. That is a stretch," Erik said, dropping the papers he'd been studying.

"You don't know him," she said. "I do."

"*Did*, Paris. *Did*. You *did* know him, and not for that long. Now he's dead! Come on. Give it a rest."

"He faked his own death," she said. "Maybe that's why he came back, so we could see him die."

"He drowned," Erik said. "You're the one who pushed him in!"

"He was a good swimmer," she said. "He could have followed the shore-line and crawled up into the woods."

Erik stared at her incredulously, and his disbelief infuriated her. "Why don't you go home?" she snapped. She stood up. She swayed a bit. Her head was light from the wine and the anger. Her face felt hot, flushed.

"Paris," Erik said, looking up at her from the pile of papers on the floor.

"Go," she said.

He stood up and stepped toward her. He lifted his arms to grab her shoul-ders and she pushed them down. "Please," she said. She picked his jeans and shirt up off the floor and threw them at him. "Get dressed and go home."

This time the bright, otherworldly light was missing. The room was dark, a change from the earlier visitations. The only thing that was casting light was his face as he bent over her. As before, she couldn't make out his features right away. They were a blur. He again flashed a knife in front of her face, slipped the blade under the bodice of her thin nightgown and slit it down the middle with one pass. He crawled on top of her and turned his head to one side, burying his face in her hair. This time he wore no clothing, nothing to melt away as in the previous dreams. The weight of his body was unbearable. She could feel his heart beating, matching the rhythm of her own.

She struggled to see his features. "Look at me," she said. "Look at me." He laughed into her hair; his breath felt like steam from a hot iron. She fought hard. The hardest she'd ever fought. She beat his back with her fists and clawed at it with her nails. This time it seemed to work. He lifted his body off hers slightly, and she was relieved. She looked into Michaels's gray eyes. But they weren't human eyes. They were the bug eyes of a fly. He put his mouth on her cheek and licked her. She could smell him, smell his cologne.

She screamed and bolted upright in bed, awake and alert. She could still smell him. She felt the side of her face. Wet, from his tongue. He's really here, she thought. He's on my boat.

She was dizzy and her head was throbbing. Too much wine. She fumbled around the top of her nightstand for her cell phone. She knocked over an empty wineglass. It shattered on the wood floor. She heard muffled ringing. On her hands and knees she crawled around on the bed until she found it buried in the covers. She froze with it in her hand, then slowly lifted the phone to her ear.

"Hello," he said. "Sorry to wake you from such a dead sleep."

"Where are you?" she asked. "Where?" With her free hand she yanked open the nightstand drawer and reached inside for her purse. Not there.

He laughed. "Come find me," he said. "I want you to find me."

She slid off the bed and went for the light switch, but stopped. This was her boat. She could get around better in the dark than he, but she needed her gun. She threw the phone on the bed and ran toward the closet. She tripped over his file in the middle of the floor, scattering its contents. She yanked open the closet door and felt around for her purse. Still couldn't find it. She felt along the closet walls, pressing against her suits and dresses and knocking them down. No one there. She needed a weapon. Something. Her hand touched a wooden hanger. She wrestled it from a knot of clothes. Better than nothing.

She picked up the phone. "Where are you?" she said. He laughed again. "Why aren't you dead?" she asked. He stopped laughing; he didn't like that question.

Murphy ran down the steps to the galley. She heard a paddleboat go by. Clearly heard it. She looked into the living room. The patio doors to the deck were wide open. She was sure she'd shut them before going to bed. She slowly walked toward the open doors, looking to her left and right around the galley and living room.

She remembered the wooden dowel she kept in the track of the patio doors for extra security. She set the phone and the wooden hanger on the galley counter. She walked over to the patio door, bent over and picked up the rod sitting on the floor next to the track. The pole was the size of a broom handle; it felt good and solid in her hand. She stepped out onto the deck. She gripped the rod with both hands, ready to swing it like a bat. The moon illuminated the deck; there was no one there. She heard thumping along the boat's waterline. Murphy held her breath, walked to the railing and looked down. A large log was floating in the black water, bumping against the boat. Slowly, she exhaled. She stepped back inside, shut the door behind her and locked it. She retrieved the phone and raised it to her ear.

"Still there, Michaels?" Murphy said.

"This is taking way too long," he said. "I'm getting bored with this game. Maybe I should come find you. Come fuck you. Fuck you hard, the way you like it."

"Don't do me any favors . . . Art," she said. "Or should I call you fly boy?"

"You're too smart for your own good," he said. "Don't you know dumb women live longer? It's a medical fact."

"Why did you come back?" she asked.

"Be it ever so humble . . . ," he said. He laughed loudly. He sounded different, more unhinged, even hysterical. He kept laughing. She took the phone away from her ear to try to hear where his laugh was coming from. Nothing. She looked up at the ceiling, straining to listen. She thought she heard creaking. Was he still in her bedroom? She lifted the phone back to her ear. He'd finally stopped laughing. She heard only his breathing. Keeping the phone pressed to her ear, she set the dowel down on the galley counter and pulled open a kitchen drawer. She felt around until her fingers touched the handle of her largest knife. She lifted it out.

She took the stairs back up. She walked slowly, with the phone in one hand and the knife in the other. When she reached her bedroom, she threw the cell phone on the bed and walked into the master bathroom, her right arm raised and ready to stab. With her left hand she grabbed the edge of the closed shower curtain. She took a breath and ripped it down. Plastic curtain rings clattered to the floor. No one there.

She walked to the patio doors leading to the deck off her bedroom. She grabbed the handle and slid the door open. She poked her head outside. Nothing. She slid the door shut and locked it.

She reached for her phone on the bed, lifted it to her ear. He'd hung up. She dropped the knife on the bed and punched in Gabe's phone number. Her hands were shaking. "Gabe," she whispered into the phone.

"Murphy?"

"He's on my boat."

"What?" asked Gabe.

"Michaels is on my boat," she said. "Or at least he was."

"Be right over," he said.

She heard something downstairs. Footsteps. She picked the knife up again. "Hurry," she said into the phone. "Please." She heard Tripod barking next door; stranger on the dock.

Every light in the houseboat was on and Murphy's living room and galley were filled with plainclothes and uniformed cops. They'd gone through every closet and cabinet, looked under and behind furniture. They'd roused neighbors on each side of Murphy to make sure the caller hadn't taken refuge on their decks. They'd waved their flashlights under the cars in the parking lot and tromped around the bushes lining the lot.

Murphy and Gabe stood alone in her bedroom. He was in sweatpants, sandals and a white T-shirt turned inside out. "Are you sure someone was here?" Gabe asked. He saw Michaels's file and its contents scattered in the middle of her bedroom floor and crouched down to pick it up.

"What a stupid question!" she snapped.

He sighed, threw the folder on the end of her bed and looked at her. Barefoot and in her robe. Hair like a nest of black snakes around her face. Then there was the knife on her bed. The broken wineglass next to the nightstand. The torn shower curtain in a heap in the bathroom. What the hell was she doing with Michaels's file all over her bedroom floor? He didn't even want to ask. If she wasn't a cop, thought Gabe, she'd be cuffed in the back of a squad headed to the psyche ward.

She walked out onto the deck and he followed her. "You've been having these dreams," Gabe said. He waved a moth away from his face. "Mix in a little too much wine and that bedtime reading you brought home from the cop shop, and you've got a ghost lurking around your boat."

"I did not dream this up," she said. "I am not drunk and I never said it was a goddamn ghost! Didn't you hear a single word I said? Michaels was here. Michaels. On my boat. He left and ran down the dock. Tripod was barking."

Sandeen walked into the bedroom and through the open patio doors. "Bergen found your husband's cell phone in the parking lot," he said. "Figure some pervert stole it from your hubby's car and then used it to rattle you. The asshole hit redial and lucked out, maybe watched you while he was jacking off in the bushes. Probably dropped it and ran when he heard us coming."

"So the dog was barking at someone in the lot," said Gabe.

"He doesn't bark unless there's a stranger on the dock," she said.

Sandeen's eyes met Gabe's.

"Get prints," she said. She turned her back on the two men and looked out at the Mississippi. She knew what they were thinking; she knew what she looked like. Cops laugh and tell stories when they get back to the station from calls like this. Calls where crazy women living alone see bogey men in their bedrooms.

"Sure. We'll get prints," Sandeen said tiredly. "Whatever you want, Murphy. Whatever you say. It's your show." Sandeen left them alone on the deck and went back downstairs.

"I know it was him," she said, as much to herself as to Gabe. She suddenly realized that she had a hangover. She leaned against the railing with both hands and focused on the downtown lights lining the waterfront across the river. "He was here, on this boat. He didn't get the phone from Jack's car. He took it right off my kitchen counter."

"Get a grip, Murphy," Gabe said sternly, folding his arms across his chest. "There's no way in hell it was Michaels who called you. No fucking way. You got an obscene phone call, a heavy breather getting his rocks off. That's all."

"You're wrong," she said. Gabe sighed, but didn't say anything in response.

She brushed a mosquito off her cheek. The night air felt like a sauna and smelled like dead fish. Under her robe, she could feel beads of sweat trickling down between her breasts. She felt like taking another shower, a cold one.

"Let's check his house tomorrow," she said.

"Why?" Gabe asked.

"Be it ever so humble," she said softly.

"What?"

"Humor me," she said.

"Jesus. You don't think he's there, do you? " Gabe asked.

"I think he might have stopped there, tried to get in, retrieve something. I'm sure he's long gone after tonight's little game. He'd be too smart to hang around. If we can find evidence that he's alive . . ."

"He's not," Gabe interrupted.

She took her hands off the rail, squared her shoulders and walked inside. Gabe followed her. "If we don't find shit, I'll keep my paranoid delusions to myself from now on," she said. "Deal?"

"Deal," Gabe said. "Now go back to bed. Try to get some sleep. I'll have a couple of uniforms hang in the parking lot until their shift ends."

"Don't bother," she said. "Thank everyone for me and then get them the hell off my boat. Tell them the nutty, drunk bitch has settled down." She shut the patio door, locked it and gave it a pull to make sure it was locked.

Gabe started to leave, but stopped at the foot of the bed to pick up the knife. "How about I put this away for you?" he said, eyeing the massive blade.

"Top drawer, to the left of the sink," she said. She walked over to the broken wineglass and bent down to pick up the pieces. The room started spinning. She grabbed the edge of the nightstand and closed her eyes.

"Did you find your gun?" he asked.

"Yeah," she said, without looking up.

"Where was it?"

"In my purse, under the bed. Right where I left it. Why? You want to take that away from me, too?"

"Don't be a smart ass," Gabe said. "What about Michaels's file? Through with it?"

"Take it," she said. "I've had enough of him for tonight."

"Right about that," Gabe mumbled. He picked the folder up, tucked it under his arm and walked down the stairs.

"Lock the living-room patio door on your way out and put that wood rod in the track," she yelled after him. "It's on the kitchen counter." She tossed the broken glass into a wastebasket next to the nightstand and then grabbed the edge of the wastebasket, fearing she was going to vomit. She stood up slowly and held her forehead.

Bergen was waiting at the bottom of the stairs, smirking. Gabe wanted to punch him. "Jesus Christ," Bergen whispered, eyeing the blade in Gabe's hand. "Look at the size of that mother."

Gabe threw the knife in a drawer and dropped the wood rod into the patio door track.

Bergen shook his head. "A butcher knife. A bat. What the fuck did she need us for?"

"Shut the hell up and let's go," Gabe said.

"What's that file under your arm?" asked Bergen, following Gabe outside.

"None of your business."

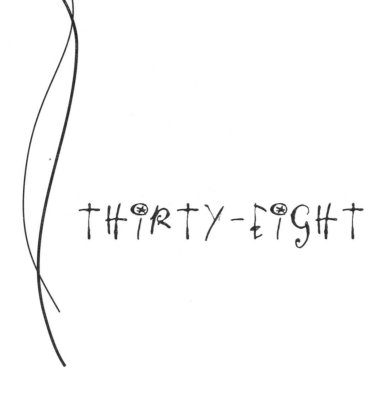

THIRTY-EIGHT

Unreal," said Gabe. "The crap keeps raining down on us."

Murphy walked into the chief's office twenty minutes after her partner. "Thanks for joining us," Christianson said, looking at his watch.

"Sorry," she said, sinking into a chair next to Gabe. She'd overslept and gotten to work late. Her head ached. All day she'd felt like her limbs were stuck in low gear no matter how fast she tried to move them.

"You didn't miss anything," said Gabe. "Chief was getting to the good stuff. The part where we drop our pants and get fucked in the ass."

Murphy raised her eyebrows; Gabe usually kept his tongue tamer around the chief. She looked across the desk at Christianson. They'd asked to meet with the chief to propose another sweep through Michaels's mansion.

"They want access," said Christianson. "Family heirlooms, legal documents and the like. We can't keep them out forever."

"Who wants access?" asked Murphy. "What are we talking about here?"

"Michaels's relatives. We're letting them into the house on Monday," said Gabe, glaring at Christianson.

"The hell we are," she said. Christianson looked down and shuffled some papers on his desk, avoiding her eyes.

"Yeah," Gabe said, slapping his hands on the arms of his chair. "It's a regular shit tornado."

Christianson looked at his watch again. "Are we finished? It's almost seven. I'd like to get some dinner tonight."

"I'd say we're finished," Gabe said. He stood up and walked out, slamming the door behind him.

Murphy stared up at the ceiling, willing herself to stay civil. She returned her gaze to Christianson. She leaned toward his desk and spoke in a low tone. "Who in the hell is coming down on you? Huh? One of those assholes up on the hill? The mayor and his cronies? Who?"

He didn't answer.

"God dammit!" she said, slamming her hand on his desk. "We've got a right to know who's pulling the strings."

He set the papers down on his desk, folded his hands together and looked at her. Murphy thought his face looked as pasty as the papers on his desk, and wondered if it was the case that was grinding him down or something else. "Murphy, they can get a court order," he said.

"Let them," she said, throwing up her hands. "Force them to get one. It'll buy us some time."

"Time to do what?" he asked.

"Give us one more shot at the house, one more pass through to see if we can find something," she said.

"The hair?" he asked.

"Maybe," she said.

He lowered his eyes and fingered the same stack of papers, straightening them so the edges lined up. "Nash tells me you think Michaels is still alive, that you got a call from him last night. Maybe even a visit," he said. "Hard to believe, but a lot of things about this case have been tough to swallow. Really tough."

A knock.

"Yes," he said tiredly. Christianson's secretary poked her head into the room. "Your wife again. Line three."

"I'm on my way home."

"She says it's important."

He glanced at the blinking light on his phone. "I don't give a damn what she says. Tell her I'm in a meeting."

"I did, sir. She says it can't wait."

"Yes it can," he said sharply. The secretary closed the door.

Christianson reached across his desk and picked up the photo of his sons. He studied it for a few seconds, running his fingers over the edges of the frame. He sighed heavily and set the photo down so it faced Murphy. "Good-looking boys, aren't they?" said Christianson. "Got my damn lantern jaw. That hair, though, that's my wife's side of the family. All the kids on her side have it."

She frowned, thrown off guard by his sudden self-absorption. She picked up the photo and studied the three youths, all in hockey jerseys. All blond. All with familiar gray eyes. She inhaled sharply and set the frame down, turning it away from her.

"How could a father do what he did?" Christianson asked, rubbing his forehead with his hand. "To kill the mother of your children, their grand-mother, and . . ." His voice trailed off. He swiveled around to face the window.

Murphy stared at the back of the chair, her mouth open. It took her a full minute to form the question. "How is she related to him?"

"Cousins," he said, still facing the window. "First cousins. Very close. She refuses to believe Buzzy . . ."

"Buzzy?"

"That's her nickname for him. Buzzy. She refuses to believe he did it. Absolutely refuses. Others in the family admit it's possible, probable. They saw his temper. The drinking. Of course it doesn't matter to them; they still want a whitewash job. Family reputation comes before everything. My wife, she's different. She sincerely believes he is . . . was . . . incapable of murder."

"Chief . . . ," she said.

"I didn't know the guy very well, and didn't care to," Christianson contin-ued. "The little I did know of him, I didn't like. He was a mean drunk. Told my wife she married a loser. Told her that at our wedding reception, and he was one of the groomsmen. Bastard. He brags that his family got me to St. Paul, into this office. That's bullshit."

"You didn't need to tell me all that," Murphy said. She stared at her fingernails and then the carpet. She wished Gabe would come back in, the secretary would walk through or the phone would ring. This was more than she ever wanted to know about her boss.

"I didn't handle this case any differently," he said.

"I know you didn't," she said a little too quickly.

A long silence. She picked the photo up again and looked at it. Very handsome boys. Big grins, like they'd just won a game. Would they grow up to be drunks, wife beaters or worse? Would it be inherited, passed down like the blond hair and the money?

"Chief?" She set the photo down. "Ben?"

Christianson swung his chair back around to face her.

"Ben," she said. "How do you want your sons to grow up? How do you want them to turn out? Like him or like you? You can stop them."

Christianson shook his head.

"It's in your power to stop them," she said. She spun his nameplate around on his desk so it faced him. "You're the chief of police. You've got the power. Not them."

"Power," he repeated. A long silence. He was thinking. His eyes went from the photo to the nameplate. A grim smile stretched across his face. "You and Nash take as many people as you need and get over there. Do it now. Spend the weekend there if you must. I'll sign off on the overtime. Come next week I'll be clean out of excuses and they'll have shopped around for the right judge."

"Can't you stall them any longer than that?" she asked. She stood up to leave.

"It would be like stepping in front of a freight train," he said. "I don't have enough power to survive that."

They took an unmarked squad, one of the last cars in the lot. The thing was a hot box and the air conditioner was busted. Gabe turned on the ignition and rolled down all the windows. "What'd the chief say?" asked Gabe. "How'd you get him to go along with this?"

"Tell you later," she said. She slapped a light on the hood. "Come on. Let's rock. It's the pedal on the right."

"What's the rush?"

"This operation's got a time limit and I want a good head start," she said. He squealed out of the parking lot and headed toward the freeway. The sun was a low, orange glow on the horizon. She looked in the rearview mirror as they got on the Interstate 94 ramp headed west. "Where's the rest of our crew?"

"Castro had to take a quick pee," Gabe said. "Bladder infection."

"Why is everyone sharing with me today?" Murphy asked.

"Huh?"

"Never mind."

Traffic was heavy with the start of the weekend. They took the Lexington Avenue exit and headed south toward Summit. Murphy kept checking the rearview mirror, wondering when the other Crown Victoria would materialize behind them. She figured Castro and Dubrowski would be help enough, but she changed her mind when they got to the house.

"The tape," Murphy said. They stood at the bottom of the steps leading to the side door off the driveway.

"Yeah. Yeah. I see it," Gabe said. "Maybe it fell off."

"Bullshit," she said. She drew her gun and started walking up the steps, but Gabe put a hand on her shoulder.

"Keep your ass right where it is until I radio for backup," he said.

Gabe ran back to the car. Castro and Dubrowski pulled up behind him and got out. Dubrowski walked up the driveway.

"What's the story?" asked Castro, leaning into the open passenger window.

"I called for backup," Gabe said.

"Why the hell do we need backup?" Castro asked.

"Tape's broke," Gabe said, hanging up the set.

Castro pulled his head out of the window and started for the house. "So where's Murphy?" he asked.

Gabe looked through the open car window and saw Dubrowski standing alone at the bottom of the steps, eyeing the loose yellow tape.

"Perfect!" Gabe said. He jumped out of the car, slammed the door shut and drew his gun. "She went inside by herself. Damn her."

Michaels's house was warm and quiet. With the place sealed tight for days, the air had grown musty and dead. It smelled like the inside of an old purse.

She quickly surveyed the modernized kitchen and saw there was no place for him to hide amid the open stainless-steel shelves. She kept walking, looking to her left and right and back to her left. The early-evening sun wasn't strong enough to filter through the heavy curtains that hung from every window on the first floor. The house was dim, getting dark, but she decided not to turn on any lights. The thick oriental carpets cushioned her footsteps. When her shoes hit expanses of bare wood, she walked a little slower. She entered the cavernous dining room. One long gleaming table, big enough for a banquet, surrounded by more than a dozen chairs. She bent over and looked under the table. A forest of chair legs. She stood up straight and looked around the room. The drapes. She lifted them away from the wall and looked behind them. Nothing but cobwebs.

She heard the floorboards squeak behind her. Her feet froze. She held her breath and turned, gun ready. Gabe, with Dubrowski and Castro right behind him. All had their guns drawn. Gabe looked pissed. He pointed to the floor. He wanted her to stay put, until backup arrived. She shook her head and pointed to the ceiling. Gabe shook his head, forming a silent "No" with his mouth. She ignored him and walked toward the staircase.

"Fuck," Gabe said under his breath. "Let's do it." He motioned Dubrowski and Castro toward the library and followed Murphy up to the second floor. By the time they reached the top of the stairs, they could hear more sets of feet on the first floor. Their backup.

"Goddamn about time," Gabe whispered to Murphy. He was at her elbow. She tipped her head toward the first door on the right. He nodded. Both had their guns raised as she gently pushed the door open with one hand. They figured it was one of the girls' bedrooms. Small, square and yellow. Posters of female soccer players taped to the walls. Poster of a shirtless male guitarist taped to the ceiling over the frilly bed. Gabe opened the closet. A solid wall of clothes. He shut it. Murphy got on her belly and looked under the bed. Dust bunnies. Soccer shoes. A flattened soccer ball. A stack of teen magazines. A lone stuffed animal, a loon. Murphy stood up and motioned toward the door. He walked out ahead of her.

The hallway bathroom. Gabe and Murphy stepped around the broken pieces of mirror. Crime-scene investigators from the first search of the house left the shards where they were. "What the hell was this about?" Gabe said, speaking low, scanning the mess on the floor.

"Maybe he didn't like what he saw," she said, looking behind the shower curtain.

The next door opened to a grim guest bedroom, a furniture museum with matching Victorian pieces that were heavy, dark, deeply carved. Even the velvet bedspread looked like a dusty antique. "Welcome to Our Home" read a needlepoint pillow on the bed. This time she checked the closet and he looked under the bed.

"Nothing," he whispered, standing up.

"Out-of-season coats," she said, gently shutting the closet door.

"Murphy," he whispered as they walked down the hallway to the next bedroom. "I don't think there's anyone home. This is another wild . . ."

"Don't say it," she said.

Uniformed and plainclothes cops went through every room in the house, from the basement to the attic, and checked the carriage house and the yard.

"Murphy. Thanks for another exciting evening," said Bergen, holstering his gun. He stood in the kitchen between Murphy and Gabe, under a ceiling rack of hanging pots.

"Drop dead," she said.

"Hey, I appreciate the overtime," Bergen said. "I'm working on a new motor for the bass boat." He walked through the side door, following a stream of other cops who were laughing or grumbling on their way outside.

"No roaming Romann," said Dubrowski, shuffling tiredly into the kitchen. "Not even his ghost."

"The tape was busted when we got here," said Murphy.

"I know it was," said Dubrowski. "Probably fell off. That shit happens." He holstered his gun and looked at the kitchen wall clock. "Hey, my shift is long over. It's Friday night, a payday and life is good. Want to grab a brew?"

"Usual place?" Gabe asked. Dubrowski nodded. "We'll meet you there," Gabe said. Dubrowski followed the line out the door, leaving Murphy and Gabe standing alone in the kitchen.

"Thank you," she said quietly.

"No problem," he said, snapping his holster shut.

"Sorry I shook you off in the dining room," she said.

"It worked out."

"You're a man of few words tonight," she said.

"I'm wiped out," he said, digging in his pockets for the car keys.

"Mind waiting while I do one last walk-through?" she asked.

"Christ almighty. Don't you ever let up?" he said. "We're coming back first thing in the morning to rifle through that pile of boxes in the attic. Murphy, the man is not here. He's at the bottom of Lake Superior. You know what else? The hair isn't here, either. We're gonna waste a nice weekend digging around this stuffy morgue looking for evidence that doesn't exist. Phantom evidence."

She looked wounded.

"Oh, fine. You hit the second floor and I'll take down here," he said. She smiled. "Afterward, you're coming to the bar with me and you're buying the first round. For everybody. Deal?"

"Deal," she said, heading for the stairs.

"Should have my head examined," Gabe said. "Should have her head examined." He flipped on a light as he walked into the dining room. Empty. He flipped off the light and walked to the library. He flipped on a light and stared at the wall of shelves filled with books from floor to ceiling. He pulled the pack of Winstons out of his pocket. One left. He lit it, inhaled deeply and walked closer to study a row of westerns.

"Hmmm," he mumbled. "What we got here? *Shootist. Hanging in Sweetwater. Day the Cowboys Quit. Last Days of Wolf Garnett.*" He stopped to pull a copy of *The Black Mustanger* off the shelf when he noticed a vertical sliver of light between two stacks of shelves. The cigarette dropped from his mouth.

"Clever son-of-a-bitch," Gabe breathed.

"That's me," Michaels whispered behind him.

Gabe reached for his gun.

Michaels slipped off his right glove and felt for a pulse. "Still alive, you hardheaded cop bastard?" He pulled the glove back on, and wiped both gloves and his gun on Gabe's shirt. He'd pistol-whipped him hard, twice, and there was a lot of blood, but head injuries were deceptive. They tended to produce a lot of blood regardless of their severity. He thought about one of the knives in the kitchen. The big carving knife. He didn't want to take the time. Not yet. He hooked his arms under Gabe's armpits and dragged him into the safe room. Michaels dropped him in the middle of the room and looked down. He didn't want to look at that ugly puss while he was doing the bitch. He grabbed one of his wife's fur coats and threw it over Gabe. Maybe he'd finish her partner off in front of her. The thought excited him.

He took the stairs to the second floor, slowly and deliberately. He avoided walking directly in the middle of each step; that's where most of them squeaked. He thought about what he was going to do to her. Rape her and then kill her and then rape her again. He'd brought condoms, though it was probably unnecessary. Everyone thought he was dead, even his own family. They'd never trace the crime to him, never even consider it. He'd take some things from the house, break some stuff. Arrange the corpses cleverly. Make it look like burglars surprised the two cops and killed them. Such a tragedy.

He'd have to remember the hatbox. Couldn't leave that behind. Then it was off to Europe to join his daughters, create a new identity. They'd understand in time. Even if they didn't, tough. They'd have to live with it.

The buzzing in his head was so loud, he wondered if it would give him away.

Murphy walked into the hallway bathroom and crouched down to study the hunks of mirror on the floor. Mixed in was a broken drinking glass. She figured he must have gotten drunk and thrown the glass at the mirror. She carefully picked up part of the broken glass by its edges and examined what was painted on the side. Some sort of bird. She put the piece in her left hand

and with her right picked through the scraps of mirror to look for another piece to match it up with.

On the floor, she saw his disjointed reflection in the jagged fragments.

He grabbed the top of her hair with one hand and with the other jammed a gun into her neck. "Should we do it on the bathroom floor, or take it to the bedroom?" he said. He yanked her up by the hair.

She held on to the broken glass in her left hand, cupping it so he couldn't see it. "Why aren't you dead?" she said.

"Shut up! Using two fingers, unsnap your holster," he said. She hesitated. "Do it!"

She did.

"Good girl. Now take it out. Two fingers. Slowly. Slowly. Set it on the counter. Good. You're a quick study. You're going to learn a lot more before the night is through."

"Go to hell!" she said.

"Shut up, bitch. No talking. Save that tongue for my cock."

He kept the gun on her neck and, from behind, wrapped his left arm around her waist. He pulled her against him. "We've danced this dance before, haven't we? This time you're going to be the one left for dead." He pulled her into the hallway. "One foot in front of the other and walk toward my bedroom. Slowly. You know where it is. Baby steps. That's it."

"Your dye jobs keep getting worse," she said. He'd colored his hair black this time.

"Yeah. Yeah. I'll tell my hairdresser," he said. "Keep moving."

He kept his arm around her waist and the gun against her neck. He smelled like sweat and whiskey; probably hadn't showered or shaved for days. She could feel him getting hard as his front pressed against her back. He was getting off on this, and it made her sick. She wondered where Gabe was, if Michaels knew he was in the house.

As if he'd read her mind: "By the way, Gabe won't be joining us tonight," he said in a low voice.

"What have you done with him, you asshole?"

"I'm afraid he's suffered a severe head injury," he said. "Bleeding badly. The doctor predicts he might not make it through the night."

She stopped walking. "Where is he?" she asked. Michaels laughed. She decided to make her move, gun or no gun. She took the broken glass she'd been cradling in her hand and ripped a jagged, red line across his left arm.

"Bitch!" he snarled. He released her and wrapped his good arm around the bad. He dropped the gun. She dove for it. He kicked it away, grabbed the back of her head and plowed his knee into her face. She fell against the wall, blood running from her nose. He bent over to retrieve the gun and she crawled to her feet and ran for the stairs. He fired a shot into the ceiling; plaster rained on the floor. She stopped, inches from the stairs.

"Arms up or the next one is in your back," he yelled. "Kill you now or kill you later. Your choice. Makes no difference to me. I don't mind fucking a dead woman."

"Someone is going to hear, call the cops," she said, raising her hands in the air.

"Old house is pretty solid, walls are thick. Neighbors are all gone for the weekend," he said. "Besides, your friends were already here. They aren't coming back. This is the last place the dumb shits will check.

"Now turn around and march your pretty ass back here," he said, training the gun on her. "You're gonna pay for this arm."

She turned and walked toward him, arms raised. "Keep coming," he said. "Coming. Stop." She was less than two feet from him. He took a step toward her, swung his arm back and slammed the side of his gun into her mouth. She fell backward.

"Stand up and peel off your T-shirt." She didn't move. "Now," he said, pointing the gun down at her face.

She wiped her split lips with the back of her hand, stood up and pulled her shirt over her head. "Give it," he said. He stretched out his bleeding left arm. She tossed the shirt over it and he held the arm close to his chest. "Arms up again," he said.

"I hate white sports bras," he said, studying her chest. "Boring. I like to see black lace against a woman's skin."

"Sorry to disappoint," she said. She swallowed a mouthful of her own blood.

"It's what's underneath that counts, right? Let's see what's underneath." Grimacing, he reached over with his left arm and unzipped the front of the bra.

"I hate your fucking guts, you sick puke," she said.

"I love it when you talk dirty to me," he said. He pushed the white material aside and with the gun barrel, traced the curves of her breasts. "Lovely."

They were standing across from the bathroom. He saw her eyes dart to the counter, her gun. "Bad idea," he said. He shoved the gun into her left breast. "Downstairs. We're gonna check on your partner, see if he's still bleeding, still breathing."

"Keep both hands on the railing while we're walking down," he said. He was one step behind her the entire way down and kept the gun buried in her back.

"Stop," he said. They were at the bottom. "To the library."

They stepped into the library. "A safe room," she said. "How long you been in there? Did you sneak into the kitchen at night to eat, like a cockroach? Wait. Wrong insect."

"Move," he said, pushing her farther into the library. His arm was starting to throb. "Stop," he said. "I'm not ready for you yet." Grimacing, he reached his left hand into the left pocket of his jeans and pulled out some handcuffs.

"Turn around," he said. He threw the cuffs at her. She caught them and looked at them; they were Gabe's. "Snap one over your right wrist," he said. "Do it!" She did.

He looked at her face and scowled. "You're a bloody mess, and whoever sewed up your forehead did a crap job. You look like the Bride of Frankenstein."

"Know a good plastic surgeon?" she said.

"Gotta clean you up," he said.

"How considerate," she said.

"Can't screw you the way you are now," he said. "I'll get blood all over myself. Walk, toward the kitchen."

He pushed her into a bathroom in the hallway between the kitchen and the dining room. "Turn it on and get in," he said, nodding toward the shower stall. She turned it on and felt the water. "Get in," he said. She stepped in. "Snap the other end of the handcuff over the showerhead," he said. She paused. "Do it, unless you want your brains running down the drain," he said, aiming the gun at her head. She obeyed.

He shook her bloody T-shirt off his left arm and, with his teeth, pulled the leather glove off his left hand. As she stood with one hand stretched over her head, he roughly rubbed her breasts with his bare hand. With his gloved right hand, he jammed the gun into her back. "Nice," he said. Blood from his arm dripped onto the shower floor and washed down the drain. "Very nice. Is it the cold water, Paris, or is it me? Please tell me that it's me."

"Drop dead," she said.

"If you don't like it, shut your eyes and pretend it's somebody else's hand getting you off. Ever do that with your lover?" He kept rubbing her breasts. "Ever shut your eyes and pretend he's somebody else? Maybe you pretend it's me. Ever dream about me?"

"Shut up," she said. "Shut the hell up."

"I hit a nerve," he said, smiling. "Good."

He pulled his hand away, set the gun down on the counter and got a first-aid kit from under the sink. He lifted the lid and dug out a roll of gauze.

"Where's Gabe?" she asked. "What have you done with him?"

"Don't worry about old Gabe," he said, wrapping the bandage around his arm. "Gonna take care of him in a minute. Worry about yourself." He taped the ends of the bandage and slipped the leather glove back on his left hand.

He opened a drawer under the bathroom counter and pulled out a large pair of scissors. She stared at them. "No peeking," he said, setting the scissors down on the counter. "You'll ruin the surprise." He figured he could still get his souvenir, but he'd have to be careful, take a small section from the back of her head.

This time she read his mind: "If you cut it they'll know it was you," she said.

"I won't take enough to flag them, and they won't catch it because they won't be looking for it," he said.

"Yes they will."

"No they won't. I'm dead. You drowned me. Remember?"

"You'll never get away with it," she said. "Never."

"Close your trap," he said. "Close your pretty fucking trap." He walked over to the shower, reached up and turned the showerhead so it hit her in the face. He grabbed the gun and the scissors off the counter. He opened and closed the scissors in front of her face. "The fly shall marry the bumblebee," he said, grinning.

"Bastard!" she screamed through the water.

"I don't want to hear you," he said. Michaels walked out of the bathroom, shutting the door behind him.

"Bastard!" Her voice bounced off the marble walls.

The water was ice cold, and she was glad for it. It eased the throbbing in her face. The shower was higher than a standard one, but she could reach the oversized head when she stood on her toes. She grabbed it with her free hand and tried to turn it. Getting a good grip with her left hand was hard, especially with the water running. It wouldn't budge. She stretched as tall as she could and hung on to the shower pipe with her cuffed right hand for leverage. "Damn," she sputtered. She kept straining. Her hand kept slipping. She relaxed for a moment, turned her head and tried to catch her breath as the shower pounded her.

She reached up and tried it again. "Righty tighty, lefty loosey," she muttered. "Come on." It moved. Water shot out where the pipe met the showerhead. She kept turning. The head popped off and dropped to the shower floor.

She opened the door and ran out of the bathroom, the free handcuff dangling from her right wrist. She stopped in the hall and listened. She could hear him in the kitchen. She recognized the noise; she'd done it a thousand times in her own kitchen. He was putting an edge on a knife.

She dashed for the stairs and took the steps two at a time.

"Bitch!" she heard him yell at the bottom of the stairs. He was on her heels. She ran into the bathroom, crunching over the broken mirror. A shot rang past her ears and slammed into the bathroom wall.

"Looking for this?" he said.

She threw up her arms and swung around to face him. He was standing in the doorway, her gun in his hands. "Don't do it," she said. "You'll get life for killing a cop."

"Life in Europe, with my daughters," he said, raising the gun. "That's what I'm gonna get."

"Your daughters? Are you crazy?" she said. "Don't you remember?"

"Remember what? What the hell are you talking about?" He looked mystified.

"They're gone!" she yelled. He still didn't get it. What she said wasn't registering. "Your daughters. Your daughters are dead!"

"Liar!" he yelled, raising the gun higher. "Lying bitch!"

"You killed them," she said. "You! We found their bodies at the lake. There were four bodies in the carriage house. Four rotting corpses."

For the first time in days, the buzzing stopped. Shocked out of his head, like with a stun gun. He lowered the gun and took a couple of steps backward into the hallway. The color drained from his face; it was coming back to him. A terrible epiphany.

"You killed your own daughters," she said. "Your pretty blond daughters."

"Shut up!" he wailed, waving the gun toward her. "Shut the hell up!"

She heard footsteps downstairs. Voices. They'd come back. She knew what she wanted to do, but she didn't have much time. "Did they put up much of a fight? Did they beg for their lives?" she asked, speaking low. "Or don't you remember?"

He fell to his knees, crying.

"You don't, do you? You don't remember."

"Stop!"

"You don't even remember murdering your own daughters," she said. "You make me sick."

"I do remember," he said softly. "They cut their hair. I told them never to cut their hair. Never."

"Did you want to do other things to them?"

"What are you saying?"

"Even worse than killing them. Did you want to? What stopped you?"

"I wouldn't," he said, shaking his head. "That's what my mother tried to do to me. I wouldn't let her. I wouldn't do that to my daughters."

So that's what had happened between mother and son. She felt a flash of pity and brushed it aside. "You killed your own daughters," she said. "How can you live with yourself?"

"I can't," he said. "I can't live." He slowly stood up, the gun still in his hand.

"Nothing left to live for," she whispered. "Nothing."

"Nothing," he repeated, putting the gun to his head. "Nothing left."

"Do it," she said. "I would. In a heartbeat. Do it."

"Murphy? You up there? Murphy!" Gabe, at the bottom of the stairs.

"Don't come up here!" she yelled. "He's armed. Don't come up!"

"You don't have much time . . . Buzzy," she whispered.

His finger was on the trigger.

"Shut your eyes and pretend you're shooting somebody else," she said. "Pull, Buzzy. It's the only way to redeem yourself. Pull."

"I can't."

Gabe was running up the stairs.

"Say the rhyme, Buzzy. Finish it and pull."

"I can't."

"You can. Say it."

"Fiddle-de-dee, fiddle-de-dee, the fly shall marry the bumblebee. They went to church and married was she . . . I can't . . ." He choked back a sob. "You finish it. I'll pull if you finish it."

"The fly has married the bumblebee," she said.

Gabe was at the top of the stairs when he heard the gunshot, saw Michaels's brains splatter against the wall, saw the big man fold on the floor. Bergen and Dubrowski came up behind Gabe and stopped. "Holy shit," said Bergen, looking at the body in the hallway and the red running down the wall. "Holy shit."

Gabe pulled out his cell phone and called for paramedics, even though he knew Michaels was gone. Murphy walked out of the bathroom. Gabe looked at her battered face and her open bra and ordered a second ambulance.

"Give us a minute," Gabe whispered to Bergen and Dubrowski. They stayed back while Gabe stepped over the body and walked toward her, holding the back of his bleeding head. "Murphy? How you doing?" he asked. "How bad is it?"

"I look worse than I feel," she said. She looked down and with shaking fingers, zipped up her bra. When she looked up, Gabe was staring at her, a worried expression on his face. "He didn't get that far," she said. "Okay?"

"Yeah. Okay. It's just . . . Jesus. We found your bloody T-shirt in the bathroom downstairs. We thought . . ."

"How are you?" she asked.

"Sore as hell."

She started shivering. "You're soaked," Gabe said. He took off his sweatshirt to give to her and saw his own blood smeared all over it. He turned it inside out and draped it over her shoulders.

"Why did they come back for us?" she asked, pulling the sweatshirt tight around her wet body.

"Missed me at the bar," he said. She nodded.

She studied the bloody wall. "I'm surprised he had the balls," she said.

Gabe stared at her.

"I tried to stop him," she said, turning to meet Gabe's eyes. "I really did."

"That's not what I heard," Gabe said in a low voice.

She didn't answer, pretended not to understand. Sirens wailed in the distance. She crouched next to the body and saw that his gray eyes were open wide. "Did you know . . ." her voice trailed off.

"Know what?" Gabe asked.

"Did you know that suicide is considered one of the worst of the mortal sins?"

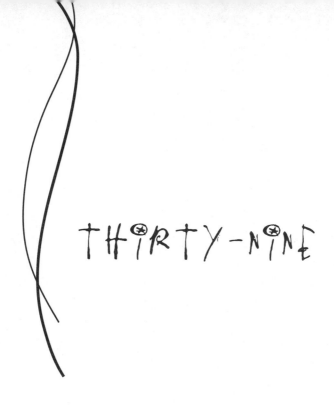

THIRTY-NINE

How's your partner?" asked Jack.

"His new girlfriend is coddling the hell out of him," Murphy said. "It's almost too sickening to watch. I'm afraid to say it, but she may turn out to be wife number four."

"More power to him," said Jack, raising his beer bottle in tribute.

She and Jack were on the deck of her houseboat, watching the rockets light up the sky across the river in the first of three nights of Fourth of July fireworks over the State Capitol building. The summer night was hot, but the humidity was down and so were the mosquitoes. She kept the patio doors and all the windows open to cool off the houseboat.

"I wish Gabe would reconsider that early-retirement bullshit," she said. "What's he gonna do with himself all day? Fish?"

"Give him a break, baby," said Jack, taking a bump from the bottle. "This case really knocked the wind out of him."

"Me, too," she said. She reached up and reflexively touched her face. The bruises were fading and her nose wasn't broken, but her mouth was sore and the stitches on her forehead still troubled her. Bride of Frankenstein.

Jack knew what she was thinking. "If it bothers you that much, let me set you up to see a plastic surgeon," he said. "I know a few who aren't homicidal maniacs."

"Had my fill of plastic surgeons for a while," she said. She carefully sipped her wine; it made her lips burn. "Maybe I'll talk to one later, if I can find a nice lady doc. Hell, a scar on my forehead might add a little character."

"Oh, please," he groaned, polishing off his beer. "I am not going to touch that; too damn easy."

She laughed.

"At least you don't have to worry about that lawsuit," Jack said. He bent over and retrieved another beer from under his lawn chair. He popped off the cap. "You surprised his asshole uncles backed off?"

"Hell no," she said. "Imagine having that gruesome hair collection dragged out in front of a jury. Poor Finch's red hair, all braided and everything. The ash brown hair from that Minneapolis murder victim. Roxanne Magnuson's auburn hair. His wife's blond hair . . ."

"Even his wife's?"

"Uh huh," she said. "We found Rue's sad, brown braid. All of it stashed in that safe room of his."

"Had pretty much every shade covered, except black," Jack said.

"Except black," Murphy said in a low voice.

"He didn't cut his daughters' hair?" Jack asked, taking a bump off his beer.

"They got their hair cut short in Europe, to copy the Danish girls," said Murphy. "That probably helped freak him out." From what Murphy and Lake County officials could piece together, the two girls had begged to come home early from soccer camp, so their mother arranged for them to take a connecting flight to Duluth and a cab to the cabin. They walked in on their father in the carriage house standing over the bodies of their mother and grandmother. He smashed his daughters' skulls with the same shovel he'd used on their grandmother.

"What about that drowning stuff? You think he planned that?" Jack asked.

"I think he planned to disappear, but not like that," Murphy said. "I think he almost got his clock punched by the lake and that made him even crazier."

"Figured out how he made it back to the cities without someone spotting him?"

"Nobody was looking for him," she said. "He had a dye job on top of a dye job, and he was driving some junker motorcycle he'd picked up. The big thing is, nobody was looking for him. He was supposed to be dead."

"You knew he wasn't," Jack said.

"Yeah, I knew."

He leaned over and patted her thigh. "My baby is smart."

"You are so drunk."

"Yeah, but you're still smart."

She laughed again. "Stop. You're making my face hurt."

"Hey, smartie, what was all that fly and bee stuff?"

"Something with his mother," she said.

"Always boils down to hating your mother."

"He didn't hate her," Murphy said.

A rocket exploded in the sky, releasing a display of red, white and blue in the shape of a sunflower.

The phone rang in the galley. It jarred her. She still half expected a call from Michaels, even though it was impossible. He'd shot off half his own head. In her report, it was a straight suicide. Gabe knew otherwise. He'd made it to the top of the stairs and heard the words she and Michaels exchanged right before he pulled the trigger. Gabe said he didn't care. Said he was glad. He told her she'd saved the justice system a lot of time and the taxpayers a pile of money. Still, he'd treated her differently these last few days. Like she was a cocked gun. She wondered if she had played a role in his decision to retire.

The phone kept ringing. She tried to ignore it. "Should I get it?" Jack asked. He set his bottle down and started to get up from his chair.

"Sit. I'll get it," she said, motioning him down with her hand. She stood up, set her glass down and walked into the galley. "It's probably my mom calling for the hourly update on my health."

Erik: "Paris?"

"This isn't a good time."

"I was on the phone with the Lake County coroner, wrapping up a few loose ends," Erik said.

"Any surprises?"

"No. The grandmother and two girls died of blunt-force trauma to the head and Jennifer Michaels was strangled."

"Anything else?"

"How you feeling?"

"I'm not suppose to say 'fine.' Right?" she said.

He laughed. She liked his laugh. Liked his hands on her. Liked Jack's hands on her, too. The status of their marriage was still uncertain. They weren't back together. Not really. Did that give her license to sleep around? She pushed the answer and the guilt to the back of her mind.

"Jack's home?" Erik asked.

"This morning," she said.

Then why he really called: "When can I see you again?" Erik asked. "I really want to see you again."

"I don't know," she said.

"I think we have something good going here."

"I don't know." She hung up and set the phone down on the counter and went back out onto the deck.

She lowered herself into the chair and picked up her wineglass. Empty. She grabbed the bottle to refill it when it suddenly occurred to her it was the 1997 Cabernet Sauvignon Michaels had rejected during his visit to her boat. She stared at the label and then poured another glass.

"Was it your mother?" Jack asked.

She paused. "Yeah."

She took a sip of the wine and remembered Michaels had said it wasn't complex enough. She smiled to herself; she was alive to drink it and he wasn't. She sipped again. "Plenty fucking complex."

"What?" asked Jack. "What did you say?" Thunderous explosions in the sky, like cannons going off. Multiple clusters in green, gold, blue and red rained down showers of sparks. The beginning of the grand finale.

"I said the fly was killed by the bumblebee," she said softly.